The Dragon

"Hali, you can fly."

"You know I can't."

"You can once you're rid of *this*." She tapped the jewel on Hali's neck band.

Hali turned her face to the patch of sky with an expression of longing. The jewel on the neck band suddenly disintegrated.

Her mer lower body split in three, two taloned rear legs and a sinuous, barbed tail. With a shudder, she tripled her size and her features elongated. Her hair flattened into a dark, lacy pattern on the shining silver scales of her lengthened neck.

She gripped the other two by the arm in her front talons, flaring her huge wings, then launched upward.

Celestra held on for dear life as the ground plunged out from under them.

Half the world seemed to cave in at once. Hali banked violently, trying to avoid the worst of it.

The opening in the ceiling approached rapidly. By Celestra's quick calculations, it was too small for Hali's new wingspan, but Hali was already adjusting.

Downstroking hard in a burst of speed, she tucked in her wings. They sailed clear just as the cavern groaned a final time. It collapsed in a deafening explosion, leaving a smoking crater in the earth.

Hali extended her wings, pumping frantically, and they soared higher and higher while the ruins of their prison dissolved into nothingness.

SWORD AND SORCERESS XVI

EDITED BY

Marion Zimmer Bradley

DAW BOOKS, INC.
DONALD A. WOLLHEIM, FOUNDER
375 Hudson Street, New York, NY 10014

ELIZABETH R. WOLLHEIM
SHEILA E. GILBERT
PUBLISHERS

First Printing, June 1999
1 2 3 4 5 6 7 8 9 10

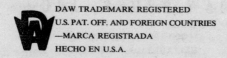

DAW TRADEMARK REGISTERED
U.S. PAT. OFF. AND FOREIGN COUNTRIES
—MARCA REGISTRADA
HECHO EN U.S.A.

PRINTED IN THE U.S.A.

ACKNOWLEDGMENTS

Introduction ©1999 by Marion Zimmer Bradley.
The Kappa's Gift ©1999 by Fujiko.
The Changeless Room ©1999 by Charlotte Carlson.
Isabelle and the Siren ©1999 by Mary Catelli.
Dragon's Tear ©1999 by Sonya Fedotowsky.
A Sister's Blood ©1999 by Patricia B. Cirone.
Changed ©1999 by Lisa Deason.
The Power to Change the Shape of the Land ©1999 by Dayle A. Dermatis.
The Frog Prince ©1999 by Linda J. Dunn.
Honey from the Rock ©1999 by Dorothy J. Heydt.
The Will of the Wind ©1999 by Christina Krueger.
Moonlight on Water ©1999 by Carol E. Leever.
Nine Springs ©1999 by Kathleen M. Massie-Ferch.
Mistweaver ©1999 by Terry McGarry.
Waking the Stone Maiden ©1999 by Cynthia McQuillin.
City of No-Sleep ©1999 by Vera Nazarian.
Daughter of the Bear ©1999 by Diana Paxson.
The Wishing Stones ©1999 by Lisa S. Silverthorne.
A Fool's Game ©1999 by Selina Rosen.
The Anvil of Her Pride ©1999 by Lawrence Schimel.
The Dancing Men of Ballyben ©1999 by Laura J. Underwood.
Salt and Sorcery ©1999 by Elisabeth Waters and Michael Spence.
Weaving Spells ©1999 by Lawrence Watt Evans.
Enaree, an Azkhantian Tale ©1999 by Deborah Wheeler.
The Day They Ran Out of Princesses ©1999 by Gail Sosinsky Wickman.
Taking Flight ©1999 by Susan Wolven.
The Vision That Appeared ©1999 by Katherine L. Rogers.

CONTENTS

INTRODUCTION

It's hard to believe I've been doing these volumes for as long as I have. Every year I realize again how lucky I am to be able to do this series, to discover new writers, and to read new stories by my old friends, many of whom were new writers when I first encountered them. I remember looking at the new books shelf in a local science-fiction bookstore one day about eight years ago, and thinking that the names on the new releases looked a lot like the table of contents of a volume of *Sword and Sorceress.* By now I have writers whose first stories I bought bringing new writers into the field, following our tradition of "paying forward"—since we can't pay back the writers and editors who helped us when we were young and just starting out.

Both the world we live in and the stories I get have changed over the years. The first few years, I got so many stories about women who *knew* that they could do traditional "men's work" and were busy proving it to men. Now that a good part of our world has figured out the truth of that (or at least passed laws to that effect), I don't get many of those stories anymore.

It's like the basic rule of science fiction: just grant your gimmicks, and get on with your story. (This is why science fiction has FTL travel and transporters, and fantasy has teleportation spells. They save travel time, so you can get right to the story.) Also, after the second year, I put my foot down and said I refused to buy any more stories about women proving they could be camel herders, or whatever it was the men said they couldn't be.

But now that so many women hold down "men's jobs" in addition to having families and homes to take care of—all too frequently without any help from the man who promised to be there and help, I'm starting to see another sort of story. A woman may be able to do *any-thing,* but that doesn't mean that she can do *everything.* And I sometimes suspect that too many of us are trying to do just that.

This year I noticed that quite a few of the stories I got were about women coping with things *they* weren't at all sure they could do. We've gone from needing to prove our abilities to men to having to prove them to ourselves. So now we have stories about women perse-vering against all odds, keeping on with their lives no matter what the world throws at them, coping with disas-ter, and surviving. Perhaps that's the motto for the end of the millennium: just keep going. When you fall, pick yourself up and try again.

That certainly applies to my writers. A very few sell to me on their first try, but most of them have years of rejection slips before their first sale. The ones who succeed are the ones who work hard and keep trying.

For anyone who wants to submit a manuscript for *Sword and Sorceress,* first send a #10 SASE (self-addressed stamped envelope) to *Sword and Sorceress,* P.O. Box 72, Berkeley CA 94701-0072. The guidelines for my magazine (*Marion Zimmer Bradley's FANTASY Magazine*) are available from P.O. Box 249, Berkeley CA 94701-0249, or on my Web site, www.mzbfm.com. The Web site also has useful information for beginning writers, including the articles I used as handouts when I taught a writer's workshop some years ago. The maga-zine is an easier market; I get to do four of them a year, instead of just one, and the story requirements, not being limited to sword and sorcery with female protagonists, are less rigid. The magazine gives me a chance to play with additional types of stories, including contemporary settings, which I don't use for *Sword and Sorceress*. But I love both the anthology and the magazine, and I wouldn't give either of them up for anything.

THE KAPPA'S GIFT
by Fujiko

Fujiko was born in Japan, near Mount Fuji; she was, of course, named after the mountain. At the not very observant age of six months, she and her family moved to Chile, where she spent "an almost embarrassingly idyllic childhood" until 1968, when her family moved to Vancouver, Canada. She spent several years in the public schools—which I know from experience can be a far from idyllic surrounding—and then struggled through four years of university to earn a Bachelor of Science degree which she has never used in her work, but which she says has enhanced her ability to understand and enjoy her surroundings.

She met her future husband, Tero, when she was fourteen, and they are now doing their best to make decent human beings of their son, Brian, fourteen, and daughter, Selene, eleven. (It doesn't matter much what you do, when they're older they'll think you did everything wrong; that's just human experience.)

She also has, as is par for most writers, an assortment of animals: an English cocker spaniel named Kelsie; three cats, Simba, Nikki, and Tasha; three guinea pigs; a hamster; and assorted fish and transient frogs. Aw, shucks! You mean you didn't have the imagination to name the fish *and* frogs? I was really looking forward to knowing what names you'd give to all of them—particularly the transient ones.

Well, for a story as imaginative and not overdone as this, I guess we'll just have to forgive you. It's nice to get some mythology that isn't Celtic, as well as a reminder that gifts can come in unexpected ways and forms.

Aki paused to listen to the sounds of the night creatures awakening around her in the growing darkness. The familiar noises made her smile, but tonight there was no time to sit and enjoy them. She still faced a long walk back to the farmhouse and wished she hadn't dawdled in the fields. The young cucumbers filling the basket on her back felt heavier with every step. Sighing, Aki adjusted the straps of the basket on her shoulders and continued to trudge along the river path.

A loud splash at the water's edge made Aki jump. With the back of her neck tingling in alarm, she scanned the reeds along the riverbank. She could detect no movement or anything out of the ordinary; still, her steps quickened of their own accord.

Suddenly, a shadow unraveled itself from the tall water reeds and stepped onto the path in front of her. She cringed back with a sharp cry, and then laughed out loud in relief when she saw that the shadow was no bigger than she was. It was only a young boy.

"You nearly scared me to death!" Aki said to him. She started forward with a smile, and froze. What stood in front of her was not a boy. Horror crawled along her spine as her eyes took in details of the creature that confronted her. At first glance it did look like a boy, but on its back it bore a shell like a turtle. The top of its head had a bowllike depression filled with water and was rimmed with long, black hair that hung in wet spikes. The amphibian face had cunning, intelligent eyes that watched her with great interest.

"*Kappa!*" Aki gasped. She had always thought *kappas* were a myth, a creepy story to tell children at bedtime. Now she faced one in the flesh, and she forced her terrified mind to remember the many stories she had heard. They were magical—but how? Water in the bowl at the top of their heads held their power and magic; without it they were very weak. They were blamed for many children's drownings. Cucumbers were a drug to them, causing a feeling of euphoria. They stole farm animals and ate them. But did they attack people? Aki couldn't remember.

Barely able to control her shaking knees, Aki swallowed hard and said, "I have no quarrel with you. Let me pass, and I will not harm you." She marveled at her own gall. It was clearly obvious to both her and the *kappa* that if there were any harm to be done, she wouldn't be the one doing it.

The *kappa* stood on thin, bowed legs and stared at her, its gray-green skin shining with a slimy glint. Suddenly, it let out a long hiss and raised its head, sniffing the air with disgusting, wet noises. Aki watched, paralyzed with fear, unable to react when it closed the space between them and grabbed the basket on her back. She fell hard on her knees and struggled to regain her feet as the creature hauled the basket toward the river, dragging her behind. Fearing that she would die if they reached the water, she redoubled her efforts. She twisted and rolled, scattering the cucumbers from the basket.

The *kappa* stopped and eyed the vegetables strewn on the dirt. It could not ignore a cucumber any more than a starving dog could ignore a piece of bloody meat. It bent down to reach for one, and Aki, seeing her chance to escape, kicked with all her might. Her foot caught the *kappa* on the side of the face and sent it rolling to the ground. It screamed in rage as it felt the water spilling from the bowl on the top of its head. Aki tried to get away from the nightmarish creature but slipped in the mud. Feeling its strength draining, the *kappa* frantically flailed its arms, clawing at Aki's kimono and slashing her thigh. She screamed in pain and terror and fell once more to the ground. The *kappa* lunged at the basket again and yanked. Aki rolled backward, crushing the *kappa* underneath her. Without its extraordinary strength the creature was unable to hold Aki down, and she managed to stand up. She tried to run, but she could still feel the *kappa* holding on to the basket. Wild with desperation she turned her head, and from the corner of her eye she saw the handle of the small hatchet, her *natta,* sticking up above the basket's rim. Whipping her arm back, she jerked the *natta* free and swung it in a wide arc. The sharp blade caught the *kappa's* thin arm above the elbow and sliced through it.

With an agonizing scream the *kappa* fell to the ground holding the stub of its arm in a webbed hand. Aki stood stunned as the creature convulsed and screeched in the mud. She closed her eyes to shut out the horrifying image, and then she turned and ran.

Aki ran blindly, with the hellish screeching echoing in her head. She ran until her lungs were bursting and she could no longer feel her legs. When she thought she could not go another step, she saw the farmhouse lights ahead and forced her legs to keep moving. Finally, she stumbled through the back door, and collapsed on the floor.

"Where have you been all this time?" yelled her Aunt Noriko, stomping toward her. "What the . . . look at you! You've ruined your clothes! And the basket, too!" she said, pulling the basket off Aki's limp body.

The inner door of the kitchen slid open, and her cousin Goro stood framed in the doorway. He watched silently as Aki slowly picked herself up from the floor. His eyes narrowed when he saw the rips in her kimono, and the blood on her exposed thigh.

"A *kappa*—" said Aki trying to catch her breath. "I— I was attacked by a *kappa*—by the river."

Goro walked up to Aki and slapped her hard across the face. The unexpected blow sent her sprawling back to the floor.

"Liar!" he yelled. His face was red and his speech slurred. He had obviously been drinking.

"No! A horrible monster attacked me! A *kappa*!" she insisted.

Goro slapped her again. Pain seared her face, but she gritted her teeth and glared at him. Goro, breathing hard through his nose, would have hit her again but was stopped by Aunt Noriko's scream of horror.

"What is that?" said the old woman pointing at the basket.

Goro picked up the basket by its rim and held it high. The *kappa's* arm swung from the bottom, its curved claws caught in one of the straps.

"It's the *kappa's* arm," said Aki. "I told you. It attacked me. I cut off its arm and ran home."

Goro studied the grotesque arm for a long time, and then he looked at Aki and started to laugh. He lifted and pulled at the arm, but it held fast. Swearing, he stepped on the basket and yanked it free. Holding the arm up like a trophy he went back to his room, Aunt Noriko following on his heels. Aki slumped against the wall as they disappeared through the door. Goro's voice reached her from the other room.

"I'll take the *kappa's* arm to the castle and present it to Lord Minagawa. He'll be so pleased he'll reward me with gold," he said and slurped noisily from a jug of *sake.*

"You better be careful," warned Aunt Noriko. "*Kappas* have magic. What do we do if it comes looking for its arm? I've heard they do that," she added in a frightened voice.

There was a silent pause as Goro considered this. "The *kappa* is badly wounded; it won't move tonight. Tomorrow, after I take the arm to the castle, I'll wait for it. If it comes, I'll trap it and put it in a cage. I bet people will pay good money to see a *kappa*," he said, guffawing.

Aki had heard enough. She quietly stepped outside and limped toward the bathhouse. A quick inspection of her wounds showed that the slashes on her thigh were not nearly as bad as she had feared. Easing into the deep tub, she let the steaming hot water soothe her battered body while her mind reeled with the unbelievable events of the day. It was almost inconceivable that she had survived the *kappa* attack with less damage than she normally received from Goro's beatings. Aki gingerly touched her swollen cheek, and smirked. She thought how ironic it was that her own flesh and blood was more savage than the greatly feared *kappa* monsters.

With a sudden shock, Aki realized that the *kappa* had never actually attacked her. She replayed every detail of the encounter again. The *kappa* could have easily killed her with one quick swipe of its claws across her throat, yet all its efforts had been concentrated on taking the basket . . . the cucumbers. The *kappa* had never made any moves to hurt her purposely. The gashes on her leg had happened while it had been flailing its arms trying to grab the basket. Looking back, her wounds now seemed almost incidental, accidental even.

The only attacks during the encounter had come from her. She was the one who had kicked the *kappa* and then cut off its arm. Could it be possible that it would have let her go unharmed if she had just dropped the basket?

The image of Goro swearing and tugging trying to untangle the arm from the basket popped into her head and she realized that the *kappa* had not been holding on to the basket. Its hand had been caught in the strap! She shuddered as a ball of guilt exploded in her stomach.

Back in her own room, Aki put out her sleeping futons on the floor and fell into them exhausted. Goro's loud voice came through from the other room. He was still talking about the fame and fortune that would soon be his. Aki snorted in disgust and pulled the futons over her head.

Long after Goro's voice had slowed to a stop and her aunt's steady snoring had started its familiar echoing through the house, Aki lay wide awake. Her mind still raced with thoughts of the *kappa*. New images of it dying in a cage added to her guilt.

Unable to live with the guilt any longer, she quickly put on her clothes and tiptoed into Goro's room. On her hands and knees she felt along the floor for the *kappa's* arm and almost yelped in surprise when her hand touched the cold, slimy skin. Picking it up with a shudder, she ran to the outer kitchen and found her basket. She put the arm in the basket and, shrugging the straps on her shoulders, she stole into the night.

Many times during the long walk back to the river Aki wondered if she had lost her mind, but she continued on. When she arrived at the spot where she had encountered the *kappa* earlier she stopped and called out as politely as she knew how. *"Kappa-san!"* Her voice sounded thin and frightened. *"Kappa-san!* I . . . I've brought your arm back!" She called a little louder and waited. Nothing happened. She was just beginning to think that the whole exercise had been a mistake when there was a soft splash in the reeds behind her.

Horror washed over Aki again as she turned to face the *kappa*. It plodded from the reeds to the path and stood stooped on trembling legs. Its webbed hand still clutched the stub of its arm. Aki could see that it was very weak, but she would not take any chances.

"Tilt your head and drain the water from the top of your head," she said, fear making her voice harsher than she intended. "Then I'll return your arm."

The *kappa* looked at her silently for a moment, then slowly tipped its head forward and let the water dribble from the bowl. As the last drops of water spilled out, the *kappa's* knees buckled and it toppled to the ground.

Aki quickly put the basket on the ground and placed the *kappa's* arm in front of it. "Here is your arm. There are a few cucumbers left in the basket. You can have them," she said, stepping aside.

The *kappa* dragged itself over to the arm and collapsed on top of it. It rolled on its side, gasping for breath, and feebly tried to connect the dead arm to its stump. The pitiful sight brought a lump to Aki's throat. She was the cause of the creature's suffering; she should help, but she didn't know how. She stood immobile with indecision while the *kappa* struggled to lift its head, then she suddenly realized what she must do.

Aki stepped to the river's edge and quickly returned with water in her cupped hands. She held the water above the *kappa's* head and said, "Before I give you this water, you must promise not to harm me or any other human." The *kappa* looked up at her and nodded. She let the water flow between her fingers and could immediately see the strength returning to the *kappa*. Sitting up, it once again attempted to join the arm to its stub. Forgetting the fear and revulsion she had felt only moments before, Aki held the arm in place and watched as the *kappa* stretched and pinched the skin and muscles along the cut. The webbed hand then covered the fissure and in a few minutes the arm was reattached. Aki stared in amazement. She would never have believed had she not seen it with her own eyes.

The *kappa* clenched and unclenched its fist and, seemingly satisfied with its arm, ate a few cucumbers from the basket and closed its eyes to rest. Aki watched the peacefully resting figure. It wasn't a monster, only a creature that belonged to the river. Feeling like an intruder, Aki stood up to leave but was stopped by a webbed hand on her leg.

"Thank you," said the *kappa* looking up at her.

The words were more of a hiss than speech, but the meaning was undeniable. Aki stared at the *kappa* with a gaping mouth. "You can speak?" she asked incredulously. The *kappa* nodded. It stood up and gently placed both hands on Aki's head. Soft warmth emanated from its hands. The warmth moved through her head to her body and to her limbs until it filled every inch of her being.

"You have saved my life and the life of the unborn son I carry," said the *kappa*. "In gratitude, I will share my healing powers with you."

"But I don't know how to use these powers," said Aki.

"You will know when the time comes," said the *kappa* and looked deep into Aki's eyes. "Your kind is so young!" Aki heard the *kappa* exclaim in wonder, and then felt her head explode with images and feelings so ancient her mind could not comprehend them. Aki drowned in the whirling sensations for what felt like an eternity, and at the first hints of dawn the *kappa* released her from the mental link and bid her farewell. It walked to the river and disappeared into the murky waters. Aki sat and watched the river for many hours afterward, but she never saw the *kappa* again.

It was mid-morning when Aki finally made her way back to the farmhouse. She heard Goro yelling her name and looked up to see him running toward her. Judging from his expression, she was in more trouble than she had ever been. The thought of running flitted through her mind, but she immediately dismissed it. She had nowhere to run.

When Goro reached her, he hit her so hard she flew backward for several feet and landed in a heap at the side of the path. Goro's rage at having his fame and fortune stolen from under his nose was so great it was not easily sated, and the beating that followed was so brutal that some farmers working in nearby fields were forced to intervene.

The men who rescued Aki carried her limp form to Aunt Noriko's farmhouse. They looked at her broken body and sadly shook their heads. They thought that she would surely die.

When Aunt Noriko saw Aki carried in, she cried out loud. She cried with anger over Goro's stupidity. What purpose did it serve to kill the girl? If Aki died, she would have nobody to help her with the chores. Goro had become a lazy drunk, and Noriko wished she had beaten some sense into him long ago. It was too late now; he most likely was already hiding and taking refuge in a jug of *sake*.

Aki could not see, or move, or even breathe. Her life was draining away and she had no strength to fight. She floated in an ocean of pain when the image of wise, intelligent eyes pulled her back. *I don't want to die,* she thought and drifted back into a void.

A few days later Aki awoke well-rested and strong. She looked at the shafts of morning sunshine coming through the window and wondered why she had been allowed to sleep so late. Then the sight of an ugly yellow bruise covering her right arm brought memories of the beating and the *kappa* flooding back into her mind. She trembled uncontrollably as she relived the memories. Although she had no clear recollection of the beating, she knew that the only reason she was still alive was because of the *kappa*. She also knew that she could no longer stay in Aunt Noriko's house.

Goro was still sleeping; Aki could hear him snoring. Aunt Noriko was out in the fields. Without anyone there to stop her, Aki simply walked out of the house and headed down the road.

As Aki slowly left behind the little group of farm-houses and everything familiar, the enormity of her action began to dawn on her. She had no plans, nowhere to go. Aki sat down at the side of the road to think, when she noticed a little yellow butterfly floundering on the dirt. It had a torn wing. She gently picked it up and wished that it could fly again. As soon as her thought had formed, the butterfly's wing began to mend, and in just a few moments it flew out of her hand and was carried away by the breeze. She stared at it in disbelief. The *kappa's* healing powers! Of course Aki knew that she was alive because of them, but she had not thought of them in terms of others.

She remembered the village tofu-maker's little boy who had been trampled by a runaway horse and could no longer walk. Perhaps she could help. No, she *would* help. And the young *geisha* girl wasting away with a strange fever. And surely there would be many others who could also use her help. With that thought, Aki was no longer afraid of her uncertain future.

Before heading for the village, Aki made a detour to the fields. She picked as many cucumbers as she could carry and took them to the riverbank. She bowed by the river's edge and sent the *kappa* a silent prayer of gratitude for the wonderful gift she had received. And to the end of her days, no matter where her travels took her, Aki returned to the river every summer and left an offering of young cucumbers by the muddy banks.

THE CHANGELESS ROOM
by Charlotte Carlson

This is as close to a horror story as I ever buy, and when I read the first paragraph I almost tossed it on the "Reject" pile. People who know me know that I usually go for very mild flavors in the gruesome, probably due to the fact that the sharer of my home and editorial duties, Lisa, is not even as tolerant of the horrible as I am, and in general I don't like buying stories that Lisa can't or won't read. But I read a page and got hooked; I predict you will, too, if you give it a fair chance. And it's really not all that scary—if Charlotte Carlson will forgive me for saying so.

This is Charlotte's first professional sale, although she has been dictating stories to her mother since she was three. (She started even younger than I did.) She was born in Florida, and now lives in California with her parents and younger sister, a Border Collie named Murphy and a cat named Sen-gen.

She says this story is a gift to her mother for her Croning.

The Changeless Room was said to be the darkest place in the world in spite of the light of the Soul Candle that it was built to protect. Cold and black— once the door clicked closed. Yet, human nature being what it is, countless adventurers from all lands, all walks of life, sought it.

At least some of them, certainly, searched for the purest of reasons: the snuffing of Cryshade's Candle. But others were drawn by avarice and a curiosity that gave no thought for the purpose of such a creation. They sought the legendary treasure that was said to grace the

15

base of the Candle (in truth a littering of armor and jewelry from those who, upon entering the Changeless Room, had failed to leave again) or the fame of having found what so many before them had striven for but never reached.

But imagine little Sihir's surprise when she went down into the cellar for more candles and found a door towering over her that she had never seen before. Really, it shouldn't have been there at all; it was too tall for the low-ceilinged cellar and hinged right into the permafrost. Sihir noted the large brass leaf in the center of the door—it was as tall as she was—and the trademark latches of interlocking leaves, and bent to pluck eight thick candles out of their storage box. Hugging them to her chest, she went back up the stairs and shut the cellar door.

Over the next few weeks every member of her family made trips into the cellar for various things (mostly candles, which went quickly this far north where the sun rose and set practically on the same horizon), and none of them ever said anything about a phantom door haunting the cellar.

Sihir knew what it was, of course. She knew all about the Changeless Room that held cursed Cryshade's Soul Candle, and had heard the tales of the fates of those stupid enough to open the leaf-decorated door. When the nights were two and three times as long as the days, the stories were the only thing that kept the house alive, and she knew them all by heart.

She went down into the cellar three more times for candles, extra blankets, and more oil and ignored the door each time. Not for her was the fate of the Gil Gnome, or Mad Sham Pete, or Lady Creamskin. And she knew that if she opened that door, she'd see all of them, and that the Gil Gnome's fabulous Ruby Torque would be loose around his bleached neckbones, and Mad Sham Pete's "enchanted" sword would be rusting in its moldy sheath (but the emeralds would be sparkling brightly), and she knew that Lady Creamskin's scrying diamond would be resting in her spiky rib cage, still attached to its thick gold chain.

Sihir wasn't even tempted. She gathered up the candles, blankets, and oil and didn't so much as glance back down.

She and her family slept in the loft of the house, all together for warmth during winter on a large mattress stuffed with down. The children in the center, the adults to the sides. Sometimes her aunts and uncles or parents would volunteer to sleep downstairs (for room, they said) and the children would usurp the entire middle of the bed, sprawled this way and that, fighting half-asleep for space when there was plenty—just out of habit.

It was on such a night that her cousin Ifhaer accidentally elbowed her in the eye. He didn't know it, of course, being still asleep, and Sihir quelled the urge to hit him back. He wouldn't know why, and it would start a big fight. Everybody would wake up, and she'd be in trouble.

She squirmed out from under the layers of blankets and expertly picked her way off the mattress without a sound or a slip. Down the loft ladder she went and quietly made her way into the storeroom. Her eye was watering badly; it felt swollen and she couldn't shake an image of it popping. The door from the storeroom to the outside creaked, but she opened it slowly and just wide enough that she could snake her arm out and pull in a handful of snow.

The wind nearly tore the door out of her hands. She gasped and pulled it closed. It smashed shut and she froze for a minute, shivering both from the chill and the possibility of a midnight scolding. But no sound came from beyond the storeroom.

She sighed and found a rag for the snow and put it against her eye. She started humming a tune her Aunt Aillin had taught her, hearing the music of the flutes and drums in her head.

But then the drums gained a life of their own. They shattered the melody. The drums were coming from outside. They were a horse's hooves crunching through the deep snow.

The crunching stopped very near to the door, and Sihir almost went up to it to greet the person—it could only be a neighbor at this hour, and there must be something wrong. But the door swung open and smashed into her, knocking her to the side, pinning her against the wall.

And a giant black bear walked into the storeroom.

At least that was what it looked like from where she huddled. But bears don't generally wear boots, and they don't wear helmets or travel with big swords strapped across their backs. Of that she was absolutely sure.

But this man—whoever he was—was huge, and his helmet and sword were gilded in places. He closed the door as though it had just occurred to him that people might be sleeping. He didn't see her.

With great purpose he studied the cellar door and lit a thin torch before swinging it open and creaking down the steps.

Sihir, being a practical soul, thought about running to wake her parents. But Sihir also thought about that big sword, and about her utter certainty that he could wield it very well. She determined that the wisest thing to do would be to lock the cellar door behind him and then call her parents. He could probably hack through it, but by then they'd be ready for him.

She crawled over to the edge of the cellar door and reached across the opening to close it, readying herself to spring up and pull the bolt, but saw something very strange. Something that told her that this man wasn't a thief—at least not in the usual sense. The top of his helmet made a gold star—four points—the sign of a Souther sorcerer.

Sihir had never heard of a sword-carrying sorcerer before, even from the South, but no one wore the Star in Gold except them; swindlers and would-be charlatans smartly kept a respectful distance from their calling. And if a Souther had trudged this far north at this time of the year, there could be only one reason.

The stairs gave a final creak as the dark-clad sorcerer stepped from them to the floor of the cellar, and stayed silent as Sihir gingerly put a foot on the top stair. She'd lived in this house all her life and knew precisely where to step. She knew that the third stair from the top always made a cracking sound like it was about to snap in two (no matter how much weight was on it), and she grabbed onto the rail and lowered herself to the fourth. The fifth step only made noise if you went down the middle of it, and the ninth step only if you stepped on the left side.

Five more quick steps and she was on the floor behind the man, in the dark of his shadow. The floor was freezing against her bare feet, and the wild shadows cast by his thin torch made the cellar a very sinister place.

As she'd guessed, he was staring up at the door, seeing it plainly as no one in her house but she had. Naturally, he reached for the leaf-shaped latch.

"No!" She couldn't help it. Even though he was a Souther, she couldn't let him do it.

He whipped about, brandishing his torch, but he had expected an adult and waved it too high to burn her. She yelped and leaped to the side. In her haste to get away from the torch, it hadn't occurred to her that she had now placed the sorcerer between her and her only exit.

Heaving for breath, the sorcerer moved in front of the stairs. He pulled back the torch and held out a pacifying hand. "Shhh. I'm not going to harm you, girl! Hush!"

His size made her doubt him. Sihir thought he could probably crush her head in one hand.

"Calm down," the sorcerer said. "I just want to see inside."

See inside and stay inside, the stories said. Sihir was still trying to catch her breath. She was shaking her head at the same time. "N-no," she breathed hoarsely. "You'll be trapped."

"How can I be trapped if I keep my feet out here?"

"It's the Changeless Room." She felt like she was talking to one of her baby cousins. "You just will."

He smiled at her and raised one hand to take off his helmet. Without it he didn't look nearly as scary. In fact, he looked quite amiable. "I appreciate your concern, child. I would never have expected it from a Norther. But I have ways of protecting myself." He showed her the Star in Gold.

Foolish, foolish, foolish. "Everyone has said that," she said. "All of them: the Gil Gnome, Lady Creamski—"

"Creamskin? Those are just stories. Here." He presented her with his helmet. "You can give it back to me when the door closes again."

No, you'll be inside the Room.

Numbly she took the helmet. It was much heavier than she thought, and she nearly dropped it on her toes. The star alone was as big across as her chest. The sorcerer nodded reassuringly and turned his attention back to the door.

For some reason she thought he would draw his sword. Maybe she'd thought it was a magical sword. But he didn't. Instead he reached a gloved hand inside his black fur coat and withdrew a small leather pouch.

He went to stand by the door and planted his feet carefully before pulling the drawstring on the pouch and crouching to sprinkle its contents over his boots. Before he opened the door, he glanced back at Sihir once and smiled one more time. His fingers curled around the handle, and Sihir ducked behind some grain sacks. His thumb pressed the latch.

He took a deep breath and jerked the door open a head's width.

Nothing.

He held his torch higher.

Nothing.

Slowly, he opened the door wider and thrust his torch into the dark beyond it.

Sihir could barely breathe. She was waiting for giant

hands to rip the sorcerer and his petty magic right off the floor and suck him inside for eternity.

Nothing.

He seemed to be getting impatient. The adrenaline was ebbing, and she could see that his stance was growing lazier. He opened the door wider, and then flung it open all the way. The phantasmic door that should not have fit in the low-ceilinged cellar did something else it should not have been able to do; it swung freely through the boxes that would have stopped a real door and crashed back against the permafrost wall.

The sorcerer spoke a word that Sihir had never heard and stepped into the chamber. He was cursing.

Sihir didn't move.

He was saying something about a dirty-rotten trick, and he was muttering something about murder.

Sihir poked her head up a little. "What is it?"

"You know damn well what it is!" he hissed. "It's the rest of your cursed cellar!"

Sihir knew it was a trick. Dirty and rotten, and it was on the sorcerer. She did something impractical and got up to peer inside. Knowing that the door was about to slam closed on the foolish man, she moved very cautiously.

But what she saw made her straighten from her half-crouch and frown through the doorway. The chamber beyond was lit by his torch, and it was filled with boxes and stacks of blankets and sacks of grain scattered across the floor.

He was kicking the sacks and cursing, still staring in disbelief around the little permafrost-walled room. One of the sacks flew at Sihir, and she whirled away from it instinctively. What broke over her back, though, wasn't the deadweight of a grain sack but a splintering rib cage.

She turned back in horror and saw the truth. The sorcerer was standing right in front of a giant waxy cylinder—he was dwarfed by it—and he was kicking through the remains of his predecessors that littered the floor.

The ice behind the door started to crackle, and the

impossible door itself began to shake, and Sihir cried out. He just looked at her as though it wasn't a funny joke.

The door freed itself from the permafrost and Sihir dove forward reflexively, jamming the door open with the helmet that bore the Star In Gold.

She heard the sorcerer's muffled shriek, saw his torch drop and sputter out in a wad of moldy clothing. In the sudden absence of the firelight the sorcerer was backlit by a faint reddish glow.

The Candle.

Cryshade's tormentors had taken her soul and given her an eternity of ghosthood by winding its waxy substance into a candle that would never burn down. And no one had ever seen the Soul Candle from the other side of the door before little Sihir poked her head into the dark.

"Souther! I caught the door, but I can't pull it back—and I think your helmet is crushing."

The snapping of bones met her ears, growing closer, and then she felt the heat of the sorcerer and his breath on her face. His huge hands caught the door and she heard him grunt with strain.

"It won't move," he whispered after a moment.

Sihir couldn't see a thing, and she couldn't think. No story about the Changeless Room had ever given a clue as to what should be done if the Room materialized in your cellar and you managed to catch the door before it could lock shut on any trespassers who were stupid enough to be inside. One thing she knew for certain was that, no matter how much force they put to the door, if the sorcerer couldn't muscle it open, it couldn't be muscled.

"Don't you have a spell or something?" she asked him. His panic was palpable.

"No." She thought he might die of fright even before his helmet gave way. "I didn't think I'd go in."

The metal of the helmet was making a strange noise as it bent, and Sihir didn't know what to do. She had a mental image of the sorcerer's face, an image of the horror plastered across it, and she couldn't turn away.

The metallic crinkling stopped suddenly and the door trembled for a moment and finally stilled.

"The Star," she heard the sorcerer breathe. Relief was in his voice, but not much.

A tiny glint of gold, imperceptible to anyone with even a little light, told her where the Star in Gold was on the helmet. "It won't break?" she whispered.

"I don't know," he replied softly. "I still can't move the door."

"Could it hold long enough for us to get a message to another sorcerer?" In the hiatus, Sihir was thinking again. She wished she wasn't the only one.

"I don't know," he repeated. His voice was shaky, as though it was only now dawning on him what was happening. And then he said, "I don't know of any who would help me."

Sihir didn't bother to ask why. Sorcerers didn't usually garner reputations as neighborly sorts. Their petty rivalries were legendary. "What about the Candle?" she asked.

The darkness that was the sorcerer moved in front of the vague reddish light from the Candle. "Burn through the door?" he wondered out loud. But then his darkness moved again, and she heard him settling back close to her. "The fire won't burn anything. It's the Soul Candle. It's not real fire."

"No, I mean put it out." Her mind was racing. "Put it out, and see what happens."

He sighed. "I can't even see the top, girl."

"Use your sword to climb the wax."

The sorcerer sighed again. "I told you, it's not a real fire."

Sihir got up off the floor and went to the other side of the cellar.

"Where are you going?" A huge man, a sorcerer, a Souther, frightened like a child in the dark.

"There's a box of kindling wedges somewhere in

here," she answered softly. Now she was keeping quiet not just from shock; if her family woke up now, they'd probably try to do this themselves. It was for their own good.

"Kindling wedges?" the sorcerer whispered also; gods alone knew why.

"Yes. Just a second." She stubbed her toe on a box and bit her lip as she felt its contents with her shaking fingers. Cold. Ridged. Splintery. She retrieved two of the wedges and felt her way back to the door. Her free hand went to the ground and followed it to the helmet. Her fingers splayed to judge the size of the opening.

The helmet was big. The opening was just big enough. She said, "Move away from the door," and heard a slight scuffle as the sorcerer did.

"You think it will burn?"

Sihir didn't stop to consider how odd it was that the sorcerer was asking her such a thing. Of course the door wouldn't burn! It shouldn't even have been in the cellar. And she suspected that if she'd tried to jam it open with anything other than the Star In Gold, the sorcerer's fate would already be out of her hands.

She turned sideways and stepped through the door. Against the dead light of the Candle, the sorcerer could finally see her.

"What are you doing?" he demanded, but he kept his voice hushed. "You'll be trapped, too!"

"Come over to the Candle with me," Sihir told him. She hoped he wouldn't simply heft her up and shove her back through the door.

But he followed her; she heard the bone cracking under his boots as he walked. She stumbled and cursed her way across the littered floor, having no boots. And then his hands were on her waist and she started to protest that she was trying to help him, but he raised her up and sat her on one of his shoulders.

"What can I do?" he asked her.

She recovered herself with effort and looked up. The glowing Candle was too tall for her to see the top. She reached out a hand. The Candle was warm (or at least warmer) and she took one of the wedges and pressed it into the wax. "Lift me up to it, so I can stand on it," she ordered.

He hesitated.

"I won't fall."

He hesitated some more. "Are you sure?"

"Yes. It's like climbing ice." But she hoped he wouldn't press her because it wasn't really like climbing ice at all—and anyway she'd never climbed ice in her life.

He lifted her up, and she put her small feet on the protruding edge of the wood. The wax was soft enough that she could dig her fingers into it if she worked at it, and she felt confident that if she had handholds, she could move the wedges up for her feet. But the wax was also soft enough that the wood started to dip as soon as she stepped on it, and she was forced to move faster than she'd planned.

She stabbed the Candle with the second piece of wood and stepped onto it quickly, scratching at the wax with an outstretched arm.

"I'll catch you if you fall," the sorcerer assured her. "Don't be afraid."

She moved carefully, hugging the soft Candle and moving the wedges up with whatever hand happened to be free, and soon she couldn't hear the sorcerer's breathing anymore. She kept going, finding a steady rhythm: grip wax, move wedge, step up, grip wax, move wedge, step up . . . higher and higher, until there was a point in the high darkness where the reddish-gold Candle stopped.

When she saw it, she lost her rhythm. Her foot missed the wedge and kicked it out of the wax, sending it into the darkness. There was a clatter, and the sorcerer, sounding smaller than ever, called up to her. "Come down, girl!"

Sihir didn't answer. She was clinging to the side of the massive Candle, both feet on one sliding wedge, trying

to catch her breath. But it seemed to her that the top
was closer than the bottom, and she got sick when she
thought of herself having to *lower* the wedge of wood.
Get to the top, she told herself. *Put out the Candle.*

What might happen then, she didn't know. But if she
didn't try, the sorcerer would die, and maybe others, too,
if the Changeless Room decided to stay in her cellar.

She made her left hand a spear and twisted it deep
into the wax until her arm was buried up to her elbow,
and with her right hand pried the wedge out of the Candle. And she dangled by one arm as she pounded the
wedge back into the wax.

The going was slower now that she had less reach, but
she found a rhythm again, and at last she stood up
straight on the wedge and peered over the lip of Cryshade's Soul Candle to the tiny, tiny flame in the center.
She knew from the stories that as soon as the door below
locked shut, the tiny fire working on the monstrous Candle would go out—only to be reignited the instant the
door was opened once again. It was a sorcerous flame,
to illuminate the stalk of the whole Candle, and though
the Candle itself was warm, she felt no heat from the
fire.

She pulled herself over the edge.

"Girl?" It was a muffled call. A concerned call.

Sihir didn't answer. She cupped her hands around the
tiny wick and heard whispers above her head.

She bent forward and puffed out the light.

The whispers became one whisper, became a scream,
became a triumphant howl so loud she clapped her
hands over her ears.

She felt the Candle starting to collapse, but she could
do nothing. Her knees sank into the softening wax, trapping her. She was screaming as the wax came up over
her waist, clawing at it with her arms as it swallowed
her torso. But she was sinking faster and faster as the
wax melted and started to run like honey in the air
around her.

There was no heat. The wax grew clear as her head

was consumed, and she found she could breathe when she at last gave in and gasped for air. The air around her was a swirling of waxy mist, winding—or unwinding, rather—as she fell slowly through its heart, becoming entangled in the thread of the wick.

The waxy air was a blanket over her ears; the cry that would have deafened her—the unified voice of those who, by chance or by design, had come to share Cryshade's fate—was faint like the whistle of wind through trees.

Cryshade's soul spread out like a fading flower, and then that muffled voice became voices, became a whisper, became a thought in her head:

Free.

And it was gone—all gone—and she was cold on the hard floor and it was dark and growing darker. But warm hands on her shoulders lifted her off the freezing floor and the sorcerer's voice reached her as though from a distance. "Stay with me, child," he whispered.

"The Candle—"

"Is gone." His voice was warm with relief and awe. "So's the door."

Her eyes snapped open. "We're trapped?"

But there was light here and she glanced up. The door to the cellar stairs was standing open, and it was the dim light of predawn that was filtering down into the cellar. She looked back at his face, seeing it for the first time in the silver light.

He seemed even younger than her father, and he wore no beard or mustache. In this light, he wasn't so big— his bulk was mostly the fur coat—and she realized that he probably wasn't much bigger than either of her uncles.

He was unwinding the wick from her ankles, coiling it like a rope.

"You could see the door," he whispered.

In the presence of a sorcerer who wore the Star in Gold, the magnitude of that seemingly small fact finally sank in. In all the time she'd seen the door, she'd only thought of the stories, not of the people in them. The Gil Gnome, Mad Sham Pete, Lady Creamskin, and all the rest had been either sorcerers, or crazy.

Her eyes widened, and she suddenly found herself glancing longingly up the stairs. Now that the ordeal was over, she wanted to go back to bed and have everything normal again.

"Practical soul," he chuckled as he got to his feet. He turned away from her and went to where the phantom door had stood and bent to pick up something; his rumpled helmet with only the Star in Gold still intact. And then he looked down at the bones on the floor and picked up something serpentine and sparkling.

A creak from above made him jump a little, and he came back and knelt at her side. He handed her first Lady Creamskin's scrying diamond and then the helmet and wick. "I wouldn't suggest that you leave your family so young," he told her quickly, "but you saved my life. When you're ready, if you wish, you may bring these south. If you come through the Pass, I will find you, and I'll find some way to repay you."

He glanced upward again. Someone was awake above. The sorcerer rose to his feet and bowed deeply to her before making his way cautiously up the stairs. She heard the outer door open and close and a moment later the sound of hooves crunching through crusted snow.

Sihir chipped a hole in the permafrost wall and put the helmet, the wick, and the diamond inside. She replaced the bulk of the icy debris in the hole on top of them and stacked boxes in front of it. When thaw came, water would run down the cellar walls from the cracks and freeze everything solidly back in place. Rubbing her swollen eye, she walked back up the stairs and closed the cellar door quietly behind her.

For a long time she sat alone in the storeroom with her chin resting on her knees, wondering what it would be like to live an impractical life.

ISABELLE AND THE SIREN
by Mary Catelli

Mary Catelli says she programs computers for a living, about which I can only say it takes all kinds—if she likes computers, well, rather her than me. I'll never get over the fact that some people pay good money for things for which I'd pay rather lavishly to avoid, like riding roller coasters. I guess that's how Disneyland makes such a fortune—something for everybody.

She's sold several short stories and, like half the human race it seems, is working on the obligatory novel. She says, "Please make sure to put this in the anthology: Isabelle is mentally ill. Her melancholia is our clinical depression. People with her symptoms, or some of them, should seek help, because we have treatments that Isabelle did not have." As a depressive of many years standing, I echo that sentiment—fellow depressives, let's all come out of our closets—and hooray for imipramine and all such God-sent medications!

A wordless melody drifted sweetly into the white-washed room with the morning sunlight. Isabelle lay in bed, contemplating the ceiling. *I should have stayed in the city,* she thought. *My melancholia made it hard to do anything, but out here, convalescing, with nothing that has to be done by a given time—why, I do nothing.* A sea breeze tugged at the white bed hangings. Isabelle wrinkled her nose. *Even get up.*

Outside she heard the townsfolk moving toward something outside the town (perhaps toward the music, but she could not rouse the concentration to tell or the energy to care).

Thoughts floated vaguely through her mind, as detached as if they had no connection to her: about how
all the townsfolk would think her a perfect sluggard,
taking two hours to get up. She had managed to get up
in the city. Then, when she had heard two townsfolk
talking about how the Professor of Rhetoric—her own
father—had debated Satan for the title Prince of Lies,
and won, she had not only *not* defended her father, she
had not cared. She rolled over. *Still didn't,* she thought.

She forced the thoughts away. *I have to get up,* she
resolved. *Now.*

Isabelle lay in bed unmoving for over an hour while
the music faded away. She vaguely registered that she
could not hear the townsfolk, which was unlike them.
Most of the fishermen went out to sea, but the townsfolk
had shops and kitchen gardens, and she had gotten thoroughly familiar with the noises of morning, since she had
not gotten up early once in the two weeks she had spent
in the town.

Isabelle sighed. There were times when she could not
figure out not only how she had gotten herself a scholar-
ship in magical zoology, but how she had gotten herself
to the town. Professor Arthurson may have suggested
that she be sent out to the countryside, like a sickly baby
with its wet nurse, but she had made the arrangements.

I have to get up, Isabelle thought again, and somewhat
to her own surprise, found herself getting up. Having
done so, she managed to keep going, to walk toward the
window, pick up her dressing gown, and look out the
window as she put it on.

The square outside was completely empty. The store
stood open, but Mistress Agatha did not stand behind
its counter. The clapboard houses stood silent among the
dunes. Down the street, an open door swung in the wind,
and over the dunes, the sea, empty of boats, glittered in
the sunlight. A thin, piercing cry echoed from the house
next to her. Isabelle turned her face toward it as the
baby's crying went on and on. She frowned. Kate might

aggravate her with perpetual chatter, but she would
never let her daughter cry like that.

Isabelle sighed and headed for the stairs. Her hand
rested loosely on the railing as she walked downstairs.
"Angel of God," she whispered, "my guardian dear, to
whom His love commits me here, ever this day be by
my side, to watch, to lead, to guard, to guide." The
prayer rattled itself off mechanically, without engaging
her mind. She reminded herself, dutifully, that she would
need all the leading and guiding she could get, but she
roused no enthusiasm in herself; she could not even
manage curiosity at what had stolen the townsfolk
away—or shock at her inability to feel it.

She opened the front door. A sea breeze came in to pull
at her pale brown hair and tug at her sky-blue dressing
gown. Isabelle swallowed and wondered if the music earlier had been responsible—strange music to be heard in
this worthy if dull town. She walked down the street,
reminding herself again that while she had not completed her studies, she had been a promising zoologist—
had even planned to write a book before she was graduated. Besides, something had to be done, however black
her mood. She forced herself to look about. The clapboard houses stood in rows, painted pale yellows and
blues and grays, neat and respectable, except for the
number of doors swinging open.

Music came floating through the air, sweet and faintly
familiar from the morning. Isabelle stopped at the edge
of town, listening to the alien notes and slowly matching
them to her studies. A siren sang there: a humanoid
winged beast, a carrion eater that made its own carrion.
She glanced over the dunes. The siren was inhuman and
unintelligent, but dangerous; even to her, the music
sounded attractive.

Isabelle turned and walked back into the town. When
Professor Arthurson had babbled about the town as a
perfect, quiet place for convalescence, she had complied
more out of being too listless to argue than of thinking
it would do her any good, but she had not thought some-

thing like this would happen. Why, Arthurson had cited
that nothing ever happened here, that its nominal duke
had never been troubled by it since the end of the Viking raids, as its chief attraction. She glanced over her
shoulder, noting that the seclusion would also give shelter to monsters.

The music came after her, growing more alluring. The
siren must have seen her, Isabelle realized as she
reached the house where she rented the room; it could
have, since its eyes were like an eagle's, and it would
eagerly draw more prey. Isabelle swallowed. The siren
might even be able to draw her, melancholia or no melancholia, if its song grew alluring enough.

She walked into the kitchen and looked around. *Wax,*
she thought, remembering Ulysses. She started to look
through Mistress Catherine's cabinets.

The song wound its way into the house, and Isabelle
felt a tug on herself, a desire to go, such as she had not
felt for months, ever since the melancholia had fallen on
her. She looked down into the last drawer she had
opened, and saw a butcher's cleaver. The music called,
more and more sweetly; her desire to follow was not
strong, but it was growing. Isabelle drew a deep breath.
*I must pick up this knife, especially since I can't find any
wax,* she sternly told herself, *even if I can find no interest
in doing so; at the very least, I must think of the townsfolk.* She reached down, picked it up, and breathed a
deep sigh of relief, flexing her fingers around this unexpected victory.

The siren sang on. Isabelle decided, gravely, that she
had best go before the song numbed her mind, while
she could still resist. She turned and walked out of the
house, down the street, and out toward the song.

The sunlight shone over the beige sand and the rip-
pling sea. Isabelle walked on through the dune grass
and the wild roses, noticing the trampled grass and the
footprints in the sand that showed she was following the
townsfolk. The song grew no more alluring, but it tugged
on her like a fisherman's line.

Isabelle looked over the cove. Ahead, the beach rose up into a rocky pile, and on the other side, there was a cliff face, and there the bent grass and footsteps in the sand marked the townsfolk's path. Isabelle's mouth pursed. Which would, indeed, be the way the siren would want them to go.

Not that way, then, Isabelle thought, setting her will as if she were resolving to get up. She started to walk along the water's edge, skirting the rocks. The song faltered for a second, and grew more enticing. Isabelle bit her lip. The lure was stronger than the blackest of her moods; she could not stop herself from going forward.

But I can, she told herself, *not go over the cliff. Even when I wanted to kill myself, and had, in my lighter moods, the willpower to do, I did not. Therefore I can go around.* Her knees smashed against a boulder; blinding in pain, Isabelle caught herself against the rock. *This is not,* she thought with grim humor, *what I meant when I said I would like to be rid of my melancholia.*

She came around the cliff face. Spread across the rocks at the bottom of the cliff were the townsfolk. Men, women, and children lay broken against the stone. Some of them had crawled on, tearing their wrecked bodies against the stones. One of them still tried to pull herself on, toward the siren; her legs were shattered, but her bloody hands dug into the sands to pull her toward the song.

Not all dead yet, then, Isabelle thought, recognizing Kate, and feeling her heart grow cold at the sight of the woman's glazed eyes. Her eyes went past them—she could do nothing for them while the siren lived, she reminded herself. Up on the slope, on the other side, stood the siren herself.

A figure like a slender woman stood there. Blue feathers instead of hair fell from her head, blue down covered her body, and two great wings spread from her back. Her face was pale and innocent as the wondrous music bubbled from her lips. She could be taken for human. Isabelle, her hand tightening on the cleaver, walked slowly toward the siren, picking her way through the broken rocks. She could not have stopped walking; the song's charm would not have let her. Her hand shook a little as she prayed that the charm would let her strike.

The siren's soulless eyes looked at Isabelle; they were brown, enormous, and as placid as a cow's. The woman drew in a sharp breath, knowing she could never mistake the siren for human. A faint expression of astonishment crossed the siren's face, but it shrugged the emotion off. Its hands came up, long black claws spreading from them. Isabelle lifted her cleaver, but the siren did not notice as it stepped forward to strike down its prey.

Isabelle struck. The cleaver sliced into the siren's unprotected side. Its song choked off into a cry of pain. Blood gouted, again and again as its heart beat. The siren stepped back, astonishment on its face, and Isabelle dodged to one side as it fell. The flow of blood slackened. The siren's eyes stared blankly at the sky.

"Mistress Isabelle!" A pain-filled voice rose over the sand. Isabelle turned to see Kate raising her hand again. The woman's eyes were human again, but Isabelle bit her lip, surveying the wreckage of the bodies. She raised her voice: "I will do what I can; first I must see how many of you still live."

Kate sank back, nodding weakly, and Isabelle started to look over the bodies. The nearest one to her was dead, but the young man next still breathed, however shallowly; blood oozed from his side. She went through the bodies, cataloging, and stopped by the worst injured living—a boy of twelve, with blood seeping from his body. It would be a long time to work through them all. She pushed back hair from her face. And then there was getting them to shelter and getting help. She closed her eyes briefly, and reminded herself that she had learned the spell to communicate across leagues, even if she had forgotten it in her zoology studies. She could reconstruct it, and the duke, if he had had no dealings with this part of his duchy for years, owed them a great deal of protection and aid for their taxes.

A gull cried, overhead. Isabelle reached for a shirt to tear it into bandages. Her hands froze on the cloth.

I'm not, she realized, *having any difficulty helping them—nothing like even getting up.* She glanced back at the siren's body. It had been earlier, she realized; she had felt horrified when she had first seen the bodies.

A grim laugh sprang to her lips, but Isabelle managed to choke it down into an unrecognizable bark. She looked around the ruined bodies, and thought that it would never be accepted as a cure. She finished binding the boy's injuries and moved on.

A crow had come to peck at the siren's body. Isabelle grimaced and hurried her bandaging. She could already hear Professor Arthurson's lament at the loss of so valuable a specimen, but she had gained enough lore about the siren to see her to a professorship.

An old man started to cough up blood. Isabelle's mouth set, and she drew her mouth back to the present. *Treat all the injured, perhaps get them to shelter.* She started to make a list, work out the spell. She almost flinched away from the length of the list, but stiffened her resolve. It did not feel as hard as getting up had been that morning, and she had managed that.

DRAGON'S TEAR

by Sonya Fedotowsky

Sonya wrote her first story when she was in third grade
(you left it rather late in life, didn't you?), and her teacher
asked if she wanted to be a writer. She says "I nodded
hesitantly, not exactly positive that writing was what I
wanted to do, because I really wanted to be an artist. My
highly active imagination has filled my head with tons of
material for stories and novels, and writing has become
what I've called, until now, my 'unseen art.'"

She grew up in New England and graduated with a degree
in Visual Arts from college in Pittsfield, Massachusetts—I grew
up just over the state line in New York—Rensselaer County,
with Pittsfield quite near. My father used to drive a mail
route or something like that, and one of my earliest memories is of driving over Lebanon Mountain to Pittsfield. I may
have had an aunt there or something, many years ago.

Any career in the arts demands the support of completely
unrelated jobs, and she currently works as a preschool
assistant teacher. Well, don't let them know you're an artist,
or they won't let you within a mile of their kids. It's sad
but true—or maybe times have changed since I went to
Teacher's College?

She would like to dedicate this story to her husband,
Chris Cimonetti, "upon whose shoulders has fallen the painful and grueling task of being my editor, and to my family
and friends who will see my unseen art for the first time."

We all need those support systems, and quite often they
come along packaged as husbands.

Amaryl inclined a pointed ear toward the cavern
opening. Her three companions also listened for

movement in the dark mouth, but of them all, Amaryl's elven hearing was the sharpest. Except for a faint movement of air that only she could hear, there was no sign of the hell-spawned beast that guarded the treasure her party came to steal; a gem of unimaginable power and the savior of Amaryl's people—the Dragon's Tear.

The Isle of Elves was slowly falling into the sea. Earthquakes were bringing down mountains and tearing great rifts through the island. The College of Mages had worked desperately to find a spell to stabilize the land, and finally they invented one that was likely to work, but it required the Dragon's Tear. For the past twenty years, many champions had set out to retrieve the Tear, but none of them had ever returned. Daneloth was the last who had attempted the perilous quest, and when he did not come back, Amaryl made sure she was the next one to go. Along the journey she had searched for signs that Daneloth lived, but as she stood before the Dragon Maw Cavern, she was certain that the day he kissed her and promised her that he would bring back the Tear was the last she would ever see of him. Maybe she would find the Tear, maybe she would fail, but she swore that either way, the dragon would die. That she was sure of.

The companions Amaryl chose to aid her were picked from the three other races for their varying strengths. Olaug, the giantess, prettier than her name suggested, was chosen because she was the strongest of her race, and giant females, as a rule, were stronger than males. Gwyneth, the human warrior, was not chosen for strength alone; she was chosen for her heart. Human hearts were a force unto themselves, driving that inferior race to take over more than half the world like parasites and overcome the strength of giants, the cunning of dwarves, and the perfection of elves. Finally, the dwarf, Fenya; obviously not chosen for strength at all but for her uncanny intelligence. Fenya was perhaps the most valuable member of the party, for she possessed her kind's knowledge of subterranean caverns and dragon killing. Fenya had placed poison inside hollow crossbow bolts, then armed everyone with several of them. She instructed the others to aim for the dragon's eye or the soft membranes of its mouth, for any other place would be guarded by stone-hard scales.

The cavern twisted downward into darkness so pressing that the torchlight barely reflected off the coal-black stone. Clanking armor, footfalls, and the occasional shifting of a shoulder bag broke the otherwise pure silence. Amaryl occasionally heard Fenya sniff the hot and stagnant air.

"Burned," said Fenya at last, with an ancient, yet childlike voice. "It's a firebreather."

Not all dragons breathed fire, but Amaryl had come prepared for the worst. After twenty years of losing the best warriors to the unconquerable foe, Amaryl knew this was an unusual dragon. All the fireproof salves, shields, and armor had not saved the previous champions. There was something else, something worse, some terror that not even knowledgeable Fenya could guess.

Gwyneth knelt down. "Footprint."

Fenya bent closer and held the torch close to the ground. An enormous five-clawed gouge was torn through the rock.

"Interesting," said Fenya, "Most dragon prints are uneven, with the middle two digits extended well beyond the others. See, there are four even digits, with the fifth significantly shorter and bending off to the side, like a thumb."

Amaryl asked, "What does this tell us?"

"We're facing a completely unknown species."

"Why didn't we see any prints outside the cavern?"

Olaug answered, "Dragons sleep for months at a time, and any prints near the entrance would have been weathered away or grown over."

Amaryl said, "Perhaps we can kill it while it sleeps."

Gwyneth added, "And if it isn't, we'll still kill it."

The cavern eventually opened to a large space, but how large, Amaryl could not guess. The torchlight no longer fell on the walls, and their footsteps began to echo. They followed a path of unusually smooth stone, interrupted by occasional claw gouges, for some time. Then Amaryl heard a quiet scrape as if something slid against stone.

"Halt," she whispered.

There was a rush of wind, and the torches went out. Amaryl held up her shield, sweating as she waited for the incinerating rush of fire that was sure to come.

The cavern suddenly lit up as if in daylight. A globe of light rose into the air from Fenya's outstretched arm. In that light, they found themselves near the brink of an abyss of unimaginable size, with walls honeycombed with hundreds of cavern openings. They were standing on one of the balconies, facing a mammoth, winged firebreather sitting on its hind legs, holding one of its forearms out in front of it, with its clawed paw closed like a fist. Suspended on the end of a long, sinuous neck was a most unusual head.

Unlike its reptilian cousins, there was something feline about this dragon's face. It had broad cheeks, a high forehead cresting its whiskered snout, and large golden eyes under feathery eyebrows. Tufted ears poked out of a mane of silky golden hair. The only thing unmistakably dragon about it were the silvery-green scales covering the rest of it, and a triad of pearly horns over the eyes and nose.

Gwyneth was the first to aim her crossbow at a blinking golden eye. Amaryl did the same, wanting to be the one to kill it. She tensed her finger to shoot, but the massive paw opened like a hand, and something small dropped out of it and rolled toward them. A perfectly round stone, blacker than ebonite, and smoother than a polished blade, stopped inches from her feet. The Dragon's Tear.

The dragon opened its mouth and spoke in a rumbling, grandfatherly voice, "I'm glad you have that light with you because so many lost their way in here and have fallen into my den. For creatures as small as you, it's a deadly drop. I can't tell you how many times I awoke and found another little one broken on my back. If I had known that these worthless rocks were what you came for, I would have been leaving them at the entrance all along for you. My den is littered with them from all the times I cried over the poor little creatures that fell."

Fenya exclaimed, "A talking one!"

Gwyneth demanded, "How do we know you're not lying! You could have eaten them, like you plan to eat us."

The dragon replied sadly, "Please take your rock and go before you get hurt in here."

Amaryl asked, "How did you know this is what we came for?"

The dragon replied, "The last little one who came here told me that others would come after him. He told me all about your island, and how these rocks help keep it safe."

"What happened to him?"

"He slipped on the edge of my den and fell on my back. He survived for a short time, and he told me that he had made a promise to someone that he would get the rock to his people. If I were to deliver it to the next one who came, then his promise would be fulfilled. When I told him that I would do this for him, he died. After he was gone, I cried for days until I nearly buried my head in these stones."

Amaryl stared at the black gem at her feet.

Fenya aimed her crossbow at the dragon and said, "Shall we finish, Amaryl?"

Gwyneth blocked Fenya, "No! This dragon is no murderer!"

Fenya replied, "It's a rare specimen whose parts might make some out-of-date potions work!"

"I'll kill you if you shoot!"

"Amaryl deserves her vengeance!"

Amaryl knelt and picked up the Tear. The sphere fit perfectly in her hand.

Gwyneth looked pleadingly at Amaryl, "If we rid the

world of this good beast, which may be the last of his kind, we will be the ones who lose. Search your heart and find peace in Daneloth's sacrifice."

Leave it to a race bent on exterminating as many other life-forms as possible to have a heart for one miserable dragon, thought Amaryl. But wasn't this why she had chosen a human for this quest—to have the strength of a heart more impassioned than her own?

Fenya snarled at Gwyneth, "How about I shoot you and then the dragon! A few rare potions I know of call for human parts!"

Gwyneth replied, "I'd like to see you try, you three-foot-tall toad!"

Amaryl stood and said to Olaug, "Get those two and let's get out of here."

Olaug nodded, then grabbed Fenya and Gwyneth and carried their kicking and hollering forms under each arm back the way they came. Before turning to go, Amaryl looked at the dragon. It bowed its head politely, then turned and shuffled down to its den where it planned to sleep for a few more months.

A SISTER'S BLOOD

by Patricia B. Cirone

I have met Patricia Cirone at a couple of conventions, I think. She either failed to update her biography or Lisa failed to pass it on to me, but Pat has been in these collections often enough that you can look her up in earlier volumes as easily as I can.

This is a story of a pair of sisters, one of whom is a sorceress. Very often we get stories of swordswomen paired with sorceresses, but I don't remember getting one as good as this for a long, long time. Pat lives presently in Maine.

> *"Sing to the Maiden*
> *of hard choices to be made*
> *Sing to the Maiden of love.*
> *Sing to the Maiden*
> *of life and death,*
> *in Circle, all are One."*
>
> refrain, Circle song of Power.

Tess strained against the bonds that held her, but only succeeded in rubbing more flesh off raw wrists. She felt rivulets of warm blood slide down the back of her hands and drip onto the dirt floor.

"Drane's teeth," she muttered.

"Don't swear," her sister whispered.

"You think the gods are paying any attention to us down in this hellhole?" Tess demanded.

Her sister just looked at her silently.

Tess subsided, muttering under her breath softly

enough so her sister couldn't hear. She twisted, digging
her heels into the floor and managed, finally, to push
her buttocks through her bound arms. Grimacing, she
thrashed about until she was able to draw her legs
through and lay, panting, her cheek digging into the dirt
and pebbles, but with her arms in front of her instead
of behind. She had tried that maneuver uncountable
times in the twenty-four hours since they had been captured—either a day's worth of starvation had lost her
enough weight to manage it, or desperation had managed to overcome the growing stiffness in her limbs. Or
maybe Drane had decided to punish her for blaspheming
with his name by adding the exquisite pain of nearly
dislocated shoulders to the already considerable tally of
bruises, bumps, blood, and hunger she had accumu-
lated. Whatever.

She lay there and gradually caught her breath, grimly
ignoring the waves of pain. Not too bad. No worse than
the time Master Broda had decided to take her arro-
gance down a peg and given her his *personal* attention
for a full hour of sword work, back when she was a pup
in training. Or the time . . . no, she wasn't going to
remember that. *Think of Master Broda,* she thought to
herself. Those were happy times, for all she had complained about him and the hours of weapons cleaning,
footwork practice, stomach exercises, and all the other
things she and her fellow trainees had felt were sadistic
excuses to make them suffer. Lying on the floor of her
cell, Tess smiled, thinking that the times she had had
cause to thank Broda and his rigorous training must, by
now, outweigh her adolescent complaints two to one.
Even the excruciating maneuver she'd just completed
had been learned at Master Broda's feet, amidst a rain
of pointed, sarcastic comments and the thrashing of
twenty similarly bound trainees. *Thank you again,* Tess
thought silently.

Where before, they had no chance, now she thought
they might at least have a slim one. With her arms in
front of her, she might be able to untie the ropes that

bound her feet or strangle the guard when he came into
the cell or . . . or staunch the slow but steady flow of
blood that was draining the life out of her sister.

She thrust her nearly numb hands into the dirt and
levered herself up into a sitting position. Then she
hunched her way over on her butt to where Sasha lay.
Her sister's eyelids flickered and opened in the dim light
filtering down from the barred hole high up on the wall.
She smiled at Tess weakly.

"I'm glad we've had these last few weeks together,"
she said faintly. "Growing up, we were always together.
I've missed that, first training in separate ways, then all
the years of assignments in opposite ends of the kingdom. At least we got one mission together, for all it's
ended like this."

"Don't speak like that," Tess said curtly. "We'll have
lots of time together. All we have to do is get out of
this blasted dungeon."

A sudden clang and the sound of footsteps on stone
made her freeze. The sisters looked at each other in
silent fear. They began to breathe again when the footsteps passed the cell door. Tess began to work on the
knots on her ankles a little more vigorously.

"How long before they begin to torture us?" Tess
wondered out loud.

"I don't like it that they haven't even questioned us,"
Sasha said.

"What do you mean?" Tess had been glad of the re-
prieve. Her biggest worry was wondering how badly
Sasha was hurt, and what would happen to her if Korl's
torturers so much as moved her.

"It's as if they've already made up their minds about
us," Sasha replied.

"Uhhh." Tess thought about that. She didn't like the
sound of it either. "Maybe they're just too busy," she
said with false, automatic optimism. Sasha just gave her
a look.

Daylight faded into night, and still no one came to
their cell. Tess managed to free her feet and hobbled

stiffly over to the corner where she spied what looked like a water jug. She bent and sniffed. Smelled all right. She managed to grab the lip of it with her still bound hands. She dragged it over to Sasha.

"Here," she said, tipping it enough so some ran onto her hands. "This smells like water."

Cautiously, Sasha licked some off Tess' hands. "Even fairly fresh," she confirmed. "I wish I could use my Power to make sure there's no sleeping potion or other drugs in it. But there's no bitter taste. It should be safe."

"At this point, we need water, drugged or not." Tess tipped the jug to where Sasha could lap more directly from the edge. That need taken care of, she began to work on the ropes binding Sasha's hands. When those were freed, Sasha was able to gather enough energy to loosen Tess' hands. The first thing Tess did, even before freeing her sister's feet, was to check the wound in her side. With a sick feeling, Tess noticed it was deep, too deep, and there was a slight whiff of decay. Carefully she bound her sister's side with strips torn from her shirt, and tried to block out the knowledge it was her little sister she was bandaging so carefully.

As dawn lightened the square of black above them, Sasha began to shiver. Tess held her close, trying to give her what little body warmth she had. But as the hours wore on, Sasha shivered harder, fever making red spots on her pallid cheeks.

Tess got up and pounded on the cell door. Anything was better than this.

"Don't," Sasha pleaded weakly.

"You need help!"

"But not their type. Don't bring us to their notice."

"I'm not going to rot away in here!" Tess gave the door a savage kick, then muttered an imprecation and rubbed her toes. Despite the noise she made, no one came. She didn't know whether to be glad or sorry.

Sasha got steadily worse.

It had been nearly two days since they had been captured, flung into this hellhole, and then ignored. And

during that time, Lord Briedan's forces moved steadily
closer to the trap only she and Sasha knew about. If
they didn't get out of here soon, all the risks they had
taken, all the misery they had suffered, would be for
naught. If Lord Briedan's forces were overwhelmed,
Korl's forces might well sweep right over the border and
endanger the capital. They *had* to get out of here!

Tess began to pace up and down the cell, prying at
the stone walls, and the edges of the door; trying to
jump high enough to grab hold of one of the bars on
the high, small window. Nothing.

"I'm not going to make it out, Tess," Sasha said
weakly.

"Don't talk like that. I'll figure a way out," Tess said,
trying once again to jump up to the window.

"Tess. I mean it. Pretending only wastes time, and I
have precious little of that left."

Tess stopped trying to jump and walked over to her
sister, crouching beside her. Gently she stroked back
Sasha's hair from her face. "Please, Sasha, just hang in
there a little longer. I'll figure a way to get us both out,
I will." She bit her lips hard to keep tears from falling.

"The only way one of us is going to get out of here
alive is by using Power, and I can't do anything right
now, not with this festering gash in my side."

"You'll get better, and then you'll be able to . . ."
Tess began unconvincingly.

"You'll have to kill me, Tess," Sasha said quietly.

"Never!" Tess said vehemently. "If . . . if it comes
to . . . I'll stay with you . . . I'll stay with you until . . ."
her voice choked with sudden tears.

"Tess. Just *listen* to me," Sasha said weakly. "You
know that I'm Circle-trained, that I have powers."

"Of course," Tess said, wondering if her sister was
beginning to wander in her thoughts. She could hardly
have forgotten her sister had been chosen to Circle!
They had been apprenticed at the same time, she to the
Guild of Swords, and Sasha, at an unbelievably young
age, to Circle. Their parents had not known whether to

weep with joy or heartbreak as the two of them had marched off together for their long, seven-year apprenticeships away from home.

"Of course, you have powers—enough to get us both out of here, I daresay, if you weren't wounded."

"Whole body, whole spirit," Sasha whispered hoarsely. "You're bruised, but not wounded, are you Tess?"

"Just scratches—but I'm not Circle, Sash. I don't have even a predisposition to Power, you know that. Not a magical bone in my body."

"You don't need predisposition for Death Gift, Tess."

Tess felt her entire body freeze in coldness—even her brain felt cold and motionless. Then, with a rasp that shook her body, her breath started again, a harsh, sudden sound in the silence. "You're not dying," she choked out.

"Tess! Don't let all we've worked for, all I've suffered for, go in vain!" Sasha said, with more strength than she had had for the past two days. "If I die, here, now, of these wounds, then Lord Briedan will never find out that Korl's allied with the mountain tribes and that they're waiting to pin him in the pass. Even if you escaped these walls, you'd never make it back across a week's worth of territory and a guarded border without the disguises my magic gave us all the way here. I would be dead, you would be dead, and, without that information, half Lord Briedan's forces will be dead! You *have* to, Tess. You have to sacrifice me before I die on my own."

"But . . . but if you live, then you'll be able to get us out of here, and back home, and we'll . . ." Tess trailed off, knowing that the chances of Sasha living were slim, that talking of it was like a fire-gather tale; more fantasy than reality, mere comfort against the cold fear of the dark.

"Tess, even if I somehow survived this, it would be months before I was strong enough to work magic again. Do you think Korl's torturers would let me live that long? Do you think Lord Briedan's forces wouldn't attempt the pass and fail in that time? That Korl would

be content to keep within his own borders while I
slowly mend?"

"No," Tess whispered.

"You have to do it, Tess. Take my life as a willing
sacrifice, and my Gift will fill you, give you the magic
you need to get out of here and back home. Warn Lord
Briedan. It's not just for me, or for you, Tess, but for
all our people! We both swore, when we entered King's
Service, Tess, that we might be called upon to sacrifice
life and limb for the sake of all. Well, it's come to that
for me, Tess."

Tears seeped out of the corners of Tess' eyes and
rolled bleakly down her face. "We can wait . . . a bit . . .
and maybe . . ."

"No time, Tess. There's no time at all. Can't you
see?" Sasha pleaded with eyes gone big in the hollowed
planes of her face. Tess knew the reality then.

"I love you, little sister," she whispered.

"I love you, too, Sis. Take care of me one last time?"

Tess nodded, slowly.

She bent and removed the small, ceremonial knife Sasha
kept hidden in a sheath in her boot. Together, they began
to say the prayers and incantations that every close relative
of a Circle-trained warden learned, but hoped never to
have to use. As Tess murmured Drane's name, and that
of the Maiden, she felt peace gather within her. It had
been a long time since she had prayed, other than lighting
a quick incense stick to the god of the Sword Guild. It
had been a long time since she had used Drane's or any
other god's name in other than a swear.

But now it felt right. . . .

Their murmured responses seemed to gather the light
from the room and weave it between their clasped
hands. Tess felt tension begin to gather, until finally, the
moment she had been dreading arrived.

She looked full into her sister's eyes. Sasha looked
calmly back.

Tess faltered.

"Don't be afraid, Tess," Sasha whispered. "I will be

with the Maiden, and you will be free to save our people." She removed her hands from the ceremonial knife and pressed it into Tess' hands.

Tess began to sob. She clenched her hands around the knife so hard she felt its ridged handle cut into the calluses on the palm of her hand. "I can't."

"You *must*, Tess. Surely, you've given Mercy, before."

"Not to my little sister!"

"This isn't just Mercy, big sister. It's Life! Life for both of us; you with our people, and me with the Maiden, my Power living on, not just wasted in pus and blood on a prison cell floor! Do it, Tess! Do it now!"

With a sob, Tess bent and pressed the knife against her sister's throat. Her eyes were so full of tears that her sister's face seemed to waver as if under water. Tess blinked, gulped, and cut through her sister's life-force, through her throat. She felt the blood spill, warm, over her hands.

"No," she whimpered, even now willing the deed undone—and then there was a singing in her veins, a rush of Power like the thrill of running. She fell forward with a gasp. All her senses became bound up with what she was feeling inside her body. Hearing, sight, touch . . . all roared, and then grew silent.

Slowly the sensations subsided.

Tess flexed her hand. It felt the same, and yet it didn't. She still had calluses, knew she could still handle a sword . . . and she could also . . .

Tess stood up. She gestured with her hand, and light flared. She snapped her hand shut, and the light ceased as if it were a candle suddenly blown out. She walked over to the cell door, the door that had defeated her many attempts to rattle, pry, or force it open and laid her hand upon the lock. It clicked open.

Tess swallowed hard. Years of training for a Circle magician to do this; yet she could do it without thinking, without knowledge, as surely as if she had learned by her sister's side all those years. Death Gift. She must be sure to use it well.

Tess turned, and gathered up her sister's body into

her arms. "Good-bye, Sash," she whispered, and felt her sister's spirit caress her one last time before lifting into the light. Gathering up her new-found power, Tess brought fire and light into her sister's broken, abandoned shell and gave it to the light, as well. When she was done, only ashes remained.

She turned and began her journey home.

CHANGED

by Lisa Deason

Nobody who has been reading either these anthologies or *MZB's Fantasy Magazine,* needs to inquire who Lisa Deason may be; she's been one of our writers for a long time. Of course, time is relative—I just realized the other day that I've been doing these anthologies for seventeen years and even the magazine is ten years old. In that time we've printed many stories about shapeshifters, but I can't remember many, if any, that asked as clearly as this what it really felt like to be a kind of lycanthrope. Of course that's what fantasy writing is all about—at least the kind I print, and Lisa writes.

"You must be certain," the shadowed man said.

Celestra growled low in her throat, swiping at a lock of tangled blonde hair as it drooped into her brown eyes. The feel of her smooth forehead elicited a second sound of annoyance.

"I'm certain," she said. Her voice still somewhat shocked her: a dull, lone instrument in place of an exquisite symphony.

As a small orb rolled across the table to her, the man commanded, "Stare into the jewel and focus on your heart's desire."

Celestra did so. The clear surface clouded, then its depths began to glow. A magnificent creature appeared, its hooves sparking with each step. Vibrant blue eyes blazed beneath the sharp jut of silver and gold emerging through its thick, white forelock. Its well-shaped equine head lifted, surveying its surroundings with an air of majesty.

"A horse?" the man said.

Horse? Idiot. She didn't even bother to correct him. The jewel suddenly swelled, filling her vision as the Change tugged at her, reshaping, remaking. Returning what had been stolen by the chop of a sword and the snap of bone.

Then it was abruptly snatched from her again. A scream of denial cut off as she was struck hard in the throat.

"Hm," the man mused. "An interesting configuration." The floor danced wildly beneath her, dizziness buzzing in her ears. Liquid black swept her mind into a deep, empty abyss.

Celestra woke, lashing out in blind panic. Then the realization that her body had been altered pierced the confusion like a ray of light. Touching her forehead, her fingers closed on a hard, spiral-twist of bone. Joy flooded through her in an ecstatic rush that just as quickly went cold.

Fingers?

And she looked down, discovering in dawning horror what had been done to her.

Her torso, from head to just below her navel, remained hatefully human. Her hips, however, blossomed into the shoulders and sleek, white, equine body she knew so well.

"No, no, no," she said softly. She tried to draw upon her power, so long denied her while she had been trapped in human flesh. It flickered, then went silent, a terrifying absence she probed like a tongue in the gap of a missing tooth.

Her attention expanded slightly. She was in a bronze cage with a packed-dirt floor, lit only by a circle of light from a mage globe on the opposite stone wall. Used to having the roam and rule of the entire Deep Forest, her instincts wailed at the confinement, urging her to plow through the bars.

"Hey. Nice horn you have there."

The female voice, so matter-of-fact, sliced through her internal chaos.

"What?"

A scaled woman with golden eyes regarded her from the cage to her left. "I was complimenting your horn. Don't tell me . . . human and unicorn, right?"

"*La faie suiateih.*"

"La what-what?"

As the other glided lithely backward, Celestra noticed that the bottom half of her cage was a water tank. "*La faie suiateih*. It's Old Tongue. I prefer it to 'unicorn.' "

"Ah. I'm a mer-dragon, if you're wondering."

"Were-dragon?"

The woman grinned, showing pointed teeth, then pivoted. A row of blunt ridges along the length of her spine poked through the wet slick of her long black hair. Two leathery wings were folded compactly against her shoulder blades.

She dove, arching to reveal a thick, tapered tail ending in flared double fins. Resurfacing, she flung her hair back with a hand that had three talonlike fingers and a thumb. Her interlocked scales shimmered in faint rainbow sheens, creating fascinating, swirling patterns.

"*Mer*-dragon," Celestra affirmed.

"Name's Hali."

"Celestra."

"Pleasure. Welcome to the Collection."

"The what?"

"You've had the dubious fortune of meeting the Collector. He promises to shapeshift you to whatever you're wanting, a real shifting, not an illusion like the other mages offer. Then he traps you between forms and puts you here. There must be a dozen of us now."

Through Hali's cage at the dim edge of the mage globe's radiance, Celestra could see a massive creature with the head of a grizzly atop a woman's body. The bear-woman's small dark eyes turned on her. She roared loudly enough to rattle the cages, then charged.

Celestra welcomed the idea of taking some of her frustrations out in combat, but the bear-woman stopped before she reached her bars. She roared again, a furred hand/paw grappling at her throat. Something glittered there—a large, clear gem on a silver band.

"She's always like that," Hali said. "Not a sparkling conversationalist, I'm afraid."

Celestra dismissed the incident as she spotted an identical band around the mer-dragon's neck, blending almost invisibly into her shimmering scales. Then she found the same thing at her own throat.

"That locks the transformation in place," Hali said. "It also keeps you from getting too close to the bars."

Celestra stretched her hand forward, and the band around her neck squeezed in warning. When she jerked back, it relaxed. She cursed succinctly.

"Such language."

"The Collector," Hali murmured as a tall, dark-haired man appeared.

Celestra recognized the face she'd last seen in shadows across the table from her. Her head lowered automatically, horn targeting the center of his chest.

Before she launched her doubtlessly futile attack, a second man came into the circle of light.

"Well, Baron?" the Collector asked.

"I'm impressed, I must admit." The short, balding man twisted his hands eagerly. "I'd be the envy of the court."

"The only one of her kind. I don't know if I can even bear to part with her."

"I'm sure an equitable agreement can be reached." The Baron must have realized he was overplaying his position because his tone became decidedly more casual. "I'd like to see her paces before committing further."

"Of course," the Collector said. "I'll be displaying a few prized creatures later today. You can see more of her then."

"Very well. Do you think she'll be difficult to break to a saddle?" the Baron asked.

Saddle? Seeing red, she started to shout, "Try it, soft-foot, and I'll crush you!"

But instead of words, all that issued from her mouth was a high-pitched, equine squeal.

"I don't foresee any problems," the Collector said as they walked away, not even glancing at her.

Once they were gone, Hali said, "Don't worry about the voice thing. It's temporary. The Collector doesn't want his 'creatures' saying anything inopportune while a potential buyer is around, you understand?"

"I'm killing the first one who comes near me with a saddle," Celestra swore passionately in her own—albeit human—voice once more.

Hali chuckled, submerging. As Celestra waited for her to return, she looked at the cage to her right for the first time.

Her heart stopped, then resumed its beat with a painful slam.

"Cieran," she whispered. The young man sat, knees pulled to his chest, his straight dark hair framing a face with vaguely felinoid features and eyes of an astonishing green. His pale skin was a sleek pelt of fur; a long white tail sprouted from the base of his spine to twitch restlessly against the ground.

It *wasn't* Cieran, but the resemblance was unnerving.

"That's Jade," Hali said. "He doesn't talk."

Celestra looked back at the mer-dragon. "Then how do you know his name?"

"Don't. Just got tired of calling him 'Hey, you.' " She jerked a thumb at the pacing bear-woman. "Same as Grizelda, there."

Celestra gave a wan smile.

Hali rolled several times then propelled herself slowly backwards. "Who's Cieran?"

"He's . . ." Words failed her. How could she explain about the human prince she'd chosen as her mate? She'd been in the process of Changing him to *la faie suiateih* like herself when a guardswoman had interfered, denying him her offered glory. Her attention had been focused on protecting Cieran, not herself, and she had been outwitted, her horn lopped off for her trouble. It was a mistake she would never make again.

But it would have been worth it, if only . . .

If only . . .

"He's someone I lost," she finally said.

"I can find a way to restore things. You have to be patient."

"Don't you understand, Celestra? We're on a new path now. We have to forget we were ever anything other than human."

"Forget? You're only saying that because you weren't fully la faie suiateih. *Once you are—"*

"I've accepted my humanity. Now you have to do the same."

"Never. Humanity is nothing but weakness, powerlessness, without a single advantage. I detest it! I won't rest until I regain what was taken from me. That is the only path I'll walk!"

Pause.

"Then you'll be walking alone, Celestra. I'm going home."

Celestra snapped free of her reverie, Cieran's last, dreadful words ringing in her ears. She brutally shoved away the memory and the pain it brought with it.

"Lunch is coming," Hali told her.

"I hope he knows I'm carnivore in either shape," Celestra muttered as a huge platter of sizzling meat and a bucket of water popped into existence at the front of her cage. From the sounds echoing through the cavern, food was appearing in a similar manner for the other prisoners as well.

She discovered she was ravenous and made short work of the meal.

Hali was occupied with chasing the small silver fish that had been dumped live into her tank. Watching that slightly unsettled Celestra—or rather the squeamish human "flicker" in her she couldn't seem to purge.

She lashed out with a kick, frustrated as much at her inability to be rid of her humanity as at the cage confining her.

"I hate this!" she spat. "The Deep Forest was mine, with its secret places and invisible paths. I could come and go as I pleased, and none could even see me if I didn't allow it."

"Sounds nice," Hali said, finishing the last of the fish in an efficient gulp. "Show me around it sometime, hm?"

Other than Cieran, her intended mate, Celestra had never made anyone welcome in her forest. "Sometime, sure," she muttered, rejecting the notion even as she spoke. "If we can ever get out of this triple-cursed prison, that is!"

"Oh, as prisons go, it's not so bad," Hali said. "At least we get fed."

"You were imprisoned before?"

The mer-dragon beat her tail in hard, upright strokes, pushing her body out of the water almost to her fins, and mimed juggling several objects. "I was born in the circus. I've been a captive all my life," she said, continuing her actions for a few moments longer. Then she stopped abruptly, dropping with a soft splash.

Celestra didn't know what to say to that.

"We were lucky to eat once a day." Bitterness crept into Hali's tone. "I lived on the dream of flying away."

"Flying?"

"I've never even seen the ocean. There's no need to go there. On land, even with legs, I would've been too easy to recapture. But I saw a dragon flying high overhead once, saw the way the men feared it, and that was when I knew what I wanted to be. So when the Collector came along . . ." She trailed off, visibly trying to get her emotions under control.

The sound of footsteps interrupted any further conversation. Half a dozen men came into the light, two pulling a flat-bedded wagon. Each carried short, animal-handler whips.

The wagon stopped at Hali's cage and one of the han-

dlers used a gold key to unlock the door above the rim
of the tank.

Hali, her face impassive, pulled herself up as high as
she could. The two men lifted her out and put her on
the wagon, then dragged her away.

The handlers had more trouble with Jade, who hissed
and fought until they had to drive him out with the
whips. Finally, Celestra's bars were opened.

"Try anything, and you'll regret it," the handler said,
cracking his whip and leaving a trail of sparks in the air.

She slowly came forth, feeling out the situation. The
remaining handlers projected a calm, watchful alertness.

The time wasn't right. She had to be patient.

Moving up the tunnel ascending the narrow cavern,
she saw the other prisoners at last. There were several
human/animal mixes, creatures like Grizelda who made
unintelligible noises as she passed by: a lion with hands,
a tailless wolf with human legs. Then there were others
so scrambled, with an assortment of hooves and fur and
feathers and paws, that she couldn't tell what they were.

The tunnel ended at a wall of solid-looking rock, but
a door rolled back as they approached. Celestra squinted
at the brightness as she emerged from the cavern. Someone appeared next to her and she shied.

"Easy there," the Collector murmured, laying a casual
hand on her equine shoulder. Pain crackled through her,
aborting her instinctual attack.

"This is what you will do," he said, the light touch of
his fingers binding her in place, unable to even fall, as
waves of agony spiked through her. "You'll obey my
commands and entertain the crowd, understood?"

"Choke, you ugly—ahh!" The band around her throat
tightened, rendering her unable to breathe for a few perilous moments. Then it relented, and she gasped out,
"I'll . . . die . . . first."

"That won't be allowed. However, keep in mind you
can still be sold if you are lame. How would you enjoy
being trapped in a body that no longer functions
properly?"

A sliver of ice went through her veins. As *la faie suiateih*, she had taken pride in her beauty. Even in human form, she had known she was at least a fair representative of the species. The very notion of being less than that, of being physically *broken*, repulsed her to her core.

He nodded congenially, then released her from his paralyzing grip and smacked her side. Startled—and more than a little spooked by his threats—she bolted.

A tall set of fences herded her into a large ring, then a gate dropped to seal her in. Faces gawked through the bars at her.

While she ran, the Collector started a theatrical speech of which she caught only the end. ". . . a beast of equal parts grace and ferocity."

Then his voice brushed her ear as though he stood next to her. "Canter."

"I—" she began, but it came out as a thin, uncertain whinny.

"Don't bother. Go."

Whether it was her imagination or not, numbness tingled down her right foreleg, as though it wasn't going to support her weight. The feeling quickly passed, but the warning lingered.

Hesitantly, she started around the ring.

"Faster."

She twitched, hating that intrusive voice, hating that a human *dared* to order her to perform like a trick pony. Hating herself because she feared lameness more than humiliation.

Jolting into a canter, she randomly changed direction without losing speed. A simple demonstration of skill, but it felt good to be moving, even in circles.

Cutting across the ring, she came to a halt, rearing as high as she could until she seemed perilously close to toppling over backward. Several onlookers gasped.

She cried out in a full-throated call. For a moment, she was in her forest, secure in her place and power. Before she'd decided she wasn't content to rule the

Deep Forest alone. Before she'd set eyes on Cieran. For such a brief moment, she was whole.

But she couldn't stay that way forever. Her weight shifted and she descended with a bone-jarring thud.

The crowd cheered. The Collector murmured in her ear, "Well done. I see potential."

His voice then came from a distance again. "In the land of the south live creatures that resemble the great cats. But the *ixbis sul* have remarkable intelligence that is matched only by their viciousness. What happens, then, when *ixbis sul* is merged with man?"

The group of people turned, filing to another ring. Celestra caught sight of Jade cowering in the center of several oddly-shaped wooden structures. Obstacles, she deduced, for him to use to display his sinuous grace.

Jade shuddered. Celestra could almost *hear* the commands the Collector was barking silently in his ear. Commands and threats.

Jade abruptly curled into a ball. A mutter darted through the crowd.

The Collector's face darkened. Celestra's flesh crawled, detecting the strength being exerted, but Jade merely rolled more tightly in on himself.

He was willing to die rather than obey, Celestra realized. Shame scalded her that she hadn't shown the same resolve.

A pure soprano suddenly drifted through the air, a siren's song ensnaring all who heard it.

The crowd left Jade behind, forgotten, following the mesmerizing sound to the small pool Hali had been put in. Her voice trailed away.

"Who has never heard of the song of the mer?" the Collector said, covering the lapse. "But who has seen a mermaid . . . fly?"

On cue, Hali dove, swimming swiftly beneath the water and then erupting forth in a geyser of spray. Her leathery wings unfolded and stroked the air. She came free of the pool, gliding over the water's surface but no higher.

Celestra glanced up, following the bars encircling the pool as they stretched well over 25 feet toward the sky. There was no top.

"Climb," she called, her voice an excited whicker.

Hali evidently could still understand her, for she started rising. It quickly became apparent that her body was too heavy for the size of her wings.

Even still, Celestra found herself leaning, muscles tensed, as though she could somehow *will* the mer-dragon over the bars.

Hali struggled valiantly, but her strength gave out just as she reached the halfway point. She fell, hitting the water in an ungainly sprawl.

The crowd applauded wildly.

"Hali? Hali, are you injured?" Celestra asked.

The mer-dragon surfaced slowly, several long black locks streaming into her golden eyes. She gazed blankly at her.

"Hali?"

"I'm . . . okay," she finally said, the words carried in a low whistle.

The Collector dismissed his audience with another speech, the words gurgling incoherently in Celestra's ears. From the hint of self-satisfaction she detected in his expression, she realized he had *wanted* Hali to try an escape.

An exciting grand finale, she thought, and it stabbed at her that she had played an unwitting part in his cruel plan. She allowed herself to be led from the ring, sudden docility masking boiling anger. They walked the long tunnel descending into the cavern, Jade in front of her, Hali being wheeled behind, without incident. But she was watching and waiting with a predator's instinct.

Jade veered to the side when his cage was opened, dropping to the ground and tucking into the corner.

The handlers cursed. When they approached too closely, Jade proved his stubby-fingered hands had claws.

"Load the others while we take care of this one," one of the men said.

Between those occupied with Jade and those lifting Hali into her tank, only a single handler was left to usher Celestra into her cage.

He pulled the cage door back. "Go on."

The predator in her wanted to fight, but she tempered the impulse, having a better plan. She went in, gathering her will, then faced him through the bars as they swung shut. He made eye contact and froze.

She formed a hasty pair of images: the key turning in the lock, the key withdrawing. "You've already locked that," she said quietly, thrusting the bundle into his mind. Enchantment, a much simpler form of mind control, required just a small bit of power.

She could only hope the bare flicker she had left would be enough.

The handler shook his head and stared at the key in his hand. She pressed harder on the images, waiting tensely to see if they would take.

Slowly, the man tucked the key into his vest pocket. Next to them, Jade was finally being contained once more.

Celestra stared into space, trying to look as animallike as possible, while she tracked the handlers with her peripheral vision. They paused before her cage, and her heart skipped a beat. If they discovered that the lock wasn't turned . . .

But then they moved on, and she breathed a soft sigh of relief. She listened for the *sh-shush* that indicated the door at the end of the tunnel had reset, then unhesitantly leaped at the front of her cage.

The neck band tightened brutally, but her momentum carried her through as both her human and equine shoulders crashed into the bars, popping them open.

Skittering to a halt, she gasped for air as the band relaxed, her throat on fire.

"Hurry," Hali hissed. "The Collector always comes after one of his little shows. Can you break the locks?"

She approached the mer-dragon's cage cautiously. The neck band tingled, then went quiescent. Either it was

sensitive just to her own bars, or her escape had over-
loaded it.

Lowering her head, she fitted the tip of her horn into
the keyhole, rupturing it with a quick thrust. Once she'd
opened Hali's door, she went to Jade's and repeated
the process.

"Celes—!" Hali began, but a second voice spoke
over her.

"I had no idea lock picking was one of your skills,"
the Collector said.

Celestra turned sharply, forming an image of her captor encased in a block of ice.

He stood just inside the reach of the mage globe. As
soon as he looked in her eyes, she hammered the image
into his mind.

"You cannot move," she said, desperation fueling the
flicker of power into a blaze.

His mouth gaped, but no words emerged. He managed
to twist his fingers in a sketchy pattern.

The neck band came alive, and she struggled to
breathe. Darkness lapped at the edge of her vision.

"Very clever," he said, letting her suffer a while
longer before ending the assault. "It's a shame to destroy
a thing of beauty, but you simply can't be trusted
whole."

Pain sliced down her right foreleg, sending her crash-
ing into the wall. A deep groan tore from her, as much
in anguished terror as physical pain.

Not again, she thought. *Not another human striking
me low!*

She screamed in the wordless anger born the moment
her original horn had been chopped off, increased tenfold at Cieran's abandonment, increased a hundredfold
at her capture and humiliation.

I am la faie suiateih, *the scream said.* I rule the Deep
Forest. I know no master.

Her human torso trembled, warming like butter on a
skillet, then was suffused in white light. The jewel on her
neck band sizzled and spat then shattered explosively.

The light drained away, revealing *la faie suiateih* in her true form, all signs of humanity eradicated.

Power filled her, *over*filled her, bubbling forth almost visibly. But as she was shaping it into a weapon, the Collector frantically carved a set of symbols in the air with his hands.

A thousand tiny, vicious needles wrenched and writhed in her flesh, disrupting her concentration. Celestra shrieked as blood appeared from knee to hock like rubies strewn on white satin.

Her wounded leg crumpled. She fell awkwardly, her legs twisting in such a manner they seemed to snap like matchsticks, one after another. She cried out piteously, violently convulsing. Then her head dropped, and she went still.

Hali yelled incoherently. Jade batted about his cage, flinging open his unlocked door.

"Enough" the Collector shouted, spinning to slam the bars shut with a wave of his arm before Jade could escape. While his back was turned, Celestra leaped up, not with the slow lumber of a horse, but with the supernatural physicality of *la faie suiateih*. Her legs uncoiled in a powerful burst, propelling her straight at her captor. Her horn took him cleanly through the rib cage next to his spine and emerged out his chest. She reared, lifting his impaled body, then came down and slung him into the wall with a tremendous crack.

The dark, lush symphony of her voice flowed like chilled honey over steel. "I learned the hard way. Always check your dead."

The pain in her leg disappeared. She reared again, hooves sparking like flint, then came down forcefully, crushing his skull.

She savored the revenge for a single moment, then concern about getting through the tunnel door took precedence. She had just started down to investigate when Hali's alarmed call brought her back.

"Celestra!"

The Collector's body was shining with a gradually

brightening radiance. Blue flames erupted forth, quickly reducing the remains to a handful of ash. An enormous gush of smoke rose from the smoldering pile, spreading across the high ceiling before seeping in.

A soft, ominous sound came from the stone, like a squeaky latch being thrown. Dust sifted down, followed by a smattering of pebbles. A delicate webwork of cracks blossomed along the face of the rock.

"We've got to get out of here," Celestra said.

The door failed to open at her approach as it had for the handlers. She probed the hard surface but couldn't find a hidden catch. Chipping at it with hooves and horn proved useless.

This required assistance. She went to Grizelda's cage.

"Listen to me," she said, the angelic choir of her voice assuming a metallic edge. "If you want to live, you've got to get through that door. Do you hear me?"

She broke the lock with her horn, then caught one of the bars in her sharp teeth, pulling them open. She was prepared to defend herself but hoped she wouldn't have to.

The bear-woman snarled as she passed by but otherwise ignored Celestra, loping up the tunnel in an odd, shuffling gait.

The ground lurched. A raucous din of squawks, roars, and shrill screams filled the cavern as the other prisoners began to panic. Celestra started down the line, freeing them. Some managed to shatter the hold of their neck bands and complete their transformation, tearing out of their cages before she even reached them.

They gathered at the door, pounding with claws and talons and whatever they possessed. Pieces of the ceiling trickled down with the deep, tortured sounds that indicated something much bigger and heavier was in motion.

"Come on!" Celestra urged, pushing through the crowd.

A bear with copper-and-black fur and glowing copper eyes—presumably Grizelda—stood at the front, her massive paws carving away considerable amounts of rock.

Moving alongside, Celestra lashed out with her rear hooves, speeding along the process. Grizelda shoved her way through the resulting hole; the others following in a frenzied stampede that swept Celestra outside in its strength.

It saved her life. A huge boulder crashed onto the place she had been standing a moment earlier.

Ahead, her former fellow prisoners wrenched the bars of the fenced-in passage to the rings out of shape. A hint of forest beckoned in the distance like the hand of a trusted friend.

The small, determined human part of her stirred. Friend . . .

Hali. Jade.

It wasn't easy to turn from the forest's lure, but she did, only to find the boulder partially blocking the ragged opening.

She pounded at the stone with her hooves, trying to either move the entire thing or break it up. Neither worked.

Bending low, she peered into the hole and shouted, "Can you hear me?"

The growing rumble was all the answer she received.

Any moment, I'll see them, she thought, knowing it to be a lie. Hali had precious little mobility on land, even with Jade assisting her.

She lowered her belly to the ground as only *la faie suiateih* could have and crawled forward. Her body, more slender than a horse's, nonetheless was still too large to fit, even in such a contortion.

I suppose I have to finally admit that this is one time when being human would have been an advantage, she thought.

A wave of dizziness caught her by surprise. Her forelegs blurred into arms and, for a few heartbeats, she felt her shape slipping. Alarmed, she drew back and her equine legs returned.

"Hali! Jade! Are you there?" she yelled with fading hope in her glorious voice.

Nothing. The cavern loudly growled its intent to collapse.

She took a deep breath. If she lost her newly restored body, the only one who had the ability to return it was dead by her own horn and hooves.

I could just leave, go back to my forest and live alone. La faie suiateih *need not care for anything beyond her own self.*

The persistent, dogged flicker she had always derogatorily termed humanity trembled in her breast. That was when she saw it for what it was.

Her conscience. Her soul.

La faie suiateih *cares for no one. But . . .* I *do.*

She pushed hard, jagged rock digging into satiny hide. The dizziness rose up and she embraced it.

La faie suiateih melted, like dross burning away to reveal the gold. In human form, she easily entered the hole into the cavern. Debris bit painfully into the soles of her two soft feet but she ignored it, shakily beginning to run.

The mage globes shivered, bathing the scene in surreal, uncertain illumination. Several of the cages had been smashed by huge rocks and, judging by the groaning coming from overhead, more were on the way.

Thick clouds of dust stung her eyes and nose. She gave a choked scream as she unexpectedly came face to face with a human man.

"Where's—?" she started to say, but he threw her to the ground atop something large and slick, then fell on her. Before she could struggle against the bizarre attack, the ceiling gave an almost living screech of agony and the ground shook as rocks drummed down like sharp rain.

"You've got to leave me," the mass beneath her said in Hali's voice.

Celestra pulled free, realizing then that the human male had very familiar green eyes. Jade, now free of his neck band and transformed, had managed to lift Hali

from her tank and bring her two thirds of the way to
the door.

"We can make it," Celestra said, then her heart sank.
The opening out of the tunnel had become a pile of
impassable rubble.

Light slanted through the thick air, a bit of blue sky
peeking through the decaying ceiling.

"Climb for it," Hali urged.

Celestra and Jade, with human limbs, might have succeeded. Hali had no chance at all.

At least, not as a mer-dragon.

"Hali, you can fly."

"You know I can't."

"You can once you're rid of *this*." She tapped the
jewel on Hali's neck band. "Think of how you watched
that dragon while you were in the circus. You can *be*
that dragon. You'll be no one's captive ever again."

Hali's golden eyes were wide. "I want to," she whispered, "but I'm afraid to fall again."

Celestra leaned closer. She couldn't enchant Hali into
doing her bidding; she didn't even have a spark of her
power left. All she had now was the power of her
conviction.

"No," she said, not in the exquisite tones of *la faie
suiateih* but in simple, honest, human vehemence. "You
will not fall. *You will fly.*"

Hali turned her face to the patch of sky with an expression of longing. The jewel on the neck band suddenly disintegrated.

Her mer lower body split in three; two taloned rear
legs and a sinuous, barbed tail. With a shudder, she tripled her size and her features elongated. Her hair flattened into a dark, lacy pattern on the shining silver
scales of her lengthened neck.

She gripped the other two by the arm in her front
talons, flaring her huge wings, then launched upward.

Celestra held on for dear life as the ground plunged
out from under them.

Half the world seemed to cave in at once. Hali banked violently, trying to avoid the worst of it.

The opening in the ceiling approached rapidly. By Celestra's quick calculations, it was too small for Hali's new wingspan, but Hali was already adjusting.

Downstroking hard in a burst of speed, she tucked in her wings. They sailed clear just as the cavern groaned a final time. It collapsed in a deafening explosion, leaving a smoking crater in the earth.

Hali extended her wings, pumping frantically, and they soared higher and higher while the ruins of their prison dissolved into nothingness.

Considering it was Hali's first landing, it went fairly well, though Celestra and Jade were sent rolling on the ground when she released them.

Hali's rear talons skidded on the carpet of grass as she fought to stop before the small clearing ran out and she crashed into the thick foliage at the edge of the Deep Forest. To avert such a disaster, her body folded in on itself, reducing from silver dragon to dark-haired human. She flipped over once and ended up in a seated position.

"Hm. Interesting," she said, poking at the legs stretched out in front of her. Then, seeing Celestra's startled expression from a few feet away, she explained, "Dragons can take human shape, too."

"*Were*-dragon," Celestra said, smiling. But the smile faded as she pushed a lock of blonde hair from her eyes, fingers pausing at her forehead.

"What happened?" Hali asked gently. "Weren't you la what-what?"

"Didn't take, I guess," she said simply, not ready to explain any further.

Hali looked distressed. "Then this was for nothing for you. You didn't get Changed. You didn't get *anything!*"

"She did," Jade suddenly said, surprising both women. Hali asked, "What did she get, then?"

"Friends," he said with absolute certainty, as though

he somehow knew how deep a difference that was for her. A Change not in flesh, but in heart.

Celestra felt the smooth expanse above her brows one last time, then resolutely dropped her hand. *A new path, just like Cieran said,* she thought. *If he can walk it, so can I.*

But this time I won't be alone.

She got to her feet, holding a hand down to both of her friends.

"Come on," she said. "Let me show you my home."

THE POWER TO CHANGE THE SHAPE OF THE LAND

by Dayle A. Dermatis

In general I don't much like titles that take up more than a line of type. Brevity may not be the soul of wit, but I normally think it highly desirable in titles. Usually if a title is more than two or three words, I imagine the writer hasn't done enough private brainstorming to find a suitable title for his or her work, and I try to suggest she do a little brainstorming. Dayle Dermatis has sold to me before, so I tend to give her more credit for knowing what she's doing than I would to someone with no record of sales.

Dayle says that she hates to be backed into a corner and doesn't believe that there is only one choice in any situation, so she wrote this story of a heroine placed in a "seemingly impossible" situation.

Dayle is about to move to Wales with her fiancé and do the things she loves: write fiction full-time, research seventh-century Welsh history for her SCA persona, and travel. In addition to reading and research, sewing medieval garb, and doing needlework, she is learning to ride a motorcycle.

She says she loves the outdoors—but hates camping, which reminds me of the late witch, Sybil Leek, with whom I was privileged to work on her astrology magazine. When some arrogant writer on witchcraft insisted that all witches worked "skyclad"—which is, in plain words, naked—she snorted that it was plain to see they had never been in the British Isles: "If the climate doesn't get you, the gorse bushes will." Gorse bushes, I found out years later, are *very* prickly. So if you can't avoid the camping, at least avoid the gorse bushes—or do they have them in Wales? They have entirely too many of them in Scotland and Northumbria.

Dayle says she has three goals in life: "To never lose my sense of wonder, to always be a source of light, and to never stop growing." Aside from the split infinitives, I would agree.

A geas bound her; she was bound never to harm the king with her sorceries.

Not even when he held a knife to her throat.

The brute force was enough to subdue her. He had left his men at the base of the tower, away from the night's storm, and entered her study alone, slamming the door back and placing the blade against her skin before she could react.

His entry had surprised her; his methods had not. This new king had risen to power by slaying everyone in his way. Even innocent children died and simple farms burned under his quest for the throne.

"You are a sorceress—a revered magician." He demanded agreement rather than asking the question.

"I am, Your Grace."

His leather armor, soaked from the rain, stank of cow and days of sweat and the blood of helpless women. "There is something I seek, something you can help me gain. If you cannot . . ."

His sour breath brushed her cheek like a malevolent spirit on the longest night of year.

"What is it you seek, Your Grace?" Her voice sounded distant. She had to remain composed.

"It is my desire to rule completely," he said. "I want the power to do that."

As he spoke, his hand tightened on the knife. The blade, warm from being carried close to him, scraped against her skin.

"And you believe that I have this power?"

"I know that sorcery is vast. As your king, I command that you use your sorcerous talents to help me."

She considered what she knew of him. He had used sorceresses in his campaign—in fact, she had known several of the women who had died, their deaths a small percentage of the total slaughter—so he wasn't ignorant of their existence. But he was ignorant of the extent of their abilities, and he was suspicious of sorcery.

"Then you also know that I cannot—I am unable—to harm you with those sorceries." She spoke with complete honesty; the geas that had been set upon her kind long ago to keep them from rising against the ruler of the land held her, no matter how she felt about him. "Your Grace, I am but a simple woman, and I live alone as my studies require. Surely I pose so little of a threat to you that you can feel safe without your blade at my throat."

The quill had fallen when he had grabbed her. Her ink-stained fingers, lying carefully complacent on the desk, seemed as distant as her voice.

He complied. Still, no geas bound him as it did her. Slowly, so as not to startle him, she turned in her seat.

Outside, distant, beneath the hiss of the rain, she heard the low boom of the surf.

"Tell me of the power that you seek." The more time she had . . . she wasn't quite sure how that would help her. She had no illusion that anyone would rescue her. She lived far enough outside the town that no one would be venturing here on this wretched, storm-soaked night. She had purposely chosen this location, because it was remote, for her year of reflection; a time of study and meditation every sorceress had after her seventh year of magic.

"I want the power to change this land—to change the shape of this land," he said, and his voice grew rough with the passion of his dream. "I want a power that men fear and cannot overcome."

She closed her eyes. If she granted his wish, the land as it was now known would be forever, brutally destroyed: trampled and bludgeoned and burned by a man who cared for nothing but power.

If she denied him, she would die . . . but her death was hardly a hindrance to his goal. He would simply continue his search until he found someone who would help him.

A choice—and soon, else he would take the choice from her, kill her, and be on his way.

"I will take you to something of great power," she said finally.

"And I will gain power from it?" he asked, guardedly eager.

"It cannot give you power, but it can teach you about power."

"You swear, sorceress, that I will learn power from this thing?"

She shook her head, carefully, feeling the memory of the blade hot against her throat.

"I can make no guarantees about your own ability to learn," she said. "I can swear that this thing has very great power—the power to change the land, a power that men fear greatly. I can swear that much can be learned from it. If you are a perceptive man, then you will learn about power from it."

He considered her words, the only sound that of sapfire spitting in the grate. She waited, still, her chest barely stirred by her breaths. He would either choose to trust her, or he would kill her.

"Very well, sorceress," he said finally. "Take me to this power."

A breath of relief, and then, "There are two final conditions," she said quietly. Vaguely, she was astonished at how steady and calm she sounded—but she knew if she gave any hint of uncertainty, he would slit her throat and leave her body to seep lifeblood into the worn floorboards.

His fingers twitched on the knife. "You said nothing of conditions."

"There are two," she repeated. "They must be met, or this thing cannot be done. You have no chance of learning otherwise."

"What are they?" he snapped.

"You and I must go alone, and you may bring no

weapons." The latter wasn't much to save her, she knew. He could snap her neck between his burly hands as easily and thoughtlessly as breaking a branch for kindling. But perhaps, in a small way, it would give her more authority.

He growled low, in the back of his throat, and despite herself, she flinched.

But, as she'd gambled, his lust for power outweighed his common sense.

"Take me," he commanded.

The rain had ceased, leaving the early morning sodden as if the clouds were made of unwrung towels. As requested, he arrived at the docks alone and unarmed.

"Must we travel in that thing?" He eyed her small boat suspiciously. He was a landborn man, unused to sea travel and unlearned of the sea. That, she knew, was the only thing that enabled her to do this—the fact that she had grown up by the sea, and he had not.

"I know of no other way to take you to your goal," she said mildly, less afraid now. His powerlust had already betrayed him; he wouldn't turn back now.

They sailed until no shore was in sight, and then she brought the boat around and fixed the sails so they bobbed, gently, on the waves.

"What now, sorceress?" he snapped.

She held a hand out toward the sea. "Now you must get in the water."

To his credit, he showed no sign of fear. In that way, he was a strong leader of men. But he also ruled by fear.

He leaned toward her, and she met his gaze with as much courage as she could.

"I cannot swim," he said. Which she had supposed, and hoped.

"This is the only way," she responded. "Here, I will tie this rope about your waist, so—" and she securely looped it around him "—and the other end of it to the boat." She deftly flipped the rope into a knot, and tugged at the knot to show him its sturdiness.

Again, her instinct of him proved true: his lust for power outweighed his common sense, and he slipped into the chill winter swells.

"Where is this thing that will show me power?" he called out to her, gripping the rope, splash-paddling in something of a circle to search in all directions.

She took a deep breath. The seasalt seared her nostrils. He didn't understand. She supposed that somewhere, somehow, she'd hoped that he would, that somewhere, humanity would prevail. But he didn't, and it didn't, so she had to continue.

With a wristflick she released the knot that held the rope to the boat. She'd based so much of this on the hope that he wouldn't know knots.

"The ocean is a powerful force, feared by all," she shouted as she snapped up the sail before he could grab the edge of the boat. The skiff began skimming the water for home.

His men-at-arms would be waiting when she docked. She was calm in that knowledge. What mattered was that he couldn't hurt anyone now; his evil ways would not continue.

She wondered if they would give her time to explain before they killed her.

The ocean was a powerful force; its waves ate at the shore and changed the shape of the land. Wise men learned its power and respected and feared it.

And truly wise men understood that there were forces far greater than them, power far greater than they could ever possess.

THE FROG PRINCE
by Linda J. Dunn

Under normal conditions, if a story with a name like "The Frog Prince" came across my desk, I'd throw it aside imagining it was the same old stuff. I would think by now that I've read every twist a writer could find on that overdone idea. That's almost the only advantage you can have in knowing an editor; I've read enough of Linda Dunn's stuff to be a little curious about why an experienced writer would try once more to slip this old idea past me for the three-thousandth time (at least).

So I read a page and was hooked. I wonder why it never occurred to anyone why a prince would let himself be turned into a frog?—or why he couldn't prevent it? Maybe marrying a princess is not so enviable a fate after all.

Linda Dunn says that like most writers she began writing in childhood and tells of writing her first stories under the blankets by flashlight. (That's a new one on me, probably because I never owned a flashlight; I just wrote them behind the barrier of another book in grade school and read them aloud to acquaintances—not having any friends—in junior high school.) Linda says that her dreams of writing vanished behind realities of divorce, single parenthood, and poverty—yes, that's par for the course, too (substituting a desperately mentally ill husband in my case). But after a divorce and a cooling-off period, she found while pursuing a college degree that it was impossible to write "while studying such black magic as 'Advanced Calculus.' " (I was lucky—I had to repeat trigonometry twice, and was excused from further math. I was never faced with calculus.)

She's had stories in *Sword and Sorceress XII, Marion Zimmer Bradley's FANTASY Magazine* and a few other anthologies. "Unable to tolerate a life without writing," she changed jobs and quit school, and now works as a computer specialist and has never been happier. Well, if she can handle computers, I don't see how calculus can have any terrors for her; between the two, I'd take calculus any day. Maybe I'm just from the wrong generation. I use mine only as a grown-up typewriter.

Linda says that she and her husband live with the usual number of allergy-inducing cats in Greenfield, Indiana. One major advantage of California is not so many mosquitoes. When I was last in Indiana, about 1962, I was appallingly mosquito-bitten.

Princess Karelia kissed one hundred and forty-nine frogs before breakfast. She stared at the crowd of frog-holding peasants awaiting her now and wished once again that there was some way to escape this unpleasant duty.

The king's voice was a mere whisper. "I never knew we had so many frogs in the kingdom." He turned to Karelia and smiled. "Courage, my dear. I'm sure we'll find him soon."

Princess Karelia allowed the king to lead her slowly back to her seat at the front of the room. The chains attached to her legs made it impossible for her to move swiftly. The king could ill afford to risk the only beautiful princess within a hundred miles of his kingdom escaping. He needed her to find his son, Prince Frederick, who had turned himself into a frog.

If only she'd inherited her father's hooked nose or her mother's mustache, she would not be here today. But no, she had to be beautiful, unlike her sister Matilda who had only to appear before the king and be sent home immediately.

She'd tried making herself fat, but the servants watched her diet carefully and insisted she have plenty of exercise and fresh air to maintain her beautiful appearance.

Once, she'd managed to find a knife and she'd toyed

with the idea of permanently disfiguring her face. Alas, she lacked the courage and instead sliced off her beautiful hair, certain that a nearly bald princess would be considered ugly.

Immediately, all the court ladies and servants adopted the style, claiming it made her even more beautiful.

The situation was hopeless.

Princess Karelia sat down and spread her gown around her. If she must kiss frogs, then she would do so with the dignity that befitted her position.

The first peasant stepped forward and extended a mud-caked amphibian. Karelia shook her head and motioned for a servant to dip the frog into a bucket of water and dry it before offering it again. She might be a prisoner in this kingdom, but she was still a princess and she would not kiss a dirty little frog.

When the mud was washed away, it became apparent that the frog was actually a toad.

The king exploded in anger. "How dare you try to trick me. I said 'frog.' I will pay no shillings for trickery."

The peasant fell to his knees. "Forgive me, Your Majesty. I could not tell the difference."

The king stood up and motioned to the guards. "Take this man to the royal wizard and have him turned into a frog. Maybe after a few days of eating bugs, he will be able to tell the difference between a frog and a toad."

The guards led the man away and Princess Karelia took the next frog from a peasant and pressed her lips against the frog's. Nothing happened, just as nothing had happened the last one hundred and forty-nine times.

One hundred and fifty frogs so far today, and a long line of peasants waited.

By nightfall, Princess Karelia had kissed another eight hundred and nineteen frogs. Her lips were chapped and sore from the effort and she couldn't wash away the smell of algae.

The guards returned her to her room in the tower and she waited for the servants to arrive with her next meal.

She would go mad if she didn't escape soon.

A voice spoke softly from the window.

"May we talk?"

She turned and saw a blue-eyed frog sitting on the window sill.

"Prince Frederick! I most certainly want to talk to you. Have you any idea what I've suffered due to your little prank?"

"I'm sorry," he said, "but you've met my father. What would you do in my place?"

"I'd turn myself into something better than a frog. Why not a white deer so you could hide in the forest?"

The frog leaped to her bed. "Ragnar is very clever in concealing his books and I only had a few moments to find a spell. The frog one looked simple and easy to read. The others looked more difficult."

Karelia grabbed him and held tight, pursing her lips together. Finally! The last frog she ever had to kiss.

"Wait! Please! Hear me out."

"Why should I? I've wasted away here for over a month with no hope of rescue. Do you have any idea how disgusting it is to spend day after day kissing frogs?"

"Do you have any idea how difficult it is to hide in a kingdom where the king is paying a month's wages to anyone bringing him a frog? I've heard merchants have been shipping in frogs from foreign lands at a good profit, taking the shilling from the peasants and rewarding them with a half-pence."

"That's terrible!" she said.

"Well, it's lucky for me. Without that trade, someone might have found me earlier."

"Where have you been all this time?"

"Hiding in the garden. I figured they'd look for me everywhere except the royal pond. It was too obvious. Please don't kiss me. I like being a frog."

"Well, I don't like kissing them, but you're the last one."

"If you kiss me, Father will insist we marry."

Karelia dropped the frog on her bed and he hopped away to sit on her pillow.

"You're right. Kissing frogs all day long might be a better fate than marriage to you."

"I thought perhaps we could come to an agreement," the frog suggested.

"What did you have in mind?"

"I've been trying to find Ragnar's book of spells so that I could change form, but it's proven impossible."

"And you think I, locked away in a tower, might be able to help you find the book?"

"If you refused to kiss another frog until the king showed you the book, he would do so."

"I've tried refusing before."

"But you never asked for a favor easily granted."

"And if I succeed?"

"See if you can find a better spell—one that makes me a fire-breathing dragon or something more interesting."

"I would hardly wish to turn you loose on the country-side as a dragon."

"Then something safe, but fun. Being a frog is grow-ing boring."

"And what would I get out of this arrangement?"

"If you make me a dragon, I'll fly you home on my back."

"Done!"

The next morning, Princess Karelia refused to kiss any frogs until the king allowed her to examine the wizard's book of spells. The wizard insisted that she see only the page the prince had left open but Karelia held firm that she wanted the entire book so she could assure herself that Prince Frederick hadn't merely turned to this page in the book after becoming a rabbit or a dog or some other animal. After all, it had been a month and they hadn't found him yet. Were they absolutely certain he was a frog?

Prince Frederick was waiting when she returned to her prison. He hopped up and down madly, saying, "You got it. Oh, I cannot believe you managed to actually obtain possession of it. This is marvelous. We can go through all the spells until we find one that's perfect. Let me see."

Princess Karelia stepped back a pace. "Oh, no, you don't. I've been reading this, and I noticed you didn't pay full attention to the spell you cast. You stop being a frog when the first snowflake falls."

Prince Frederick hopped onto her bed and crossed his legs in a most unprincely manner. "So? Winter is still several weeks away and besides, I don't want to return to the boring duties of a prince. Do you think it's fun rescuing princesses from dragons and escaping their loving fathers? Do you think I enjoy wearing silk shirts and being warned by my mother not to get them dirty? I just wanted a little fun, and I don't want it to end come winter."

"You don't return to being a prince when the first snowflake falls."

"No? What do I become?"

"A beautiful princess."

Princess Karelia held the book in front of her and gestured to the window. The words were foreign and difficult to pronounce, but she managed somehow.

"No!" was the soprano shout from her bed as a most unusually early snowstorm began to blanket the land.

Princess Karelia looked down at the beautiful princess and smiled. "Have fun, Princess Frederica. Use salve on your lips after kissing frogs. It helps keep them from growing too chapped."

She closed the book and muttered a few carefully memorized words.

A few moments later, the wizard Ragnar walked out of the room carrying his precious book. Princess Karelia smiled as the servants backed away, accepting her illusion. She walked to the stables and tucked the book carefully into a saddlebag before mounting a horse and riding home.

HONEY FROM THE ROCK

by Dorothy J. Heydt

Dorothy Heydt presents here her Greek stories of the sorceress Cynthia, who has appeared in these *Sword and Sorceress* volumes for lo, these many years. At the University of California, she mostly learned fascinating trivia about biochemistry and office politics; now she stays home with her "Chronic Fatigue Syndrome, two or three cats, two or three grown children, and a couple of outrageously cute kittens who will probably be muckin' great cats by the time this anthology is in print."

Yes, cats, like children, do grow up with truly appalling speed; I am hardly accustomed to my nephew being out of diapers, or to my niece being too old to toddle at my side holding a finger, when I get an invitation to her wedding or to the christening of his twins.

Dorothy says that she knows that bees have a queen, not a king, but they didn't know that in classical times.

Dorothy published a full-length novel of medieval chivalry, tournaments, and computer espionage, *A Point of Honor*, with DAW in April 1998.

"We've docked at Panormos," the captain said through Cynthia's door, and she felt herself go cold and fought the feeling down. This wasn't the Panormos of Sicily where Komi had died, but the one in Asia Minor, the port of Miletos. She unlatched the cabin door and saw the sun just rising above the rocky shore, behind the captain's head.

"We'll be unloading and then loading again, all day," the captain went on, "and we'd be greatly obliged if you either stayed in your cabin, or went ashore." His tone was respectful. The passenger had paid well, and besides, she had lanced a boil on the mate's neck and had the reputation of a witch. "We'll sail an hour before sunset."

"I'll go ashore," Cynthia said. It was an easy choice between a day shut into a cabin with one small window and a day spent wandering a lively Ionian port. No sense in taking chances, though. She packed her simples and the turtle shell full of books into her bag. Her remaining supply of gold was sewn into her hem; just enough, if her reckoning was right, to get her to Athens. Maybe. She took her small change in her mouth. Any quick-moving thief would find nothing to steal but a worn black gown and her bedding, both of which she'd cheerfully replace if someone else paid the loss. She slung her bag over her shoulder and went ashore.

Parts of Panormos were waking with the sun; parts had been up all night. Right at the foot of the dock a man was unrolling a faded red carpet and laying out his wares: a dented copper pot, a pile of cheap pottery, a clay statue of Artemis with her arms and nose chipped away. Farther on, little fish were grilling over a fishwife's brazier, filling the air with a scent sweeter than honey. "LOU-ka!" the woman screamed, "I need more CHAR-coal!" So much for that story in Herodotos that Milesian women never called their husbands by name. Maybe it had been true in his day. Cynthia spent her small change on little fish on hot bread, and a flask of wine and some ripe apricots, and wandered through the market watching men and women haggle over prices and children run about underfoot. Over the rooftops she could see the first of the pilgrims climbing the road to the Temple of Apollo Didymaios, not quite visible in its hollow in the hills above.

She was licking the last of the juice from her fingers when the little girl tugged at her sleeve. "Please, lady. Aren't you Cynthia, the witch of Syracuse? Please come and see my mother; she's very ill."

Cynthia looked the girl over and decided she was

probably in earnest: a little maiden of ten or twelve years, if Cynthia was any judge: in a year or so her breasts would bud and her father would be seeking a husband for her. Her eyes were red and her cheeks streaked with half-dried tears. Her little white gown, however, was as clean and bright as if it were new, and she had tucked into her hair a few flowers that were still unwithered. "What's the matter with your mother?"

"She's weak and tired all the time. She lies abed all day. She has vomited many times, and now she won't eat." (That could be any of some dozen ailments and at least six of the spells in Cynthia's turtle shell.) "And at times I think she's going mad. She said her hands and feet were numb, and that the light was whirling before her eyes. And now she seldom speaks, and what she says makes no sense."

These words lit a candle in Cynthia's mind, a tiny pale light that illuminated nothing, not yet. "What had she been eating before this?"

"What she always ate. Now she only drinks water."

"I'd better go and see her. Take me there."

"This way," the girl said, and led her through the town and up into the hills behind it. This was a major road, stone-paved throughout its length, that led to the temple of Apollo for those who didn't care to take the hundred-stadia march along the Pilgrim Way from Miletos to the north.

There were others on the road, travelers and peddlers and beggars and thieves; and a gang of workmen with a stonewagon, ready to continue the rebuilding that had been going on since Alexander's day; and a party of Hellenes with an ox for the sacrifice, its horns wreathed with flowers, its eyes placid and dull.

They climbed to the top of the plateau and turned a corner 'round a well-placed stone, and saw the temple of Apollo, its painted and gilded pillars shining in the sun, nestled into its sacred grove, the village of Didyma huddled at its feet. All the temenos was ringed with whitewashed boundary stones.

Close to the road stood the shrine of Hekate Propylaia, Hekate-at-the-Gates, where worshipers paused to pour unmixed wine. Here peddlers lurked with charms and amulets and figures of all the gods and goddesses by turns. "Ey, sir! It's a fortunate day for you! The god will smile on you, answer all your questions, see! the very finest pewter—" "Probably lead," Cynthia muttered, and cursed as the man turned her way. But he went straight past her as though she had not been there, to cry, "Ey, lady! Such a bargain! The four gods on one medal!" to some other victim. Perhaps Cynthia and the young girl didn't look prosperous enough.

The priests on duty at the entrance must have thought the same—nobody took any notice of them—or perhaps they would be asked for contributions later on.

Inside the great gate marking the entrance stood a round building with no roof and many doors, the altar of ashes, the place of sacrifice. A pair of priests standing outside it caught sight of the Hellenes with the ox and moved forward to take charge, arrange them in a procession of suitable length and lead them forth.

The girl led Cynthia straight past the village and along the Sacred Way toward the temple of Apollo. So the mother had not been living in Didyma when she fell ill, then; perhaps she had come to seek the help of Apollo the Healer and had not received it, and was now too weak to walk. They passed by the temple entrance and turned to the west.

Here a smaller ring of boundary stones enclosed the shrine of Artemis Pythie. Between the stones, through the trees of the grove, they could see the outcrop of rock that brought forth the goddess' sacred springs; and at the entrance stood the Hydrophor herself, her chief priestess, carrying a golden cup, with several of the attendants. The girl led Cynthia between them into the shrine, weaving back and forth as between close-growing trees. None of the women took the slightest notice. It was as if the ring of Gyges shielded both of them from sight: and Cynthia, who had seen already many strange things in the homeplaces of goddesses, felt the hair rise on the back of her neck.

She took a step into the temenos, and another, and suddenly a great flash of light flowered in the cool western morning sky and blinded her. She tripped and fell flat, and heard a deep voice rumbling like a stormwind, like thunder over her head,

"Is that the best you could find?"

Foolish people (knowing no better) frequently are tricked into taking a man's voice, heard through an actor's speaking mask, for the voice of a god. No one who has heard the voice of a god will ever mistake it for the voice of a mortal. Cynthia pulled her stole over her head and wondered if this was death at last. But she heard the little maiden saying,

"Uncle, don't be foolish. If you burn her to ashes, she can't do *any*thing. Cover yourself; you can't talk to her like that."

The light that blazed through the woolen stuff of her stole and through her eyelids dimmed, and the deep voice rumbled, "Woman, look at me."

She uncovered her head and obeyed. The figure before her might have been man-sized and within arm's reach, or mountain-tall and far away. He stood naked, a bow in his left hand, a little animal sitting in his right palm. It turned its head to look at him. She had seen his likeness on coins and medals all morning. His hair was long and curled; there was a little smile on his lips, such as one saw on the old *kouroi*, the figures of young gods. A cruel little smile, with nothing human in it.

"Listen, mortal," he said. "If you cure my sister of her illness, you shall have my favor. If not, not. If you fail to cure her—" He raised the bow in his left hand—

"Yes, Uncle," the little maiden said, "you've made your point. Now let the woman do her work. Don't you have somewhere you're supposed to be?"

The god favored his niece with a look of annoyance that would have turned a mortal to cinders, and vanished.

"He's always wanted somewhere," the girl explained. "Now he has to be in Delphi, and soon after, he runs to Kolophon and from there to Xanthos, and then back on a run to Klaros, then to Delos or back here, or wherever the oracle drinks from the sacred spring, or chews the bay, or shakes the tripod, and calls him." In the darkness he left behind, the little maiden shone like the moon behind a cloud.

"That was Apollo," Cynthia said.

"Yes."

"And his sister is—"

"Artemis. You know: Leto's twins."

"And she's your mother?" Artemis was, going by the tales, the most virginal of the gods, saving only Athene who had sprung motherless from the brow of Zeus. "What is your name?"

Now she smiled, like the moon breaking out of cloud. "Aretë," she said.

Virtue. And it explained why her gown was so clean and white, her flowers unwithered, why none had seen her unbidden. "But I know you," Cynthia said. "I knew you in the form of a man. Komi was his name."

"Oh, yes." The maiden's eyes glistened with tears. "Yes, he was one of mine. *I'll* not threaten you. Only, please: for the love we both bore him: cure my mother."

"If I can."

Cynthia got to her feet and looked around. This was not the same temenos she had seen before she had stepped into it: tiny, close-walled naiskos here, altar over there. Only the outcrop of rock was the same, with its springs that bubbled out of the clefts and fell into golden basins below. The white pillar-stones marking the temenos boundaries had receded to a great distance, and beyond them the pale shapes of mortal worshipers moved about, dim as clouds. Within the vast plain of the temenos there were a few trees here and there, and over against the west a dark grove. One great oak stood nearby, and in its shade a woman lay on a bed inlaid with ivory. The cloth that covered her was rich with

Tyrian purple, interwoven with threads of gold. From a branch hung a bow and a quiver.

Cynthia came close and knelt down to look at her. She seemed a woman of some forty years, thin and pale, with a few lines in her face and throat. A little of her daughter's light seemed to shine out of her, and indeed Cynthia felt she could almost see the sheet and pillow through the goddess' skin.

There was no point in asking why Apollo Paian, the Healer, could not heal his sister himself. If he could, he would; therefore he couldn't. If she lived long enough, she might discover the reason why.

"First, study the patient's appearance." She could almost have recited the description in Hippokrates word-for-word: the nose sharp, the eyes sunken, the ears cold and drawn in and their lobes distorted, the skin of the face hard, stretched, and dry, and the color pale. "How long has she been like this?"

"Like this?" Aretë had come close; she bent down and brushed the fair hair away from her mother's face. "She's been feeling poorly ever since I can remember: two hundred years, maybe, as mortals reckon time. But *this*—the vomiting, seeing things that aren't there, speaking out of madness or not at all—that began this spring."

"What was the weather like this spring? I mean, what was it like here (if she was here)? I was at the other end of Greater Greece then, halfway to the Pillars of Herakles."

"The *weather*," Aretë said, frowning in concentration. "It was a very cold, rainy, late spring. You'd think such things would not bother us immortals; but if they *did*—why didn't she recover once the weather got warm?"

"Well, I don't know that yet. A mortal, at least, might take such a chill in such a spring as he'd never recover from, no matter how warm it got." She looked around. A bowl lay on the ground beside the bed, made of gold with an ivory spoon in it, and a golden cup. She picked up the bowl; it was half full of something clear as water and firm as soft jelly. Ambrosia, she supposed, the food

of the immortals, prepared in a soft form like to the
barley gruel fed to sick mortals. She raised the bowl to
her nose and sniffed: there was no smell so far as she
could tell.

"You shouldn't taste that," Aretë said.

"I hadn't planned to. What's in the cup? Water?"

"The water from her own spring. It's all she will
take now."

Cynthia took a cautious sip. The water tasted pungent,
almost, and slightly bittersweet. The candle in her mind
burned a little brighter. It was like, it was like— Curse!
she couldn't put her mind to it. She got up from the
bedside and looked around again. The great plain within
the temenos seemed perfectly flat, or even bowl-
shaped—or maybe that was just a trick of the light.
There were stretches of green grass, and she could see
deer wandering out of the woods to graze. (A white stag
raised its head to look at her, and lowered it again.) But
much of the plain was a powdery cracked limestone with
bushes of laurel and heather and rhododendron growing
out of it, the sunlight bright on their rustling leaves. And
as she stood looking blank-faced across the plain, a bee
flew by her ear with a loud buzz and hurried away into
the distance. But the light in her mind blazed up and
illuminated that bee, lit up the golden fur on his body,
his glassy wings, his tiny dark-eyed head. Stories welled
up in her mind like the springs of Artemis: poisoned
armies, raving warriors, foragers who should have stayed
on beans and horsemeat. She turned back to Aretë.

"What place is this?" she asked. "This vast plain that
fits so neatly within a little ring of stones?"

"It's the plain of asphodels, the plain of immortal
things," said Aretë. "The little patch of ground inside
those boundary stones stands for, or in a sacred sense it
really is, this wide plain where the herds of Artemis
graze without fear, where all healing plants grow."

"Oh, it is, is it? May your words be as true as the
truth." Cynthia almost gripped the young goddess by the
shoulders, but thought better of it. Yes, almost at her

feet grew a clump of spiky asphodels. The only flower
that grew in both worlds, some poet had said. Well, he
was wrong: the heather was wearing ten shades of soft
rose and purple, and the rhododendrons must have been
a glorious sight when they were in bloom. "Now tell me:
is this plain on earth?"

"I'm not exactly prepared to answer that question,"
said Aretë after a moment's thought. "I'm only a young
goddess, lady; give me a little time to learn."

"Does the same sun shine on it, that shines on earth?"

"Oh, yes."

"Does the rain fall on it, water its plants, and sink
deep into its soil?"

"Yes."

"And does that water, presently, bubble up out of the
ground into these springs? And this is what your mother
has been drinking all year?"

"Yes, yes. What is it? Is she poisoned? Can you cure
it? How could any poison harm an immortal goddess?"

"Yes, it's poison; yes, I know a treatment. As to your
last question, I'm not prepared to answer *that,* not yet.

"Listen. Xenophon tells of a band of soldiers traveling
overland near the region of Colchis. They found wild
beehives, ate the honey, and fell ill. They acted mad—
or drunk. They fell to the ground in their thousands,
unable to stand, miserable and despondent. It took them
days to recover. Later they found out the honey they
had eaten came from the flower of the rhododendron.
The people of that region know better than to eat it
themselves. 'Mad honey,' they call it. Medea lived there,
princess of Colchis, witch and poisoner. Dionysos danced
there with his Maenads."

"Mad lads," said Artemis suddenly. "My skip, the
moondering wan, high with Castor's brother and his
brother Castor."

"The rhododendron blooms here every year," Aretë
said, "but this never happened before."

"That's where the weather comes in. The spring was
cold and wet and late: there was nothing for the bees to

feed on, except the rhododendron. They made it into thin, greenish, watery honey that dropped from the combs: and if, as I guess, their hives were not well-shielded from the weather, then every time it rained, the honey washed right out of the uncapped combs. And into the water your mother has been drinking all year."

"Water," Artemis said. "Wetter. Wether, wither, whether. Why not."

"No, don't give her any," Cynthia said. "I dare say in her good days it still wouldn't have harmed her. But with this weakness upon her, bringing her down almost, no offense meant, to the feeble strength of a mortal—"

"About half of that seems to make sense," Aretë said. "Let's assume it does. You said there is a treatment?"

"Sound honey, and pure water," Cynthia said. "Or rue as an emetic, but I don't want to make her vomit now, she's too weak. There'll be nothing but traces inside her anyway. I'll go find the honey; can you get water that doesn't come from these springs? Rain water would be fine."

"Yes, I can have it brought. But the honey—" she gestured toward the plain. "Won't it be poisoned, too?"

"Not the new stuff, that they've made since the other flowers bloomed. Sometimes you can get good and bad within parts of the same comb." She knelt beside the bed again, where she had laid down her sack, and found flint and steel. "I'll be back as soon as I can."

"Wait." Aretë ran her hands over Cynthia's face and hair. "That will protect you from stings—as long as you don't become afraid."

Out on the plain, time was still passing as it did on earth; the sun had risen almost to the noon. Cynthia looked back to mark the place where the great oak grew by the outcrop, and set off to look for flowers.

The grassy lawns where the deer grazed were more clover than grass, thick with white blossoms, and the bees were foraging over them as greedily as newborn babes at the breast. The white stag lifted its head again to look at Cynthia, sighed as a weary man might have done, and stooped down to graze.

The bees were no ordinary bees. If there were bees of the gods, they were these: bees the size of sparrows, bees that hummed under their breath like a whole chorus of deep-voiced Scythians, bees that flew off with pollen clumps on their legs the size of horse beans. They could fly faster than she could walk, but when one flew out of sight, another came into view over her shoulder, steadily leading her toward the hive.

It was plain enough that none of the spells from the scrolls in the turtle shell would be of any use to her here. There were charms to keep bees from swarming or, once they had swarmed, to coax them to settle in a new hive. But Cynthia had had as friend a farmer who kept bees, and she knew the value of smoke.

The bees led her to a huge oak, still green and hale but split up the side to a point higher than she could reach. Cautiously she knelt and peered inside. It was dark, and it murmured, and smelt of wax and honey.

Piles of green heather branches at the entrance, on a bed of dry leaves and grass to catch the spark and fire the whole stack. The grass flared, the heather smoldered; the little leaves and flowers blazed up, crackling like hail, and then settled down to pouring out clouds of thick, pungent smoke. The hollow tree drew it in like a chimney. Inside the murmuring rose sharply and fell again, more slowly. " 'Tisn't that the smoke fuddles them, nor makes them more peaceable," her friend had said. " 'Tis that they think the woods are afire and they must fly for their lives. So they go to fill their bellies with honey. And once their bellies are full, look you, they're happy and they don't sting." She gave them a little longer, till their song had dwindled to a thick gluttonous hum. Then she picked up a branch of heather by its unburnt end and stepped inside.

The comb hung like curtains of thick-woven homespun from unseen ceilings far overhead. Here and there, where the cells were not yet capped, bees hung in clusters drinking their fill. Long-fallen combs crunched underfoot like shells on the seashore.

She looked overhead, peering through the thick smoke, with only the fitful light of the torch to see by. She *thought* she caught a glimpse of the king bee, his long body as large as a wood pigeon's, but she could not be sure of it.

What she needed was a piece of filled comb that she could break away with her hands, and most of these combs were entirely too big. Each separate cell must hold several spoonfuls of honey. Wait—there was a small piece, growing out of a great hanging comb like a wart on someone's earlobe. If she could break it loose—

She laid the torch on the ground and tugged at it with both hands. It bent, and swayed, and came loose with a chorus of pops. Honey oozed over her hands. She picked up her torch again and turned to go.

But the larger comb was still swaying and popping, and the anxious bees rose from it in a great cloud as it collapsed to the floor, folding up on itself with a sound like a long sigh.

The cloud of bees swirled and thickened into a pillar the size of a man, that bent its shapeless top this way and that as if to search for the person responsible. The song rose into a bellow of rage, a war chant for an army of myriads.

It had been a mistake to lay the torch down on the floor. Everywhere a twig or leaf or strand of dry grass had blown in across the wax, a little candle flame had sprung up on a slender wick. It made for a lot of bewilderment and not much real light, and where in Hades was the doorway?

The pillar of bees was circling now, like a beast closing in on its prey—but no beast went upright, none but man, the most dangerous of all. She fancied that it would soon put forth a head to see her with, arms with poisoned talons to grasp and kill. She took in a last deep breath, dropped the torch and trod it underfoot till it was out.

Then she trod out the little candle flames, one by one, till they were all quenched and the place was dark again.

The bees roared like swarms of lions around her head, but none of them touched her. Perhaps they didn't sting because of the smoke; perhaps they didn't sting because of the blessing of Aretë, and because Cynthia was just too busy to fear. After some time her eyes grew used to the darkness; she saw a faint light glimmering through the smoke, and groped her way outside. Eyes watering, her clothes reeking of smoke and sticky with honey, she made her way back across the plain of asphodels to the oak tree beside the welling rock.

Two of the Hydrophor's women were there, their faces empty as in a dream, carrying between them a cask full of water. "Rain water," Aretë said, "some housewife's laundering water from the village." The women put down the cask and turned to go. As they passed between the pillars of the gate they vanished and reappeared cloudlike on the distant horizon.

Cynthia poured out the spring water from the cup, the watered-down ambrosia from the bowl, and rinsed the vessels with rainwater. Then with the golden spoon she uncapped one of the cells and held a spoonful of honey to Artemis's lips. The goddess drew in a long breath, as if the smell were sweet, sighed, and swallowed.

Cynthia got four more spoonfuls into her before she opened her eyes, pale blue as the clouds on the horizon, and said, "Water." Aretë brought the cup, and her mother drained it without stopping. "More," she said, and drank another cupful before falling back into sleep.

"Two sensible words together," Cynthia said. "This might work."

They watched by her all afternoon, as the sun slowly descended the sky toward Panormos. *Four hours,* Cynthia reckoned, counting handsbreadths above the horizon. And then, *Three hours. If she mends within the hour I could still get down to the dock before the ship sails—* If, in any case, Apollo did not blast her to ashes. Neither piece of good fortune seemed likely. If worst came, at

least she wouldn't have to worry about stretching her
dwindling gold as far as Athens. Artemis took more
honey once, and water several times, but she did not
speak again.

It was some time before Cynthia realized that there
were others sitting beside them—and there was no excuse for it, since they were not pale and transparent like
Artemis, but ruddy and hale, with rounded arms and
sparkling eyes. "These are my sisters and cousins,"
Aretë said. "Philia, Elpis, Tychë."

Friendship, Hope, Luck: the young goddesses whose
names were abstract qualities, whose worship was dis-
placing the Olympians in the hearts of men—along with
Tammuz and Cybele, Isis and Osiris, and even men
themselves. The rituals went on unceasing—no one was
anxious to break with long-held traditions, least of all
those who made a living from them. But their hearts
were no longer in it.

> *"For other gods are either far away or have not ears,*
> *Or do not exist, or heed us not at all;*
> *But thee we can see in very presence, not in wood and*
>   *not in stone,*
> *But in truth, and so we pray to thee."*

So they had sung to Demetrios, ruler of Athens, while
he still lived. And being a Hellene, Cynthia could not
but wonder which was cause and which effect. Had men
turned from the Olympians because they had faded and
grown distant? Or were they fading because men no
longer adored them in their hearts? But she did not say
any of this aloud.

As the day wore on, other watchers became visible,
pale and dim but perceptible, especially if she looked at
them out of the corner of her eye. Zeus, Hera, Poseidon,
Hermes, Hestia, Dis. None of them looked as ill and
wasted as Artemis, but she could see straight through
them, and they sat without moving and their expressions
were grave as they watched at the bedside of their kins-

woman to see if she would live or die. Pale, anxious; but
maybe no worse than they had ever been.

So she thought until Athene appeared. Not pale, not
transparent, she was as solid as Aretë herself, bright as
her painted statues in the temples. Her saffron-colored
gown fluttered in the wind, and her gray eyes were as
deep as the sea. The little owl on her shoulder fluttered
its feathers and said softly, "Hoooo." Then it flapped its
wings and nearly fell off as the goddess rushed forward.
Artemis woke, and said, "Sister. Welcome to my house,"
and reached up a thin arm to Athene's embrace.

The gray-eyed goddess rose and took Cynthia firmly
by the shoulders. "Cynthia! Well met," she said, and
kissed her on the cheek. The touch stung like hot iron,
but only for an instant. Then all the weariness fell from
her body and her filmy eyes cleared, and she stammered,
"Forgive me, lady, but have we met?"

"You called on me," the goddess said, "long ago, in
the middle of the sea. I haven't forgotten."

"Oh. Oh, yes. I called you Minerva, among the Romans." In fact, she had taken her name in vain, to cover
up a spur-of-the-moment deception, but she wasn't going
to mention that.

"But you called me," the goddess said, "and it was as
though I had woken from a long dream. So, seeing you
were in a tight place and needed an idea, I sent you
one."

Cynthia was fairly certain she had had the idea before
she called on Minerva, but she wasn't about to mention
that either; and besides, another idea was coming to her,
one that swelled and bloomed like all of spring and summer in a moment. A great light was sweeping over the
plain, and she turned her head and squinted behind her
hand as Apollo burst into view.

"Uncle," said Aretë, and Apollo said, "Oh, yes," and
dimmed his light again. He came and knelt by his sister's
bedside, and she smiled weakly and took his hand.

"She's not cured," he said, glaring at Cynthia.

"As we mortals say, lord, 'she's not right, but she's

better,' " Cynthia answered. "Aretë, would you say she's
back to the way she was before this spring?"

"About that."

"And you, my lord, who travel so widely around the
lands and seas: do you visit Rome?"

"What has that to do with—?" he began, but his sister's soft voice interrupted him.

"Yes, he does," she said. "The Romans did not know
him before they started dealing with you Hellenes; but
they know him now, sing hymns in his praise and offer
sacrifices for his favor." She coughed and groped for her
cup; Aretë held it to her lips.

"And under what name do they call on him?" Cynthia
asked when Artemis had finished swallowing.

Apollo bellowed, "My own!"

"Uncle," said a new voice, soft but entirely firm, "you
will do better to let the physician do her work." This
was another little maiden like Aretë, even younger in
appearance, perhaps eight or nine. Her hair was dark
and her eyes serious, and she wore one great pearl on
a ribbon around her neck.

"Thank you," Cynthia said. She got to her feet and
marshaled her wits. The more this sounded like a formal
spellcasting, the better.

"Artemis, daughter of Leto," she began, "today I give
you a new name. Far to the west, in the hearts of the
people of Rome, temples of virtue and honor, your name
is Diana."

And the goddess drew in a great breath and let it out
in a wail, like a newborn child drawing in its spirit with
its first breath, with her new name. She was opaque and
solid; the color stood in her cheeks; she kicked off the
coverlet and rose to her feet. The white stag came 'round
the bole of the oak tree and nuzzled at her hand.

She laughed and embraced her brother, Cynthia, and
Aretë. Then snatching her bow and quiver from the
branch of the oak, she cried "Rome!" and vanished.
Apollo disappeared a heartbeat later.

"You also, my lords and ladies Olympians," Cynthia

said, "can do the same. Jupiter, Juno, Neptune, Mercury, Vesta, Pluto."

There was a great flash of light and color and they were gone, had been gone for some time. Only the five young maidens were left, the young goddesses, embodied virtues. "Well done," Aretë said softly.

"That should last for a few hundreds of years," the youngest said, "or as long as the Romans remain temples of virtue and honor."

"What about you?"

"Oh, we already have our Latin names: Virtus, Amicitia, Spes, Fortuna, Sapientia."

"Sophia, in Greek," the littlest maiden said, leaving Cynthia to wonder how Wisdom could be so young—until she took a look into her eyes.

"Now, then," Aretë said, "there's the matter of your fee."

Cynthia shrugged. "I can say I've put my head into the lion's mouth and brought it out again. What I really want isn't in your gift."

"Well, no. Korë, I mean Proserpina, wasn't here today, was she?"

"No. I haven't seen her in a while."

"She's probably in Eleusis," Sophia said.

"You could go there," Philia said.

"I'm not Orpheus," Cynthia said. She glanced at the sun, barely a handsbreadth above the horizon. "I've missed my ship anyway. And he didn't succeed either, did he?" And crying aloud, "But if I had his chance, my head would fall from my shoulders before I turned it to look back."

"Go to Eleusis and ask," said Tychë. "There's always a chance."

"We'll all come and speak for you."

"And meanwhile—" Sophia held out a little coin, tarnished bronze and not worth much, and gave it to Tychë.

"When you get back into the town, you'll see a merchant on a red carpet, offering for sale a very poor statue of Aunt Artemis," said Tychë. She gave the coin to Aretë.

"Buy it with this." And Aretë pressed the coin into Cynthia's hand, and for several long moments that was the only solid thing there was, as the red light of sunset washed her in a sea of flame.

When she could see again, she was standing at the edge of the dock, her feet on the pavement, her bag on her shoulder, the coin in her hand. Beside her sat the merchant on the red rug. She tossed him the coin—the man smiled—and picked up the battered figure of Artemis. It was unusually heavy for a piece of clay, and it was no surprise when by chance she stumbled over her threshold and dropped the thing. It shattered and spilled out a hoard of gold coins: enough to fill all the empty places in her hem, enough to get her to Athens or even farther. Eleusis, for instance. She stripped off the honey-wet gown and put on the old worn one. Enough even to spend a little at the next market—Samos, probably.

She undogged her window latch and let in the salt breeze and the sun's last hour of light. What had the other maiden's name been, the one who seldom spoke? Elpis, that was it: Hope. Outside the anchor thudded on the wooden deck and the captain shouted to raise sail. Eleusis, maybe, and back again.

THE WILL OF THE WIND

by Christina Krueger

Almost every year I get half a dozen stories which take place in a school of sorcery, and every year I resolve not to print any more—and then a story like this one comes along, and I find I have to print just one more.

Christina seems to have thought out more carefully than usual what would be the curriculum in such a school, and how the students would react to it. I think it was Ted Sturgeon who defined the art of fiction as that of creating "passionate emotional relationships," which is as good a way of describing it as any and better than most. Ted has left us now, but his legacy as a great—and a wise—writer lingers on.

Master Stormcaller Yvarlin Grayfeather swept into the room and silenced her chattering class with a brisk *snap!* of her white-and-gray wings before folding them against her back.

The twelve acolytes settled, and the *avir* priestess began the day's lessons in the meditation and emotional discipline necessary for controlling the fickle element Air. Those blessed with the Windlady's Gifts were fey and temperamental by nature, and a great deal of patient effort was needed to help them grow into their abilities. Yvarlin inwardly glowed with pride as she worked with her talented group, all of whom were nearing graduation.

This year's students were all Mage talents, with no candidates for the Priesthood. Yvarlin accepted this with equanimity, knowing through long experience not to question the will of the Gods. With one exception.

That exception sat at the students' common table with his hands folded before him, his black eyes bright with intelligence. This student possessed such a natural ease with Air that he didn't need instruction so much as simple guidance. Yvarlin relished the chance to work with such a gifted pupil, but she often felt a surge of bitterness for the unfairness of his situation.

Sallik Citarha was of the shape-shifting *nimir*, a people faced with even more prejudice and misunderstanding than the winged *avir*. He had been born *tayec*, which meant "Balanced One" in the *nimir* tongue. The hermaphroditic *tayec* were born only once in a handful of generations and were treated with near-worship. *Tayec* children were raised in a cloistered environment of awe and mysticism, and were groomed from infancy to become shamans and oracles. Unfortunately, such children had little chance to *be* children, or to be cherished for themselves.

Nimir were the children of Amaevith Earth Mother, and they rarely developed any Elemental talent besides earth. When Sallik had developed an unmistakable Air affinity shortly after his fifteenth birthday, his clan had been in turmoil. After months of intense debate, they had reluctantly bowed to the will of the Gods and delivered Sallik to the Temple of Yris in the Arthamian Mountains.

Sallik was the first *nimir* most of the students had met, and the superstitions about his mysterious race made them uneasy around him. He had coped with his feelings of ostracism by adopting an attitude of aloof serenity that would have done a High Priest proud. This mask was easy to maintain due to a strange characteristic that set him even farther apart: his silence. Sallik's father had informed Yvarlin that in Sallik's entire lifetime, no one had ever heard him speak. Whether this was a physical oddity or a voluntary silence, none knew.

Sallik's exotic looks were also of no help. He was taller than most, with long slender hands envied by every girl who saw them. His bone-straight hair was the color of moonlight on snow, making his liquid black eyes stand out in stark contrast. Naturally graceful, he exhibited none of the physical awkwardness that was the bane of most pubescent boys.

Whether conscious of it or no, Sallik exuded an air of charismatic enigma that created distance between himself and his peers. Yvarlin had recognized the façade for what it was: impenetrable armor against loneliness, homesickness, vulnerability.

Yvarlin herself had worn that armor. When her Stormcalling talents had manifested during her teens, she had been sent to learn from the only other known Stormcaller in her half of the world. The Ittimar Island Temple was far from her home in the Arthamians, and she had been the sole *avir* in residence. She understood exactly how alone Sallik felt, and her heart ached with sympathy when she sometimes saw his expressive eyes fill with silent pain.

Yvarlin had appointed herself Sallik's champion, vanquishing the teasing and rumors. A few of the bolder students began making friendly overtures to him, drawing him out of himself. He was hesitant at first, but he quickly learned to like being treated as a *person* instead of a religious icon. That change had been like summer rain on a parched garden. Most Air talents had impish personalities, and Sallik proved no exception. He grew to love his surrogate clan, expressing his affections with gestures and eloquent body language.

But as his two years of schooling neared their end, Yvarlin saw her lively pupil become quiet and introverted, withdrawing from his circle of friends. The priestess felt heartsick every time she found him standing alone somewhere, wistfully studying his surroundings as though he expected never to see them again.

In the last few weeks, Yvarlin had gone to the Temple Sanctuary again and again, pleading fervently with Yris to intercede with Her sister Amaevith for a way to heal the rift in her student's soul. The only answer she had received was the sound of empty mountain wind.

The priestess dismissed her class for the day, and the children bounded energetically down the halls of the Academy Building, accompanied by the breezes that filled the Temple complex.

A tendril of air tugged at Yvarlin's silver-white hair, and she looked up from her papers to see that Sallik had stayed behind. She smiled and said, "Is there something you need, my Silent Breeze?"

A gentle pressure of air lifted her left hand from its place on the desk and turned it palm-up to expose the white Eye of Magic tattooed there. A finger of wind traced the Yris Rune at the Eye's center, set there by the Goddess Herself, affirming Yvarlin's Priesthood. Sallik held up his own long-fingered left hand, its bare palm toward her.

The priestess' gray eyes widened. "You're asking to apply to the Priesthood?" she breathed, unable to believe it. "Has the Windlady called you?"

Sallik smiled brilliantly. Through breezes and graceful gestures, he explained that the Goddess had sent him a powerful dream of taking the Trial of Air, soaring triumphantly as Yris' breath filled him with Her acceptance.

When he finished, Yvarlin felt a great weight lift from her heart. She surged out of her seat and unfurled her wings. "Yris be praised!" she sang, seizing his hands and squeezing them hard. "I'll send a message to your clan immediately!" She felt the overwhelming urge to throw herself out the open window behind her desk and sky-dance until she dropped from sheer exhilarated exhaustion. Well, why not? She jumped lightly onto the broad windowsill and looked at Sallik over her shoulder, grinning mischievously. "Coming?"

Laughing at his mentor's very unpriestlike display of exuberance, Sallik followed her out the window, shifting to his *nimir* form in midair. A huge swan joined the jubilant *avir* in a joyous aerial dance that drew a delighted audience from all corners of the Temple.

* * *

Yvarlin reread Clan Citarha's message, willing the words to change before her eyes. Sallik stood in front of her desk with his hands clasped behind him, impatiently shifting his weight from foot to foot. The priestess desperately wanted to offer a word of comfort to soften the blow, but none came. Silently, she handed him the parchment.

He snatched it, eyes darting swiftly from word to word, trying to see them all at once. Yvarlin's throat closed convulsively as his expression fell from anticipation to disbelief, then down into despair. The scroll dropped from his trembling fingers and lay disregarded on the floor.

In a few terse sentences, Clan Citarha had adamantly forbidden Sallik to apply to the Priesthood, citing his religious birthright among the *nimir* more took precedence over any other calling.

Tears tracked down Sallik's pale cheeks. Yvarlin rose and walked around her desk to place a gentle hand on his shoulder. "You have the questionable honor of being held by two Goddesses, my Silent One," she said with soft compassion. "It seems Amaevith needs you more, as do your people. Use what you've learned here to become the great leader you were born to be, and I know you'll find peace."

Sallik shook off her hand and angrily wiped his sleeve across his face. He dodged past her and fled, a hard gust of air slamming the door behind him.

The priestess almost went after him, but stopped. He would need some time alone to assimilate the shock of the news. Air talents never stayed angry for long; emotional control was too deeply ingrained in their psyches. Despite that truth, Yvarlin wafted a gust of air under the discarded scroll, viciously shredded the parchment, and swept it out the window like a cloud of gnats.

The falling sun painted the white granite Sanctuary a radiant orange-gold and gilded Yvarlin's snowy feathers as she knelt before the altar. The tranquillity of the open-air shrine was shattered by the angry echoes of her voice as she flung questions to the evening sky.

"How could You do this to him!" She pounded the marble altar with her fists, her fury lashing the wind into sharp whips of air. "To offer him the hopes of his heart and then let Your Sister snatch them away! *You* were the one who called him here!"

Her body bent forward until her forehead rested on her bruised hands. Tears wet the cold marble as she breathed words even closer to her heart. "I thought You took care of Your own. How can I serve You when You show such cruelty?" Her arms crossed over her knotted stomach as she curled into a tight ball of wings and misery. "How can You test my love for You so harshly?"

A warm hand of wind ran through Yvarlin's short hair, making her lift her tear-stained face from the floor. The many windchimes strung among the columns went still as palpable silence fell over the Sanctuary.

The delicate silver windbells hanging directly above the altar began to swing, playing an icicle melody in the vast quiet. The priestess' eyes went beyond the altar to the Reliquary, an exquisitely crafted chest of white granite and flawless rock crystal. Important Temple relics were housed within: books penned by the Founders, feathers from prominent *avir* priests, holy talismans, and a coiled length of white silk rope.

Yvarlin's focus narrowed until only the rope filled her consciousness. Her heart drummed in her ears, filling the uncanny silence with its thunder. Feeling strangely detached from her own actions, she rose slowly and rounded the altar, drawing a silver key from the pocket of her robe.

The night wind had risen until the simple act of walking was a muscle-straining chore. Against her training, Yvarlin recklessly diverted the wind away from Sallik and herself as they crept through the dark to the Promontory.

The priestess had expected questions from Sallik when

she had shaken him awake an hour earlier. He had blinked only once at her standing at his bedside with the ritual rope in her hands before throwing off his covers and donning his robe. Silent as a windless winter morning, they had slipped through the dark halls of the dormitory and out to the barren cliffs where Priesthood candidates had been Tested for time out of mind.

Ordinarily, the Trial of Air would begin the previous twilight with fasting and meditation. At sunrise, every student and teacher in the Temple would gather in the Sanctuary to offer prayers and hymns to the Windlady. The postulate and his Initiator would then undergo elaborate blessings and ritual cleansings. The day's celebrations would culminate at sunfall where Sallik and Yvarlin now stood, on the cliffs overlooking the rocky valley of Yris' Mirror far below.

Yvarlin smiled grimly. This postulate's Trial would occur at the deepest hour of night, unwitnessed except for an Initiator who was breaking every oath she had ever sworn to Test him.

Sallik watched Yvarlin uncoil the rope, the whites of his eyes showing like a skittish horse. His hands asked, *Are you sure you want to do this? You know the cost of failure.*

The priestess' mouth went dry at the reminder. A Tribunal of priests would invoke a curse to strip Yvarlin of her powers, and her wings would be brutally broken before she was flung into the chasm to die. Or they would give her to the *nimir,* and the Gods alone knew how they would extract retribution.

Yvarlin cleared her throat and said, "It doesn't matter. I'd rather die than live with broken faith." Somewhere among her roiling emotions she found humor enough for a wry smile. "Besides, I think the Gods would be disappointed if we didn't force Their hands occasionally. But are you still sure *you* want to do this? It's not too late to stop."

Sallik nodded calmly, but the priestess could see him trembling. Impulsively, she pulled him into a tight hug, and he squeezed her ribs until she gasped. They stood that way, drawing strength from each other, until Yvarlin remembered herself and pushed him firmly away.

The priestess wound the rope around his body, binding him securely from neck to ankles. After tying the final knot, she turned him by the shoulders to face the precipice before him. His frightened gasp almost made her halt the rite, but she hardened her heart and placed the ritual kiss on his cheek.

Raising her hands to the overcast sky, Yvarlin intoned a soulfelt prayer: "Lady of the Winds, Your child stands before You on the edge between Death and Life." She barked a harsh laugh tinged with hysteria. "Your *children* stand before you on the edge between Death and Life. We lay our souls at Your feet in total trust. I pray You accept us and fill us with the breath of Your love."

Sallik's chest heaved rapidly, sweat trickling down his face despite the night's chill. He turned his head to give his mentor a long look filled with a mixture of fear, elation, and gratitude, then forsook his safe rock perch and fell toward his fate.

During the day, the gathered crowd would be able to watch the postulate's descent. Yvarlin strained to see Sallik, but the darkness swallowed him the instant he left the cliff. Instead, her mind's eye provided her with a vivid picture of his body scattered in red fragments on the rock teeth below. The strength drained from her legs as the ruthless truth seared her soul; if her intuition proved false, she had just sent a beautiful, trusting boy to his death. Her control over the wind slipped, and relentless fists of air buffeted her like an autumn leaf as she slumped to the ground and buried her face in her hands.

Over and over, she sent the litany to the wind: "I lay my soul at Your feet in total trust. I lay my soul at Your feet in total trust."

The gales around the cliffs died abruptly. Yvarlin's head snapped up to discover the clouds had vanished and the world was drenched in silver radiance. The night seemed to hold its breath with anticipation, but of success or failure, Yvarlin couldn't guess. Then, like a brilliant incarnation of living moonlight, a blazing-white swan shot skyward with a great rush of his powerful wings.

Tears of gratitude blurred the priestess' view of Sallik's flight. "Oh, my Goddess," she breathed, "forgive me for doubting You." Far above her, Sallik wheeled like a falcon and folded his wings tight to his sleek body, executing a spectacular power dive before pulling up at the last possible instant to shoot effortlessly into the night sky. The wind of his passage dried his teacher's tears and made her laugh out loud.

The *avir* leaped to her feet. Two long steps carried her over the cliff and she threw her wings wide to catch the sky. Elated, she joined her student in thanking their Goddess with a dazzling display of aerial joy.

Yvarlin and Sallik stood in the courtyard of the main Temple complex, where a group of white-haired, black-eyed men and women waited patiently to escort their clanmember home.

Sallik's decision to return to his clan had surprised Yvarlin. The Yris Rune in his palm entitled him by Divine Providence to remain at the Temple as a full Initiate. His clan could not dispute the physical evidence of the Windlady's favor. He could continue his education and become a teacher himself, if he wished.

When Yvarlin had asked his reasons, he had explained that during his Test, the Breath of Yris had caught him in mid-fall, unwinding the ritual ropes with spectral fingers of Air. This was the normal order of the Trial, but Sallik had found himself shifted to his *nimir* form without having caused the change himself. He believed in his heart that Yris had reminded him of his true self and the destiny he had been born to fulfill.

Sallik had not only accepted his destiny, but he had resolved to shape it for the benefit of himself and those like him. He would be the wind of change to his people, teaching kindness and compassion and freedom of will so no *nimir—tayec* or otherwise—would ever again be forced into a life he or she did not want.

The priestess in Yvarlin had wanted to argue, claiming that the Goddess Rune indicated that Yris wanted Sallik for Her own. In the end, she had held her peace out of respect for his courageous decision. She was tremendously proud of him.

The two turned to face each other, no longer student and teacher, but priest and priestess. Yvarlin took his hands in hers and said, "I'll miss you terribly, but I know you'll be well." She turned his left palm up and traced the white Eye newly tattooed there. "You will always have somewhere to go, if you have need."

Sallik smiled gratefully despite the threat of tears in his eyes. He abandoned decorum and flung his arms around Yvarlin's neck.

The *avir* affectionately wrapped arms and wings around him and whispered, "Be strong and true, my Silent Breeze. Yris hold you always."

A flock of magnificent swans took wing, filling the courtyard with the wild wind of their passage. Yvarlin followed their flight until they vanished in the sky. Head high, heart light, she turned and walked smiling into the Temple, where a Tribunal of senior priests waited to discipline her and issue her penance.

MOONLIGHT ON WATER

Carol E. Leever

Carol Leever currently works as a high school English teacher in California. I'd rather teach sixth grade; at that age they're housebroken, but they still want to learn. In college some of them get a little of the conceit knocked out of them. And by the time they're thirty they're positively human by contrast. She also owns up to being an avid reader, martial artist, and amateur—very amateur—musician. She sold her first story to *MZB's Fantasy Magazine,* and is delighted to have made her way into an anthology. She likes to pretend she understands both science and philosophy, but suspects that her three cats ate the secrets of the universe for breakfast one morning and have been snickering at her ever since. (So *that's* what happened to my Rice Krispies.)

When I first read this story my initial comment was—scribbled on the cover sheet—"too nailed down in time and space." But then I reread it and reconsidered—something I very rarely do. Make that "almost never." Few things annoy me more than having somebody return a rejected story, begging me to reconsider. (Believe it or not, some sophomoric types still do it. A word to the wise: DON'T!)

The goddess Ameratsu's golden light shone out across the heavens as the rising sun heralded a new day. The warm light brightened the woodland clearing where Neko danced slowly and gracefully through her martial arts kata beneath the colorful falling of early autumn leaves. Around her sprawled her teachers—twenty-nine golden temple cats. They lounged in the autumn foliage, some rolling in the colored leaves; others stretched amid the flowered branches of a pink crepe myrtle tree. Their slanted green eyes watched Neko's every move, the twitch of their tails displaying their pleasure or displeasure with each strike or kick in the kata. But despite their intent feline stares, it was the absent cat—the thirtieth—that most distracted Neko. The thirtieth cat had gone to summon two of her other teachers, two other members of the sacred kami, gods of the woodlands.

Who would it be, Neko wondered as she turned swiftly to deliver a high spinning kick to an imaginary opponent. One of the white cranes who taught her moves of grace and delicate beauty? One of the mischievous foxes who taught her the devilish craftiness of all the kitsune?

She dropped into a low stance as she struck a series of blindingly swift blows to the side, her bare feet sinking deep into the moss-covered earth. Each member of the kami had their individual lessons to teach, but lately they had begun speaking in tandem, offering her strange cryptic words that she was supposed to translate into some infinite knowledge. She wondered sometimes if the samurai of the noble houses learned in such a fashion, or if this was a torture reserved by the kami solely for her.

She heard them approaching before her kata ended, heard the soft tinkling music of crystals and the whisper of silk. She caught their scent in the wind—the mingling of spices and cherry blossoms—and she smiled. To her, the kami always smelled of springtime, even in the dread dark of winter.

Mindful that her teachers could not abide distraction of any type during a kata, Neko continued her dance. She finished out the martial arts form, her hands moving with flowing grace delivering deadly punches even as her body spun and twisted through the long, silent pattern. And when at last the form ended, she bowed respectfully to her teachers, her long dark braid falling across one of her silk-clad shoulders.

She looked up then, her own cat-green eyes flashing eagerly at her teachers for some sign of approval. Her kata had not been precisely perfect—she'd slipped slightly on the second movement, had stretched too far on the twelfth. But she believed she was improving, never mind the fact that the cats kept telling her that she was still thinking far too much. If she didn't think about each individual movement, how was she supposed to perfect them?

The sprawling temple cats blinked at her as the three newcomers stepped out of the shadows and into the sun-lit clearing. Red-and-gold autumn leaves fluttered in the air around the tall humanoid shapes clad in shimmering white kimonos. The three kami wore crystals around their necks, carried flutes instead of swords, and pos-sessed a glowing aura that mingled with dawn's radiance, but it was their animal faces that set them utterly apart from humans. Neko smiled at them—a cat, a dragon, and a fox.

It was the dragon who spoke at last, his long trailing whiskers twitching from his scaled snout as his multifac-eted eyes gleamed with a deep power. "Tsuzuki noko-koro," he intoned mysteriously. Then he turned, and with a rustle of white silk, disappeared back into the shadows of the woods.

Baffled, Neko stared after him, her eyes widening with bewilderment and irritation. "Mind like the moon re-flecting on the water?" she demanded of the fox and the cat still watching her. "That's it? That's my lesson? What's that supposed to mean?"

The fox giggled, his furry ears swiveling even as his long fluffy tail shifted the silk of his kimono. "Poor little Feline," he crooned, speaking the use-name the kami had given Neko. "Is it truly so terrible?"

Neko sighed, blushing under his amusement. "I don't understand, Kitsune-san," she complained. "Mind like the moon reflecting on the water? What moon? What water?"

"If you understood the lesson, then there would be no need to teach it," the fox laughed before he, too, turned and followed the dragon into the cool shadows of the forest.

"Wait . . ." Neko called in protest. The cat, however, folded her arms, blocking Neko's pursuit of the fox. "Your kata, little Feline," the cat commanded, green eyes gleaming brightly. "Begin again."

Frowning in confusion, Neko bowed to the kami. She stepped back into the center of the woodland clearing, fully aware that thirty discerning cats now watched her every move. She began her kata again, but her mind was distracted, her head filled with so many questions she could not concentrate. Moon on water? What could it mean, what did they expect her to learn from so cryptic a sentence?

She put extra effort into her form, working out her frustration in each kick and punch, changing the kata from something graceful and serene into a swift dance that better suited her mood. Maybe if she tried harder, kicked higher, spun faster? She was only halfway through the form when she heard all thirty of the cats huff in annoyance, fluffing their golden tails in irritation before they, too, vanished into the forest, leaving her alone in the clearing.

Neko broke her pattern and dropped resignedly down onto the blanket of golden leaves coating the forest floor.

"You think too much," a voice called from the woodlands, the voice of one of the cats filled with irritation and reproach.

"I'm trying!" she called back, wondering if she'd get any points for effort.

"Think on this, little Feline," the voice echoed softly, fading away as the cat left her alone in the woods. "When does a baby learn to walk? When she's trying, or when she ceases trying and just does it?"

Neko hit the ground with her fist, fighting the wave of frustration that swept through her. Now they were comparing her to a baby! She'd messed up the kata, letting her own emotion ruin the perfection of each graceful movement. Such carelessness always drove her teachers away, and sometimes Neko despaired of ever mastering their lessons. Three years ago when she'd left her father's home, cast out for a dishonor not her own, she'd been accepted into the ranks of the kami as a changeling child. She'd given up her dream of becoming a samurai and had become instead the kami's student, a masterless warrior who had yet to earn a sword from her demanding and mysterious teachers. In all that time, Neko had never regretted her decision to join the kami, but there were times when she wondered if the kami regretted claiming her. The very thought depressed her—without them she was nothing, she was . . . she was alone.

A sound, soft and far off, distracted her, catching her attention. She turned, lifting her chin and cocking her head slightly to catch the sound on the morning breeze. Shouts and cries of alarm floated through the woodlands. Someone was calling for help, and a quick glance around confirmed that the kami were quite gone. She was all that was left to answer the cry. Quickly, Neko pulled on her sandals and raced into the forest, heading north toward the voices.

Inhumanly sharp hearing led her toward the far-off cries, and she emerged from the dense woodlands to find herself poised on a hill overlooking a wide valley. Much of the valley was cleared for farming, and a great crop of rice grew along a winding river that flooded regularly and kept the ground fertile and moist. Protected along the rise of a hill was a small town, and beyond that Neko could see the great flared roofs of a warlord's castle.

A small army had emerged from the castle. Armored samurai on horseback, faces hidden behind hideous war masks, rode behind a group of foot soldiers. The samurai waited at the entrance to the town while the foot soldiers tromped through the streets kicking in doors and dragging peasants out into the sunlight. Other peasants who'd been tending the fields, rooting out weeds with their bare feet, now stood timidly along the stone streets, watching in horror as the soldiers destroyed their homes.

Neko had seen such scenes before. The samurai wanted something from the town: food, treasure, women, servants—it didn't matter what. They took whatever they wanted and left the peasants to repair the damage they left in their wake. In theory the samurai protected the people of Ameratsu's land, the master of this castle named guardian of this particular village. But in truth they were more like giants in a playground, tromping around and destroying everything with their own wars of honor.

Neko sprinted down the green hillside. She spied a group of foot soldiers dragging an old man from his home. They pushed him to his knees before the samurai, and beat him cruelly with bamboo staffs. He raised his thin arms protectively over his head and cried out for mercy, but the blows did not cease. A few more blows and Neko feared they'd crack open his frail skull. Already his arms were battered and bloodied, and she could hear the wrenching sobs of his family watching nearby.

"Leave him be!" Neko cried, and she dove into the fray. Three well-placed kicks laid out the old man's main tormentors. Even as the last one fell, Neko snatched his bamboo staff out of his hands. She stood over the beaten body of the peasant and swung the staff forcefully at the remaining foot soldiers. Four more soldiers dropped from Neko's resounding cracks to their heads. Others moved in to stop her.

Quick as a cat, Neko danced past all of them, her blows and kicks landing so swiftly that the men fell in a tangled heap in her wake. But one loud bark of command from the samurai warlord ended the battle. The rest of the foot soldiers backed away, leaving Neko standing in the center of her fallen, unconscious foes.

Staff still in hand, she moved to the old man's side, catching hold of one of his arms and dragging him to his feet. She motioned with her head toward his weeping family. They rushed swiftly to her side and carried their old father away, leaving Neko alone before the angry warlord and his samurai.

Neko turned to face the warlord, staring defiantly up into his masked face. His long braided hair was streaked with gray, and the demonic mask he wore was painted with jeweled colors befitting royalty. His samurai, forty in all, sat frozen and silent on their horses, each man perfectly schooled in his discipline. Their hands rested upon the hilts of their katanas, the swords a mark of their rank and honor.

Neko's hand tightened on the bamboo staff as she gazed balefully at the warriors before her. A group of common foot soldiers she could handle, but forty armed samurai were another matter entirely. She could escape to the rooftops as swiftly as any cat if her life was pressed, but she'd stepped into this confrontation to save the peasants. If she saved her own life only to lose theirs, her interference would have served no purpose at all— save perhaps to rouse the warlord's anger.

She had one chance, and she took it. She picked a samurai out of the forty at random and pointed her finger at him defiantly. It was challenge enough. Honor demanded that he face her. The warlord nodded, and the samurai dismounted from his horse and strode forward. Around them all grew silent.

The two of them bowed to one another. "Tsuzuki no-kokoro," Neko informed him with a wry grin.

Through the eye slits in his mask, Neko saw the samurai narrow his gaze in confusion. She smiled grimly—let him worry about the cryptic lesson of the kami. Perhaps it would distract him enough to give her the advantage.

He drew his sword, the bright blade of the katana gleaming in the morning sunlight, and Neko knew immediately that the man would be no match for her. A master swordsman would never waste such a movement of his sword—the very act of unsheathing should have been the killing blow, the graceful motion of drawing a weapon the only strike needed in a fight.

With a loud battle cry the samurai rushed forward, his
blade blazing like the sun as it flashed down toward
Neko's head. Unblinking, Neko stepped aside, spinning
the bamboo staff and sweeping the samurai's feet out
from underneath him. As he fell, Neko caught his hand,
wrenching the sword from his grip. He struck the road,
and Neko lowered her own blade to his throat. The samurai froze momentarily, then quickly removed his mask
so that he could gaze defiantly into the face of the warrior who now held his life.

Neko slowly removed the blade from his throat and
stepped away. The samurai hesitated a moment as he
realized that she was not going to kill him. His only
move then was to sit up, resting upon his knees, head
bowed as he waited for events to unfold. Neko, heart
pounding from the confrontation, turned toward the
warlord, schooling her features to remain calm and un-
emotional despite the nervous energy sizzling through
her body.

"Green-eyed girl," the warlord remarked, his gruff
voice echoing with displeasure at the way events had
transpired. "Are you perhaps Neko-Butou-san, the
changeling child called Cat-Dancing by the kami?"

Surprised that the warlord had heard of her, Neko
could only nod her head. "I am Neko-Butou."

Behind the war mask, the warlord's eyes gleamed
brightly. "I am Kokou, Daimyo of this land. I came to
this town seeking the master swordmaker Hibashira, but
you will serve my purpose far better."

Neko frowned. "I'm not yours to seek."

Her words caused a stir among the foot soldiers, and
they milled about uncertainly, waiting for their master's
orders. If the samurai were surprised by Neko's defiance,
they did not show it, remaining unmoving and stoic.

For a long moment Kokou said nothing, and Neko
could feel him staring hard at her, looking perhaps for
some sign of weakness. She schooled her features to remain as uncaring as a cat's—had she a tail, she would

flick it in nonchalant boredom the way her teachers so
often did.

Finally the warlord came to a decision. With swift gestures, he removed his war mask, revealing stern and
deeply lined features. "This evening my enemy Daimyo
Hokorashii dines with me in my castle. There our best
samurai will compete at kata in a contest to prove who
has the superior fighting style. We need an unbiased
master to judge the contest. I came here to find Hibashira to judge the contest—but you, a student of the kami,
would serve far better in that capacity."

"Why should I care which of your samurai has the
better style?" Neko demanded.

He smiled grimly at that. "Because if you agree to
judge, I will spare this village. These peasants claim that
Hibashira is no longer here. I do not believe them. If
you do not stand in Hibashira's stead, I will tear apart
this village in my search for a judge."

Neko stiffened, her gaze moving swiftly toward the
frightened villagers. They watched her hopefully, their
dark eyes pleading for her aid as they trembled beneath
the unmerciful stares of the stoic samurai. It seemed she
had two choices—fight or judge. As the kami would tell
her, it would be foolish of her to fight when there was
no need.

She brushed a few strands of dark hair back from her
forehead as she glanced longingly toward the quiet forest
she'd left. Were her teachers watching her now from the
safety of the trees? Would it concern them that this warlord had tricked her into service, however brief it might
be? She could see no alternative. "I will judge your
contest."

Kokou bowed curtly, and then pointed a finger at the
defeated samurai still kneeling on the ground. "You
must deal with him first, Neko-Butou-san."

Neko bit her lip pensively and glanced at the samurai—he had been defeated. If he or any of the other
samurai judged him also dishonored, he'd have no
choice but to take his own life. At the moment she held

his life in her hands—how she chose to give it back to him was entirely up to her.

She took a step toward him and thrust the tip of his sword into the ground before the kneeling man. He gazed impassively up at her. "There is no dishonor in being defeated by a superior foe," she informed him, trying to strive for the same tone of voice her kami teachers used on her. With one sentence she gave him back his life—but she couldn't help adding a final warning to both him and the warlord. "The dishonor would have been in attacking these unarmed peasants. I have spared you that."

She could feel the hard glares of the samurai, but no one spoke against her. The defeated samurai bowed his head deeply to Neko and stood. He took back his katana and immediately set it against the stones of a small retaining wall. With one mighty blow, he snapped the shining blade in two. The blade had been unsheathed without drawing blood, and had been taken from his hands by an opponent—in his eyes it was now useless. Neko sighed regretfully, but she supposed it was better the cost of a blade than the cost of a life.

Evening found Neko in the warlord's castle, seated upon a silken mat in an enormous open courtyard. No single room in the castle could contain all the visitors, so they'd moved outdoors beneath the light of the full moon. Against the coolness of autumn's breezes large fire pits had been set alight in the courtyard, and the flickering lights of the colored flames danced shadows across the walls. Hokorashii and his samurai arrived and greeted Kokou with stoic respect despite the heightened tension in the air.

At Kokou's bidding, they were all seated around the courtyard on the silken mats provided while artfully painted women in brightly colored silk kimonos served an evening banquet. The samurai all knelt at attention, hands on their katana hilts—the aggressive posture a sign of respect toward their fellow warriors. Only the

war masks had been set aside in concession to the evening's peaceful gathering. As guests in Kokou's house,
no one would fight unless unduly pressed or offended.

It had been a long time since Neko had been present
at such a gathering of samurai. Not since her father's
great banquets had she been forced to sit and listen to
talk of great battles and wars fought over insults and
possessions—ideas that now seemed foreign to her after
spending so much time with the peaceful kami.

Bored, she let her mind wander, her gaze drifting
about the courtyard. It was a beautiful night, the air
scented with the sharp aroma of spices burning on the
fires. High overhead the moon glowed brightly, reminding her of the kami's lesson that morning. Moon
reflecting on water—it still made no sense to her.

"Neko-Butou-san?" Hokorashii interrupted her
thoughts. "Kokou-san tells me that you are a student of
the kami." There was a question in his voice, even
though he did not fully vocalize it. To do so might infer
he thought Kokou was lying, and such an insult would
not be borne.

"I am," she nodded.

Hokorashii's eyes narrowed deeply as if he were trying
to perceive something worthy in her to warrant such an
honor. "It must be a great experience," he pressed.

"It is a humbling experience, Hokorashii-san," Neko
corrected with a smile.

The samurai laughed at that, and even the women of
the court hid their faces behind their hands and giggled
at her answer.

"And will you judge our contest fairly, Neko-Butou-
san?" Hokorashii continued. "Will you watch everyone
in this courtyard and tell us who has the most perfect
form without bias for allegiance?"

Neko nodded her head. "I will judge. As a ronin warrior, I have no allegiance save to the kami."

Her reply satisfied Hokorashii, and he nodded to
Kokou. Kokou waved his hand, signaling the start of the
contest. Servants rolled out huge drums, and as their

pounding music echoed through the courtyard, the fires were built higher. Neko watched in some fascination as the evening meal was cleared away quickly and efficiently. Servants ran about preparing the center courtyard for the samurai who would perform their katas.

A group of very young, richly dressed boys brought out a large silk mat and began unrolling it, covering the center flagstones with the bright material. Kokou's sons, Neko guessed, judging by their rich jewels. She frowned in sorrow when she saw one of the boys roughly shove an ancient servant woman out of his way as he prepared the center court. Apparently Kokou had taught his sons his same disregard for peasants.

The old woman, bent and gray-haired, had been sweeping ash from around the large fire pits. Young men tended the flames, but the old woman was responsible for keeping the hearths clear of any ash that might escape on the wind. She fell when the boy shoved her, but once the boy moved on, the old woman righted herself and continued with her sweeping as if nothing had happened. Her brush strokes were slow and precise, and the plain grayness of her hair and clothing let her blend into the background largely unnoticed.

Once the courtyard was prepared, a dozen samurai rose to stand opposite Neko. All had been dressed in white robes at the request of Hokorashii—white with no sign of rank or house on their person so that Neko could not tell who served whom. The first one came forward, standing proudly on the mat. He bowed to Neko, Hokorashii, and Kokou, and then to the pounding music of the drums he began his kata.

His movements were straight and strong, his lines perfect and clean. He moved with a violent swiftness, his war cries deafening as he fought imaginary foes. Neko watched closely, seeing a myriad of things in his movements—strength, stamina, speed, and, above all, pride. He crashed through the form with a violent flurry that left all watching breathless, and when at last he came to a swift stop, his eyes were blazing eagerly as the approval of his fellow samurai washed over him and increased his pride tenfold.

He stepped aside then, and the second contestant stepped forward. In contrast, his kata was circular, a swirling dance of graceful movements delivered with violent accuracy. He stretched and twisted, his strikes reaching both high and low as he kicked and spun. He was like a dancing cobra, ever moving, never resting. Neko could see from his features that he was caught up in the form, reveling in his own speed and finesse. When he finished, he added a flourish to his bow, and the corners of his mouth twisted with pleasure.

When the third man began his form, Neko guessed at last the nature of the argument between the two houses. One school taught linear movement, the other circular. As the contest continued, Neko began watching the others in the room as well, trying to guess which Daimyo favored which style. Faint signs gave them away, the twitch of the mouth, a gleam in their eyes, the prideful set of their features. A quiet communication was taking place between the warlords and the contestants. Each man sought not only Neko's favor, but the approval of their master as well—and Neko could tell by the set in their stance at the end of each kata if they had won their master's favor or displeasure with their kata.

It reminded her distinctly of her own kata practice that morning. She, too, had sought the approval of her masters, the kami. Even during the pure concentration of her form, she had been focused on the temple cats studying her from the sidelines, watching intently for the twitch of a tail or the fanning of whiskers. It had been a mistake, she guessed now—a mistake she had compounded later when she'd faltered in her kata through confusion over the dragon's cryptic words. She'd let outside influences fill her mind with too many thoughts. Kata, her teachers had once told her, was the perfect union of body and mind—movement without thought; thought without conflict.

She could see the same thing happening here, despite

the intensity of the skilled forms being danced before them all. All the samurai were distracted by the subtle byplay of their masters, thinking too keenly about the outcome of the contest—win or lose, pleasure or displeasure.

A movement caught her eye, distracting her from the current samurai displaying the wonders of circular motion before her, and she realized then that there was one person after all who did not care about the politics burning brightly in the courtyard. The old ash sweeper was still hard at work, focused solely on the simple act of cleaning the hearths. She swept away, undisturbed by the noise of the drums, the yells of the contestants, or the tension of the two opposing houses.

Her actions were completely natural, done without thinking. She swept with the same ease as—realization struck Neko—the old ash woman swept with the same ease as the moon reflected off water. Disturbances, obstacles—to the old woman they were like nothing more than ripples in the surface of a pond—something that would pass in time and leave the reflection as clear as ever. She did not care what others thought of her actions, did not care that one sweeping motion was not as straight or as long as another. Her actions were as natural as breathing, and in so being not one ounce of ash escaped her broom. It was a pureness of focus Neko knew she lacked herself.

You think too much. Her teachers' words filled her mind, and Neko slowly smiled. Would the moon, she wondered, be able to maintain such a perfect reflection in a lake or a pond if either it or the water had the ability to think? Doubtful, she decided, and all joy at gazing at such a sight would be lost.

The contest came to an end, the pounding drums finally stilling in their beat. The twelve samurai presented themselves, all bowing before their masters and judge. They knelt then on the mat, awaiting Neko's decision.

Kokou and Hokorashii turned toward Neko. "You

have seen our best samurai," Kokou declared. "You will tell us now who in this courtyard has the superior kata."

Neko bit her lip, the answer that sprung immediately to mind one she knew would displease many in this room—possibly to the point of bloodshed. But she'd given her word, and she had no choice but to speak the truth.

"I will tell you," she agreed. "But before I do, I wish to ask a favor as a guest in your house, Kokou-San."

Kokou's gaze darkened, but to refuse a guest's request would be bad form. "You may ask."

"I wish to take the winner of this contest with me," she explained.

Her words caused a stir among all the warriors, and she heard the murmured speculation—the winner would get to train with the kami. It was a privilege beyond any previously offered to these samurai.

"You would take one of my samurai from me?" Kokou demanded.

"Or one of mine," Hokorashii protested. "She has not yet declared the winner—you do not know if it will be one of your samurai!"

"Nevertheless," Kokou interrupted. "The loyalty of any samurai is to his master—they have a duty to serve even if offered such a chance at study as you have suggested."

"I have no intention of taking any samurai's loyalty from either of you," Neko assured them both. "I simply wish to take the winner from this house tonight—the winner is free to return at any time, whenever duty demands it."

Her words brought more speculation—a chance to meet the kami this very night. A chance to go into the spirit-haunted woods and come face-to-face with the woodland gods themselves. It did not violate any oath of loyalty, and there wasn't a samurai present who could resist such a chance.

Kokou and Hokorashii finally agreed, nodding their consent for Neko's odd request. "Now name the winner,"

Hokorashii demanded. "We would have this matter settled once and for all. Whose form is superior—which fighting style wins, linear or circular?"

Neko rose from the mat to face them all. "You have asked me to tell you who in this courtyard has the most perfect form . . ." she began only to be cut off by Kokou.

"Not fair!" he cried in protest, discovering the flaw at last in his request. Anger blazed in his eyes. "You will name yourself and leave us still undecided!"

Outraged, Hokorashii began to protest, but Neko raised her hand to silence the outcry. "No," she said quickly, shaking her head. "I will not name myself. That would be a lie. As I learned today from my teachers, I still have far to go with my kata." She glanced at the expectant faces. "Consider this—if you thought about every single movement that went into the simple act of walking, would you still be able to walk? Kata should be no different—it is the perfect union of mind and body. For any form to be perfect, your mind must be clear and uncluttered. Your body must be able to act and react with instinct. Ultimately, it should be the most simple thing in the world. There is only one person in this courtyard who has mastered that."

She stepped toward the ash woman and placed one hand on the old servant's shoulder. "You are the winner of the contest, Old Grandmother. Your form is perfect."

The old woman smiled even as the samurai all leaped to their feet in protest. "This cannot be!" Hokorashii cried in fury. "You mock us!"

"No," Neko assured him. "All of you are so concerned over which is better—circular or linear motion, that you forget the simple fact that movement is movement. Your samurai are so concerned with their power and position in your courts that their katas are filled with conflict. There should be no conflict in kata."

"You will choose another," Kokou demanded.

"I have chosen," Neko replied with a shake of her head. She took hold of the old woman's arm and led her toward the double gates of the castle. "You have promised I could take the winner from the castle this night. You will keep your promise."

Kokou's eyes blazed with anger as Neko made her way through the crowd of warriors in her path, but he did not make any move to stop her. To do so would be dishonorable.

"You are wrong," he told her before she could depart the courtyard. "Life is conflict!"

Neko laughed, imagining what her lounging feline friends would say to that. More likely than not they'd giggle and tell her that people take themselves far too seriously.

"Yes," Neko agreed. "Life is conflict. But kata is not life. It's just a dance."

"We must know which movement is superior!" Hokorashii insisted.

"Somehow, I don't think the movement really cares," Neko shrugged, and she left the castle, slipping out into the moonlit shadows with the old ash sweeper beside her.

They made their way slowly to the village, and as they climbed the hill to the town's boundaries, they saw Hokorashii and his samurai riding out of Kokou's castle. They rode swiftly, thundering back toward Hokorashii's home while war fires were lit upon the castle walls. The sound of the deep war drums echoing across the land roused the village, and at Neko's urging, the peasants all gathered a few meager belongings and began a trek into the hills and the dark woods beyond.

At dawn Hokorashii returned, armed for battle, war masks hiding the faces of his samurai. Kokou and his men rode out to meet their enemy, and as the villagers looked on in silence, the two forces met on the battlefield to decide for themselves which fighting style was superior. Flags waved in the autumn breeze, battle cries echoed through the valley, swords blazed in Ameratsu's light. The two forces met with a bloody clash, metal against metal, as they fought with a fearless viciousness unique to the samurai.

The war was swift and deadly, and when it was over, the few remaining men stood on the blood-soaked field and shouted their victory to the gods. One man, coated in blood, battle mask cut and scarred, made his way from the field and climbed the hill where he saw Neko and the peasants watching.

As he approached, he removed the mask from his face. Through the sweat, blood, and grime of battle, Neko recognized Hokorashii's features. He sneered at Neko, blood still dripping from his katana.

"I have proven my style is superior," he declared proudly.

Sadly, Neko shook her head. "You are scarred and injured. You must return home with most of your men dead. And with Kokou gone, the Emperor must find a new Daimyo to govern this territory. It seems to me that it is these peasants who have won. They alone have not suffered for the sake of movement."

Hokorashii's face hardened, and he raised his sword. "That can be remedied."

With one swift spin, Neko kicked the sword from Hokorashii's hands. As the blade fell, the Daimyo screamed in outrage. A second spin, and Neko swept his legs out from under him, dropping him to the ground. She retrieved the bloody sword, and bracing it against a protruding boulder, broke the blade herself.

"Not today," she informed Hokorashii with a feline snarl. "That single act just dishonored you and your men. Go home! We have no use for you here."

Pale and defeated, he climbed swiftly to his feet and made his way back down to his men. They gathered their dead and quit the field, returning home.

"What will you do now?" Neko asked the villagers, worried that there might still be danger for these simple people.

One old man just shrugged and smiled. "We will tend the dead, and then return to our fields. It is nearly harvest, you know. These wars are always so disrupting . . . but life goes on."

Neko laughed and nodded. "It does, indeed." She joined them as they walked back to the village, and on the way she spied the old ash woman she'd rescued from Kokou's home. Neko touched her arm, stopping her. "Old Grandmother, who are you?"

The old woman bowed to her. "I am called Hibashira."

"Hibashira-San?" Neko asked in amazement. "The master swordmaker Kokou spoke of?"

The old woman nodded. "On Kokou's last raid he stole me from my home to work in his castle—he did not even bother to ask what skills I had."

"So he set you to sweeping ash!"

At that the woman just shrugged. "It was no great hardship. When I was a little girl, learning swordmaking from father, my job was to sweep the ash from the forge. Now that I am too old to pump the bellows or hammer the metal, I sweep the ash again while my younger apprentices do the hard work."

They reached the village, and the old woman led Neko to her forge. The fires were cold, but young men entered and began tending the coals. Neko watched for a long while, noticing then the cats that had crept from the woods and were now slinking into the various nooks and crannies of the forge. They climbed onto shelves, leaped into unused cooking pots, and sprawled on the window ledges. Golden cats—thirty in all—making themselves as at home in the forge as they had once been in the temple Neko had grown up in.

The forge workers spied the cats, and all whispered in amazement, noting the similarities between the green-eyed cats and the young girl who watched them from the doorway. Neko smiled, gazing curiously at her kami teachers and wondering if the idea stirring within her would please the cats.

"Hibashira-san," she said formally to the old woman, bowing respectfully. "I wish to learn from you."

The old woman's eyes widened in amazement, and she

glanced uncertainly at the thirty cats who had invaded her domain. "You wish to learn how to make swords?"

Neko laughed and shook her head, thinking again of all the things she had yet to learn about kata. "No, Hibashira-san, I wish to learn how to sweep ash."

Throughout the forge, thirty golden cats blinked their green eyes in approval. Their soft purr filled the forge with earthen music.

NINE SPRINGS

by Kathleen M. Massie-Ferch

Kathleen was born and raised in Wisconsin and worked her way through college, earning degrees in astronomy, physics, and geology-geophysics. I'd say that disproves once and for all (not that it needed disproving as far as I'm concerned) that old slander that women aren't good at hard science. One of my housemates is a paleontologist as well as a physiotherapist; also being quite an exceptional musician, she wrote some very funny songs about a paleontologist's life, from the paleontologically oriented "Digga Bigga Bone" to "The Everlasting Outcrop in the Sky" where presumably all good geologists go when they've finished their last Earthly rock hunt and found that last perfect geode.

Kathleen specializes in sedimentary rocks as well as computer applications. (Personally I think sedimentary rock are very dull. I prefer crystals, especially calcite, but then I'm a romantic.) She also teaches creative writing—which I think is great—I never got into a good class of creative writing, but I've been told that despite my prejudices and experience, it *can* be taught, so good luck to you, Kathleen. She lives on land called Stone Gardens, with a wonderful husband, two Scottie dogs, several telescopes, numerous rocks, and more books than she cares to count. Me, too; right now one of the young women who works here is cataloging and reshelving all of my books.

Kathleen has sold to various magazines and anthologies other than mine: *New Amazons, Warrior Princesses*, and *New Altars*. She has also coedited two anthologies for DAW: *Ancient Enchantresses* and *Warrior Enchantresses*— so she also knows that contributors come in all flavors.

Lyra watched as the old nun carefully washed Rheta's face and body before changing the dressing on each wound. Rheta was asleep again before the woman was even two steps away. Lyra followed, her own wounds slowing her and causing more than a little pain.

"Where is her medicine?" Lyra asked. "Rheta must have it to fight the demons poisoning her blood."

The sister motioned her farther from Rheta's pallet, and still she spoke softly. "We have little medicine and many wounded. Our supplies run low."

"They aren't low yet," Lyra said.

"Your friend is beyond any potion's skill to heal."

"You lie!"

"No, you know I speak the truth, and so does Rheta. While you slept last night, she made her choice to refuse the drug. She understands and accepts the Goddess' will."

"But I do not!"

"Rheta is beyond our help. We will make her as comfortable as we can, but—"

"There has to be something I can do. She cannot die. Your own prophetess said I would save her life." Lyra looked from the nun to her friend and back again. "Tell me what I must do."

"There is nothing—"

"No, there is something. I see it in your eyes!" Lyra grabbed the woman's arm. "Tell me!"

The nun pulled her arm free and rubbed it before she slowly walked to a nearby altar. She was silent as she stared at the Goddess' many images painted on the wall. Finally she spoke. "If you believed in the Goddess, there might be something, but you don't believe."

"Don't question my beliefs. You don't know me."

The older woman shrugged. "You are a warrior."

"Yes, we are at war. Only the nuns refuse to take up weapons to protect our land. I sought to protect our people, villages filled with children and the old."

The nun nodded. "My sister told me how you saved her life and that of her grandbabies. I know of several villages which speak your name and Rheta's in great honor. For this I thank you, and I have prayed for your friend, but death comes to us all."

"I know, but must it be so soon?" Lyra couldn't keep the tears from her voice, though her eyes did not betray her.

"Your love is as great as your passion for what is right and fair. That passion saved my sister. Perhaps prayer isn't enough." She took a deep breath. "The Goddess has nine sacred springs where one may receive her healing powers. Only by drinking of these waters will Rheta be healed."

"I don't need a child's myths for comfort. I need—"

"They are not myth, but real, though they are difficult to reach. You are a soldier. If anyone can reach them, you will."

"How far is the nearest?" Lyra asked.

"A day's ride by swift horse."

"Rheta can't travel so far. What if I bring the waters to her?"

"That would heal her, too. But there is little hope in your venture, for you must cross those same enemy lines that almost took your life. You suffer, too, from your wounds. Such a journey might kill you."

"Tell me where I must go."

Lyra followed the old woman through the crowded temple to where scenes of their land were painted on the wall. "The map is old; the landmarks might have changed over time," the nun said before she returned to her duties. Lyra memorized the wall before she went back to Rheta's pallet. The sick woman woke at Lyra's light touch.

"Dearest sister, I have to leave for a short time."

"No, stay," Rheta begged.

"I'll be back soon. Wait for me! You must wait."

Rheta quickly fell back to sleep. Lyra found her sword and knife among her own pallet's bedding. She strapped both on and threw Lyra's dark brown cloak over her shoulders. The color would give her more protection

than her own red cloak of command. The old nun waited
not far away and stopped Lyra.

"Rheta may not live long. I would counsel you to stay
an share her last moments so that they may carry you
both until you meet in the next life. You need the peace
this time together would give you."

"I'll be back soon, you'll see, and then there will be
no leaving by either of us."

The woman handed her a filled waterskin. "Then go
in the Goddess' care, for I think you need her healing
powers as much as Rheta, perhaps more."

In the days since staggering into the Temple, Lyra had
not stepped outside. Now she saw that the Temple's
outer courtyard was crowded with improvised shelters
and wounded. Only a few narrow paths meandered
through the sea of dying.

"All this in three days," she muttered to herself. Now
she understood why the nun worried over supplies. She
took a deep breath, too deep. She pressed a bandaged
hand to her left side. It was a serious wound, but she
lived, and she would mend. The way would be slow, but
once she got to the spring and drank its waters, she
would travel like the wind on her return. Lyra found her
way to the stables, but instead of finding hers or Rheta's
horse, she found more wounded. Lyra stopped an
attendant.

"My horse was here three days ago. Where is it now?"

"King Stefan's men took all horses and weapons away
yesterday, after his victory."

Lyra touched her own sword hanging from her belt.

"Well, most of the swords," the woman amended.
"Someone will suffer for that oversight." She pointed to
Lyra's sword. "Our new king doesn't like to be
disobeyed."

"He's not my king," Lyra said through clenched teeth.

"He thinks he is. You must ask him for your horse,
if you dare. His guards are beyond these walls. Have
care of where you travel and what name you claim as

your own. Pick a name they will not know." She went back to her patients.

Lyra left the stable and made her way through the temple compound. She hid in plain sight among the wounded and waited until the guards were farthest away before she slipped into the surrounding forest. From the cover of the trees, she could see guards patrolling the outer compound in the distance. They wore colors she was well familiar with. She had killed many of their number, but not enough. She wondered how the enemy's strength had changed now that the war was done. It was late afternoon, and clouds darkened the forest even more. The coming night would be a good time to steal a horse.

Lyra made her way along the forest's edge, using the cover of brush to hide from the patrols. Always she worked her way north, for over a mile. But for the trees she'd be able to see the slopes of Mount Titos where the goddess' nearest spring lay.

She rested a few minutes. A day's journey? She was already tired, and she had yet to begin it. Then she heard the sounds she needed: drunken laughter, cheering, and the snorts of horses. The two young guards seemed to show less than their usual alertness near the horse corral. They, too, had drunk to their victory and their lives. Lyra snuck through the trees to the back of the corral. Even in her injured state, she easily removed several rungs from the fence. She pulled out some long grass. Horses milled around her seeking the sweet grass, hiding her from the guards. A number of the beasts still wore saddles. Their owners would be back soon, before full dark, Lyra guessed. She found one horse to her liking: a stallion with rich ornaments on the tack and saddle. Stealing a lord's horse suited her mood, but more than that, the horse had likely not seen too much battle and would be a strong runner. He looked fresh, and she had need of his speed even if she would be traveling forested, highland paths. She walked the horse away from his pen for several minutes, and then she silently and painfully, climbed into the saddle. Lyra held on. With every step, pain flared along her side. She calmed her mind and ignored the pain as best she could. They walked even farther until she knew the trees would swallow the sounds of their passing. As the sun painted the treetops in brilliant colors, she urged the stallion faster, as fast as she dared, along the forest path until it was too dark to safely run.

After two hours, the forest thinned, and the path grew steadily steeper. They were traveling the flanks of Mount Titos. By morning she'd have the spring water and be on her way back. Returning would not be nearly as easy as escaping. She knew they'd be looking for the thief by then. They might even be following her already. She'd have to stay alert for the sounds of pursuit, though she felt faint and wondered if her fever had returned. Ahead, she could see where the road crested a hill. She hurried to the hilltop and looked back, but saw no one traveling the dark road. She wished for a moon, but that would also give her away. The bright starlight through the treetops would be enough. All night Lyra traveled the winding path through the forests and grasslands flanking Mount Titos. As dawn approached, she knew she had reached the main split in the path. She took neither the right nor the left, but instead headed northwest. The horse complained about the tall, spiny grass and prickly brush. She forced him forward. At a small stream they both drank. The water cooled her fevered face. She wanted to rest, but dared not. If she fell asleep, she'd never make it back in time.

Past the stream, the slope increased. Lyra led the horse up the pine-needled and leaf-covered mountain sides and through the trees which seemed to go on forever. The thicker the forest became, the closer Lyra knew she had to be. Soon the horse would be useless. Night passed slowly into morning, so unlike the sudden dawns of her youth on the great plains. By the time full morning arrived, Lyra could barely see under the dense canopy. She tied up her horse and pushed on through the wall of leafy and spiny brambles. Suddenly she was in a clearing. The sun shone on her and the surrounding grass. A stream bubbled from the mountain side and fell over rocks and into a wide pool before it continued down the mountain. In the hillside near the waterfall was a small shrinelike building of wood timbers and stone. Many varieties of flowers grew along the water's edge and before the shrine.

"Well, this looks like a holy place," Lyra muttered to herself. "Pretty and utterly useless to almost everyone who needs it." She wondered if any water was acceptable, or did she have to take it from the source. She quietly walked toward the spring, her hand on her knife. She felt foolish, but she'd not give up after so hard of a night's ride. Birds continued to sing in the trees as if she weren't there.

Lyra knelt beside the spring and cupped her hands in the cold water. She drank deeply and splashed the coolness over her face. She wasn't certain what she expected to feel, but there should be something. Instead, one moment she hurt and the next she did not. She thirsted for more and drank again. Her head felt light.

"If you drink too much, you will become drunk."

Lyra started and reached for her knife, but the woman across the stream from her carried no visible weapons. She wore only the thin robes of the Goddess' order, the same as the healer nuns caring for Rheta.

Lyra reached for her waterskin, emptied it completely and began to fill it with springwater. "Are you the keeper here?" Lyra asked the stranger.

"Yes, for the moment. Taking the water with you will not help you any further."

"What do you mean?" Panic began rising in Lyra's chest.

"The water will only heal you once. You may not save it for another day's hurts."

"Oh, it's not for me, but my friend. She is gravely wounded." Lyra stood and turned toward her horse.

"You take the Goddess' favor and offer no thanks in return? Your gratitude is most warming."

"I give her thanks in my own way," Lyra said. "My need is great, and I am short of time."

"You may not go," the woman said.

"You would stop me? Are you perhaps better with the sword than I?" Lyra chuckled. "I think not. I don't wish to insult you, but I don't have time for this. I will come back in a few days and—"

"You may not go!" The woman's voice bore through Lyra's body as if she were made of mist and not flesh. She found her feet would not move. Ice gripped her heart in dread.

"If you had taken the time to ask, rather than just steal the waters, I would have warned you, but you chose your path and now you must live with your actions."

"I don't understand."

"Of course not." The woman's shoulders sagged and suddenly she looked older than she had a few minutes before. "I didn't understand either, when I came here." Her voice was softer, older, and far less harsh. "But not understanding does not release you from your destiny."

"Destiny?"

"You are the ninth soul to drink the Waters during my watch. Now my watch is over, and yours will begin with the next day. I have but one day to teach you what you must learn to survive in this forest. There is much to learn, so listen well."

Lyra shook her head no. "I have no intention of staying another moment. Release me!"

"I was so much like you when I first came. Then for years I denied the healing waters to people because they were not worthy of the waters or my position as caretaker, as I would have denied you. But you are a thief, and now you must pay for your actions. It serves your temperament that you are forced to remain in this holy place. I was honored, but perhaps it was also my punishment, just as it seems to be yours."

"You don't understand. I can't stay. I have to leave now. I swear I will return in two days, but I must go now."

"And you don't understand that you can't go. Come here," the woman commanded.

Lyra found herself walking toward the stream, then through the water to stand beside the strange woman.

"What draws your heart from this place?" She asked.

"My dearest friend is dying. Only this water will save her. I must leave now."

"You cannot. I'd release you if I could, but it is the Goddess' will."

"I should have known the prophetess lied," Lyra said.

"Explain," the woman asked.

"A prophetess from your order said I would save Rheta's life, and we would enjoy a quiet life as we raised our children. I long for a rest from this cursed war."

"Perhaps Rheta is not as ill as you believe? Would it ease your worries to see?"

Lyra felt hope for the first time in many days. "How? What is the cost?"

The woman laughed. "You learn quickly. But there is no cost in this simple magic. It is a gift to the caretaker from the Goddess so we may not miss our friends and family too much during our time here. Come." The woman moved toward a quiet pool away from the waterfall. She knelt. Lyra found she could follow.

"I am Cealla," the woman said. "What are you called?"

"Lyra."

Cealla placed her hands before her and over the water. "Still the currents of life. Show us Lyra's dearest treasure and heart's desire."

"My treasure?" Lyra asked, suppressing her smile. "Her name is Rheta."

Cealla shrugged. "The waters give you what you ask for, but I had to learn how to ask for what I truly wanted to see."

They waited as the waters grew murky and then a picture began to form. Lyra leaned forward, but did not touch the water. The picture was now clear. She could see a cottage. An unknown woman lay in bed. She was

clearly in pain as she screamed, though there was no
sound. Still, Lyra had witnessed this event all too often.

"Who is this?" Lyra asked Cealla.

"I do not know. I assumed it was Rheta."

"Rheta is a soldier. I left her in the care of healing
nuns. Her wounds were worse than mine. It was my
fault, since her actions saved my life. She is the bravest
soul I know." Lyra pointed to the image. "This woman
will not likely survive the birth of her child. It will be
great luck if her child lives." They watched as a girl was
born to the woman. The midwife held the child for
mother to see, but the mother was already beyond caring. Lyra took in a ragged breath. "Why have you shown
me this?"

Cealla opened her mouth as if to speak. Instead she
looked at the birthing scene again. "Show us the soul of
Rheta," she commanded the waters. The image on the
water did not change. Cealla reached out and placed her
hand on Lyra's arm. "I am sorry."

"What does this mean?" Lyra asked.

"That even if you could leave here, your journey is
finished."

"No!"

"Rheta is no longer in need of the waters. You left
her just yesterday?"

Lyra nodded silently as she stared at the image on
the water.

"The Goddess does not often return souls so quickly
to us. Rheta must have truly been a blessed soul. You
said she was brave."

"The bravest," Lyra said softly.

"This newborn child will have to be brave to grow in
a world without her mother and most likely without father, too, or he would be there holding his daughter
now. I suspect your war took many fathers and mothers
from their children.

"The prophetess lied?" Lyra's voice held bitterness.

"Perhaps it was not this past life of Rheta's of which
the prophetess spoke, but another life—the life Rheta

now holds. You have it in your power to save nine lives. How long it takes you to choose those lives is your choice, almost your only choice."

Lyra stood up and walked away a few steps and then turned back. "What happens to you tomorrow?"

"I die," Cealla said softly.

"Why?"

"I have been here for a very long time, too long to have any life left out there beyond the trees."

"If I take only a year to find another caretaker, will I be able to go on with my past life?"

"Yes, you will leave here only a year older than when you came. You wish to go to Rheta and raise her?"

"Yes, she will not know me or remember our life together, but she needs me more than ever now."

"The love you shared is strong, I think she will know you in any life and in any shape. But do not hope for a quick end to your stewardship. Few people come here now. This place is a shrine out of myths. Not many remember it." Cealla waved her hand over the waters, and the image vanished. "Sit here and I will tell you of this place, so you will understand your task ahead."

For several minutes Lyra just stared at Cealla, and then she finally sat nearby. Lyra listened to Cealla's words as the morning turned into the day and then into the night. As dawn approached, Cealla lay on the grass. Lyra held her hand and watched as the lost years quickly took control over the older woman. When dawn had nearly arrived, Lyra left for a minute. When she returned, she embraced Cealla and supported her shoulders.

"Please don't go again," Cealla began. "I have not been the best of caretakers, but I fear dying alone. Stay with me until the end."

"I'll stay." Lyra looked around. "It will be dawn very soon."

"I can feel it coming."

"And I feel a power entering me. Oh, I feel so odd. Is it . . . ?"

"It is the Goddess entering you and filling you with her power. She is gone from me now. I already miss her."

"How wondrous! I understand now why you didn't want to abandon this." Lyra took in a deep breath, then she held her waterskin to Cealla's lips and forced the fluid down her throat despite the woman trying to push it away. Lyra watched as years faded from Cealla's features, though she remained an old woman. After a few minutes, Cealla gained enough strength to sit up on her own.

"Why did you do that?" she asked. "You knew I had already drunk of the waters once. And why did it work? I should not have been healed again!"

"But that was on another caretaker's watch, not on mine. I asked the Goddess to heal. You are my first soul to have tasted the waters. Eight souls left."

"Why? I was content to die. It was my time."

"Perhaps, but I need your help. I can't stay here for one hundred years. I want my life back, such as it was. I want to see Rheta again."

"What if the Goddess wants otherwise?"

"Then you'd be dead now. I left my horse tied up just beyond the trees. Take him away from here, but since I stole him, I suggest you trade him for a mule rather quickly, or you'll likely hang for my theft. Visit the towns ravished by war, and send the sick here and to the other springs. Keeping the waters a secret does no one any good."

"I'm not certain. My shouting their existence will bring some that will not be worthy of healing."

"So if the Goddess wants them dead, she will take them no matter how much water they drink."

Cealla laughed. "She has the power. I'm not certain she'll think that is fair. I never asked her. I will send pilgrims your way. Not all at once, and not everyone I meet, but some."

"Still deciding who lives and who dies, Cealla? What gives you the right to make that judgment?"

"I was not alone during my years here. Living with the Goddess for over one hundred years taught me something. The Goddess spent many hours talking to me." Lyra opened her mouth and started to ask something, but Cealla held up her hands. "No, I'll not say any more. You'll meet her soon enough, and then you'll know what I mean. I was chosen to come here by her and I think she must have chosen you as well. Perhaps I bored her? You'll not bore her, I think." Cealla embraced Lyra briefly and then she walked away from the springs without looking back.

Lyra wondered how long it would be before she saw Cealla again, or any other person for that matter. She rested her hand on the hilt of her sword. She contemplated removing it, but decided against it. Her sword was part of who she was and who she would always be. She'd not remove it even for a conversation with a goddess.

MISTWEAVER
by Terry McGarry

Terry McGarry's work has appeared in magazines and anthologies—from *Amazing Stories* to *The Confidential Casebook of Sherlock Holmes* and *Blood Muse.* Her poetry collection *Imprinting* was published by a small press with which I'm not familiar—but I could tell she was a poet by reading "Mistweaver." As a motivational tool for getting stories written she started a weekly "story dare" in the on-line community SFF Net—well, whatever works.

Personally, I can't make head or tail of the Internet; I guess I'm intimidated by it. Maybe I'm the wrong generation. (Funny how aware of that I've been since my last birthday.)

She works in New York City and recently acquired a house with a backyard that hopefully will make a nice garden some day. Well, good luck; in every house in the five boroughs I lived in, the backyard was full of broken glass, nonarable musty soil, and the like! So I prefer California. But lots of luck!

The mistweaver had served the court long and well. She had conjured armies of wraiths to frighten off attackers, she had wrapped foes in mist to confuse and dishearten them, she had even summoned fogs to deter rude court visitors from staying on another day. But she had wearied of her work at last; outlived all those she cared for. She retired to the deepwood, where dew dripped from ferns, where the smell of mulch was a richness in the nostrils, where sunlight diffused into a vapor, where greenshadow was a soothing balm and there was no stink of middens, only the fecund natural decay of moldering leaves. The most complex intrigue was a snarl of roots below an ancient oak.

These woods were no shortcut from one place to any other. No one came here. No one logged these trees; many had stood for as long as there had been trees. This was first-growth forest from the time of the world's beginnings. An old, old place, fit only for the old. The willows wept, the aspens laughed, the oaks endured.

Her skin was brown as bark tea, steeped in tannins. She slept on a bed of bracken, with fog for her blanket. Cold did not affect her. There were no fires in the wood; lightning strikes smoldered but did not ignite. The dead-fall was too sodden to catch flame.

For days or months or years she existed thus, until her world-battered heart was healed, her spirit whole again.

One night a wind came up, sudden and aggressive. Dappled moonlight was flung in sprays of quicksilver from jostled trees; then the clouds came, sensed rather than seen, sky-mist thick as wool. The storm battered the ancient wood, sweeping to the floor dead branches and dry husks of trees.

Lightning flashed, illuminating the deepwood, casting a second wood in stark relief, a wood within the wood: a forest of shadow branches, barely glimpsed between heartbeats.

It was to that wood the mistweaver would go.

Lightning strikes, she knew, cleared room for new trees to grow, fed by the old as they crumbled year by year into mulch.

She found the oldest, strongest oak she knew, a massive growth in the center of the forest. She stood in the whipping, howling, rainless wind and waited.

Lightning rent the great oak—once, and then, impossibly, again.

The mistweaver cried out, inarticulate, yearning. Thin bones aching, threadlike sinews straining, she pulled herself into the smoking V of the split trunk and stood in heartwood fresh-opened to the air.

The third strike took her squarely, as if the blazing,

jagged river of light originated in her and streaked up
into the sky. For an eyeblink, the forest of shadows was
blinded by a glare more intense by a hundredfold than
any sunlight filtered through its canopy. Then darkness
closed in, a hand fisting around a retaken possession.
Where the mistweaver had stood, in the crotch of the
smoldering tree, lay a pale, human form.

The infant rested placidly in the sticky heartwood.
When it thirsted, it gathered damp from the air with a
curl of its pudgy fingers, catching a fine spray in its open
mouth. When it hungered, it sucked oozing sap—regard-
ing, perhaps, the ovals within ovals of the grain, like
patterns on the tips of great fingers pinched to keep it
safe. When it could crawl, it left the tree and sank into
soft bog, steeping in tannins, fed by the nutrients of de-
composition, turning brown as a nut.

When she could toddle, she foraged for berries, stain-
ing her lips and hands purple and dark red; sometimes
she craved bitter herbs. She twined the evening mists
around her fingers like a string toy, learning how to ma-
nipulate them. She conjured legions of playmates, and
cavorted with diaphanous specters in the gloaming. Her
hair came in pale, grew to her waist, was dyed a lucent
silver by the moon as she slept; her eyes never lost the
color of smoke.

The moon intrigued her. She could never see the
whole of it, strain though she might to make it out
through the dense weave of leaf and branch above her.
How big was it? Was it round, or oval, or crescent?
Her mistwraiths eddied about her, dimly suffused with
moonlight, but they could not appease her now. They
drifted slowly off through the trees. When she followed—her steps, in spongy moss and damp bracken, as
silent as the wraiths—she found herself at the deepwood's edge.

She had not known it had an edge. She had not known
the moon was so small, centered in a profusion of stars.

The creations of her chill heart beckoned her forward—into moon-bright meadow, a terror and exhilara-

tion of open space, then through a thin barrier of firs
and onto a road of molten silver.

Where did it lead? Some half-memory surfaced briefly,
along with snatches of sound—words spoken in tongues
she did not yet know.

She set off down the moonroad, puzzled, pulse quick.
Her wraiths dissipated into the clear night air. She would
summon them again should she need them. For now, the
sensation of openness was a novelty to be reveled in.

The road was long, and silent in the night, and ended
with the night's ending: at the gates of a towering, dark
structure, frozen shadows spun into walls and arches,
turrets and galleries, charcoal against the moonset but
paling to opalescence as the blush of morning caught up
with her.

The drowsy gatekeeper, stirring, seemed to recognize
her. He admitted her through a complexity of wrought
iron as if she were coming home.

"I knew your mother, though she had no name—only
mistweaver, as we have called you."

The prince was slim and supple as a sapling, his hair
the yellow of oxalis root. His nose was crooked, his
mouth was thin; his eyes were kind. When he smiled, it
was like coming upon an expanse of meadow in sunlight.

"What is my purpose here?"

"I don't know. To weave mists, I suppose. As the
others have done before you."

So she wove mists. She conjured an army to frighten
off the prince's foes; she hid the palace in a fog, that
attackers could not find it; she entertained children at
court with cat's cradles of dreams and vapor. She loved
the prince but did not make love to him; that was for
the woman he took to wife, who bore him golden children. But often she sat with him on his high balcony,
pale as the moon beside his sunlit glow; and when he
was crowned king, it was she who placed the circlet of
gold upon his head.

"Are there others like me?" she asked him, surveying the teeming life below the balcony.

"In far Linroeven, they say, the mistweavers ebb and flow like tides, created by the mating of moonbeam and wave froth. In Golsk, rainweavers are common as droplets. Indrilan boasts stoneweavers who make mountains dance; such as they move slowly, and come but once in an age. The flameweavers of Yorr wage war with fire legions who cannot be defeated, but they are fickle and brief, quick lives that gutter when there is no war to stoke them. When Ktharon's waterweavers leave, others come on their heels, a river of weavers that flows through the years like a current. Windweavers are rarely seen, except by sailors, who claim they sleep on beds of cloud, and will hang you by a noose of air if they feel you've insulted them—which they always know, for the winds carry all words to them in time."

"I would like to see these marvels," said the mistweaver.

"You cannot," the king replied. "It is not done."

She did not believe him. She summoned her wraiths and set out for the borderlands, the sere no-lands that separated one realm from another, one world from another. But the wraiths lagged behind her, reluctant; it took all her will to keep them from flying apart on the hot border wind. With each farm she passed, each hill she surmounted, she grew weaker. Then there were no more farms, there was no more life, only an endless dusty plain; so she turned and set her eyes on the opal tower, her mind's eye on the deepwood somewhere beyond it.

"It is the order of things," the king said, kind eyes sad. "A mistweaver could cause a sailing ship great harm; a flameweaver's fire soldiers would be quenched by a waterweaver; a lightweaver could weave arrows of sunlight to disperse a mistwraith army. Each could do equal harm to the others. So the weavers keep to their own quarters, aiding men as they will, but never encroaching on each other. Among yourselves, you would destroy the world, and what would you have then?"

The king aged, fell, was supplanted by his golden sons, and they by their golden sons in turn. Each time a prince came of age, she asked him, "What is my purpose here?"

"To weave mists," he would say, "as you did for my father before me."

To weave mists. It was enough—to spend a lifetime engaged in gratifying work, then to return to the deep-wood, sink back into the soft loam, steep again in the waters of childhood.

It came to her that she was old, and weary of the palace air, the strain of pulling moisture from it and molding it into useful forms. For the second and last time she walked the long road to the meadow, dusty rose now in the setting sun—a bent, brown crone, skin striated as bark, hair a moonfall over hunched back, eyes a gray-smoke swirl. She sighed into the balm of greenshadow; and at last a night came when the moon was swallowed by clouds, and a great, rainless storm racked the ancient forest. She stood in the crotch of an oak twice lightning-blasted, and opened her heart to the third strike.

In the crumbled ruins of other trunks, green shoots strove for the sun. Courts came and went; one day, soon now, the palace would have its mistweaver again.

The willows wept. The deepwood endured.

WAKING THE STONE MAIDEN
by Cynthia McQuillin

The title of Cynthia's story reminds me of the very first fantasy story I can ever remember reading. I was only about seven years old, and it scared the heck out of me; it's a wonder I didn't swear off fantasy forever. It was Prosper Merimee's "The Venus of Life," and I still get the creeps remembering the little kid I was then. It wasn't till three years later that I encountered "The King In Yellow" and was imprinted by it. But—if it needs saying, which it shouldn't, Cindy's story isn't scary at all—which anyone knowing her would expect. Although I gather she is turned on by vampires, a taste I don't share, to put it mildly.

When I first encountered Cindy McQuillin at a convention many years ago, I was moved to ask in wonder, "Is there anything this gifted young woman can't do? I'm still astonished by her many talents. She paints; sings professionally; and, in addition to being one of the very few people I allow to see my manuscripts, has written a handful of very fine stories and is now trying to find a market for her first novel—hey, all you book editors out there, here's an opportunity!

With a groan of frustration Arrek rolled stiffly out of bed, sweat-slicked and aching with an overpowering compulsion to flee from the safety of all she knew, and seek her destiny in the unknown wasteland that the once-fertile plains of Itar had become. It had been nearly seven years since she had sworn herself to the Stone Maiden. So long, that now that her calling had finally come she could scarcely credit the truth of it.

But the dream had returned every night for a quarter-moon now, and with each dreaming the compulsion to seek out the shrine of the Maiden had grown stronger. The time to act had come at last, but she must proceed wisely—prepare herself for the long trek ahead. And Mama must be told.

With a sigh, she rose and poured a small amount of water into the basin on the table beside the bed. Unable to bear her own stench or the sticky feel of old sweat on her skin, she washed thoroughly, rinsing herself twice. It was a shameful waste of water, but it was wonderful to feel clean again, if only for a few hours. By the time she had dressed and plaited her long dark hair, Mama had a cold breakfast of meal cakes set out in the common room.

"You've had the dream again, haven't you?" Mama said.

The words were more an accusation than a question, spoken with a strength and clarity that belied the look of weary acceptance the harsh life of an Itari tribeswoman had etched into her mother's sun-darkened features.

Arrek nodded, trying not to let her own growing sense of excitement show in her expression. Seating herself, she took a bite of meal cake, chewing it with thoughtful determination while she decided what to say next. She washed it down with a mouthful of the tart beverage they brewed from dried sourgrass.

"The call of the Stone Maiden has grown too strong to deny," Arrek murmured, setting the half-emptied cup gently on the table. "I must seek her shrine or die."

"The Harvashti have forbidden it!" Mama hissed, lowering both her eyes and her voice as if she feared some unseen spy.

She ground the dust of the floor beneath her heel in the customary gesture of disgust when she named the fierce hillsmen who had subjugated their tribe. The followers of Harvash had stripped the plains of everything precious, forcing the once-proud people of Itar to eke out whatever miserable existence they could from their leavings.

"That for the Harvashti!" Arrek spat, grinding the precious moisture into the floor, true profanity in their drought-stricken land. "Are we not the people of Itar? If the Stone Maiden calls, then I have a duty to answer. When we served the Maiden, the rains came; the plains were green and rich with life. If we have the will, they can be again."

Arrek had a storyteller's turn of phrase, like her father's sister Yolko, who had been a spinner of tales and the last stoneweaver born to their tribe.

Stoneweaving was a magical gift peculiar to the Itari women, and always rare. In other times Arrek, whom Yolko had sworn had the talent, would have taken up the calling after her aunt—weaving charmed necklaces from bits of stone and cord, and keeping alive the history and lore of their people through stories and song.

But Yolko was long gone, tortured to death for refusing to abandon her devotion to the Stone Maiden. In the new order, all things Itari were forbidden. Now, there would be no more stoneweavers, just as there would be no more priestesses to rouse the spirit of the Stone Maiden who had for so long tended and protected their once fertile plains.

"Oh, indeed you are right, daughter. Things *were* different once." The scathing tone of her mother's words brought Arrek's thoughts back to the present. "But the past is dead as my husband's sister is dead, and as we will all be if you and your hotheaded friends can't learn to accept the world as it is. You were too young to remember what it was like when the Harvashti came. . . ."

A look of anguish darkened her mother's eyes as she suddenly clenched work-worn hands to her breast and averted her gaze.

"But I do remember, Mama, I do," Arrek fiercely whispered, laying her own fingers over her mother's to stop their twisting.

She had been six, nearly seven, when the warriors of Harvash swept down from the hills, overwhelming the peaceful Itari with their ferocity. The memory of their

brutality, the joy with which they drank in the suffering
and death of her people was etched forever in her memory. And what she didn't remember, she had heard from
Yolko often enough before her death, that it seemed
like memory.

"And I was no child when Yolko died."

"She died a fool's death!" her mother angrily retorted.
"All for nothing."

"Never say that!" Arrek hissed, shaking her.

"But the price she paid—"

"I know better than you what price she paid for defy-
ing Harvashti law. I was there, Mama."

"No!" Her mother's face turned pale. "You were only
eleven, and if you'd been caught, too . . ."

"When she heard the Harvashti war steeds approaching, Yolko saw that I was hidden safely away in
the secret cellar where she kept her charms and stones.
She was nearly dead by the time they left her, but she
still had breath enough to speak the Maiden's blessing.
I swore the oath of service as she painted the rune-
charm on my breast in her own blood!"

"Then it was she who laid the geas on you," Mama's
voice shook and her eyes widened. "She had no right!"

"She did," Arrek said, meeting the accusation with a
steady gaze, "for she was the last stoneweaver, and,
poorly schooled and inexperienced as I was then and
still am, there was no one else left with the talent. Did
you never wonder at how strange and distant I became
after that day, Mama? How I come and go when the
lamps are dark and everyone sleeps?"

"I hoped I was wrong." Her mother reached out a
hand as if to touch her. But the gesture fell short, and
the line of her mouth hardened once more. "So, now
we're all doomed by an old woman's fervor and the rash-
ness of youth. But tell me, if you're so knowledgeable,
where was the power of the Stone Maiden when we
needed her protection? Was she too weak to stand
against the Warrior God, or just uncaring lifeless stone,
after all, as the Harvashti claim?"

"The Maiden would have protected us if we hadn't turned from her in our weakness and fear. It was we who broke faith. We who paid willing tribute to Harvash, giving up our crops and our herds, our very lives, and we who stood by like stupid sheep while they defiled and murdered her priestesses and desecrated her shrine!"

"Acceptance was the only way!" Mama returned with equal heat, pulling free of Arrek's grasp. "The Regosi would not bow to Harvash and see what their pride bought them. We survive, at least. They are no more."

"We survive," Arrek bitterly agreed. "But we don't live. If we'd keep faith with the Maiden, *she* would have protected us."

"So the Regosi thought of their Spirit Guardians. Oh, what's the use," Mama broke off, throwing her hands up in a gesture of resignation. "You'll do what you've decided to do, whatever I say, and I'll weep over your grave too soon."

"Perhaps you're right," Arrek replied with a sad smile, squeezing her mother's hand. It was a gesture of apology left over from childhood. "But the dreams have taken root in my soul, and I must answer their calling or go mad."

"Then I suppose you must go," Mama replied. With a long-suffering sigh, she pick up the stoneware platter that held the meal cakes and, after putting away the leftovers, carefully set it into the bucket of water she would mete out to the plants in her meager garden at the end of the day.

"But I don't understand what you hope to accomplish," she said, wiping her hands on her skirt as she turned to face Arrek once more. "You've no real training, you admitted that yourself, and nothing but the bits and pieces of Yolko's stories to guide you."

"It will be enough," Arrek murmured. "It must be."

"What shall I say when you've gone? Luka and Ghari must be told something; they're expecting you to help with the sourgrass cutting tomorrow, and there must be

an answer for the governor's men. You know they'll
come as soon as word gets around that you're missing."

"Luka and Ghari will know where I've gone and why.
As for anyone else, tell them you've sent me to cousin
Touvi's family at the caravansary to seek a husband. I'm
certainly the right age for it." She laughed. Truthfully,
at eighteen she was overripe for the picking, as the old
women had been all too fond of telling her this last
season.

Mama's answering chuckle broke the tension, and
Arrek knew then she was forgiven.

When Arrek came to say good-bye that evening, she
asked for the traditional blessing and was surprised tó
receive not only her mother's well-wishing, but also the
small pot of honey they had hoarded since spring for its
curative powers. Once the *siba* hives had been plentiful
and their guardians less fierce. Now the slick, sweet jelly
was treasure indeed.

"A fit offering for the Maiden," Mama said, in reply
to her startled protest. "Let it be my gesture of faith
and atonement." That said, she sent Arrek on her way
with the ritual kiss of parting, first on the lips, then the
eyes and finally the forehead. Mama's cheeks were dry,
save for one small tear, but her sun-faded eyes spoke
her fear more eloquently than any words.

"Save your tears, dearest," Arrek whispered, smiling
bravely as she rose. "I'll return within a quarter-moon,
just see if I don't!"

Mama made a brief attempt to return her smile, then
turned her face away. It was bad luck to watch a loved
one go. Some habits died hard, even in such times as
these.

Arrek had chosen to travel by night, sparing herself
the heat of day, and allowing her to use the stars as a
compass. The Shrine of the Stone Maiden, which Yolko
had described as a single gigantic block of granite set in
the eastern section of the plains, lay three days' journey

to the east, more or less. She had only to keep the
Southern Crown to her left as she walked, and she
should be able to see it by the middle of the second
night.

The first leg of her journey passed uneventfully; she
made good progress, choosing a cluster of weathered
rocks for shelter when she could go no further. But
unused as she was to walking so far, she slept fitfully,
tossing uneasily on the hard ground. Her dreams were
filled with the sound of weeping, and it seemed that she
was walking still, this time through an endless sea of
waving grass.

Unable to rest despite her weariness, she moved re-
lentlessly onward. The sun grew brighter and brighter
until the grass began to wither beneath its unforgiving
heat. The tough sticky blades clung to her legs as if
trying to hold her back, but still she staggered on, driven
by the certainty that she must somehow reach the Shrine
or the sun would devour the world.

Suddenly the thigh-high blades became tongues of fire
which licked at her legs, reaching upward to sear her
loins with their whip-like caresses. . . .

Arrek woke with a start, moaning low in her parched
throat. The sun burned brightly overhead and to her
surprise she found that she had risen in her sleep and
was indeed walking. Sinking down in the dry, brittle
grass, she sat for a moment trying to make her eyes
adjust to the brightness of the late morning light. Somehow the dream had translated itself into the physical
world.

When she turned to survey the ground she had covered, Arrek saw that she had left the stones she had lain
beneath at dawn far behind. In fact, they were nearly
out of sight.

Too stiff and weary to rise, she crawled into a nearby
stand of scrub for what little shade their twisted
branches and ragged leaves could provide. But tired as
she was, her thoughts were too disturbed to allow her
to sleep. Sitting with her back to the trunk of the

stoutest tree, she tried to sort out the meaning of her dream.

The "sun devouring the world" must be Harvash, she reasoned, for the Warrior God carried a golden shield with the image of the sun embossed on its gleaming surface. But why had she been driven by such a sense of urgency? Harvash was certainly a threat, but an old one which moved slowly and inexorably over the land. And why should she be driven to walk in her sleep?

Turning that last puzzling bit over in her mind, she sipped a mouthful of water from the skin bag she carried tied to her belt; then she lay down once more, determined to get what rest she could. But only a moment or two had passed when she was jolted awake by the distant jangle of metal on metal and the steady thud of hooves drawing nearer: Harvashti war steeds in full battle harness!

The Governor's Patrol was out on one of the pointless exercises Petralli insisted they routinely undertake to keep their fighting trim. Under other circumstances Arrek would have been grateful, for when the Harvashti troops were out playing soldier they weren't harassing Itari citizens as they went about their business.

Crouching among the twisted trees, she murmured a prayer to the Maiden as she watched. Her dusty clothing should allow sufficient camouflage, but even at such a distance there was no sense taking chances. The patrol proceeded at a good pace, turning in the direction from which she had come. Her heart nearly stopped as they passed the stand of rocks where she had lain not long before.

When they had passed out of sight, she lay down once more determined to rest, though she doubted she would sleep. But her fears dissipated as quickly as they had flared, replaced by an inner calm that fed the growing sense of purpose and expectancy that had been blossoming within her since the dreams had first begun. Within a few moments she had dropped into a light, restful sleep.

*   *   *

By the middle of the second night, Arrek had begun to make out what appeared to be a low mound rising from the moon-drenched flatness of the plain. When dawn lightened the sky, it had grown large enough to be clearly seen. The great rectangular slab of granite was far larger than she had imagined, looming against the deepening rose and gold of the sky like a gigantic altar. An almost imperceptible sound like the overtones struck from metal sang to her from the stone, tantalizing her with its nearness, so that she kept on until the thickening heat of day finally drove her to seek shelter.

Pausing to wipe the sweat from her eyes, she spotted a tumble of stones that must have been a range house such as the herders used when these were still grasslands. Moving the debris from the only corner which still stood with a section of roof intact, she lay down in the pool of shadow it provided. But with her goal in sight she was too excited to sleep. She lay for a long time facing the shrine, the magical energy which infused the stone humming like current through her blood, and never knew when her eyes finally closed.

An hour or two past sunset Arrek woke to find herself once more on her feet and walking toward the shrine. The granite block loomed before her as she trudged mechanically onward. The bulk of it blotted out the sky. When hunger rumbled in her belly, she took a meal cake from her provision sack and ate. When her mouth grew painfully dry, she sipped water from her skin, but never paused.

Suddenly her ankle turned on something hidden in the tall dry brush and she staggered, falling to her knees. Her single-minded and unseeing advance had allowed her to stumble over a fallen door frame. She paused before going on to examine the charred and weathered wood of the lintel and the worked stones that were scattered nearby. There were half a dozen more such ruins, marking the site of the village that had served the

Shrine. Human bones were scattered among the fallen masonry and the scent of burning still lingered faintly even after all these years, with no rain to wash it from the parched soil.

So many lives wasted! She sighed, laying a child-sized skull gently back in its resting place.

When she lifted her gaze, the shrine stood directly before her. Its mass obscured the full moon which rose to flood the plain on the other side with light, outlining the granite slab with a silvery glow. The sight of it forced all thought of death and ruins from her mind. But upon reaching the foot of the Stone, Arrek could find no immediate way up. With a growing sense of dismay, she examined the base more carefully, certain that the stairway which led to the altar above must be there as Yolko had said it would.

What she found could hardly be considered a stairway, however. The Harvashti had done their best to obliterate the narrow steps that had been painstakingly carved into the rugged face, but what remained provided ample holds for fingers and toes. Scaling the narrow ledges as a child might go, Arrek clung to the rugged, sometimes crumbling surfaces as best she could. It seemed like hours passed as she felt her way along the shadowed face of the Stone, but at last the top was in sight. She heaved herself over the edge and lay gasping and unable to move for several minutes, muscles knotted from the strain of her long, hard climb.

When she caught her breath at last, Arrek rolled away from the edge and sat up. Turning toward the center of the shrine, she stopped, her eyes dazzled by the moon's brilliant face as it inched slowly from behind the rectangle of darker basaltic stone which served as an altar. A shrill sound like the chiming of bells seemed to resonate through the breathless night.

The altar stood about a hundred feet away, but through some trick of magic or moonlight, it seemed much nearer. Arrek found she could make out the figure of a woman's body: the Stone Maiden! Her vision con-

tinued to sharpen until she could see the gigantic statue
quite clearly.

The sculpted figure was pale and naked in the cool,
clear light; each muscle seemingly taut with anticipation.
The woman's head was thrown back as though she were
laughing and her hair fanned out to trail across the stone
beneath her.

Stunned by the magnificence of her vision, Arrek sat
staring, all to aware of the sudden ache in her heart. As
she continued to watch, the massive breasts began to
rise and fall as if filled with living breath. Stretching like
a *sabo* cat, the woman sat up, limbs now as supple and
tawny as a *sabo's*, where before they had been hard
and pale.

Overwhelmed by the distinct impression that she was
being studied in return, Arrek began to tremble. The
gigantic figure stepped from the altar and began walking
toward her with powerful rolling steps, and Arrek scrambled awkwardly to her feet. But as the woman drew
near, her body seemed to shrink, taking on more
human proportions.

"What seek you here?" the woman demanded, her
voice low and challenging.

"I seek the Stone Maiden," Arrek replied, finding her
courage in disappointment. What she had earlier seen
must have been a trick of the moonlight. This was no
goddess, only an ordinary woman after all.

In fact, as she looked more closely, Arrek realized that
the woman was very ordinary indeed. Blunt-featured and
stocky, she had no prettiness or grace, and was much
older than she had first appeared.

"Why do you seek the Maiden?" The stranger's expression gave away none of her thoughts.

Arrek knew she should answer, but found herself unable to speak for staring. The moon had cleared the edge
of the altar and rose high enough to flood the shrine with
its brightness. In that unforgiving light, ever imperfection
in the woman's face and form seemed to stand out as if
magnified, but Arrek found to her amazement that the

scars and lines only made her seem somehow beautiful and noble. The desire to touch the broad features, to tenderly caress the disfigured limbs grew nearly unbearable.

"I would make an offering," Arrek murmured, at last, reaching out her hands in supplication.

"Then come to the altar," the woman said, holding out her own rough, square-fingered hands. Hesitating for only a moment, Arrek took one, then allowed the woman to lead her to the stone slab.

Neither spoke as they sat together on the hard, time-pitted surface. The woman turned away as if she were weeping. Arrek longed to comfort her, but she could only sit staring at the woman's hair which flowed across her body as if stirred by a soft breeze though not a breath of wind was stirring.

That hair, which had appeared silvery in the moon glow, had taken on the color of dust and the woman's skin had darkened to Arrek's own hue. Was this an Itari woman from another village drawn by the same power as she to the Maiden's shrine? Perhaps she was a hermit or madwoman, living alone with the dead all these years—a sad and frightening thought. She seemed old enough to have survived the massacre. Perhaps there was a hidden chamber in the Stone where she had taken refuge.

What did it matter, though? They were both here now, drawn by the Maiden's calling. Succumbing to the spell of the moon-drenched night and the soft singing of the ancient stones, Arrek laid her hand gently on the other woman's arm.

"In this and all things will I serve my people and my land," Arrek murmured. "Only guide me, for I do not know the way."

As though her words were a signal, the woman turned to smile at her, kissing Arrek lightly on the cheek in the formal gesture of kin-greeting, then drew her down to lie on the altar beside her. Made to hold a statue half-again human size, there was more than enough space for the two of them to lie side by side.

The stone, surprisingly warm beneath Arrek's flesh, seemed alive, conforming itself to the contours of her body, and the essence of new spring growth seemed to rise from it. *Or is that heady perfume the scent of the stranger's body?* Arrek absently wondered as she was drawn into the woman's comforting embrace.

"All will be well now," the woman murmured stroking Arrek's head as she began humming a wordless tune so old and familiar it had no name.

Smiling into the woman's face as she recognized the tune, Arrek suddenly realized that though her face was indeed as plain as the stone upon which they lay, her eyes shone green as spring grass as they caught the glow of the moonlight. Awe flared in Arrek's soul and something deep within her responded to the hunger she sensed within those verdant flames.

The night shimmered as some heretofore unguessed-at gateway opened in Arrek's mind allowing her whole being to resonate to the energy which coursed through the stones of the shrine—welling up from the very plain itself. As if echoing that resonance, her senses came alive as they never had before.

Gazing in wonder through her new-found senses, Arrek saw that this woman, whom she had thought so plain before, was suddenly transformed. Reverently she caressed the weathered flesh, tracing the web of cuts and scars—some old, some new—that covered her body like a shroud of fine lace. A few were very new indeed, still oozing.

Stricken with sorrow and pity, Arrek sat up to kneel beside her. Slipping the carry sack from her shoulder, Arrek dug out her spare robe. She carefully tore a strip from the hem to moisten it with precious drops from her waterskin, and began bathing the woman's wounds. The skin was empty and her robe in tatters by the time she brought out the honey pot.

The honey had been meant as an offering, but what

harm if she used a little to soothe the deeper cuts? Dipping her fingers into the pot, she slathered the sweet gelatinous stuff into the worst of the open sores, working with the gentle competence of experience.

The woman gave a little cry like the calling of a wild bird when Arrek was finished, and clasped the startled young woman to her with surprising strength, breaking the enchantment.

"Daughter of Itar, know you what you have done this night?" she murmured, taking Arrek's face between her hands to stare into her eyes. "I have been nearly dead for lack of caring, and you have restored me. As you have given, so shall you receive. Speak your fears and pain to me now, so that I may ease your wounds as you have eased mine."

Arrek could scarcely believe her ears. Did this woman really believe herself to be the Stone Maiden? But the ceaseless song of the stone was building once more to its overwhelming crescendo. It broke like a wave across her senses, opening all the secret places in her soul.

Tears streamed down her cheeks as she allowed herself to be drawn once more against the soft comfort of the woman's body. With childlike simplicity she murmured every fear, hurt, and secret shame she had ever harbored; each failing and fault—imagined or real. And as she spoke, each one magically faded to insignificance or took on its rightful perspective, freeing her heart and making her soul once more whole. When all had been said, she lay spent in the woman's arms, at peace for the first time in her life.

The sun was hot on Arrek's back when she woke. Rivulets of sweat ran down her sides, where the tattered robe wasn't plastered to her torso. She moved slowly to spare her aching muscles and scraped skin, pushing herself up from the rugged surface upon which she lay, to discover that she was kneeling between the legs of an enormous stone statue. The Harvashti had indeed sought to destroy the Maiden; her once-smooth body was marred with ugly gouges and cracks, but she had otherwise withstood their desecration.

Arrek's guilty surprise quickly faded, to be replaced by an overwhelming sense of awe as she reverently caressed the weathered stone. Tears of joy suddenly welled in her eyes to spill down her cheeks and drip into the Maiden's breasts as she embraced the living statue. Their moisture mingled with the offerings she had made the night before, and the scent of *siba* honey filled her nostrils.

Why do you weep, Daughter of Itar? The voice that filled her mind, accompanied by what she now recognized as the singing of the stone, was as soft and sweet as spring rain.

"I weep for all we've lost and all I've found," Arrek replied.

What have you lost?

"Truth."

And what have you found?

"Truth," Arrek's said, with a dry laugh and a wry quirk of her brow.

The answer is the same. There was an echo of Arrek's own amusement tempered with compassion in the Maiden's thought-tone. *So why do you weep?*

"How can I go home, now that I have seen the truth?"

And what is the truth, Daughter of Itar?

"That we are the land as you are the land, all things are joined. But the land withers and dies for want of the people's nurturing, just as we must die without her care—without your care."

Weep no more. All who serve the land shall be one with me, and all who are with me shall thrive, for I am the spirit of Itar made manifest.

"What of the Harvashti?" A troubled expression creased Arrek's brow.

In the fullness of time such men are nothing. Their day in this land is nearly done. Spread the truth you have learned among the people and return with those who will follow you. With them you will build a new and better way, serving me all the days of your life, if this is your will.

"It is!" Arrek unhesitatingly replied.

Go then and tell all who will listen that I have awakened and await the return of my people with love and joy.

The climb down the face of the shrine had been easier in the light of day, though no less perilous, and as Arrek began the long journey home, she found that the longing which had driven her before had transmuted itself into a sense of purpose. She paused as the ghost of a shadow swept over the plain obscuring the sun. Gazing skyward, she saw the Maiden's eyes again as she had seen them the night before, green as new grass and soft with caring.

Arrek smiled at this, but her smile turned to joyous laughter as the first gentle rain of the new age of Itar began to fall.

CITY OF NO-SLEEP

by Vera Nazarian

Vera, who was one of the youngest writers I ever published, says she's excited by having made it into this year's anthology. I'm now getting more than twice as many stories as I can use, though years ago when I began these volumes, I really had to go out and beat the bushes for them. Now every year I have to reject stories I'd have greeted with what my younger son would have called "great squeechs of joy" when I first started. I can't even make room for my own stories anymore.

Well, neither Vera nor I are all that young these days (four presidents later, including some two-termers), and instead of being a young and inexperienced editor, I'm an old hand. Vera is now working for a printer company doing tech support, specializing in barcode technology, whatever the heck that may be. (On second thought, don't tell me, I don't want to know.)

This story is in her Compass Rose universe, and she got the idea for this story while driving home late at night from her ten-year Pomona College reunion. She got a speeding ticket, which upset her so much that she thought "some good has to come out of all this," and then a story idea popped into her head: "What is the true meaning of law?"

She dedicates this story to her friend Lauren Elaine Oliver, who helped her brainstorm it on Mount Baldy, and—to a lesser degree—to the cop who gave her the ticket. I guess that goes to show that "all things work together for good," as Saint Paul said.

Congratulations on constructive use of a traffic ticket—I'd even give you some of mine, if I could still drive.

If you ever get lost, somewhere West of the Compass Rose, look for a city called No-Sleep.

The city is young—as each new day is young. And it's filled to the brim with miracles.

But the King here is old and mad like a mangy goat. They say his mind is broken; a fractured mirror, filled with disjointed ever-changing images which are his dreams. They reshape the fabric of the city every night.

The old madman spends his waking hours attempting to put together the shards of the mirror in order, and then sleeps erratically, during which time, chaos returns to him. And the residents are known to keep themselves awake for as long as possible, so as to delay the inevitable changes, for they come only after sleep's oblivion.

You are welcome to visit this place if you like, to marvel at the wonders.

Only, whatever you do, don't fall asleep here. For the next time you wake, the city will have rearranged itself.

*   *   *

Ierulann stood above the woman. The woman lay prostrate at her feet, groveling, and her tears were watering Ierulann's boots.

"Please forgive me, Guard of Law, grant me mercy! I wouldn't have been driving my wagon so fast if I'd realized I was on the King's Road, for it wasn't here yesterday! And my employer will pay me a pittance for tardiness! I must deliver these goods or lose my job, and I have children to feed. I beg you not to judge me by the letter of the law! Mercy, just this once!"

"It's true, the King's Road was to be found two-and-a-half leagues to the South of here, last night. But so what? You should've known better than to be late in the first place," said Ierulann impassively, holding her tablet, and about to mark down the woman's name and today's place of residence. Guards would be dispatched there in a hurry to collect the fine, before the King dreamed and the city was rearranged overnight according to some new chaotic pattern that lived in his mind. A day later the woman's residence might no longer exist, and her meager possessions (that now belonged in full to the King) wouldn't be there to be collected and deposited in the treasury. No doubt, these worthless items will likely disappear from that very treasury again on the morrow—indeed, the woman herself might end up on the opposite side of the city, and her children who knows where else—but that was not the point. The law was to be upheld.

The woman continued weeping, her sobs turning into dry heaving shudders of desolation. She was one of thousands.

There were so many of them, thought Ierulann, each one often having gone without sleep for days now, in a hopeless attempt to curtail the changes. This one's reason was obvious. One of the starving multitudes, she was attempting to keep her family together, but was slipping up due to exhaustion and had committed the trespass of carelessness.

Everyone knew to drive slowly on the King's Road. It was his earliest—and possibly most irrational—decree, and one he expected to be followed unfailingly. Most people took smaller inconvenient side streets to avoid the King's Road wherever it may have popped up that day, and the patrolling Guards of Law such as herself. For no one wanted to crawl along at the speed of fifteen paces a minute. And no one wanted to pay the ridiculous fine of all of one's life possessions.

Poor sleep-deprived idiot, thought Ierulann, and she jotted down the woman's name.

Beyond that, Ierulann felt no mercy.

Zuaren crawled silently along the edge of the roof of the tallest structure in the city. Vines of verdant hue sprung and wound like snakes on both side of him. They had grown hundreds of feet, clinging to one another all the way from the ground, like messengers of the earth straining to convey something vital to the sky.

From way up high as he was, perched dangerously on the edge of the abyss, on top of the world, he could see the whole accursed city illuminated by sunset like a terrible broken jigsaw puzzle, with rich buildings of rose granite intermingled in patches among pale bleached limestone of the rabble poor. He could see chunks of roads and streets doubling upon themselves. He could see alleys ending in cliffs, and houses bursting from hillsides.

All of this would be different, he knew, the next time he closed his eyes in sleep, the next time the sun rose. All he had to do was stay awake long enough to accomplish the deed that he had come here to do.

Soon, he would rid this place of its malediction.

Having dispatched with the sad business of the King's Road, Ierulann made her way toward her own austere residence. She walked confidently along the twisting clumps of uprooted and disjointed buildings—their foundations were oddly protruding in places, and patches of varicolored stone hinted at recent displacements—and meandering streets that often turned into dead ends. She had an odd true sense of the nature of the structures around her, and was never really lost in the impossible maze of the city.

That was one of the reasons she had been chosen to be a Guard of Law. Guards preternaturally knew the physical pattern of things in all its fractured disarray. They alone could traverse the city daily and find any given destination with the ease of a hungry dog following the scent of roasted lamb.

Guards were also the elite warriors sworn to protect the very soul of this bizarre place. Ierulann's swordbelt held a fine long blade, and a Serpent Whip. She had no fear when walking these streets, for she was, possibly, the best.

The sun began its golden leavetaking ritual of the night.

And now, there was another scent in the air of early evening.

Death . . .

Ierulann absorbed it like a jackal. It plucked her senses, and suddenly a loud heartbeat was born in her temples.

Danger . . .

She stilled. And then, she turned about and rapidly began walking the way she came from, back to the center of the city. Alleys surfaced out of nowhere, and she took turns lightly, predicting their appearance seconds before openings came into view. She moved with her eyelids half closed and her lips parted to the inrushing air that preceded her.

Something terrifying was about to happen. . . .

And she was the only one who was close enough to stop it. She felt the pressing of many minds upon her, the entities of other guards calling into her mind, directing her to move, faster, faster. . . .

Even now the immediate future was unrolling before her, before them all, like a map of this renewing city.

She must reach the palace that stood higher than all other structures at the heart of this place, and which alone stayed in one place day after day. She must then gain entrance and come within, passing innumerable corridors of marble and walkways trimmed with gold and sandalwood. She must race the final steps to the arched doors of the old King's bedchamber, where even now he was being readied for sleep—an esoteric ritual in itself.

There, she must bare her sword and wait, hidden behind a drapery, or in the shadowed corner.

When the candles would be extinguished at last, their gentle aromas fading among the musk of precious wood and oils, the old one would sink into immediate slumber, releasing the nightly chaos of mirror-shard images inside.

And at that precise point, someone would come to kill him.

He dropped down softly in the crouch of a panther, and stayed still beneath a marble overhang of an ornate balcony. Where he was exactly in this place of nightmares, he wasn't sure.

Ahead, several arched windows, opening upon dark chambers. Behind him, an indigo, darkening sky.

And yet he needn't guess, for the scent of musk and myrrh was strong here, and all he had to do was follow it, in the absolute darkness.

Which he did.

Zuaren moved slowly and silently, having withdrawn a short slim dagger from somewhere on his body. Its blade was dull, hueless metal, and sharper than a razor. It would slice cleanly and effortlessly through decrepit flesh and bone. . . .

Moments later, he had passed through a corridor with extinguished torches on the walls, which terminated in a gaping maw of darkness. From beyond closed doors came the strong lingering aroma of incense.

Soon . . .

Zuaren stilled his heartbeat to the level of a dead man, and his breathing became almost nonexistent. Only assassins of the highest discipline could aspire to such living silence.

He placed his fingers on the cool metal and pulled the door handle toward him. Then he slipped within.

Inside, the curtains were drawn over the grand window, letting in minimal glimmers of the night.

Directly ahead, sprawled the royal bed. Like a turtle the size of a world it crouched in the sea of shadows, taking up the center of the room.

In the middle of the bed, drowning in silk and pillows, lay a tiny shriveled form.

It was the old King himself.

His breathing came shallow and faint, ragged upon occasion as he moved restlessly in the very middle of his fractured dream.

The feeling of illusory chaotic images of madness was so strong here, it was nearly overpowering. Zuaren felt them encroaching upon his own mind, clamoring with the great tumult. . . .

Soundlessly, he moved closer—so close that he could see the outlines of the shrunken skull of the old King,

and the sunken bones around His eyes—and began the
measured strike with his dagger.

From behind him he felt another mind, like his own.

Zuaren whirled around, beginning to leap into a de-
fensive crouch, but it was too late.

A thin coil of agony struck his cheek, slicing him as
cleanly as though he'd turned his own razor dagger on
himself.

And only an instant later, there came the hissing recoil
of the Serpent Whip.

"Do not move." came a woman's intense voice. "Drop
your weapon by relaxing the grip of your fingers only,
else you die now."

Zuaren was not a fool. He let go of the dagger so
softly that it came down upon the floor like feather. He
remained frozen, biding his time, recognizing this bitch
out of the shadows to be one of the occult Guards of
Law.

"Good," she continued, "Now take three steps slowly
toward me, away from the King."

In the darkness, he grinned. He knew she would not
sound an alarm, for that would take too much of her
concentration. She was clever enough to recognize that
any extra action on her part could cause the balance
between them to topple. . . .

"Move!"

"Why don't you just kill me?" he said then, beginning
to pace toward her while speaking for the first time, and
his voice was like song. "You know I will not give up
so easily, that I will be back to finish this job—"

"I know nothing," she interrupted. "And if you speak
another word without being prompted, I will strike you
down."

He laughed openly this time. "You will not. For that
would be unwarranted, and you are a Guard of Law.
Yes, I know your kind very well. . . ."

In answer, he felt lightning strike the other side of his
face, as her whip came cutting down out of nowhere.

Damn, but she moved fast! He had never seen one

with such a classic minimum of movement. Almost as good as himself. He stood pondering it while both of his cheeks now screamed with agony.

"You do not know me," she said, like ice.

And that was the moment he took to strike.

Zuaren drove forward like a maelstrom, and out of nowhere two short swordblades snapped open and extended from his hands like angry twins. He lunged forward with both simultaneously, and fully expected her body to crumple under the impossible onslaught. This move had worked with all other opponents, over a dozen times.

And yet—she was not there. It was as though she had predicted his move before it was even conceived in his mind.

He swung, regaining his balance instantly, and this time saw her lunging shadow. This time, his steel met hers with a clang, and they exchanged a blazing volley of hits and parries in the darkness, by preternatural sense alone, then disengaged.

To his wonder, they were perfectly matched.

"Why do you defend the mad one?" he hissed, stepping back, now trying to unbalance her with words. "Why not let me finish him off and rid you and this city of this excruciating curse of madness and mutability?"

"You are an idiot," she replied coldly, and then struck at him again. "You have no idea what you are about to do, and I promise you, I will not let you do it."

"Don't you want to be free?" he exclaimed, this time angry in earnest. The execution he had been sent to perpetrate was an issue of perfect justice in his mind. He had been hired to rid the city of madness, and that was what he would do.

"No one is free," she replied suddenly. "Not even you. Indeed, there is no such thing. And if you believe it, then you surround yourself by an illusion greater than this city."

"Why?" he mocked, lunging below her guard on the left. "Will you now tell me that we are all but pieces of

the same great mad pattern, akin to this city? That we
are all fated by the gods to bear another's madness?
That it is our destiny?"

"No," she said, eluding his attack like an eel. "I will
tell you only that there is more to this than you think."

At that moment, there came a moan from the bed,
while the old King turned on his side and continued to
sleep restlessly. Nothing would wake him now until the
dawn, not even the clamor of battle. The sensation of
whirling madness came closer than ever to touch the
edges of their minds.

Zuaren moved with impossible speed past the woman,
and was again at the old one's bedside.

She gasped softly, revealing for the first and only time
the true extent of her unease.

"What would happen if I wake him now, before I
extinguished his life?" said Zuaren, sensing her sudden
fear with his very mind, past the whirling sea of madness.

"Please don't! Harm him and you will regret it," she
whispered, suddenly moving in on him from another
side, and was almost between him and the old King.

Almost, but not quite.

The King moaned again, like a sad old banshee. His
form was skeletal in the semidarkness. And for a moment it seemed to Zuaren that he could see the very
dream surrounding him like a cloud, a vision of whirling
city images, streets sliding apart and coming together
like snakes, all striving to enter an almost coherent pattern, and above, a rose-gold sun. . . .

And in that moment, a stab of pity entered Zuaren's
heart.

But then the assassin slammed the feeling down inside
of him like a wall, the way he always did.

"No!" cried the woman, while at the same time down
he struck with his right blade.

Steel penetrated the ancient flesh, and passed deep
inside.

In the cruel dark, the old one made no sound, only a

single harshly expelled breath. Even in death, he never woke up.

What came next was chaos.

But foremost, Zuaren felt terrible blinding agony. . . .

"No!" cried Ierulann, as she felt the weight of minds come slamming down upon her, the storm of madness breaking free at last, no longer contained by the poor husk of the ancient King.

Around her, the darkness howled. The assassin bent forward, the blade still embedded in the dead one, as though suddenly stricken by a direct bond with his victim.

You must contain it! cried the familiar minds into her own consciousness, straining against passion, against abandon that was all around them now, ready to swallow up the world.

The outlines of the bedchamber began to grow transparent, to fade in and out of this plane. Curtains blew open on the great window, letting in weak moonlight and a screaming wind.

And suddenly, Ierulann saw ghosts of a million cities superimposed like crystals outside the window.

Transparent towers came into focus and were displaced by tall spires and walls of violet marble; obelisks sprung up into the marrow of heaven, only to collapse into sand; structures of pale sandstone and clay spilled and popped like mushrooms after a rain; ancient gilded domes stood up like bubbles of water, globules of dew from a distance.

The vision danced, and times were mixing, and madness was upon her. . . .

Guard of Law! cried the voices of her fellow minds from afar, *Contain the destruction! You must do it, for you are the only one close enough to touch it!*

And Ierulann knew that if she did not, then the city—indeed, the whole world—would collapse around her into a common dream of insanity.

And thus she allowed herself to look forward into the

future for just an instant longer, using the very clairvoyance of her being to piece together the fabric of things just behind and just ahead of her.

I am the moment. Nothing exists outside of the moment, and the past and the future line up to fall in tandem to precede and follow me.

I am the order and the law.

The madness howled around her tiny point of calm. For an instant, grotesque contorted faces out of hell threw themselves at her, and the walls around the room were gone, while the floor of what was once the palace sank and reformed below her feet.

The forms of the man who had killed and the ancient one who had died froze into stone of timelessness upon the royal bed of firmament which once contained pillows and silk coverlets, but now was the surface of an ocean.

Contain the chaos, now, or never!

Even the voices of the minds had grown muffled, and were coming from such a great distance now, receding in the maelstrom.

"How can I?" cried Ierulann desperately in her mind, "How can I hold it and not be overwhelmed, and not myself go mad?"

And suddenly she saw a second ahead, into the future, and she saw the assassin before her. She saw him from an odd, tripled perspective—present, past, and future. His body was strong, his mind vital, and he was young. . . .

And seeing him in temporal chorus thus, Ierulann reached out with her mind, and she drew a part of her being that was cold calm order, and she forced it to come and wrap around the whole city like a great net.

Inward she pulled the madness, forcing it into her and then directly out into *him*.

She moved near him, and took hold of his stilled hand.

His name danced into her mind immediately, with a shock of contact.

Zuaren.

She saw and knew him inside-out, past and present

and future. She knew what he had been, what he was now, and what he could be.

And then Ierulann released the river of chaos, letting it flow through her fingers into his ice-cold palm, into him. . . .

The one who had once been Zuaren shuddered, opening his intense eyes—pale as water—upon the world of moonlight and swirling homeless dreams, and in they rushed to populate him, their new strong vessel.

The night had grown still all around them. Transparent palace walls thickened and began to solidify, and once again shut out the outside. But this time there was something solid and definite about their shape, something very new. . . .

Permanence.

Having dropped both his swords, Zuaren stood looking out, past Ierulann, past the walls, and past this reality into the dreams that were now forever anchored within him. And yet, the insane spark was barely contained under his strong wilful surface.

"What has come to pass?" he said softly, "What am I?"

"You are the new King of this city," said Ierulann, watching his glassy eyes, "It is your lawful punishment. You who have come in ignorance and death, now carry the burden of the law which is impassive order and can alone contain chaos. Now, at long last, we can trust the oblivion of sleep."

"Guard of Law!"

Ierulann turned. She was walking slowly along the King's Road, having gone automatically to her morning patrol along a fractured carcass of a city that had somehow stilled, frozen in time—for her senses no longer felt a doubling, a shifting. . . .

The woman from the night before stood a few steps away dejectedly, holding onto a small sack of belongings.

"Here are all my earthly possessions!" she said, "I've come to deliver them myself, since no one had come for

them last night, and I want no more punishment. When
I woke up, everything was the same as before! Is it not
strange? My children are crying with hunger, but at least
they are at my side!''

Ierulann watched impassively the joy in her eyes.
"Keep your belongings," was all she said, "The new
King cares not how fast you drive on the road."

At which point the woman started to weep in joyful
hysteria, and once again ended up on the ground watering her boots. "Law is indeed merciful!" she repeated
between her sobs, "Blessed law!"

Ierulann said nothing, not wanting to spoil this one's
last illusion—since there would be none tonight. Law is
law, she wanted to say. It is neither harsh nor merciful,
merely new or old. But it is your position in relation to
it that makes it deadly or gentle.

I, too, am like the law, neither one nor the other.

Or, at least I had been once. . . .

And then Ierulann yawned deeply, watching the sun
of morning ride up over the stilled city. It was time for
her to sleep, and possibly, to dream.

For she also contained madness now, a tiny bit of it—
would harbor it forever under her still surface, secretly
helping to share the burden of the one who was now
King.

No law had required her to do that.

* * *

The city of No-Sleep is said to be old now, older than
the world itself, ever since it stopped reshaping itself
every night.

But the king is young here, and sane, and filled with
peaceful reason. They say he has no memories of his
past, but sleeps soundly every night, and never dreams
at all.

Miracles fill the city, for multitudes are now rebuilding
their lives, and the greatest miracle of all, contentment,
stands in a cloud above the rooftops.

If you visit, you will surely find something to your liking.

But you must promise to find one woman, once a Guard of Law, now storyteller. Supposedly, she still owns a sword and a Serpent Whip, and is the only one who can tell you your dreams.

DAUGHTER OF THE BEAR

by Diana L. Paxson

Around the time of my second marriage, my two brothers, Paul Edwin Zimmer and Jon DeCles, followed me into the profession of writing—which I'd been doing for about fifteen years. They began dating, and later married, two young women; college friends, who also followed me into the family business. One of the women was Diana Paxson. When both Paul and Jon became writers, Diana was encouraged to try it, too, and the rest is history.

When I moved from being a writer to an editor, the first writer I discovered was Diana; I was privileged to buy one of her first printed stories. I've discovered many writers since, including the enormously successful Mercedes Lackey and Jennifer Roberson, but I still feel Diana's stories have as much quality and will endure as long as any one of the others. After the first story, the enormously original tale of a shapechanger, "Kindred of the Wind," she produced a fine fantasy series set in an alternate future California, *The Chronicles of Westria*. She then went on to work on historical fantasies such as *The White Raven,* the splendid story of Tristan and Iseult. More recently she has been collaborating with me on the "Avalon" novels, and working on her own Arthurian novel, *Hallowed Isle*. Her special historical knowledge has greatly enriched my own work, but she still writes her own finely crafted stories set in various historical periods. Here she tells a story from the Viking period of which she writes so often . . .

Bera balanced with the ease of long habit as the wagon jolted over the rutted road, but her belly was knotting anxiously. The white trunks of the birches on the hillside glowed against the dull green of fir and pine, a few last leaves bright gold in the sun. The thrall Haki's shoulders flexed and relaxed again as he kept a steady pressure on the reins.

She had been making such journeys since she was fifteen, when Groa the Voelva took her from her father's farm to train in the mysteries of seidh-magic. But Groa had retired to Raumsdale now, and Bera—with her teacher's thrall, her cart, and a ring from the Jarl to serve as introduction—was on her way to Vaerdale to winter with one of his chieftains, Narfi of Stav.

In the middle of the day, the autumn air was warm, laden with a tantalizing hint of smoking meat as the wind changed. Bera lifted her thick dark hair, a legacy from the Irish thrall-woman who had been her mother, and wound it into a loose knot. The morning had dawned clear, but now wisps of high cloud were beginning to veil the sky. Common sense put to flight any thoughts of turning back. She had longed for independence—she must pray now for the power to use it well. . . .

Something crashed among the trees ahead, and Bera clutched at the side of the wagon as Haki hauled on the reins. The changing wind brought a rank, familiar scent as the branches shivered, and a massive brown form emerged onto the road. Bera caught her breath, suspended between present terror and a memory of the visions she had experienced in which bears had devoured her the previous spring when she lay prisoned by snow in an abandoned den.

The horse snorted, trembling, and the bear turned, half rising as it peered toward them. It was an old male, fat with autumn feasting, and more curious than hostile or afraid. Haki shot her a panicked glance, fists tightening on the reins. Bera gripped his shoulder in warning, knowing that any sudden move might startle the beast into attacking them.

Slowly she rose to her feet, knowing that the taller she appeared, the less she would look like prey. A whisper of melody surfaced in memory and she began to

hum as the Bear-Smith in her initiatory vision had
hummed while he hammered her bones, but now the
tune had words. She sang:

> *"I am the daughter of the Bear,*
> *Devoured was I, and dead in the den,*
> *yet swift with the spring, I sought the sunlight.*
> *Now I salute you as your sister—*
> *Brown One, be gone—seek bright berries,*
> *Fare onward, friend, and take my blessing. . . ."*

Whether it was some magic in the tune or her own af-
firmation of power, by the time she fell to humming
wordlessly once more, all her fear had gone. The bear's
heavy head lowered as if in homage, then the rest of
the body followed. The beast whuffed explosively, then
lumbered across the road and disappeared among the
tangle of berry bushes there. Bera sat back with a sigh.
It had been a real bear, not Brunbjorn, the bear-spirit
who walked with her in the Otherworld, but its appear-
ances seemed to her a good omen.

When presently all sounds of his passage had faded
and they moved on, Bera realized she was no longer
afraid of going to Narfi's hall. The road sloped downward, and now and again she glimpsed the blue gleam
of the fjord between the trees.

"There lies the hall," said Haki. Ahead, the ground fell
away in a long slope toward the fjord. The bronze of turning oaks and beech trees dappled the forest. Between the
trees she glimpsed thatched outbuildings surrounding a
high-built hall like cygnets around a swan. Its beam ends
were richly carved, and interlaced dragons twined
around the door. They had come to Stav.

At the time of their arrival, the Hunting month was
halfway past and the moon was on the wane. The feast
of Winter Nights would be held when next it shone full.
Narfi, a big man with a habit of stopping to clear his throat
when he was thinking, noted Bera's arrival with a grunt of

greeting, told his wife to assign her a cupboard-bed in one of the smaller buildings, and appeared to forget her. Already, more important guests were arriving. Bera realized rather quickly that, to him, she was only part of the entertainment.

That suited her well enough, for she could use the time to make friends with the land wights here and the spirits of house and barn. Quietly she unpacked her box of herbs and proceeded to make herself useful to the household.

The moon faded to a sliver and disappeared, and the lengthening nights moved toward equality with the hours of day. Bera could feel the tension growing between them as the season turned toward the moment when light and dark would strike a precarious balance before the inevitable slide toward winter began.

At the beginning of the Blood Moon, a trader called Sigvat arrived with two companions: Ospak, a weasely fellow who was his servant; and a big man called Thord, who had the look of a fighter. Narfi wished to be known for his hospitality, and he thought it a fine thing to allow his guests to pick through the trader's wares. Also, the trader was a good talker who had traveled from Bjarma-land to the Färeyjar Isles.

As the days grew shorter, the men whom Narfi had invited to share the autumn sacrifices began to arrive. Honoring the gods was the excuse for the gathering, but it also provided a chance for men to debate matters that they wished, through Narfi and Jarl Sigurd, to bring before the King.

This season, many spoke of the ship levy, which some felt bore too heavily on the Tronds. The other shires should bear a greater share, said some, while others observed that as the Tronds were the richest of the Norse-king's lands it was just that they should bear the weight of their protection. But with each day, it seemed that men spoke more and more often against the king.

"And what think you, Ketil?" said the trader Sigvat one evening when they sat over their ale in the hall.

"You have fought for the king. Is what he asks beyond what is right?"

There was a murmur from among the men. Bera turned to watch them. She had heard such a sound before, when hounds were uncertain whether to challenge for a bone.

"What is right? The king knows what he needs to fight our foes." Beneath the bristling brows, Ketil's dark eyes were watchful. He had been in Narfi's service a long time, and often accompanied him to war.

"If they *are* foes . . ." came a whisper.

"Do you wish to see Harald Gormson deal with the Tronds as we dealt with him and his Danes?"

"It is not the Danes against whom Hakon is arming, but the sons of Eric." Sigvat spoke then, his tones mellow as butter against Ketil's rasp.

"Why should we spend our substance to war against those whose blood is every bit as kingly as Hakon's own?" said a farmer who had come to talk about cattle with Narfi a few days before.

"Those are strange words to hear in the hall of Jarl Sigurd's man."

"I say what I please. I am a free man. And I say that King Gamle Ericsson would not rule us with so heavy a hand!" A murmur of mingled objection and approval echoed the farmer's words.

"What *you* please, or what this peddler persuades you is true?" rumbled Ketil. "It seems to me that you and these strangers have been talking about more than the price of hides, and the rest of you as well. Sigvat is very quick with praise for the Blood-Axe's sons; a fine trader in treason is this guest in Narfi's hall!"

"It is not for you, a landless man, to accuse him!" the farmer answered furiously. Sigvat looked from one to the other, calculation sparking in the eyes beneath the sandy lashes.

"Jibe as you will," Ketil answered with a deadly courtesy, "but no dishonor has ever stained my blade."

"Nay then, lads, let us not break the peace of Narfi's

hall. You, girl—" Sigvat gestured toward Bera. "Bring us a pitcher of ale that we may drink ourselves into fellowship once more!"

Bera stiffened. "I am no thrall to jump at your bidding," she said tightly. "But I will ask one of the maids to serve you—for the peace of Narfi's hall."

"Oh, ho!" Sigvat grinned unpleasantly and looked her up and down. "I see that your tongue is as sharp as Ketil's sword! But bond or free, in the dark all women are alike to me."

Her face flaming, Bera stalked away, trying not to hear the men laughing behind her.

She tried to put the incident out of her mind. But now that she had come to his attention, Sigvat seemed to consider her a challenge. He watched her, undressing her with his eyes. Ospak and Thord, his companions, were just as bad. But so long as they did not try to maul her, it was beneath her dignity to complain. Still, as the Festival neared, Bera spent more time alone, giving out that she needed the privacy to prepare for the space ceremony.

At sunset, on the day when her inner senses told her that the balance was about to shift toward the dark time of the year, Bera went out to make offerings to the spirits of the land where the stream rushed over a tumble of rock to fall into a little pool. In the dusk the droplets struck the still water with a sound like harpnotes—the fossegrim was making music for the nixie who lived there.

Drawing her own power like a cloak around her, Bera climbed carefully down to the waterside. She had brought mead and a silver coin to throw in as an offering. There was a soft splash, and the night stilled, listening, as she made her prayer. As she rose to return, the sound of the waterfall returned, but as she made her way back through the forest it seemed to her that it was singing "Beware! beware. . . ."

When she reached the farm, the sounds from the great

hall told her that the drinking was already well under-
way. She might as well go directly to bed, she thought
wryly, for there would be no sensible conversation to be
had until day. She turned to cross the courtyard, pausing
to let a man who was returning from the privies pass.

As he reached her, he halted, trying to see her face
by the light of the torch that burned beside the door.

"C'mere, little one, and gimme a kiss—" He giggled
softly, and Bera recognized Sigvat. She stepped back as
he reached for her.

"Sir, you are mistaken," she began, thinking he had
taken her for one of the thrall-women who sometimes
shared the beds of guests in the hall.

"You're the little sorceress!" He grinned, "An' I
know where you been, out with the she-goats on the
hill.'

"You're drunk. Go back to the other sots in the hall."

"You come with me! Why not? You offer your bum
to anything with a cock. Oh, yes, you an' Freyja the
whore!"

Bera stared at him. She had herd that some men blas-
phemed the goddess, especially those who had spent
time in Christian lands, but Groa's prestige had always
protected her. Still stunned by outrage, she did not realize Sigvat was moving until he grabbed her.

The next few moments were a confusion of grasping
hands and foul, ale-fumed breath. Drunk the trader
might be, but he was strong, and her heavy cloak and
skirts hampered her attempts to fight him. For a few
awful seconds he ground his lips against hers, then Bera
got an arm free and pushed. He grabbed her by the hair,
and she twisted round and bit his hand.

Sigvat yelled and let go. She saw his return blow coming, hiked up her skirts and kicked upward with a force
that sent the trader sprawling. It was only then that
she realized they were surrounded by onlookers from
the hall.

"Ha-harrum—" The hubbub stilled as Narfi shoul-
dered through the crowd. He pulled at his beard, looking

around him. "What happened here?" All eyes turned toward Bera, appraising, or narrowed in speculation.

"He was drunk, and thought I was one of the thrall-women—" she said finally. "I will not ask a fine."

Narfi shook his head in annoyance and gestured toward Sigvat, who was sitting up and moaning. "Pick him up, and put him to bed. He'll be punished enough by the head he'll have in the morning. And you, woman, should get to your bed as well. I'll have no one stirring trouble in my hall."

He might as well have told her to go back to her kennel, Bera thought bitterly, as if she were a bitch in heat that had gotten in among the dogs.

When at last she got to bed, sleep was long in coming. She had never thought of herself as defenseless, but she saw now how Groa had protected her, not only because men feared the older woman's powers, but because Bera was viewed as her property. Now she was alone, and being small in stature, and not worn out with child-bearing, she looked less than her thirty years. When the power was in her, she could put on a guise that any man might fear, but she had been unprepared. Must she live braced for attack until she grew old and ugly?

Bera woke, heavy-eyed, to a chilly morning and a cloud-covered sky, very much in need of the hot porridge that would be simmering over the fire in the hall.

But when she started across the yard, the thrall-woman who was feeding the geese made a warding sign and backed away. Then the door to the hall swung open, and she saw Sigvat's squint-eyed servant, with two of Narfi's guard behind him.

"There she is! The *seidhskratt,* the sorceress! She has killed my master with her witcheries!"

"Ha-harummh . . ." Narfi sighed and rubbed his forehead. "The matter is thus. Sigvat of Jorvik lies dead in his bed with no mark upon him, and his man here says that you cursed him after he attacked you."

Bera swallowed, seeing only hostility in the faces

around her, or an avid curiosity. "He lies. You were there. I did not even ask compensation—"

"Because you meant to work seidh upon him and get your own vengeance!" Ospak exclaimed.

"Why should I—" she began, but the little man was still shouting.

"You were alone in the outbuilding. Can you prove you did not?"

"I will swear on Thor's silver ring that I did no evil!"

"But if you *are* evil, what good is your word?" said someone. The murmur around her grew more threatening.

"This tale will get around the countryside, and the Voelva Groa, who trained me, will hear whether you have dealt justly with me—" Bera said desperately. And what Groa heard, Jarl Sigurd would know as well. The unspoken threat hung in the air.

Narfi frowned. "If you were a man, you could clear your name in battle. I will not touch your life, but you cannot remain when we make the offerings to the gods."

He will grant me lesser outlawry— she thought, *as if I had already been judged guilty.*

"Sir, you condemn me without a trial. I am a Voelva, but what man will welcome me to his hearth when this is known? I have here no kinsmen, no powerful friends to take oath in my support. Only the spirits who help me can clear my name."

"What do you mean?" He looked doubtful, but at least he was listening.

"In the forests above the fjord, there are wolves and bears, is it not so? At this season they are hungry. Let me sit out through one night outside the garth, with neither steel nor fire for my protection. If morning finds me safe and sound, you will know that I speak truly. And perhaps my spirits will help us to understand this mystery."

This, truly, is Utgard. . . . Bera settled herself on the rock and looked around her. The footsteps of the men who had brought her here had faded, and with them, the last of the daylight had gone. She was accustomed to travel in spirit in that Utgard which was part of the Otherword, but here, her body was at risk as well. The granite outcrop on which she sat was a pale island in a sea of shadowed trees. She took a deep breath, willing her beating heart to slow. There was nothing to fear. She had kept such vigils before as part of her training, although usually at a warmer time of the year. At this season there would be frost on the ground before the sun rose again. And as for the animals, if she sat quietly, she should be perceived neither as a threat nor as prey. She was safer here than she had been in Narfi's hall. Thus, the voice of reason, but when a branch fell somewhere among the pines, she jumped all the same.

With the setting of the sun a chill wind had come up that whispered through the trees. Bera pulled her cloak tightly around her and moved down from the rock to huddle in the hollow left when some previous storm had brought down a big pine. Out of the wind, she was warmer, but for a time, physical discomfort kept all other fears at bay.

By the time the moon, by now only two days from being full, had fully cleared the trees, the wind had ceased. Bera straightened and loosened the folds of her cloak, listening. Without the wind, the night sounds of the forest were painfully clear. That rustling could be a nightbird or perhaps a fieldmouse. The smallest creatures could sometimes make a surprising amount of noise. Or perhaps it was a weasel, or even a fox, hunting the mice to their holes.

She found also that she could sense the rock even with eyes closed. Her mind filled with images of men in short breeches and shirts and women with gathered skirts and shawls, disjointed as a dream. She thought they were aware of her, but they did not seem to mind her presence, and as the night drew onward, they faded away.

She lay curled in the hollow, half-dozing, half-listening, while the moon wheeled slowly across the sky. It was in the out-tide, sometime after midnight, that a new sound brought her suddenly upright, pulse fluttering like a trapped bird.

The crunch of a branch, crushed beneath some heavy tread . . . Bera waited, not breathing. Foliage rustled. Was it a man, blundering among the trees? Then she heard the sound of bark being ripped away, and in the same moment caught the scent, vividly remembered from the encounter on the road to Stav, of bear.

I am the daughter of the bear . . . she chanted silently. In her vision, when the bears had dismembered her, she had felt no pain. But the dangers of the spirit world were of a different kind. She had seen what was left of a human body after a fight with a bear, and shivered despite her determination to be still.

Foliage whispered as the tree was shaken; the ripping continued. She thought the bear must be harvesting insects, torpid with the chill, and prayed they would satisfy him. Presently the sounds ceased. She heard the bear coming closer.

He must have caught her scent then, for she heard him grunt, and her eyes, widened by fear, saw a darker bulk upreared against the sky. "Brunbjorn . . ." she whispered, calling for protection against the beast before her by appealing to the beast within.

The bear grunted again, then dropped back to all fours. The sudden sharp reek of its piss filled the air. The creature moved off to the right, pausing to urinate again, and then around behind her. Twice more it repeated the procedure before returning to its original position. For certain, she thought wryly, no other beast would trouble her with that reek in the air. But had the bear meant to protect or to claim her, as if she were a honey-tree?

Whichever was meant, the beast knew she was there. Bera took a deep breath and got to her feet, determined to meet her fate standing.

The bear also had risen on its hind legs once more. For a long time, it seemed, she faced it, and presently, forced by stress beyond normal awareness, her vision altered, and she saw the great furred body overlaid by a glimmering double image, an image she recognized.

Why not? she thought giddily. *If a god can walk in the body of a man, why should Brunbjorn not possess the body of this bear?*

"You sleep now—" his thought came clearly. *"No forest beast will do harm."*

"The harm will come from beasts that walk in the bodies of men," she replied. "They think I killed a man by seidh-craft. How can I prove myself guiltless so they will trust me?"

"You can't prove what you didn't do. Better turn the attack against your enemy. Then they respect you."

Bera stared at him, remembering how men would look at Groa after she had worked seidh for them, how often she herself had been asked to bear messages, as if they feared to address the Voelva themselves. But they honored the wisewoman as they honored fellow warriors. Bera's heart sank as she realized that she could not afford to appear vulnerable. Her safety lay in knowing how to inspire fear.

"Is it then my wyrd never to know love?"

"What is 'never'? You find a man who likes a woman strong as he is, you can love him. And women who know a few things themselves—they will be your allies or your enemies. But now a man is your foe."

"The man who tried to force me is dead—" she said then.

"And so, not an enemy. His brothers remain."

Bera nodded, remembering Thord's burning gaze and Ospak's malicious grin. It was they who had accused her.

"Sleep. . . . Dream. . . ." Brunbjorn's words came once more. *"Sleep will open the door of memory that fear has bolted, and you will know what to say when they come."*

As the glowing form began to fade, Bera felt her eyes growing heavy. She sank back down against the tree root and huddled into her cloak. The bear thudded heavily back to all fours as the force that had overshadowed it was withdrawn. It shook its head in confusion and then wandered off through the trees.

Bera scarcely heard it go.

As she lost awareness of the outer world, inner vision sharpened. She was walking in an oakwood; not the evergreen-clad mountains of Norway, but some other land. From ahead she heard squealing, and a black boar trotted across her path. A black sow came after him, with nine piglets running beside her, and about the fore-leg of each of them gleamed a golden ring.

Then she heard dogs baying in the wood, and the black boar was brought down. The sow and her piglets fled, and a whale swallowed them and carried them across a great water. After that things became confused. When she could see once more, the piglets were grown to young boars, but there were only eight of them now. One of them slipped off its armring and gave it to three rats who carried it away northward. She saw them scuttle beneath Narfi's high seat, but when they came out, only two remained.

Bera was awakened by the quork of a raven, calling to his mate as they flapped across the brightening sky. *Looking for carcasses,* she thought, watching them. *If it were not for Brunbjorn, they might have fed on me.*

In the growing light she could see markings pecked into the stone—line drawings of men with spears and ships and the sunwheel. In the hollow, there were old stains where offerings had been made. It was a holy place of the alfar, the old ones of the land. She understood why Narfi had chosen this spot for her ordeal.

By the time Narfi's men came to fetch her, she had tidied her hair and brushed the pine needles from her cloak and was waiting for them upon the stone.

"Phew— This place stinks of bear!" said Ketil, glancing at her uneasily.

"That is so. One came during the night, but it did not trouble me." One of the other men stepped back. Bera continued to walk, her face serene, but she felt a pang of regret as she sensed his fear.

Narfi came out from the hall to meet them.

"As you see, I am unharmed," Bera said boldly. "Will you believe in my innocence now?"

"I will believe, at least, that my landwights find you no threat to me," he replied.

"Then hear the wisdom that this night's out-sitting has brought to me." For a moment she closed her eyes, ordering the images. Then from her lips came the story, cast in the staves of prophecy.

> *"Seeds of the oak, the black swine seek,*
> *Turf the boar tears, trots his sow after . . ."*

Line by line, she recounted her dream.

"Eric and Gunhild must be the boar and the sow," whispered someone, "and their sons are the nine shoats she farrowed . . ." There was a laugh, quickly cut off, and an uneasy murmur ran through the crowd. Bera continued to chant.

> *"Seek for the cheese-stealers who whisper treason,*
> *Hiding the hoard in Narfi's high hall."*

"Rats from the south . . . ha-harrum," echoed Narfi reflectively. His gaze fell upon Ospak, who took a quick step backward and was stopped by Ketil's heavy hand.

Bera glared at him. "As he has accused me, so I challenge in return. Seek for the gold the Ericssons gave to Sigvat and his companions. If it is not found in their gear, then look for a hiding place beneath your high seat, my lord."

Narfi saw the sudden panic in Ospak's eyes and began to grin.

"I slept safe," Bera said then, "but stones and tree roots are not a comfortable bed. Take what action seems good to you. I am going to rest." Several of the men made signs of warding as she stalked away, but Brunbjorn had been right. It was wary respect that she saw in their eyes.

Bera had withdrawn more for effect than because she expected to sleep, but once she lay down, the effects of an anxious night overwhelmed her. It was nearly noon when she was awakened by shouting in the yard. She dressed carefully in the blue cloak of a Voelva and all her amber, and took her carved staff in her hand.

She found Haki waiting on her doorstep. He fell in behind her as she started toward the hall, but she needed no protection. There was awe as well as respect in the looks she got now. Narfi was sitting in his high seat, a horn of ale in his hand. She came to a halt before him.

"It needs no seidh-craft to see that something has happened," she said, smiling slightly. "What did you find?"

"Gold from the mint at York, with the image of King Æthelstan," Narfi answered heavily.

"Such gold as Gunhild might have brought away with her when she fled Northumbria," said Ketil, nodding agreement, "for every seven years the English kings mint all their gold anew, and you will only find coins with Edmund's name on them now."

"And there are many here who will tell how Sigvat and the others often spoke against the King and praised the Ericssons," said another man.

"It was to distract us from inquiring too closely about Sigvat's origin that Ospak accused you," Ketil said then.

"And what have you done with him and Thord?" Bera asked Narfi.

"They are gone. I left them only so much gold as will buy them a passage back to the Daneking's lands and sent them under guard to Nidaros. The remainder I will send to King Hakon. It seems only fitting that the gold with which Gunhild sought to seed treason be used against her. But what weregild shall we pay for the insult to you?" he went on.

For a moment Bera frowned, thinking. In truth, she was grateful to Narfi, for her ordeal had taught her something she very much needed to know, but she would not be wise to tell him so.

"Tonight begins the feast." She looked up at last, holding his gaze. "When you have made the offerings and blessed the hall, bring out the seidh platform. With the aid of the wights, I shall answer such question as are put to me, and men shall reward me as they see fit, for you know now that what I say is true."

THE WISHING STONES

by Lisa S. Silverthorne

Lisa Silverthorne has a knack for much-used titles—but the stories they describe are never overdone or hackneyed.

She's been with us since my earliest days as an editor and we've had our ups and downs, but we both seem to have survived undamaged. She says her bio is not much changed; no job changes, no wild excursions to exotic places. She's written two more novels and one of her short stories made it onto the preliminary Nebula ballot, and other than that things haven't changed much. That's a consequence of getting older; not so many highs, but not so many lows either. Life is less of a roller coaster, but one acquires a taste for stability, if not for monotony.

But in this story things are very far from monotony as a young prisoner uses her magical powers against her captor.

Shoshona stood at the tower window, the wishing stones cold in her hand, and watched the remnants of another sunset fade into darkness. She'd forgotten how the sun felt against her face and dark hair. Abruptly, the wind rose, whipping past the tower. Behind her, torches guttered. She began to tremble, feeling Terach's approach like the rush of a dark horse. Her eyes welled with tears.

For five years, he had kept her in this tower, trapping her and her magic within these cursed walls. Every time he sought to take over another kingdom, he came here to drink of her magic. With every stolen sip went a piece of her soul. She'd long given up thoughts of escape or release, for he had even cursed her ability to cast. Shoshona's well of magic was endless, so she'd become only a vessel to him. Tonight, Terach returned to gorge himself on her magic and use it to destroy yet another keep. But this time, he would regret it.

Hooves beat against the ground. The air smelled of musk and cinders, and clouds hid the moon. He'd ridden a long way out to these plains of exile. There wasn't much time.

She hurried away from the window and knelt on pillows strewn across the floor. Holding the wishing stones up to the light, she studied them. She remembered how Terach had thrown them at her last time, mocking her with the worthless trinkets sold by every merchant in the countryside. Closing her eyes for a moment, she summoned her magical essence—it was the only spell left to her.

His heavy footfalls echoed in the stairwell, leather creaking, breath huffing. The familiar jangle of his key ring filled the stillness.

Taking the stones one by one, Shoshona pressed each to her lips and in the soft syllables of her magic, she named the stones. Then she dipped each stone into the magical essence in her right hand. When all three stones had been named and immersed, she spread them in a colorful array across the pillows. They glimmered with pearly sheens: a garnet stone, a sapphire stone, and an amethyst stone. Only Terach, drunk with her magic, could cast the spells on the stones.

A key rattled in the lock, and her breath caught in her throat.

Terach shuffled his stocky frame into the room, leering at her. His blond hair looked sallow; his mustache was the color of mud. Eager to drink her magic, he moved toward her, his brown eyes wary. He expected a fight. He reached for her right hand, but she jerked her arm against her side. The magical essence dissipated into a puff of smoke.

"Always you make this difficult, Shoshona," he said

with a snarl and his hand snapped around her wrist, squeezing.

She bit her lip, fighting down the cry of pain that bubbled up. He let go of her arm, and she thrust it against her dark robes, rubbing her wrist.

"Every year, I fight you for your magic."

"And this year, I am tired," she said in a drained voice.

She cupped her hands and summoned more of her magical essence. When the pearly essence filled her hands, she presented it to Terach, who eagerly held out his own hands. She poured the essence into his cupped hands, and he drank it in quick gulps until the pearly sheen wrapped around him. Sated, his eyelids closed to slits, and he sank down onto the pillows.

Shoshona slid closer to the wishing stones. She waited until the moments of calm passed and his fervor returned. Abruptly, he bolted up from the pillows, his eyes wide. Shoshona let him pace the room for a moment, allowing the waves of magic to course through him. Only when his eyes burned fever-bright did she speak.

"I've made the magic simpler to use. No longer will you have to ride back to your troops. You can use my magic from here."

He spun around, grinning. "I could take over keeps from here?" He took two quick steps toward her. "How? Tell me how?"

She pointed at the stones. "I infused my magical essence into three wishing stones, named and charged. Remember the stones you gave me last time? They await your use."

Suspicious, he stared at her for a moment. "Wishing stones?" He scoffed. "They are little more than trade beads."

"What do you seek to own this night, Terach?"

He pointed north. "My neighbor, Odran. My troops surround Odran's inner gates, awaiting my return with your magic."

She pointed to the garnet stone. "This stone will destroy enemies. Fling it toward Odran, and there will be destruction."

Warily, Terach picked up the stone, turning it over and over in his palm. Finally, he walked to the window. It opened wider to his touch. He threw the stone northward. A brilliant red flash arced across the dark sky and thunder echoed. In the distance, flames roiled. Grinning, Terach moved back to her.

"I am glad you've given up fighting me," he said and ran his hand over her cheek.

Repulsed, Shoshona tried not to recoil. She closed her eyes, blocking out the view of his clammy hands touching her skin.

He let go of her and turned his attention to the other two stones. Shoshona picked up the sapphire stone. She pressed it into his hand. "This stone will cause capture. Throw it toward Odran."

Moving to the window, Terach tossed the stone north. Screams and shouts shattered the calm.

Terach rushed back to her, a feverish look in his eye. "I will bring you more wishing stones from the marketplace!" He swept the amethyst stone from the pillows and held it up to the light. "And this one? Tell me, what does it do?"

She smiled and rose to her feet. "That one will bring victory."

Once more, Terach hurried to the window and threw the stone northward.

Nothing happened.

He waited. Nothing.

Angry, he whirled around. "Nothing happened!" Gritting his teeth, he rushed toward her. "Why?"

In both hands, Shoshona summoned pearly coils of her magical essence. She raised them over her head.

He laughed. "What will you do with those, Shoshona? Your casting abilities are cursed, remember?"

"I forgot to tell you the names I gave the wishing stones, Terach," she said with a smirk.

Puzzled, Terach frowned. "Why do I care about their names?"

"To the name, dear Terach, goes the wish. The first stone I named Odran, and to Odran went the garnet wish to destroy enemies."

"What have you done?"

"Your troops were destroyed. I named the sapphire stone for your keep. So, to your keep, went the sapphire wish of capture."

His face paled, the realization becoming clear. "You've destroyed my troops? And given my keep over to Odran?" He fell silent and stared at the stone floor. Finally, he looked up, shock evident in his eyes. "What of—the third stone?"

She grinned. "To Shoshona, went the amethyst wish, the wish for victory."

With newfound words on her lips, Shoshona cast magic for the first time in five years. Chains of fire wrapped around Terach, binding him to his own cursed tower room. She snatched the key ring from Terach's belt and ran toward the stairwell.

"What are you doing?" Enraged, he screamed and lunged at her, but the stairwell was just beyond the fire chains' limit. "Release me at once!"

Shoshona paused for a moment and turned to him. "I'll return in five years, and we can discuss the matter."

She ran down the stairs and surged into the cool night air. She'd saved up a lot of wishes in five years. It was time she began pursuing them.

A FOOL'S GAME

by Selina Rosen

Selina Rosen sent her bio in on the letterhead of something called Yard Dog Press, which sounds formidable. She says that ten years of heavy armed combat (for fun, not for profit) was the inspiration for "A Fool's Game." Ten years of fighting doesn't sound much like fun to me, but hey—whatever turns you on! She admits that as one gets older, one tends to feel the bruises, bumps, and lacerations of one's youth more keenly. Well, if it spawned a fine story like this, maybe the bumps and bruises were worth it.

She has self-published two horror novels (through Yard Dog Press) and has a novel which will be released from Meisha Merlin Press in Spring 1999 and has another coming out sometime in 2000. It's funny, when I was a child, the year 2000 was used only in science fiction; now it's on our publishing schedules.

She must have been fifty if she was a day. She looked battered and road-tired, but when she walked into the pub, people gave her a wide berth. If she noticed that people were moving out of her way, she didn't let it show.

Her black hair had gray streaks in it and was braided in one tight braid that went almost to the middle of her back. There was a jagged scar over her right eye and cheek and another that ran the whole length of her right arm. She was above average height, which was good because otherwise the bastard sword she wore on her back would have looked ridiculously large. Her dark brown eyes were bright and seemed to take in everything and nothing.

She strode straight up to the bar, flopped down on a stool, and waited for the bartender to bring her "her usual"—even though she probably hadn't been in for a drink in six months. She took the mug he handed her and downed it quickly. Then she pointed at the empty receptacle and grunted. The bartender quickly filled her mug again, and this time she sipped at it seeming to taste and savor every drop.

No one talked to her, and she talked to no one. One of the serving girls brought her a bowl of stew and some bread. The woman gave the girl a silver coin, and the girl ran off to show the other serving girls who started whispering in awe. The woman picked at the stew, occasionally making a face and fishing something out of the bowl. At last, she picked up her bowl and her mug and moved to a table in the corner that had just been vacated. She set the vessels down, then took her sheathed sword off her back and placed it on the table as she sat down behind it. The whole time she ate, the sword's hilt was never more than a few inches from her hand. When one of the serving girls dropped a platter, the sword was instantly in the woman's hand and just as quickly released when she realized there was no near or present danger.

Danad had watched the woman carefully from the moment she'd entered the pub. Her own meal had gone uneaten and her ale untasted. Finally, she grabbed one of the serving girls by the arm.

"Hey there!" the girl protested.

"Sorry," Danad said releasing the girl. "Is that . . . is that Agnes of the Black Rock?" Danad pointed, and almost instantly the older woman's eyes met hers. Danad dropped her finger and looked quickly away.

"Yes. Yes, it is." The girl whispered so quietly that Danad could hardly hear her.

"She's old, looks like she's seen better days. I think I could take her," Danad said talking out loud but to herself.

The serving girl laughed. "Please tell me before you

do anything as foolish as challenging Aggy the Giant Killer so that I can stand clear. I'm wearing a new dress, don't you know."

"I don't want to fight her," Danad said. "I was just saying she doesn't look that dangerous."

"Neither is a spider until you get too close." The girl moved quickly away from Danad as if her brash stupidity might somehow rub off.

Danad picked up her ale and attempted to down it the way she'd seen Agnes of the Black Rock do, but she choked and wound up spitting ale all over her tunic. She picked up a rag and tried to dry herself off without much success.

After several more minutes Danad found her courage, got to her feet, and strode purposefully toward Agnes of the Black Rock. The woman didn't move. She just sat there bent over her stew and seeming not to notice the younger woman. Then, when Danad was a sword's breadth away from the woman's table, the old warrior made a few quick movements—far too quick to follow. The next thing Danad knew, the sword mistress' blade tip was against her throat. A silence fell across the pub. The only sound to be heard was an old man in the back yelling, "What's going on? What's going on?"

Danad's hand was nowhere close to her sword, and she realized she might have been too quick to judge the older woman feeble.

Agnes spoke then, the first words she had spoken since she entered the pub. "Did you come to challenge me or just fawn over me?"

"Neither, ma'am. I want to learn from you. I, too, am a hired sword, and I was hoping . . ."

Agnes started to laugh then, and the noise in the pub started up again as if nothing had happened. Agnes quickly sheathed her sword and returned it to the table.

"Child, if you are a hired sword, then you are already without hope. Remove your sword and sit." Agnes began to pick at her stew again. "When you get to be my age, you can't eat just anything anymore. It messes

with your stomach. It is less likely every day that a
sword, arrow, or magical spell will kill me, and more
likely that I will be killed by an onion or a bad piece
of meat."

"I have heard stories of your excellence with blade
and with hand-to-hand combat . . ."

"Oh, and some of the stories are even true." Agnes
laughed.

". . . how you smote the giants at Eagleswood single-
handed." Danad finished.

"They weren't really giants. They were just two really
big, ill-tempered men. Truly, it wasn't any great accom-
plishment. I waited till they were drunk, then snuck into
their camp and cut their throats," Agnes said.

"But at the battle of Asher you killed fifty men in a
single day!" Danad said.

Agnes laughed. "Did I really now! You know, I wasn't
really keeping track."

She pushed away her bowl, stood up, and put her
weapon back on her back. She stared at the younger
woman. "Do yourself a favor, girl. Find yourself a nice
young woman, or man if you fancy, settle down, and
start farming. Steel is worse than any other vice—put it
away from you before it gets into your blood."

Agnes started out of the pub. Danad grabbed up her
own sword, clumsily put it on her back, and started after
the woman. "But I want to be like you!" Danad said as
she rushed after the woman.

Agnes stopped dead in her tracks, turned, and stared
at the girl with cold brown eyes.

"Nobody wants to be like me, girl. Not even me."
Agnes strode out of the bar, and Danad didn't follow.

The horse made a whoofing noise. Aries was a little
slow today. Aggy had figured out they were being followed about three miles back. She was pretty sure she
knew who it was, too.

"Stupid girl. Thinks she wants to be a hired sword."
Aggy snorted and pulled the horse up short, then backed

him into some bushes and waited quietly. In a few minutes the girl rode past on a horse that was as green as she was. Aggy waited for her to pass and then started to follow her. She smiled to herself as she wondered if the girl was even aware of the fact that she was now the stalked instead of the stalker.

She watched from her seat above Aries as the girl stopped and made camp. She was a handsome young woman of average height who was as dark as Aggy herself was. She was carrying a little extra weight on her, but if she was serious about her sword work, she wouldn't be carrying it for long. She reminded Aggy strongly of a woman she had once fought with who had died of a terminal case of stupidity. But worse than that, she reminded Aggy of herself at that age.

She'd squandered her youth, wasted her life, and she doubted she could stop this one from doing the same thing. But she'd try. At the very least she could teach her how to stay alive.

She waited till the fire had been built up and the girl had gone off to get more wood. Then she went down into the camp and made herself at home.

Danad didn't know when or where she'd lost Agnes of the Black Rock's trail, but she had. She'd try to pick up the trail in the morning when it was light and she'd had some sleep. She was tired, and her rear was sore from being thrown around on the back of a freshly broken mount that thought every terrain was suitable for trotting. There was a full moon out. On the road it had been plenty light enough to see, but in the woods under the cover of the trees she could barely see her hand in front of her face. She kept thinking that at any minute she was going to pick up a snake instead of a twig. Quickly gathering what she hoped was enough firewood to last her through the night, she stumbled back through the dark to her camp.

"That's not nearly enough wood for the night."

Danad jumped, and the wood went flying in several

different directions. She made a feeble attempt to draw her sword before she realized who was standing warming her hands by the fire.

"Ya . . . You! But I was . . ."

"Following me. I don't like to be followed. It's not a very strategic position to be in. So I followed you instead, and now I don't have to build a fire. But you're going to need more wood than that," Agnes said.

"Are you going to help me, then?" Danad asked.

"I never said I wouldn't," Agnes said. "Get some more wood."

Danad nodded eagerly and ran back into the woods.

When she got back, Agnes had already removed the saddle and gear from her horse and apparently let him go. He was just wandering around the camp grazing. Agnes had taken out her bedroll, unrolled it by the fire, and was apparently already asleep. Her sword, which was in her right hand, lay unsheathed across her chest.

Danad decided to test Agnes; she moved quietly toward her. Agnes opened one eye and glared at Danad's sneaking form.

"That's a good way to get yourself killed," she said and closed her eye again.

Danad was exhausted. She rolled out her bedroll and crawled into it. She smiled. Agnes of Black Rock! Aggy the Giant Killer was going to teach her the trade, and someday she would be a legend. Someday people would move out of her way when she walked into a pub, and the bartender would bring her a mug of ale without being told.

In the morning Danad awoke to the sound of creaking leather and bone. She looked out from under her covers and saw Agnes stretching. Her hands on her hips, she stretched back, groaning in pain as her bones rattled back into place. Her armor was beautiful black leather, and while it looked to be pretty lightweight and flexible, it couldn't have been very comfortable to sleep in. Danad's own armor consisted of a burlap gambeson and a leather gorget she never fastened because it made her feel like she was choking. And she never wore either one of them to sleep in.

"You all right?" Danad asked.

Aggy laughed. "I haven't been all right since the first time a two-hundred-pound man tackled me to the ground from a running horse. Every bone in my body that hasn't been broken has been bruised, and I've been cut so many times I now bleed dust." She bent over, touched her toes and groaned again. She continued these stretching exercises for some ten minutes while Danad watched.

Finally, Danad asked, "If it hurts you so much . . . why do you keep doing it?"

"Because if I don't keep doing it, I won't be able to." Agnes caught Danad's gaze and held it. "You want to be a swordswoman. I'll teach you to be a swordswoman. I'll make you the best. But first I want you to take a good look at me, because what I am is what you will become. People will fear you, respect you, but they won't love you. They won't even like you. No matter when or where you work, you will always be too hot or too cold. When you don't need the money, you will have more work than you can handle, and when you do need the money, you won't be able to buy a job. People will sing your praises when you are victorious in battle, but they will scorn you and send wizards to curse you if you fail them. You will go to bed tired and wake up exhausted. Your body will become as an enemy to you, causing you constant pain. When you find the person you were destined to be with, you will already be tied to your mentor, to whom you owe too much to betray. And when I die because of your ignorance, you will be left with nothing except a memory of what might have been."

"Just because that is what happened to you does not mean it will happen to me," Danad said with a smile. "Surely a woman's fate is her own."

Agnes laughed loudly.

"What's so funny?" Danad demanded angrily.

Agnes stopped laughing and frowned. "Those are the same words I spoke not very far from here some thirty years ago. What I have explained to you is not just my life. It is the life of any person who earns a living with the sword. If you do make a name for yourself, you will never be able to relax because there will always be some fools who want to make a name for themselves by taking you out. You'll rarely get to finish a meal or a mug of ale. When you do, you'll savor every drop and every bite because you know it might be your last. You will make friends and then watch them die on the end of a pike, an arrow, a spear, or a sword. In the end, you'll ride alone because you can't handle the pain of loss anymore, because you've forgotten how to care. This is the life of every person who makes their money with steel. And any person who would willingly choose it is a fool."

Danad looked at Agnes of the Black Rock and knew the words she spoke were true. "Then teach me to be the greatest of fools."

THE ANVIL OF HER PRIDE

by Lawrence Schimel

Lawrence Schimel is now an editor himself, and when other editors send you their stories, that's some kind of validation. Which reminds me of the old joke of the mother who says to her son, "By you, you can be a comic, and by me you can be a comic, but by comics you ain't no comic!" Well, Lawrence, by editors you're an editor. He is the author of the story collection *The Drag Queen of Elfland* and the editor of more than twenty anthologies.

He now lives in New York City and writes and edits full time. That's the only thing wrong with being an editor; you just about have to live in New York City—even I did when I started.

The blade sliced the air in front of him. Teresa held the weapon before her and looked at Connor, steadily, over the sharp steel edge. Then she laid the sword down before him.

"I can do better," she said.

He stared silently at her, as if still appraising her, trying to determine her skills and weaknesses from the way she'd wielded the sword, wondering at her motives.

"So I've heard," he said at last. "That's why I'm here."

Teresa voiced no response. They waited, each studying the other in silence. Finally, he spoke again.

"I want a sword that's fast as lightning."

Teresa nodded. She could do that.

"As you know, no man-made weapon can harm me."

Teresa knew the tales well, even in her isolation. Who

did not? The exploits of Connor the warrior were the stuff that ballads were made of. Though he was barely twenty, he was already a legend; young boys playing games with sticks pretended to be Connor in any of his famous battles, or ones of their own devising. Single-handedly, he had defended his liege's kingdom from armies of hundreds.

"I wear no armor when I fight. I want a blade that will take advantage of my freedom. This," he indicated the sword that lay between them, "has been the best that I could find thus far. It's good—remarkable, even— but I want better. They say that you can make one better."

"I will fashion such a blade as you desire."

"And the price?" Connor asked.

Teresa answered immediately. "A child."

"Impossible!" Connor shouted, stepping forward as if he intended to shake some sense into her. "I won't kill an innocent, not for the best sword in the world! I'm no butcher."

"Not the death of a child," Teresa said. Her face looked as calm and in control as ever, though inside excitement was racing through her stomach as she thought of what she'd just committed to. "A new life."

Connor shank back, staring at her, comprehension slowly dawning on him as to what she demanded of him.

She was not a handsome woman, she knew. She never had been so in her youth, and time had not been kind to her. Time and her grief, ever since the death of Wilfred, nearly twenty years earlier.

Her body was unwomanly now, her skin dried and thick from the flames of the forge, her arms muscled from wielding the heavy hammers she used to make swords.

When Wilfred died, she had thought she could not go on living. She knew she could never love again, never care for anyone or anything again. So she'd fled from everything she'd known: her family, her friends, the memories of her life with Wilfred. The memories were the hardest to outrun.

Eventually she wound up here, in her mountain home, visited only by the men determined enough to find her and ask for what only she could provide them with.

Her loneliness kept her as sharp as the keen edges of her blades. This was useful in dealing with those who came to her, wanting their instruments of war.

But she was still a woman, and her body craved a child. Especially now, when it was almost too late for her body to bear one.

Teresa was the best there was at what she did, and she knew it. She, too, was sung of in the ballads: Teresa, the female swordsmith whose blades were better than those fashioned by any man. Her commissions had even included the occasional young god, come down from the heavens to seek out her services. That was how enormous her reputation was.

She had thought it would be enough to satisfy her.

So why, now, did she suddenly strike this bargain, set this price? Why with Connor, who was no butcher, he claimed, and yet he had killed thousands of men in his short life?

It was true: he was no butcher. She could tell that just from the few moments she'd spent watching him. His eyes knew the sorrow of death: of his fellow warriors and friends, the many he had been responsible for. He did not start the wars he fought in, for all that he was born to the warrior life. He fought with a sense of honor and justice, as all the ballads agreed. She wanted her child to be born with such ethics.

He was arrogant from the cockiness of his youth, which annoyed her patience. But unlike most young men, he truly was invulnerable. Yet he did not choose to use this gift to evil ends. He still held himself to a morality higher than himself and his personal needs. This was a temperament she desired for her offspring.

And she hoped her child would inherit his father's special gift, the immunity from all the myriad of weapons that man had devised. Some nights Teresa did not sleep, thinking of all the death she had brought into the world. She was ready, now, to bring life into it.

Connor was also strikingly beautiful. In a completely different way from her beloved Wilfred, and perhaps that was why she was able to consider Connor—had more than considered him, had decided. Connor was the dark to Wilfred's light; with raven hair that hung past his shoulders, dark eyes peering out from a thickly-knit brow, a rugged face that often hid a smile teasing at its corners. Wilfred had been fair as fresh milk, his face kind and gentle, though he had determination and fortitude as well. It was through no lack of courage that he'd died, at the claws of a dragon; he'd held his ground, when other knights before him had fled, unwilling to relinquish his stand until he'd been victorious. And then that sickening moment when his sword snapped in twain against the dragon's scales. There was nothing he could do, no chance for escape. He'd relied too heavily on his bravery to carry him through, his faith in his weapon.

His sword had seemed as well-made as any other blade. But it had failed him.

Teresa had stared at the broken halves of the blade they brought back to her, and her grief enraged her. She swore she would avenge Wilfred's death somehow. If not to kill the dragon herself, then in a larger sense.

In the white-hot flame of her grief, she picked up the broken halves of his sword that had been returned to her by his squire. She cut at her palms with their broken edges. Wilfred's squire moved to stop her, to save her, but she stared at him, wild with loss, and he dared not approach her further.

Her blood pooled in her palms and then trickled down the edges of the sword, as if it had found its mark in flesh—the flesh of her heart.

Holding that broken sword, she swore that she would fashion blades so true and pure that no other wife would need ever face this moment again because of this same accident. Men might die by the sword from lack of skill or lack of precaution, from ambush or from overpowering numbers, but they would not die from a flaw in one of her swords.

This was the oath she swore, and it was sealed with her blood.

And since that time, she had dedicated herself to that one unwomanly goal. It had kept her alive all these years, giving her purpose and determination, the will to go on. It was the one thing she clung to, and it did not fail her, cold comfort though it brought her. She took pride in her work, her reputation, devoting herself completely to her craft. She had no room in her life for anything else.

But from the moment Teresa had first seen Connor, she knew what she would request, though she showed no surprise at the sudden beating of her heart. It had little to do with him, and everything to do with her heart, suddenly rebelling at its aloneness, wanting something more.

At that same instant she realized what her body and her heart demanded, she recognized who he was, this hero stepped out of legend onto her doorstep. She did not want to win his love or keep him; she held no illusions about what it was she asked for.

Their offspring, her child, would be a marvel to behold. Someone for her to, again, love.

Teresa held out her hand. "Come," she said. "Let us begin your first payment."

She had never intended for Connor to fall in love with her, or she with him. Of that she was certain. She had meant to raise her son—for she was certain it would be a son, with the same unerring instinct that had let her know that Connor would be his father—in the solitude she had grown to know as intimately as a lover. But over the weeks that followed, as he dutifully tried to father a child with her, they each found a bond growing between them.

Teresa suspected it was the fact of their child, conceived at last after three months of trying, from harvest's end until the first part of winter.

In that same time, she had fashioned Connor's sword, which was indeed swift as lightning. It fairly pulled his arm with it as it sliced eagerly through air and shield, armor and, yes, even flesh and bone.

She could not keep Connor from going off to fight, nor did she wish to. To do so would destroy him, she knew; it was the life he was born to, and the life he was sworn to. She wanted her life back again, to be left with her own thoughts, her own space, without forever wondering where he was and what he was doing, if he would interrupt her work.

He left, but he came back to her. First, to her surprise, and then to her relief, for by the third time she had grown to expect it.

When he was away from her, she occupied with the myriad details of eking out her spare existence on the mountainside, as if her life continued as ordinarily as it had for so many years before.

But she also found herself eager and hopeful for Connor's return, though she told herself again and again that she had no ties on him, none other than the child they had made together, this price she had demanded of him to pay for his sword.

As she bellowed the flames in her forge to work the metal, she often wondered if it was simply the human warmth that she had missed all these years, the contact with another body, the presence of another soul—any soul—in her life. Let alone one so remarkable as the legendary Connor.

Perhaps because they had both been so extraordinary and unusual, they were comfortable with one another, able to be normal and mundane together.

Soon, Teresa reflected, pressing one hand against her belly, she would never be alone again.

One day while Connor was off following his destiny, and giving Teresa space for her own, a man appeared on her doorstep and requested a sword from her. He was a foreigner, a fact as obvious from his dress as from his accent. But Teresa was used to men traveling a great distance to seek out her blades. She was apart from all squabbles over territory, taking no sides; she did not care to know, and did not ask. She cared only about the blades she made. And now, about her son.

Before she had a chance to set a suitable price, the stranger offered her a white cloak, which he claimed was woven from the manes of unicorns. It was exquisite, shimmering in the afternoon light as if it were alive. Teresa hesitantly reached out to touch its soft nap with one hand, half-afraid that the merest touch of human hands would sully it. She could not doubt its authenticity.

It was finery greater than any she had ever known. She had not allowed herself any luxury in the years since Wilfred's death. The world she inhabited allowed for none; the world of the forge, the mountainside.

But something—her child, the way her heart had somehow woken again to fall in love with Connor—had softened her, even while her hands and skin were as hard as ever, her body lean and firm with muscle. Though she had no use for such a cloak, no friends to show it off to and preen beneath their admiration, no desire to live again in a world where such behavior was the norm, she could not resist this marvelous garment. She agreed to the commission.

"What of your condition?" the man, Racmel, asked, indicating her belly swollen with child.

"I can fashion the sword you request," Teresa repeated.

She bade him return in two weeks' time.

The following day, Connor returned to her from the war on the border, tired and victorious. Teresa was almost alarmed at how pleased she was to see him, that he had chosen to return to her instead of to his liege's castle. *I endanger my heart,* she thought to herself, but she could not help but smile when he looked at her and held her close. She had thought to raise her son alone, but for him to know his father would be better.

Connor told her of the battle, of how her sword had turned back the invading army when the enemy leader, Racmel, had disappeared from their ranks. They did not know to what purpose: perhaps, they wondered in the war council, Racmel planned some other attack while they were distracted; perhaps he'd simply abandoned his men to save his own hide. It had ruined the invading army's morale, allowing Connor to sweep through and rout them quickly.

The others now dealt with the prisoners, with the bloody aftermath of war. Connor had instead come to her.

Quietly, Teresa told him of her recent visitor.

"How dare he come here! You should have skewered the villain where he stood!" Connor threw up his arms and paced across the room. "It's not as if you're lacking for weapons here, you know."

"I am no butcher," Teresa said quietly.

Connor crossed back to her and took her in his arms. "I know, my love, I didn't mean that. I'm just so disturbed by the idea that he was here, and that I wasn't here to protect you. I can never leave you, now, without fearing for your safety."

"I have managed to protect myself here since you were newly born. I am no stranger to the sword."

They had never argued like this before. They crossed wills now in a duel as sure as if they each held swords. Teresa did not wish to fight with Connor, but she knew she must hold her ground or lose all that had sustained her for these long, cold years.

"You must refuse his commission," he said.

"I cannot."

"But—"

"I cannot. I have already accepted his payment." She did not tell Connor what it was or show it to him. Somehow she felt he would think less of her, because it was such a womanly instinct that made her crave that marvelous, magical cloak. She did not doubt that even a man would understand the cloak's mystery. It did not matter why she wanted it, she had accepted the payment and given her word.

"My reputation is at stake," Teresa continued. "I have never yet refused a commission. It would look as if I could not fashion this simple blade he has asked for."

She would not yield. The matter lay between them like an unsheathed sword, placed in their bed to keep them apart.

Connor left almost immediately.

Teresa did not try to hold him back.

She had what she wanted from him, she told herself, feeling the life that grew within her and stretched her belly. At night she wrapped herself in the unicorn mantle, trying to isolate herself from the pain of Connor's leaving, from the idea that he might not return.

By day, she fashioned Racmel's sword.

As she worked over the gleaming metal, she couldn't help realizing that she was fashioning a sword for Connor's enemy. She felt temptation rise within her to place some flaw in the sword, so that it would betray Racmel when he crossed blades with her love, could not block his lightning-swift thrusts.

But she remembered that moment of seeing Wilfred's sword, broken in half—all of him that was left to return to her. She could never knowingly fashion a blade that was not perfect, would not betray its wielder under any circumstance.

It was cold satisfaction as she quenched the metal for the final time, then held it up to admire its deadly edge. She had done her work as excellently as ever, and for once, she regretted it.

Later that summer, Teresa bore a baby boy. She delivered alone, crying out from the pain that seemed to split her in half.

She named the boy Cedric. He was fat and pink and hale, with a hearty cry when he was hungry or lonely, a bright laugh when tickled or something made him happy.

He grew quickly, as babies are wont to do in those

first few months, growing heavier, watching the world around him.

By autumn, Connor had not returned.

Teresa feared that she had lost him forever, that her accepting Racmel's commission had been a betrayal he could not stomach. She knew she had been right to hold her position, that Connor was just expressing his jealousy over her. But, despite herself, she felt the loss of him like a knife to her chest.

Was this a betrayal of her love for Wilfred, she wondered? But that love still lay within her heart, the ache of his death still tender even after so many years.

"You are just lonely for another's touch," she whispered to herself, rocking Cedric to sleep. "Any other's touch. Conner is simply the most recent, so he is the one your body craves."

Her mind agreed with her, but her heart wasn't so sure.

Telling herself that she did not go in search of Connor because of love, but simply to present his son to him, that Cedric might grow up having known his father's blessings, Teresa prepared herself for travel.

She wondered where she might find him. She would go to his liege's castle first; they would know where he was, if nothing else.

She wondered what could have kept him from her. Perhaps his affections had found another. She did not fault him for other lovers. He was young, and she knew she was neither young nor beautiful. That she was not warm and loving, for all that she wished for warmth and love in her life again, after all these years. She had never expected him to stay with her, but she had grown to want him when he had, and now she felt the theft of that companionship like a breath of icy wind across her skin.

Perhaps he had realized, at last, the enormity of what she had demanded of him. The price he had paid: this was not his child, it was hers.

She cherished Cedric to her breast, adored him and loved him. He brought a new meaning to her world, which had been without meaning—though it had purpose—for so long.

She held Cedric in her arms and wrapped the white unicorn cloak about the two of them—gleaming in the morning light, the opposite of a mantle of mourning, a cloak full of hope and renewal—and set off on her journey.

Her isolation, years of living alone and this new feeling of incompleteness without Connor, wrapped around her like a shell that kept others at bay. Men did not trouble her—a woman, traveling alone save for her infant—but neither did anyone befriend her.

She walked slowly, surely—for Cedric's sake if nothing else. Though she longed to see Connor again, she was afraid of what her reception might be. Would he ignore her, even spurn her? Would he acknowledge her and his son?

Simply to be on this journey, to have set off in search of him instead of waiting for his return that did not happen, set her heart at ease. She would at last find answers to the questions that had plagued her sleep, the doubts and wonderings. Even if the answers were not the ones she desired, the certainty of knowing would be better comfort than this bewildering, agonizing ignorance she lived with now.

And Teresa was not sure that she did not make this journey for other reasons than finding Connor, to bring her back into the world of men—the way her son had brought her back into the cycle of life.

She had coin to pay her way at inns and taverns, money earned from the swords she had forged. She had coin enough to buy a mount, but she chose instead to walk, though the weather was sometimes inclement, though the road was long and dry; the unicorn mantle kept them warm, protected them from rain, which slid from the white weave without soaking through.

She did not look for company, either while walking or when she was in a town, though she watched everything around her carefully, drinking in the sights and sounds and smells, the experience of humanity and the countryside between. She searched for one man, and he alone could ease the ache she felt within her breast. At night, she sang her son to sleep with songs about his father.

Late one evening, she arrived at a town and entered the tavern. She sat down at an empty bench. No one paid her any notice; their attention fixed on the bard who sat in one corner, in the midst of a song. Teresa listened to the voice, slow and low, sing:

> *"No man-made blade*
> *could claim his life.*
> *He made a widow*
> *of many a wife.*
> *Until a sword made*
> *by a woman's hand*
> *spilled his blood*
> *red upon the sand."*

She did not need to hear more to know who the bard sung of, or what happened to Connor. A cry escaped her lips, though still no one paid her any heed, caught in the spell of the bard's music.

If only she had chosen to listen to Connor instead of her pride! She knew with a certainty she could not explain that Racmel had killed Connor with that sword she had fashioned, "a sword made by a woman's hand." Why had she sworn that earlier oath?

And why had it served her so poorly? Again she faced loss because of a flaw in a sword—a flaw of her own making.

Sitting in the tavern, Teresa's heart—which had woken again to love after years of sleep—broke, like a sword quenched too soon, a hammer blow shattering the flawed metal blade across the anvil of her pride.

A cry from her lap recaptured her thoughts. She looked down at Cedric, wrapped in the dazzling pureness of the unicorn cloak.

How much of that instinct, she wondered, the moment she first saw Connor, had been her own heart and body? How much of it was his own destiny, the beginning of the prophesied end?

She did not know, and she did not care.

If some god up in the heavens shaped their fates, so be it. She had tried to resist fate once, to deny it, and her actions had only brought her more heartache. Vengeance brought cold comfort, and Teresa now longed for human warmth. If a god checked the balance of justice in the world, she could not know, but from where she sat it seemed as if no one cared.

"He's adorable!" a voice cooed.

Teresa looked up, startled. She had forgotten there were others around her—that anyone else even existed.

"Can't be more than a few months," the bar wench continued, peering down into Connor's face and making gurgling noises. Connor smiled and reached toward her gold braids that hung toward him.

"Four months," Teresa said at last. She was surprised that she could speak at all. But she smiled at the obvious pride in her own tone. Which quickly turned sour as she continued, "And six months since his father went off to war and got killed."

She didn't say who his father was. Or who she was, for that matter. It was no longer of any import. She could never return, even as she longed to crawl back into the past, to before she met Connor, to before Wilfred went off to fight the dragon, secure in his prowess and his weapons. She could not change time, and Teresa no longer wanted her old life back, a life that kept verging off into epic, the stuff of songs that bards would sing. Now she was just an old woman with a newborn child, and that was enough.

The barmaid's concern was obvious and immediate. "If you be needing someplace to stay, I can talk with the keeper about taking you on. He's a bit coarse, sometimes, in his humor, I do admit, but he's got a good heart."

Teresa considered this offer, this simple spontaneous kindness, made by a stranger to another stranger. By someone who had to someone who was in need.

She thought of who she had been, what she had done, the men who had sought her out for what only she could give them. Teresa looked down at her smiling son and put aside her pride, the oath she had sworn so long ago. She would not go back, not when the past was filled with so much heartache, and the future held such promise.

THE DANCING MEN
OF BALLYBEN

by Laura J. Underwood

With twenty-three fantasy short stories to her credit, Laura has been writing as far back as she can remember. Her career as a writer of nonfiction and book reviews has spanned twenty-five years, and her first fiction appeared in *Sword and Sorceress V* ten years ago. How well I remember!

When not writing or working at the library, she spends her time hiking the mountains of East Tennessee where she was born and raised. It must be something in that Tennessee drinking water; I remember once, passing through Tennessee, noticing that they had the best spring water I ever tasted. Tennessee also produced another fine writer with a silver-stringed guitar—Manly Wade Wellman's "Silver John" stories collected in *John the Balladeer.* Laura has a harp, Glynnanis, instead. I once said the advantage of a harp as one's principal instrument is that one can't make any sound on it which isn't beautiful. I wonder how many would-be musicians, especially violinists, have been put off (as I was) by the sounds they made while still inexpert?

This is Laura's third story featuring these characters and she is currently working on a novel set in their part of Keltora. Personally—for all you book editors out there—I'd love to see a volume of the collected stories about Glynnanis, Meanwhile we have this story.

The Dancing Men looked like nothing more than an irregular circle of thirty-two stones to Ginny Ni Cooley. She leaned against her staff and stared at broken teeth of gray wearing splotches of lichen green. They ranged about in the fading light and sparse mist of the mountain glen of Ballyben, a grim reminder of what could happen to any unwise enough to provoke the Old Ones from whom mageborn like Ginny were said to descend. She stood at the lower end of the circle and stretched mage senses around her, touching the life-force within each stone. Some were ancient, some were young, and all were bone-weary from the curse they shared.

"Are you certain he's here?" Ginny asked, watching as Thistle wandered from stone to stone. The moor terrier would sniff the base of each one in turn before disrespectfully hiking his leg to mark them as his own. Ginny sensed that the spirits within were not pleased to be decorated in that fashion.

"Aye," the old woman who gave her name as Granny Nora replied, pulling her common plaid shawl tighter about her. "My grandson Aiden come up this way just two nights back, and when he did not return from his foolish quest, I came here myself and counted the stones, and found one more had joined the ranks."

Ginny twisted her face with a scowl. If what the old woman said was true, this could be tricky. One could not defy such a curse without paying the price. Ginny could still recall the old rhyme about these stones that she had learned as a tiny child from her mother's Great Uncle Tamis.

> *The Dancing Men of*
> *Ballyben,*
> *Do dance around the*
> *Mountain glen.*
>
> *And any man who*
> *Joins their dance*
> *Must flee before the*
> *Sun's first glance.*
>
> *Elsewise, as stone he's*
> *Forced to stay,*

> *And dance until he*
> *Wears away.*

"Are you certain he came here?" Ginny asked. "I thought everyone in these parts knew about the curse."

"Aye, 'tis well known indeed," Granny Nora said. "But youth is headstrong and makes its own rules. He heard that one clever and quick enough could make his fortune if he caught the gold that fell from the Dancing Men's sporrans as they danced about the glen."

"And any foolish enough to gather that gold until dawn would be forced to dance their lives away for an eternity," Ginny said with a sigh. "And you're certain he didn't fall victim to bandits?"

She cast a cautious glance about the glen at her own suggestion. Ballyben had a reputation as the haunt of desperate men, for just over the summit, it gave them quite a view of the moor road as well as the merchants and tinkers who used it to travel through the kingdom of Keltora.

"Haven't seen any bandits about these parts in months since our good laird MacAnle rousted and hanged a large quarter of them last autumn," Granny Nora replied.

"So which stone is he?" Ginny asked and studied the circle once more.

Granny Nora shook her head and spread her fingers in a futile gesture. "I don't know. You being one of the mageborn, I thought you could tell."

Horns, Ginny thought, refraining from voicing a stronger epithet. Bad enough that folk were wary of her kind without attributing greater powers to them than they possessed. Ginny came into her mage power at the proper time in her life, but she had studied the use of magic much later. And in spite of getting that training from Manus MacGreeley before he met his end on a bandit's blade, she knew there was so much more she needed to learn.

"All right," she said. "Go back to your cottage, and I'll see what I can do."

"I've no gold to pay for your services . . ."

Ginny waved a hand. "I'll gladly accept a fresh loaf of bread and any old bones you can spare for the dog," she said.

"Thank ye," Granny Nora replied. Without another word, the old woman hurried down the path, eager to be out of the glen before nightfall.

Ginny waited until the old woman was well out of mage hearing before calling, "Manus?"

"I'm with ye, lass," came the ethereal reply. A tag of mist broke free to swell before her in the shape of a tall, handsome man with merry eyes full of mischief. Manus MacGreeley grinned as his incorporeal form became visible. He had not been of this mortal world for several years, though that did nothing to deter him from staying around to make a nuisance of himself.

"So you heard?" Ginny said and started around the circle of stones, glancing at each in turn.

"Aye," Manus said, trailing after her. "The lad was foolish not to keep one eye out for the dawn."

"His eyes were more likely filled with gold," she said.

"And just what does the old woman expect us to do for her? Once the lad became part of the circle, he's bound to its dance for as long as his stone stands among them."

"Maybe," Ginny said. "You do know how the Dancing Men came to be, don't you."

"Aye," Manus said. "Back before the Great Cataclysm when the Old Ones still roamed among mortal men, a foolish pack of wealthy lads full of their manhood and heather ale came staggering upon a ceilidh in this glen. 'Twas no ordinary feast, but the wedding bonds of a Seelie lass and her Seelie lord. The lads blundered into the merriment and soon turned it to chaos. They offended the Seelie lord and his guests by throwing gold at the revelers. In anger, he asked them to leave, but they refused, dancing about the glen like madmen. And when they dared to drag his lovely bride into their drunken revels against her will, the Seelie lord lost his temper and put his curse on them. Stone-hearted and stone-headed they were, and stone they would be, except between the dark hour and the dawn when they would be forced to dance for an eternity, and any man unwise enough to join their mad revel in search of the gold that fell from their sporrans would be doomed to join them."

"Your sort of revel, I imagine," Ginny said with a smile, but Manus politely ignored her. He had been full of the heather ale when he met his own death.

"So what do you plan to do?" he asked instead.

"Wait until the dark hour, I imagine."

"This is no safe place for a lass alone," Manus said with a glance toward the forest of tall thick pines that ranged the lower levels of Ballyben. "In spite of what Granny Nora says, bandits do like to hide in this glen because folk think it's haunted as well as cursed."

"I can take care of myself," she assured him.

"I'm sure ye can," he said, "but what makes ye think ye can free old Nora's grandson?"

He followed as Ginny stepped out of the circle and found herself a flat enough place below a hummock and just out of sight of the stones. There, she lay out a blanket she had bundled across her back for the journey. She opened her pouch to have a bit of the bread and cheese she had brought along and seated herself there to enjoy the simple fare. Thistle knew that food was about to be consumed and rapidly bolted toward her to beg for a share.

"There was another story I heard when I was small," Ginny said. "It was about a lad of lowly means who loved the daughter of a laird, but in order to win her father's consent for her hand, he had to find his fortune. And the lass had a nurse who told her about the Dancing Men and their scattered gold."

"And she told her bonny lad, aye?"

"Of course," Ginny said, popping a bit of cheese in

her mouth and handing another small chunk to Thistle, who in true terrier fashion forgot to chew and nearly choked himself in the bargain. "Lovestruck lads and lasses always practice such foolishness in these tales. At any rate, the lad went out and was collecting the gold, but alas, he fell victim to his own greed."

"So what did the lass do?" Manus asked.

"At her nurse's suggestion, she came up here and waited until the dance began, and when she saw him passing by among the men, she seized him and dragged him from their ranks and fled into the woods, clinging to him for dear life, to wait until dawn. He was saved, they eloped, end of story."

"So you plan to wait for the dark hour and drag Granny Nora's lad from the circle and elope with him, aye?" Manus asked with a teasing grin.

"Sometimes I wonder why I bother sharing anything with you, Manus."

"I amuse you," he said.

"Not by half," she said and drew her shawl about her to wait for the dark hour. "Will you keep watch while I sleep?"

"Gladly, lass," he said and sank to the ground at her side. "Enjoy your dreams."

"Thank you," she said and lay down on the blanket, hoping the weather would stay fair.

And it did, though there was a bit of a chill, but she managed to sleep a while until Manus roused her with a whisper.

"Ginny," he said. "It's time."

She opened her eyes to find the world bathed in shadows under a gibbous moon. A moor owl's lonely trill echoed across the glen; a haunting sound most worthy of the moment. Ginny barely got herself off the ground and drew up her blanket when she heard Thistle growling. The moor terrier stood on the hummock with hackles raised on end as he glared up the mountainside. Ginny crawled up to sit beside him and study the glen.

The gray stones were starting to tremble and shiver

like so many stalks of grain in the wind. Yet the world was a still place, and from somewhere, Ginny heard an ethereal tune begin to play. A reed whistle's breathy whine broke into a jig. She watched as the stones of the circle began to sway in time with it.

Then, one by one, the stones unfolded from their repose on the ground, growing tall and erect and becoming young men kilted in the ancient style with nothing but their plaidies and leggings. Their skin was gray, blotched with bits of faded green washed milky under the wispy light of the moon. Slowly, they began to move about in an irregular circle, their movements stiff and jerky like those of a wooden puppet.

Thistle snarled and crouched as though he might leap at them. "Wheesht!" Ginny said softly, not wanting to break the spell. Besides, she doubted men of stone would care what bit them, but she laced fingers through the moor terrier's shaggy rough coat and pushed him down to keep him from charging.

The lumbering jig picked up its pace, and the men began to move more freely. They flung their arms about, and set their plaidies twirling, and Ginny could see the glitter of gold as it was flung from their sporrans while they danced.

She ordered Thistle to stay, not that he was apt to obey her, and moved cautiously closer, Manus still at her side. His spirit watched the circle as anxiously as she until at last, she saw that one of the men looked much younger than the rest, and that his skin, though pale, was not terribly gray nor blotched with green.

Aiden, she thought and motioned toward him. Manus glanced at the lad and nodded.

Ginny kept eyes on Aiden as he lumbered about in the clumsy dance of one unused to such skill. Closer she stepped to the circle, readying the blanket in her hands. She watched him going around until he came just abreast of her, and with a shout, she threw the blanket over him and pulled it about him like a net.

He gave a cry of dismay and tried desperately to con-

tinue the dance, but Ginny threw her weight into the
effort, using the blanket to drag him out of the circle
and toward the trees. He struggled to escape the blanket's grasp and hers, only to fall on his back. Ginny kept
a firm hold of the blanket, grateful that the forest was
downhill of the mad revels, and quickly dragged him
into the stand of dark pines. And even then, she kept
dragging him until they were well away from the wheez-
ing jig of the reed whistle.

"Leave go, leave go!" he cried as she hauled him into
a clearing and turned toward him to catch her breath.
Neither Thistle nor Manus had followed, and indeed, mage
hearing revealed the faint baying of the moor terrier who
had apparently scented some prey in her absence. And
like as not, Manus would be on Thistle's heels in a futile
attempt to bring him back. She shook her head. There
were more immediate matters to attend just now. She
seized the young man's shoulders an shook him.

"Aiden!" she said, using the fact that he was tangled
in the blanket to help pin him. "Listen to me! Listen to
your name! You are Aiden and not one of the Dancing
Men of Ballyben. You are Aiden, and have no need of
faery gold that fades with the sunlight!"

"Leave go!"

"Aiden!" she repeated, knowing that sooner or later,
his name had to register.

At last, his struggles against the cloth slowed, and his
breath became ragged sobs, and only then did Ginny
dare to draw the blanket away and whispered, "Solus."
Mage light of pale blue flickered to life overhead, illuminating the thin young face of a lad barely old enough to
have gained his manhood plaidie. Pale eyes blinked up
at her.

"Are you a bogie maid?" he asked.

"Hardly," she said with a smile. "But I am mageborn.
Now your Granny Nora is worried ill about you, so I'd
best get you back down to the village. . . ."

"Not so fast, lass," a voice hissed from the dark, and
Ginny gasped when she suddenly felt a length of steel

laying across her shoulder just far enough to give her a glimpse of the first few inches. She froze, not daring to move, for mage flesh was as mortal as any, cursing to think she had let her guard down after boasting of her ability to look after herself.

"So what have we here?" the man said gruffly. "A maid and her lad wandering about in the dark. That's a foolish thing to do, you know. There are bandits about these parts, aren't there, lads?"

Crude laughter echoed through the trees. Ginny let her eyes flick sideways, giving her a better view. Four men stood about in the dark, surly men wearing common plaidies and bits of old leather armor that had seen better days.

"What do you want?" Ginny asked cautiously.

"Well, you don't look as though you've got much more than yourself to offer," their leader said. He had a grizzled beard, and a scar slashed one cheek with a puckered crescent that had been badly stitched.

"Who are you?" she said.

"They call me Dall," he said, then gestured to the others. "Their names won't matter. I get first call on you, and by the time I'm done . . ."

Her stomach tightened, especially when Aiden shot up from the ground with some misguided notion of gallantry and threw himself at the bandit. Dall merely jerked out of range, the blade deserting Ginny's shoulder, and with a shout of rage, the bandit struck at the lad with a heavy fist. She heard a resounding thwack that knocked Aiden back into the nearest tree and crumpled him to the ground. Dall sighed and glanced at Ginny once more . . .

. . . and cursed when he saw her raise her hand and whisper *"Loisg!"*

Mage fire flared about the hand, and with a shout, she tossed it at him. He gave a cry and backed away as the magical flames flew at his face, stumbling in his attempt to avoid their burn. Ginny used that moment to leap to her feet and started running up the side of the mountain toward the glen.

At once, the men were after her, shouting threats of what they planned to do when they caught her. It was a struggle to take the rise at a run, but she knew she had to keep going. Behind her, the bandits led by Dall pressed on, taking the slope a little slower under the burden of leather armor and weapons.

If she could just get to the circle above before they stopped her . . .

She continued to rush up the hill in the dark when she heard the twitter of the reed whistle gibbering the strains of that unearthly jig. Ginny fled toward the sound, and as she ran, she sensed the presence of mage essence on the air around her.

"Ginny, are ye all right, lass?" Manus said as he appeared at her side.

"No time," she said between gasps for air. "We've got company."

Manus glanced down the hill into the thin edge of the pines and said, "So I see, lass. Is there a reason you're leading them this way?"

"I thought they'd like the view," she sputtered indignantly, pushing on though her lungs ached from the effort. She struggled over the uneven ground, and she could hear the bandits getting closer, could hear their rough breathing at her back.

Ginny stumbled over the hummock and found herself at the lower end of the circle of Dancing Men. They continued to cavort around, oblivious to her presence or that of the moor terrier who suddenly came leaping after her with high-pitched barks of glee. She ignored Thistle and raced on into the circle of men. The ground at their feet was littered with what looked like gold, but mage eyes could see that it was naught but the glitter of shiny stones.

Still, it would serve its purpose, she felt sure as she headed for the center of the revels and turned back toward the four figures racing over the heather on her heels.

"What in the name of Cernunnos!" Dall said.

"Horns, look at the gold!" one of his companions cried and swiftly, the man dove into the dance, trying to capture the glittering faery coins. But there were so many of them scattered about, he could never carry them all. He shouted for his companions to come help him, and the other two raced into the revels, following the Dancing Men as they twirled and leaped and sent more of their strange coins skipping across the ground.

Only Dall held his place, glowering at Ginny where she stood in the center.

"Damn you, mage!" he hissed. "You'll pay for what you've done to them!"

He charged into the circle, brandishing his long dirk with an angry shout. The cry was quickly countered by another as Manus suddenly swelled out of the ground in the path of the raging bandit. But Dall was going too fast to stop and marvel at this newcomer. That, or he knew from experience that mageborn spirits had no power to cast spells in death. He passed through Manus, who gave a startled cry. Ginny backed away, only to stumble over the uneven ground and fall.

At that point, Thistle decided to add his opinion to the disagreement. Dall was still rushing toward Ginny when a small furry bundle of fury gave a savage snarl and snapped at the bandit's heels. The distraction did nothing to deter him. With a shout, he kicked at the moor terrier, sending Thistle sideways with a yelp of pain.

How dare you! she thought in anger, her hands scrabbling at the ground and coming away full of the glittering stones. With a shout, she threw them at Dall's face. He raised his hands and caught a few and paused.

"Gold," he muttered, entranced by the sight.

Ginny got her feet under her and rose as Dall continued to stare at the false coins in his grasp. Then his eyes strayed to the ground, and like a man possessed, he reached for more of the faery gold.

"That's right," Manus said, his voice taking on a hollow sound like the wind. "A man who is quick and clever can claim a fortune if he so desires."

Almost mechanically, Dall began to clamber about, gathering the gold as his companions did. Within moments, he was caught up in the staggering dance, following the Dancing Men around the circle of Ballyben.

"I think you'd better go now, lass," Manus suggested. "Looks like it's going to be a long night for these lads."

She nodded, catching up the moor terrier and heading for the woods, making her way to the place where she'd last seen the lad. Aiden was sitting up clutching his head. She sat down with him, making certain he'd suffered no more than a tender lump before encouraging him to lie down and sleep while she waited for the night to wear away. Just before the break of dawn, she left Aiden asleep in the forest and with Thistle at her heels, she crept back up the mountain to the glen.

The dance was starting to wane. She found Manus sitting on the hummock, smiling with wicked delight. As she sat beside him, she could see Dall and his companions still stumbling about the circle like drunkards, wearily chasing the gold that would never really be theirs to spend.

Should I help them? she wondered. There was still time. She could fetch the blanket and come back up here and set them free. . . .

But then she thought of those they might have caused harm, and of what they would likely have done to her and the lad. How many bones rested in secret graves because of these greedy men? The mercy that tried to seize up her heart quickly fled when she pondered their wicked deeds.

So she watched the sun rise over Ballyben, and as the first rays washed pale light across the bandits and the Dancing Men, they took a last step, sank to the ground, and became a circle of irregular stones once more.

Manus fled with the dawn, returning to his cairn on the moors about Tamhasg Wood as was his geas. Ginny sat on the hummock a little longer, then rose and walked the circle one last time. Thirty-five stones now stood about the glen. One less and four more than before, she thought wryly. A worthy end for unworthy men, as Manus would say.

She sighed, and gathering the scattered remains of her gear, she headed back into the woods to awaken Aiden and take him home.

SALT AND SORCERY

Elisabeth Waters and Michael Spence

As a number of contributors to these volumes will tell you (Diana L. Paxson and Susan Shwartz come to mind, among others), academia can be a fantasy world unto itself, with senior faculty more fearsome than any dragon and the longed-for "sheepskin" more elusive than the Golden Fleece. Sometimes you'd swear the only way you could survive it was by magic of the highest order.

Elisabeth Waters, as regular readers of this series know, is my secretary. She has sold many short stories and one novel, *Changing Fate*, and she is now working on another novel. She and Michael Spence met when they were 17 and in high school in Charlottesville, Virginia. They became friends, and he introduced her to science fiction. Separated by college in different states, grad school in different time zones, and her moving to California after finishing her Master's degree, they didn't see each other for twenty years, until the 1997 Worldcon, where they found that their lives had taken parallel paths through music, church work, computers, and SF and fantasy. They started talking and soon moved on to collaboration.

While Elisabeth was developing her talents as writer and amanuensis, Michael was editing study Bibles and assisting Bible translators for a major religious publisher, writing encyclopedia articles for another, and creating corporate and foundation grant proposals for a prominent medical school. Ultimately he and his wife, Ramona, moved to Dallas, Texas, where he is working toward a Ph.D. in Systematic Theology. By the time this sees print, we expect he will have passed all his Senior Ordeals—sorry, comprehensive exams—and will be hard at work on a dissertation currently entitled "Author and Reader-based Hermeneutics for Imaginative Literature as an Aid to Analyzing Popular Worldviews, with a Focus on the Fiction of Harlan Ellison." (And you thought sf titles in the sixties were long and rambling.) The title does, however, provide an easy way to tell his seminary friends from his science-fiction friends; the former ask, "Who's Harlan Ellison?" and the latter ask, "What's hermeneutics?"

Collaboration is a fascinating process, especially for any outsider who happens by during the necessary discussions. So much of a writer's work is done inside his or her head that one has no understanding of the process until it has to be put into words; when one overhears conversations that start with, "We have to give Melisande a reason to want Stephen to pass his Ordeal" and progress to, "Wait a minute, I'm giving her reasons for homicide."

Michael and Elisabeth wish to dedicate this tale to Ramona, who with faith and long suffering has endured the years of watching her husband preparing for major examinations. I'd say watching anyone collaborate by computer qualifies Ramona for instant canonization without even waiting the fifty years which ordinary saints need to qualify for naming to sainthood.

Melisande was lying on the sofa in the living room of the tiny apartment she shared with her husband, Stephen, reading one of his grimoires, when she heard the angry voices in the hallway. One was her husband's; the other his little sister's.

"It's bad enough I'm constantly being compared to my prodigy of a sister, but— How *could* you, Laurel? You're only seventeen years old, for heaven's sake!"

"It was easy, Stephe —something you'd find out if you could be bothered ιɔ try it yourself!"

"Well, I'll have to try it now, won't I?" Stephen's voice was as disgusted as Melisande had ever heard it. She shoved the grimoire under a sofa cushion and went to open the door.

"Hello, Melisande." Stephen stood there frozen in place, his hand grasping at empty air that seconds before had contained a doorknob. "Did you hear us coming?"

"I should think half the building did," Melisande replied. "You know how thin the walls are."

"They are?" Stephen was looking distracted as he entered their apartment. Laurel followed him in tight-lipped silence. "I didn't know that."

We've been living in married student housing for the past four years, and he's never noticed his surroundings. Melisande sighed.

"So," she said brightly, "how was your grandmother's birthday party? Was she angry that I couldn't make it?"

"No," Stephen said. "I told her you were sick, and all she said was 'what a shame' and she hoped you'd be better soon. That's not what she's angry about."

"Angry is a rather mild word," Laurel said. She turned to look at her sister-in-law. "I'm really sorry, Melisande; I had no idea she'd do this."

"Do what? What made her angry?" *This time, that is.* Stephen and Laurel's grandmother ruled the family with a style that could only be described as despotic. One of the strongest wizards of her generation, she was rarely argued with. Certainly not by her children, who, since strong magical talents tended to skip generations, hadn't the power and thus the status and influence to match her. Her son's Talent wasn't even enough to keep him off of the more disagreeable committee assignments at the college where he was tenured faculty. Stephen and Laurel, on the other hand—ah, they were the strong ones. They were expected to do Great Things.

"Laurel passed her Senior Ordeal," Stephen replied glumly.

Melisande was struck dumb for a moment. Stephen had been studying for his Senior Ordeal for the past eight years, ever since he had taken his Junior rank at nineteen, and didn't feel ready to undergo the tests yet. And Laurel had passed it at the age of seventeen? Melisande quickly pulled herself together and let her manners take over. "That's wonderful, Laurel! Congratulations! I didn't even know you'd passed your Junior one."

Laurel shrugged. "I hadn't. I took them together."

"Isn't your grandmother proud of you?"

"Oh, she's *thrilled* with Laurel," Stephen snapped. "But now she's furious with me. She says that if Laurel can pass Senior this easily, there's absolutely no excuse for my 'shilly-shallying.'"

Melisande could see a certain logic to that viewpoint. She'd been wishing he'd hurry up and pass the Ordeal for the past three years. Until he did, they were stuck in married student housing, and Melisande wanted more out of life. She wanted to be able to travel and come home to a real house. She wanted to decorate and have things of her own. She wanted a garden. She wanted to entertain and be involved with the outside world.

She wanted to stop drowning in Stephen's *books!*

"It's not as if you *couldn't* do it," Laurel told Stephen impatiently. "You passed your Novice Ordeal before I was even born, and I didn't pass mine until I was twelve! You could have passed the Senior Ordeal ages ago!"

Stephen just glared at her.

"So Grandmother put a *geas* on us," Laurel explained, turning to Melisande. "I'm compelled to stay with Stephen and tutor him. Until he passes his Ordeal, neither he nor I will be able to leave the campus." She looked apologetic. "I'm afraid you're stuck with me for a while."

Melisande looked around the apartment. In addition to the room they were standing in, there was the bedroom she and Stephen shared, which barely held their bed and clothes; a kitchen into which only one person could fit at a time; and an even smaller bathroom. And the apartment was made even more crowded by the inescapable books, which were crammed into any space Stephen could find for them, and piled high on every flat surface. She swore they were mating and reproducing every time her back was turned, like buckram-covered rabbits. "You'll have to sleep on the sofa, Laurel," she said. "I'm sorry, but there's just nowhere else to put you."

"I know," Laurel said. "I'm really sorry to be intruding on you like this. I guess Grandmother wanted to give us all lots of incentive."

"I think she's succeeding," Melisande said dryly.

"I'm going to my workroom," Stephen said. "I'll leave you girls to get settled in." He beat a hasty escape before either of them could stop him.

Melisande sighed. "Some weeks he spends more time in his workroom than he does at home. We won't wait dinner for him. And I'll have to see if I can find you some extra bedding."

"No need for that," Laurel said, lifting a travel bag from the floor beside her. "I brought a bed-roll, and now that I'm a Senior Wizard, I can wear a robe all the time, which usually keeps itself clean. I was planning to come back here and do some tutoring anyway; I'm still too young for most Mage assignments, and, besides, there's this guy—"

"A student here?" Melisande asked.

"Yes. His name's Edward, and he passed his Junior Ordeal not too long ago. If things get too crowded here, maybe I could stay with him—he's got a single in the main dormitory."

"Just how close are you and Edward?" Melisande looked sharply at Laurel.

"Just good friends," Laurel assured her. "Strictly platonic."

"How old is he?"

"Twenty."

"Then you are not moving in with him," Melisande announced firmly. "I'm sure his intentions are all that you say, but having you living in his room would be putting a bit too much stress on human nature."

"Maybe he can help us, though," Laurel said hopefully. "After all, he's studying for Senior, too; we could invite him to dinner a lot and discuss studies over the table—if that wouldn't be too boring for you, of course."

"Look around you, Laurel," Melisande directed. "What do you see?"

Laurel flopped on the sofa and scanned the room, then wriggled her hip and pulled the grimoire from under the sofa cushion. "Books. Lots of books."

"Right. Books. Now, first, you're not looking at a home, you're looking at a library. We may have half the knowledge of civilization here, but we don't have any room for entertaining. We can get you in, but only by Divine Providence and a shoehorn.

"And as for boring me—do any of them look like mine?" Melisande paced across the room, all three paces of it. "Hah! Where, if I had any of my own, would I put them? I've been reading Stephen's books for years. If I had his magical talent, I could probably pass that wretched Ordeal myself!"

Laurel looked up abruptly from the grimoire's table of contents and stared at Melisande. "That's it." Her eyes brightened. "That's *it!*" She jumped from the sofa and gave her sister-in-law an enthusiastic hug. "Melisande, you're an absolute genius!"

"What's 'it'?" Melisande said. This was a member of Stephen's family. And she was enthusiastic. For Melisande these added up to *lock up your sanity; we assume no responsibility for its loss.*

"The Spouse's Ordeal." Laurel spoke as if that explained everything.

It explained nothing, but it seemed to trigger everything. Melisande hadn't known there were any barriers inside her to break loose, until at that moment they broke. "Spouse's Ordeal? *Spouse's Ordeal?*" she repeated incredulously. She stepped back and ticked items off on her fingers. "I've lived in this drafty breadbox they call married student housing for four years, while everyone my own age graduated and moved on. I have to watch while my husband refuses to take any genuine steps forward in his program. On top of that, he comes home to tell me he's found yet another branch of study to fiddle around with! And now you tell me there's something that *they* call an ordeal?!''

She grabbed a stack of books off the nearest chair, flung them to the floor, and sat down. Instinctively, her sister-in-law knelt and held her while she sobbed. "Oh, Laurel, if he really loved me, wouldn't he be doing all he could to *get me out of here?* Do you know what his latest elective is? Fine arts! He's doing *sculpture!*''

Laurel was silent for a moment, then said, "It's not an elective; the category really is part of the program. I did music. You have to take some sort of art class; they think it broadens your horizons. I chose flute because it's the smallest and easiest to carry musical instrument I could get. I'll spare you my playing.'' She grinned. "Unless, of course, you have some mice or small children you'd like to have lured into the next parish.''

She sank back onto the sofa and patted the place next to her. Melisande, drying her eyes, sat down and looked at her suspiciously. "There actually is a Spouse's Ordeal,'' Laurel said. "It isn't in the catalog—I only found out about it by accident—but they came up with it years ago. From time to time there's a wife or husband who has either read all the books or heard so much of the studies that they have the academic knowledge, if not as much magical power. Do you have any, by the way?''

"A little bit,'' Melisande said. "Mostly it's the green thumb sort. My mother could grow the most incredible gardens. Sometimes I thought she talked with the flowers and trees about what would look pretty and they did the rest.''

"She might have been doing just that. What about your father?''

"Master fisherman. They said he could smell a storm two days off and that fish practically leaped into his nets.''

"Sounds like you're the daughter of two Strongs, then, which means you'd be a Weak Talent.'' Laurel's eyes widened in sudden realization. "And your children should be Strong, which would offset Stephen's tendency to father Weak. No wonder Grandmother was pleased when he married you."

Melisande thought Grandmother had hidden her pleasure quite well. "So why would it be a good thing for me to take the Spouse's Ordeal?"

"Two reasons: first, Stephen can 'help' you study for it, which will make him review all the things he should be studying; and second," Laurel grinned, "I'll bet he doesn't know this, but when they schedule your Ordeal, they automatically schedule his for the exact same time—so that he can't be linked with you and helping you magically."

"Are you telling me," Melisande asked slowly, "that when I take my Ordeal, Stephen has to take his, whether he 'feels ready' or not?"

"Exactly."

She whooped with delight. "Where do I sign up?"

"We'll go see his advisors in the morning." Laurel pulled a small pouch from around her neck and spilled the contents into her hand. Two identical amber spheres were strung on silver chains. Laurel hooked one around her neck and the other around Melisande's so that the amber rested in the hollow of her throat. "Just sit still for a moment and concentrate on your breathing."

Laurel chanted something in a language Melisande didn't recognize, and the amber grew warm, feeling as if it were melting into her skin. When Laurel finished, she asked, "What are these?"

"Link stones," Laurel explained. "They're family heirlooms; Grandmother and Grandfather wore them until he died, and now that I've passed Senior, they're mine. They'll let you draw on my powers. The spell also makes them invisible."

"Draw on your powers? For the Ordeal? Isn't that cheating?"

"Oh, it would be; you'll have to give it back before the Ordeal. But for Stephen's Ordeal, in addition to the theory, there's the practical part: discerning and dispelling illusions, dealing with elementals, magical defense—

that sort of thing. And we have to make him practice for that part."

"Domestic disasters," Melisande said, getting the point at once. "And I can't help him because I'm a poor helpless thing with no magic—do you know he actually called me 'the salt of the earth' once?"

Laurel giggled. "Men have funny ideas of what constitutes a compliment. Edward once said that my nose was 'like a Tower of Lebanon, overlooking Damascus.' I think he was quoting from the Song of Solomon. As for Stephen, if I'm setting up tests for him—or playing practical jokes on him—I'm not going to help him out. Besides," she said virtuously, "he's supposed to be learning to cope with this sort of thing on his own. But with the link stone, you'll have enough power to set up things that will drive him nuts, and you can probably come up with more than I can. After all, you know him a lot better. Just play around with the power, and see how it works for you. Have fun."

Melisande didn't even have to think hard. "I think Stephen's peaceful home life is about to become much less so. Oh, Laurel—you were kidding about the small children, weren't you?"

"Oh, yes. The use of magic against someone's mind or will without their consent comes under the heading of black magic, and we steer clear of it."

"Good. I admit I was tempted, for a moment. The walls here really are thin, and there's this kid two doors down—but no."

Laurel grinned. "Just Stephen. I'll leave you to plot disasters; I'm going to go tell Edward the news. I'll eat dinner in Commons tonight, so you don't have to worry about feeding me."

Melisande realized she had suddenly become the *de facto* mother of a teenage daughter. "Be home by ten."

Laurel cast her a startled look, and then smiled. "That's so sweet, Melisande. Nobody has worried about where I was in years."

Melisande opened her mouth again, and then smiled.

"That's so sweet, Melisande. Nobody has worried about where I was in years."

Melisande opened her mouth again, and Laurel said, "All right, ten o'clock. I promise." She dropped a shy kiss on Melisande's cheek and ran out the door.

Laurel was home by ten and asleep on the sofa by eleven. Stephen came in sometime after both women were asleep, but when Melisande woke up in the morning, he was sleeping beside her. He looked so vulnerable and innocent that she felt qualms about her plans, but the thought of another five years in that apartment gave her strength. Besides, he'd be happier once his grandmother was off his neck—and Laurel was off his sofa. She got up, dressed, and made breakfast.

"What's the noise?" Laurel asked, halfway through breakfast. "It sounds like singing."

Melisande tilted her head as if listening, although she knew perfectly well what the noise was. It was her first attempt in the use of power. "It sounds like the kitchen sink; it's been leaking for two months."

"Oh, that's right, I promised I'd fix it, didn't I?" Stephen looked up from his cereal. He frowned, listening. "It does sound different."

He got up to take a closer look, and stopped in the doorway. "There are drops of water moving around in the sink," he said, "and they are singing."

"If those are nixies," Laurel said, "you'd better get rid of them. Fast."

Stephen made a quick pass with his hands and muttered a short phrase. "There. That's stopped the leak."

"Weia! Waga! Woge, du Welle! Walle zur Wiege! Wagala—"

"But not the singing," Melisande said.

"Right." Stephen sounded distracted. "Laurel, would you be good enough to banish them?"

"I couldn't possibly, Stephen," Laurel said in one of the most unconvincing displays of innocence Melisande had ever witnessed. "It's your house, and they're your spirits. I'm just a guest. You'll have to do it."

Stephen grumbled through the entire twenty minutes it took him to find the proper tools and do the banishing, but he did it. He did not, however, finish his now-cold cereal before taking himself hastily off to his workroom.

"Do you think this will work?" Melisande asked, looking after his retreating form.

"Oh, yes," Laurel grinned. "I said you were brilliant, and I was right. What were they singing?"

"Wagner."

"Oh, my. It's a good thing that was a small leak. Imagine what the shower would sound like." That thought was enough to make both of them collapse, laughing, on the sofa.

"So, who are Stephen's advisors?" Laurel asked, once she had her breath back.

Melisande frowned, trying to remember, "I haven't met them, but I'm pretty sure their names are Logas and Sarras."

Laurel nodded. "That sounds right. Grandmother's first grandchild would get the Lord High Wizard, and Sarras works with him. She's nice; I had lots of classes with her. We'll go see her; I think she's more likely to appreciate our plan."

Twenty minutes later the two women climbed the four flights of stairs that led to the Lady Wizard Sarras' office at the top of the Gray Tower. The door was ajar, so Laurel tapped on it and stepped into the room. Melisande followed her reluctantly. Something felt wrong about this. Very wrong. Maybe this wasn't such a good idea. . . .

"Greetings, Alyssa," Laurel said cheerfully. Obviously she knew and liked the young woman standing by the window, wearing a pale blue robe with a dagger in a black leather sheath at her side. Melisande, however, could almost literally feel her skin crawling. Alyssa's smile was friendly, but it felt as if evil flowed from her in waves. Melisande was barely aware of the stone wall pressing against her back as she tried to sink through it.

"Laurel!" Alyssa gave the younger girl a quick hug, though some small part of Melisande's brain which wasn't screaming noted that Alyssa kept the side of her body with the dagger away from Laurel. "Congratulations; I heard you passed your Senior Ordeal."

"Yes, I did. Thank you." Laurel turned slightly. "Melisande, this is Alyssa, she's a Guardian. Alyssa, I'd like you to meet my sister-by-marriage—Melisande, what's wrong?"

Alyssa's eyes met Melisande's, and Melisande was suddenly sure that Alyssa knew exactly what was wrong with her, which was more than she did herself.

But Alyssa addressed Laurel. "She's Stephen's wife?"

Laurel nodded. "We're here to talk to Sarras about having her take the Spouse's Ordeal."

"Why isn't she taking the regular Ordeals?" Alyssa asked. "She's obviously a Sensitive."

"Who's a Sensitive?" A middle-aged woman in the dark blue robe of a Master Wizard entered the room. She looked straight at Melisande. "You are, obviously. What are you called?"

"Melisande." She could manage only the one word, but it was enough. It was an unusual name.

"Stephen's wife." Sarras identification was instant. "He never mentioned that your talent was so strong." She crossed to a cupboard next to the window, pulled out a wooden box, opened it and extended it to Alyssa. "Put the Blade in here."

"The last time I let go of it," Alyssa said between clenched teeth, "my own mother tried to kill me with it."

"I don't care if she disemboweled you and you're a walking spirit; put that Blade in this Shield Box. Now!"

Alyssa reluctantly removed the dagger from its sheath, and the evil filled the room like waves hitting a cliff. Melisande slid to the floor, barely noticing the tears flowing down her cheeks. Alyssa set the Blade in the box, and Sarras slammed it shut and put it back in the cupboard, which she then locked with a key from her belt.

She crossed the room to kneel beside Melisande and gather her sobbing body into her arms. "It's all right, child; it's over. It can't hurt you now."

Melisande wept helplessly on Sarras' shoulder, unable to stop. Fortunately Sarras didn't seem to expect her to. "Laurel," she said, "did I hear you talking about the Spouse's Ordeal?"

"Yes, Lady." Laurel sounded a bit subdued. "I don't know what's wrong with her; she's normally very calm."

"I can't take the Spouse's Ordeal!" Melisande sobbed. "I don't have any magic, and I'm not even a decent wife. If I were any good for Stephen, he'd have passed his Ordeal years ago. I should kill myself, and then he could marry someone whom he really loved, someone he'd want to be proud of him, someone whose opinion he'd care about—"

"Hush." Sarras put a hand lightly over Melisande's mouth. "You don't know what you're saying." She looked up and frowned at Alyssa. "Just how close did she get to the Blade?"

"She's been flat against the wall ever since she came through the door," Alyssa replied. "She never got any closer than she was when you came in. And it was in its sheath the entire time. You know I don't wave it around!"

"And even Stephen should have noticed this degree of Sensitivity in all the time they've been here—how long have you been married, Melisande?"

"Four years, Lady." Melisande swiped at her cheeks with the sleeve of her undertunic. Sarras handed her a handkerchief.

"So something just changed," Sarras said. "What was it?"

"Oh." Laurel sounded as though she wanted to sink through the floor. "The link stones."

Sarras twisted to look at her in disbelief. "Your grandmother's link stones? You gave one to Melisande?"

"Last night."

"Get it off her." It was a tone that Melisande wouldn't have argued with. Laurel hastily dropped to her knees and fumbled with the clasp. Melisande could feel the amber and chain drop away from her neck, but all she could see in Laurel's hand was a faint shimmer. Looking up, she could see a matching shimmer at Laurel's throat.

"Can you see the stones?" Sarras asked her.

"Sort of," Melisande replied. "I can see that something's there, but if I didn't already know what they looked like, I wouldn't be able to tell from what I'm seeing now."

"I'm really sorry about the Blade," Alyssa said, dropping to sit on the floor at Melisande's other side. "I had no idea you were a Sensitive; there aren't many on the campus. And don't worry about the things you were saying; the Blade makes most people feel worthless and suicidal."

Something from one of Stephen's books flashed into Melisande's head. "The Blade of Unmaking . . . did Laurel say you were a Guardian?"

"Yes, I am, and it is." Alyssa make a face. "I'm sorry you got hit so hard; most people have to touch it to be affected."

"And most of the people who touch it kill themselves with it," Melisande said. "I read that, but now I really understand why. It's horrible!"

"Yes, it is," Alyssa agreed. "I can feel it, too, but I'm used to it, so I can handle it."

"I wouldn't want *that* job," Melisande said fervently.

"Not that one," Sarras said, "but with your Talent, there must be a job that you should have."

"But I don't really have Talent," Melisande said. "I've just read a lot of Stephen's books, and the rest was the link stones."

"Ah, yes, the link stones." Sarras turned to Laurel. "Laurel, you've accomplished a lot in a short while, and I grant that you have a remarkable intuitive feel for wizardry—but Senior Ordeal or no, you obviously are not ready to handle those stones. Please take them to Lord Logas and have him put them into safekeeping for you."

Laurel nodded meekly. "Yes, Lady Sarras." She looked anxiously at Melisande. "How are you feeling now?"

Melisande leaned back against the wall, breathing evenly, closed her eyes, and concentrated. "I can't feel the Blade anymore, and I don't feel suicidal; I can tell where the link stones are, but I can't draw power through them," she frowned and raised her hands to her temples, "but it feels as though someone is trying to rearrange my head."

Alyssa gasped. "Control or influence without the consent of the other—that's black magic!"

"But that can't be right," Laurel protested. "Nobody wants to harm Melisande."

"Black magic may not be precisely what we have here," Sarras said quietly. "Is there a direction to that feeling?"

Melisande pointed without even thinking. "That way."

Laurel's hand brushed the top of her head lightly. "I've got it, Lady Sarras. I'll go check on it."

"Go, then, with caution," Sarras directed, "but don't forget to take the link stones to Logas."

"I promise." Laurel was on her feet and out the door before Melisande could protest.

"Come, Melisande." Sarras helped her to her feet. "We'll go into my workroom; it's shielded. Then we'll put some shields on you, as Laurel's little present seems to have blasted open any that you might have already had. Alyssa, I'd like you to help me, please."

"Yes, Lady." Alyssa stood up and went to bolt the outer chamber door before opening a door to an inner chamber. She stood back and waited for Sarras to enter first, then followed them in and closed the door behind them.

The inner chamber was circular and made of gray stone, as if the present tower had been built around an earlier one, which, Melisande thought, it probably had. It had a wooden altar in the center, with four candles burning on it, surrounding a box which looked like the one Sarras had made Alyssa put the dagger in. There were also several comfortable-looking armchairs arranged in a circle around the wall. Alyssa pulled three of them into a triangle, and they sat down.

Melisande sank gratefully into the cushions, feeling limp with relief and exhaustion. It seemed like days since she and Laurel had first entered the tower, although she knew it was still morning.

"So you've read of the Blade of Unmaking," Sarras said. "Tell me what else you've read."

Thinking that Sarras was simply making conversation to calm her down, Melisande began to describe how she had first started reading Stephen's books for lack of anything else to read, then become interested in the subject of magic, and before she knew it, she, Sarras, and Alyssa were deep in a discussion of the grimoire she had been reading the day before. Then she told them about Laurel's arrival and their plot to get Stephen to take his Ordeal.

"And how do you feel about Power?" Sarras asked.

"It was sort of fun while I had it," Melisande said. "Stephen had been promising to fix the leak in the kitchen sink for two months, but he didn't do a thing about it until this morning, when I made the drops that were leaking into the sink start singing."

"Do you think that was a legitimate use of Power?" Sarras asked.

"It was pretty frivolous," Melisande admitted, "more of a prank than anything else. I admit I was trying to force Stephen to use his Power, to get him ready for his Ordeal, but he could have gone on ignoring the leak—the singing was harmless and not very loud. I didn't want to disturb our neighbors."

"And if Stephen hadn't fixed the problem?"

"I would have waited until he went off to his workroom and fixed it myself."

"Or had Laurel do it?"

"It was my spell; it was my responsibility. That's why I started with something small, most of which already existed."

"Good enough. I can see why Stephen once used the word *salt* when telling us about you. You have a stability he lacks, and without it he would probably spoil like month-old beef." Sarras rose, went to the altar, and opened the Shield Box. She removed a cup from it and handed it to Melisande. "Hold this."

Melisande took it warily. It was a cylinder of hammered silver with a pattern of grapes and vines incised into it, about four inches tall and two inches in diameter. It felt pleasantly warm in her hands, like sunlight shining on them.

"What do you feel when you hold that?" Sarras asked.

"Love." Melisande said the first word that came into her head. "And light—it's as if all the light in the Universe flows through this cup."

Sarras nodded silently and lifted the cup from Melisande's hands, but Melisande could still feel its warmth.

"Alyssa?" Alyssa put out her hands eagerly, and Sarras gently set the cup into them. Alyssa held it reverently, obviously basking in its energy. After a few moments she rose and returned it to the Shield Box.

"Thank you, Lady," she said.

"You are welcome," Sarras replied. She handed Alyssa the key from her belt. "You can take the Blade back now, and would you see if Laurel has returned yet, please."

Alyssa nodded and left the room, closing the door behind her.

"Do you know what that was, Melisande?" Sarras asked.

"A kiddush cup," Melisande began, "used by the Jews for wine at festivals . . . but that particular cup," she looked up at the ordinary-looking woman in front of her and realized what she was seeing. "You're a Guardian, too, aren't you?" Sarras nodded, and Melisande finished, "and that's the Grail."

"And you've been sitting unnoticed in Stephen's shadow all this time." Sarras shook her head. "Didn't any of his professors ever meet you?"

Melisande shook her head. "Married student housing doesn't give much room to entertain, and I never went to the receptions. Too many people in a room at once make me nervous; it gets so noisy."

"Student wife activities?"

"I used to go to them, when we first came here," Melisande said, "but I haven't been in years. They're all in their late teens and early twenties, and I'm twenty-five. We just don't have much to say to each other anymore."

Sarras smiled. "Well, I think we'll be able to give you something more constructive to do from now on." There was a tap at the door. "Come in."

Laurel entered alone. "Lord Logas has the link stones, Lady," she reported. "And the rest was Stephen, making a present for Melisande. He's going to give it to her at dinner tonight. It's a sculpture, a bust of her."

"That would explain quite a bit," Sarras said. "Did he happen to mention how long he's been working on this project?"

"Three weeks."

"Three weeks that was supposed to be study time," sighed Melisande.

"And three weeks' worth of magical energy," added Laurel. "Just wait until you see it."

"I think I'd like that," Sarras said.

"You are welcome to join us for dinner, Lady," Melisande said, "if you don't mind eating off a plate balanced on your lap."

"That sounds like fun," Sarras said. "Thank you, Melisande; I would be delighted to join you for dinner."

She turned to Laurel. "Stand there." She pointed to a spot on the floor, and Laurel positioned herself there. "Melisande, you stand here," she said, pushing Melisande gently into position. "I'm going to put a shield on you myself, and I'm going to link it to Laurel's. And, Laurel, if anything tries to get across this shield, I want to hear about it immediately." Laurel nodded. Sarras walked around the two of them in a figure-eight pattern, chanting what Melisande was surprised to recognize as a very strong shield spell indeed. "That should do it," Sarras said. "I think it's safe for you to leave this room now, Melisande."

"That's a good thing," Melisande said. "I have to go make dinner."

"What about the Spouse's Ordeal?" Laurel asked.

"We'll talk about it tonight," Sarras replied.

Melisande spent the afternoon cleaning and cooking, but she found that by dinnertime she was looking forward to the meal, instead of feeling frazzled and exhausted. She even found time for a quick shower and a change of clothing.

Stephen came in twenty minutes before dinnertime, carrying a package, which he set carefully on the floor beside the sofa. Melisande greeted him with a kiss on the cheek and, wiping small flecks of marble from her lips, suggested that he shower before dinner.

"Laurel has seen me look worse," he assured her.

"I don't doubt it, but Lady Sarras is joining us."

"Lady Sarras! Laurel's dragging my advisors into this already?" Stephen gasped. "It's only been a day!"

"Just go shower, all right?"

Stephen was out of the shower in five minutes, which gave Laurel just time to use it when she dashed in ten minutes before dinnertime.

"Cutting it close, aren't you?" Melisande remarked. "What did you do, stop by to see Edward?"

Laurel blushed as she ran for the bathroom, while Melisande found a clean robe in Laurel's pack and passed it in when the water stopped running.

By the time Lady Sarras arrived, everyone was clean, properly dressed, and ready for dinner. After general talk over what Lady Sarras proclaimed to be an excellent meal, she said, "I've heard so much about your present for Melisande, Stephen, that I really feel I must see it."

Stephen looked profoundly embarrassed, but he picked up the box and handed it to Melisande. With some difficulty—*is this thing actually made of marble?*— Melisande lifted it out of the box. Laurel's description hadn't done it justice, not that Laurel had tried very hard to describe it. It was recognizably Melisande, but not the self she saw when she looked in the mirror. The face had a calm serenity Melisande had never thought of herself as possessing, and the smile looked almost angelic.

"It's beautiful, Stephen," she said, not knowing that the smile she gave him was the same as the one on the bust, "but I think it's much more beautiful than I really am."

"No," Stephen said positively. "It's a perfect likeness. It's exactly the way I see you." He gave a small, rueful smile. "When you're not feeling trapped, that is."

She caught her breath, and then she looked squarely at him, her disbelief suddenly tinged with suspicion. "You mean . . . you *really* know? You're not simply saying that because you think I might want to hear it?"

"If he didn't know before, he does now," Sarras interjected. The better artists become far more observant of their subjects in the process. That's one reason we look for them." She ran a practiced hand over the bust, keeping an inch away from physical contact with it. "This is indeed you, and it is indeed how he sees you. And now you will probably appear this way so often that others will see it, too. Do you have any idea, Stephen, what you've done here?"

"A special project for my sculpture class and a present for my wife."

"Does the phrase 'Law of Similarity' ring any bells?" Laurel asked pointedly.

"You make it sound like I'm making voodoo dolls," Stephen said. "Don't be such a brat."

"I'm afraid she's making a valid observation," Sarras said. "There is a great deal of magical energy in this." She smiled at him. "Obviously, you are ready for your Senior Ordeal."

Stephen opened his mouth to protest, but she continued before he got the chance. "Your Ordeal will begin at Terce one week from today, simultaneously with your wife's Spouse's Ordeal. Lord Logas and Lady Alyssa will judge yours; Laurel and I will judge Melisande's."

"But I can't be ready by then!" Stephen protested. "And you can't force Melisande to do it."

"Melisande has already started the process," Sarras informed him. "Alyssa and I examined her this afternoon, and we were quite impressed by how much she's learned from you. I expect both of you to do very well next week." She stood up. "Melisande, thank you for a lovely evening. Laurel, have her review Junior level and work on Senior; she got halfway through Junior today. Stephen, I'll see you for tutorial at Nones tomorrow; we should do a bit of review before your Ordeal—and I think," she said, looking again admiringly at the statue, "you'll find its direction interesting. Good night, all." She was out the door before any of them could stop staring.

Stephen and Laurel turned to Melisande. "Halfway through Junior Ordeal?" they said in unison.

"What did you do?" Stephen asked.

"Mostly we just talked about all of your books that I read," Melisande said. "And she had me hold a cup and tell her what I felt."

Laurel's eyes were wide. "She let you hold the—the cup?"

Melisande nodded. "Haven't either of you ever—?"

Laurel shook her head. "I don't rate that high in Sensitivity."

"What are you talking about?" Stephen asked.

"If Sarras wants you to know," Laurel informed him, "she'll tell you." She looked at Melisande. "I think I

have just enough energy left to do the dishes. Why don't
you two just go to bed?"

"Thanks, Laurel," Melisande said. "We'll do that."

She was in bed in ten minutes, four of which had been
spent clearing a place for the bust on her dresser so she
could lie in bed and look at it.

Stephen joined her a few minutes later. "It really is
beautiful, Stephen," she said, rolling over to give him a
hug. "Thank you very much."

"You're not mad about 'the waste of study time'?"

"That wasn't a waste of study time."

"You're thinking about what Sarras said about magical energy," he said, "but she's wrong. It wasn't magical
energy. It was love."

"I know." Melisande turned out the light and smiled
into the darkness, remembering a room of stone and a
cup of silver. "But what makes you think that magical
energy and love are different things?"

WEAVING SPELLS

Lawrence Watt-Evans

Lawrence Watt-Evans is the author of more than two dozen books and over a hundred short stories: science fiction, fantasy, horror, humor, etc. He won a Hugo for his story "Why I Left Harry's All-Night Hamburgers."

He was president of the Horror Writers of America from 1994 to 1996; has done comic books for Marvel, Dark Horse, and TeknoComix; and "meddled in various other things better left alone."

He's been happily married for more than twenty years—which in these days is close enough to fantasy for all too many people—and has two children and a cat.

His most recent novel is *Touched By The Gods*. This is his first appearance in *Sword and Sorceress*, although his work has previously appeared in *Marion Zimmer Bradley's FANTASY Magazine*.

Kirinna had been staring out the farmhouse window at the steady rain for several minutes, worrying about Dogal, when she got up so suddenly that her chair fell backward and crashed on the floor. Her mother jumped at the sudden sound, dropping a stitch. The older woman looked up.

"I'm going after him," Kirinna announced.

"Oh, I don't . . ." her mother began, lowering her knitting.

"You are not," her father announced from the doorway; he had risen at the sound of the toppling chair and come to see what had caused the commotion.

"Father, Dogal and I are supposed to be *married* to-

258

morrow!" Kirinna said, turning. "He should have been back home days ago, and he isn't! What are you going to do tomorrow, keep the whole village standing around while we wait for him?"

"If he's not here, then the wedding will be postponed," her father said. "You are *not* going to go running off in the rain looking for him—what if he comes home while you're away, and *you're* the one who misses the wedding?"

"Is it any worse that way? It's still early. I'll be back tonight, I promise."

"That's what Dogal said," Kirinna's mother said worriedly.

"Which is why you aren't going *anywhere,* girl," her father said, pointing a hand at Kirinna. "Now, you pick up that chair and settle down to your work." He gestured at the bowl of peas Kirinna had been shelling before her worries got the better of her.

Kirinna stared at him for a minute, then sighed; all the fight seemed to go out of her.

"Yes, Father," she said. She stooped and reached for the chair.

Her father watched for a moment, then turned to resume his own efforts in the back room, polishing the ornamental brass for tomorrow's planned celebration.

Kirinna fiddled with the chair, brushed at her skirt, adjusted the bowl—and then, when she was sure both her parents had settled to their work, she ran lightly across the room to the hearth, where she reached up and snatched her great-grandfather's sword down from its place on the mantle.

"What are you . . . ?" her mother began, but before the sentence was finished, Kirinna was out the door and running through the warm spring rain, the sheathed sword clutched in one hand, her house slippers splashing noisily through the puddles as she dashed through the village toward the coast road.

A moment later her father was standing in the doorway, shouting after her, but she ignored him and ran on.

She didn't need anyone's permission, she told herself. She was a grown woman, past her eighteenth birthday and about to wed, and the man she loved needed her. It wasn't as if she intended to run off blindly into the wilderness; she knew where Dogal had gone, knew exactly what he had planned the day he disappeared, a sixnight earlier.

A strange stone the size of a man's head had fallen from the sky during the winter and landed in Dogal's back pasture, melting a great circle of snow and plowing a hole in the earth beneath, and everyone knew that such stones were rare and of great value to magicians. When the spring planting was done and the wedding preparations in hand, Dogal had set out three leagues down the coast, to sell the sky-stone to the famous wizard Alladia, said to be one of the richest and most powerful in all the western lands.

He had teased Kirinna about how she might spend the money once they were married, and she had laughed and given him a shove on his way.

And he hadn't come back.

Some of the village children had teased her when Dogal didn't return, far less kindly than had her betrothed, saying he had run off with someone else—that he hadn't gone to Alladia at all, but to some rival's house, rather than stay to wed crazy, short-tempered Kirinna.

Kirinna knew better than that. Dogal loved her.

Other villagers had suggested that perhaps Dogal had angered Alladia somehow, and been turned into a mouse or a frog, or simply been slain. *That* possibility was far too real, though she couldn't imagine how poor sweet Dogal could have annoyed the wizard that much. She had been telling herself for two or three days now that Alladia couldn't be so cruel.

But then there was a third suggestion—that Alladia had decided to keep handsome young Dogal for herself, and had ensorcelled him. Kirinna found that theory all too easy to believe; certainly *she* had wanted Dogal from the first moment she had laid eyes on him, and Alladia was said to be young for a wizard, certainly young enough to still appreciate the company of men.

If the wizard thought Kirinna was going to give her man up without a fight, though, she was very wrong indeed—and that was why Kirinna had snatched her great-grandfather's sword. It was said that during the Great War, old Kinner had once killed a Northern sorcerer with this very blade; Kirinna hoped she could do as well with it against an Ethsharitic wizard.

Of course, Kinner had been a trained soldier, with years of experience and all the magical protection General Gor's wizards could provide, while Kirinna had never used a sword in her life—but she tried not to think of that as she marched down the road.

She had gone less than half a league when she paused to mount the scabbarded weapon properly on her belt; carrying it in her hand was tiresome and unnecessary. She settled the sheath in place and drew the sword, just to test it.

She was startled by how fine and light the blade was, how the weight of the sword was so perfectly balanced that her hand seemed to almost move of its own volition as she took a few practice swings.

She remembered to wipe it dry before sheathing it again; then she jogged onward down the road, trotting to make up the time she had spent trying the sword.

The rain stopped when she had gone a little more than a league from her parents' home, and the skies were clearing by the time she finally came in sight of the wizard's home.

She had left the ill-kept road for the rocky beach half-a-league back, scrambling across grassy dunes and wave-polished rocks. Alladia's house was perched on a bluff overlooking the ocean; as Kirinna watched, the sun broke through the clouds and painted a line of gold along the water that seemed to burst at the end into a shower of sparks that were the reflections in Alladia's dozens of windows.

It was the biggest house Kirinna had ever seen. She wondered whether even the overlord's Fortress in Ethshar of the Rocks could be larger. Three stories high, not counting a tower at one end that rose another two levels, and easily a hundred feet from end to end— Kirinna had never imagined anything so grand.

The main entrance was on the other side, she knew— that was one reason she had come along the beach. She had no intention of walking up to the wizard's front door and politely asking if anyone had seen a young man named Dogal; she planned to get inside that house and see for herself. She began clambering up the bluff.

At the top she heaved herself up over the final out- cropping of rock and found herself staring in a window, her face just inches from the glass.

She was looking into a wizard's house, and she half- expected to see all manner of monstrosities, but instead she saw an ordinary room—paved in gray stone, as if the entire floor were hearth, but otherwise unremark- able. An oaken table stood against one wall, with a pair of candlesticks and a bowl of flowers arranged on it and chairs at either end; a rag rug covered perhaps half the stone floor. There were no cauldrons, no skulls, no strange creatures scurrying about.

She hesitated, considering whether to find a door or simply smash her way in, and compromised by drawing her belt-knife and digging into the leading between win- dowpanes. A few minutes' work was enough to loosen one square of glass, and she pried at one edge, trying to pop it free of its mangled frame.

The sheet of glass snapped, and shards tumbled at her feet. She froze, listening and peering into the house, fearing someone had heard the noise.

Apparently no one had; the only sounds she heard were the waves breaking beneath her and the wind in the eaves.

She reached into the hole she had made, unlatched the window, and swung it open; then she climbed care- fully into the house.

The room was bigger and finer and cleaner than most she had seen, but looked no more outlandish from inside than it had through the glass—she had thought there might be some sort of illusion at work, altering the room's appearance when seen from outside, but if so, it worked inside, too. She crept carefully out to the center of the room and stood on the rag rug, looking around.

Doorways opened into three other rooms—one appeared to be a dining hall, another a storeroom stacked with dusty wooden boxes, and the third she couldn't identify. None were visibly inhabited.

She transferred her belt-knife to her left hand and drew her great-grandfather's sword. There should be guards, she thought—either hired men, or supernatural beings of some sort, or at least spells. In the family stories of the Great War, wizards were all part of the Ethsharitic military, and always had soldiers around, as well as their magic.

Kirinna saw no soldiers here—and for that matter, no magic. Breaking in the window might have triggered some sort of magical warning somewhere, but she no sign of anything out of the ordinary.

She also saw no sign of the wizard Alladia, or of Dogal. All she saw was a big, comfortable house.

She crept to the nearest doorway and peered through, half-expecting a guard to jump out and knock the sword from her hand; she clutched the hilt so tightly that her knuckles ached.

All she saw was a dining hall, with a big bare table and half a dozen chairs and a magnificent china cabinet.

Something thumped, and she froze; it sounded again, and she realized it was coming from the cabinet.

Was someone in there? Could Dogal have been stuffed in there, somehow? She moved nervously across the room, dashing a few steps and then pausing to look in all directions, until she reached the cabinet and opened one of the brightly painted doors.

A cream-colored ceramic teapot was strolling up and

down the shelf on stubby red porcelain legs, bumping against pots and platters.

"Dogal?" she asked, wondering if her beloved had somehow been transformed into crockery.

The teapot ignored her and ambled on until it tripped over a salt cellar and bumped its spout on the side of the cabinet; then it stopped, and somehow managed to look disgruntled as it righted itself and settled down on the shelf.

There was magic here, certainly, but nothing she could connect with Dogal; Kirinna closed the cabinet and moved on.

She made her way through room after room, from study to kitchen to privy, without being challenged or impeded and without finding anything else out of the ordinary except general displays of wealth and a remarkable number of storerooms. She began to fear that the house was deserted, that Alladia had fled somewhere with Dogal.

Finally, she heard footsteps overhead—the house was not deserted! Someone *was* here! She hurried to the nearer of the two staircases she had discovered and crept up the steps, sword still ready in her hand.

At the top of the stairs she found herself at one end of a hallway; she could smell incense and other, less-identifiable scents, and could hear an unfamiliar low rattling and thumping. Warily, she made her way down the hall, following the sounds and odors.

She came at last to an open door that was definitely the source; she crept up beside the doorframe and turned to peer in.

A woman was seated with her back to the door, working at a sort of loom—but a loom quite unlike any Kirinna had ever seen before, as it had odd angles built into it, and extra structures projecting here and there. The whole construction was wrapped in a thick haze of incense, but she could see levers, weights, and pulleys in peculiar arrangements. Although a high window let daylight into the room, three tall candles stood atop the frame, burning brightly amid mounds of melted wax, while the fabric being woven glittered strangely, as if points of light were being worked directly into the pattern.

Kirinna had sometimes heard people speak of magicians weaving spells, but she had always assumed it to be a metaphor, a description based on the intricate gestures wizards used in their conjuring; now she saw that perhaps it could be meant literally. This woman was surely Alladia, working some dire magic on her wood-and-rope framework.

The woman seemed oblivious to everything but her labors, and Kirinna stepped around the doorjamb, intending to march in and demand an explanation at swordpoint of Dogal's disappearance.

Instead she collided with someone, or something, that had been out of her line of sight and had turned to come through the door at the same moment she did. She had a glimpse of a bearded face and a thick homespun tunic, and then someone was grabbing her wrists, shouting, "*Hai!* Out! Stay out!"

Here was the guard she had been expecting. She tore her hands free and tried to raise her sword to strike, but the flat of the blade slapped into the underside of the man's arm and was harmlessly deflected; then his knee came up and caught her painfully in the belly, and she staggered back into the hallway. That dragged her sword's edge across the man's raised thigh, and he yelped in pain and stepped back.

Kirinna swept disarrayed hair from her face with her left hand, raised the sword with her right—then stopped.

The bearded man was Dogal. He was bent over, clutching his leg, where blood was seeping from a slash in his breeches; his hair and beard were somewhat longer than Kirinna remembered, and far more unkempt, but it was unmistakably Dogal.

"Augh!" Kirinna said. "She's ensorcelled you!" She lowered the sword—then raised it again.

Dogal looked up from his wound, and got his first clear look at her face.

"Kirinna?" He stared, his bleeding leg forgotten. "What are *you* doing here?"

At least he remembered who she was, despite being in the wizard's thrall. "I came to get you," she said. "We're to be married tomorrow—has her spell made you forget?"

"What spell? Where did you get a *sword*?"

Kirinna hesitated. Dogal didn't *sound* enchanted—just confused. And the wizard herself was still busily at work at the loom, ignoring the discussion just a few feet away.

"It was my great-grandfather's," she said. "From the war."

Dogal looked down at his ruined breeches. The blood had stopped; the cut obviously wasn't very deep. "It's still sharp," he said.

"My father cleans it every year during Festival," Kirinna said. She felt foolish explaining such mundane details while facing her beloved at swordpoint in a wizard's workshop, surrounded by incense and magic, but she could not think what *else* she should say.

"I hadn't forgotten the wedding," Dogal said. "I would have been there, really—at least, I hope so. We should be finished tonight if nothing goes wrong."

Kirinna looked at the wizard. "Finished with *what?*" she asked. "Is she tired of you already?"

At that the wizard glanced briefly over her shoulder at Kirinna before returning to her work; the face Kirinna glimpsed was rather ordinary, round and soft, with a large nose and wide mouth.

"*Tired* of me?" Dogal looked utterly baffled. "No, the tapestry will be finished, that's all."

Kirinna looked from Dogal to the wizard and back; then she lowered the sword warily.

"What's going on?" she said. "Why didn't you come home?"

She was not necessarily convinced yet that Dogal wasn't under a spell, but he seemed so normal, so much himself, that she was willing to consider it unproven either way, and the wizard's complete failure to intervene had her fairly certain that she did not know what was happening.

Dogal sighed. "Can we go somewhere else to talk?" he asked. "Somewhere I can sit down and get away from the smell of incense?"

"She'll allow it?" Kirinna asked, pointing the sword at the wizard.

"Of course she will; I just finished my turn at the loom."

"Go on," the wizard called, the first words Kirinna had heard her speak. "Go away and stop distracting me."

Now completely defeated by awareness of her own ignorance, Kirinna sheathed her blade. "Come on, then," she said.

A moment later Dogal and Kirinna were seated in one of the downstairs rooms, and Dogal began his explanation.

"When I came here to sell Alladia the sky-stone, I found the front door standing open, so I came in, calling out," he said. "She heard me and replied, and I followed her voice up the stairs to that workroom, where she was laboring at the loom. She looked half-dead from exhaustion, spending as much time repairing her own fumble-fingered mistakes as weaving new cloth, but she couldn't stop without losing the entire spell. She'd been working on it for six nights, with the help of her apprentice, but a few days before, he had gotten scared and run off—he'd even left the door standing open, the inconsiderate brat—and she had gone on without him, trying to finish it by herself. She was ready to collapse."

Kirinna, who knew Dogal well, suddenly understood. "So you stayed to help."

Dogal smiled. "Yes, of course. I brought her food and water, and she showed me what had to be done so I could work on it while she slept, and since then we've taken turns."

"Wasn't there some way you could have let us know?"

He turned up a palm. "How? I didn't dare leave for long enough to go home and come back—besides, I knew that our families might not let me return here. And she can't work any other spells until this one is completed—that's part of the magic—so she couldn't send a message."

"Would it really have been so terrible if she couldn't finish the spell?" Kirinna asked wistfully. "We were so *worried* about you!"

"It might have been. You must have heard the stories about spells gone wrong."

Kirinna couldn't argue with that; she had, indeed, heard stories about catastrophes caused by interrupted wizardry. The Tower of Flame, somewhere in the southern Small Kingdoms, was said to still be burning after more than three hundred years, and that had been simply a spell meant to light a campfire in the rain—a spell that had been interrupted by a sneeze.

"What *is* the spell she's working on?"

"It's called a Transporting Tapestry," Dogal explained. "When it's finished, touching it will instantly transport one to the place pictured." He added, "They're extremely valuable, even by the standards of wizards."

"I can see why," Kirinna admitted.

"She's promised to pay me well for assisting her, as well as for the stone," Dogal said. "Once it's done."

"So you're staying until then." It wasn't really a question; Kirinna knew how stubborn Dogal could be.

"Yes."

"Then I'll stay, too," Kirinna declared. She could be stubborn, too. "And I can help with the weaving."

Dogal frowned. "That's not necessary," he said.

"Yes, it is," Kirinna said. "I'm not leaving *my* man alone here with a grateful woman!"

Kirinna saw from Dogal's expression that he knew better than to argue with her, but he said, "What if it takes longer than we thought? Your parents will worry."

"And we'll have to put the wedding off for a few days," Kirinna agreed.

"Your parents *will* worry," Dogal said. "In fact, they may come here after us."

"We'll send them a message," Kirinna declared.

"Kirinna, if you go home to tell them, it's hardly worth coming back. . . ."

"I'm not going *anywhere*," Kirinna declared.

"Well, I'm not either, until the spell is done. And I already told you Alladia can't work any other spells. So how do you propose to send a message?"

Kirinna sighed. "Dogal, I love you, but sometimes you just aren't as clever as you might be. Didn't you explore this house while you were here?"

He simply stared at her blankly. It wasn't until she led him into the dining hall and opened the cabinet that he finally understood.

Kirinna's parents had just sat down to a late, lonely, and worried supper that night when a thumping brought her mother to the front door. She opened the door, and a cream-colored teapot promptly walked in on stubby red legs, a roll of parchment stuck in its spout.

The wedding was postponed a twelvenight, but at last Kirinna and Dogal stood happily together in the village square, speaking the ceremonial oaths that would bind them as husband and wife.

They were dressed rather more elaborately than Kirinna had expected, due to a sudden increase in their personal wealth, and the rather modest wedding supper that had originally been planned had become a great feast. Alladia had paid Dogal a full tenth of the Tapestry's value—more money than the village had ever before seen in one place.

And Alladia herself watched the vows: Kirinna smiled so broadly at the sight of her that she had trouble pronouncing the words of her promises to Dogal. The wizard stood nearby, slightly apart from the crowd—the other villagers all stayed at least a few feet away from her, out of respect or fear.

When the ritual was complete and she had kissed Dogal properly, Kirinna quickly gave her parents and Dogal's mother and sisters the traditional embraces, signifying that the marriage was accepted by all concerned, then hurried over to hug Alladia.

"Thank you for coming!" she said.

"Thank you for having me, and congratulations to you both," Alladia replied. She lifted a pack that lay by her ankle and opened it, then pulled out a wrapped bundle. "For you."

Kirinna blinked in surprise. "You already paid us more than enough," she said.

"I paid Dogal," Alladia corrected her. "This is for you."

The villagers had gathered around to see what the wizard had brought. Wondering, Kirinna opened the bundle and found a fine decanter of glittering colored glass. "It's beautiful!" she exclaimed.

"It isn't animated, like my teapot," Alladia said, "but I thought you'd like it. It's from Shan on the Desert—I bought it there myself."

"But Shan on the Desert is more than a hundred leagues from here!" one of the neighbors exclaimed.

Kirinna smiled. She knew what scene was depicted on the tapestry she and Dogal had helped create.

"She knows a shorter route," Kirinna said.

ENAREE, AN AZKHANTIAN TALE

by Deborah Wheeler

Deborah Wheeler, like many of us, juggles many interests: motherhood, a black belt in kung fu, living in France, and whipping the local library into shape. She has published two novels, *Jaydium* and *Northlight*, both from DAW—and both very readable—and many short stories. She is one of the very few writers to appear in most of the volumes of *Sword and Sorceress*.

In the lingering summer twilight, the sweet wild musty smell of plainsgrass danced on the breeze. Camels lay chewing their cud, their double humps round with fat. Roach-maned ponies stood head-to-tail along the picket lines, idly switching away the last flies of the day. Tents spread outward from a central fire, many of them ornamented with the clan emblem, the black-winged hawk. From the smaller cookfires rose the smells of dried camel dung and charred meat.

On this night, the *enaree*, one of the fabled eunuch-seers of Azkhant, had commanded that everyone, even the untried children, gather together to witness, to remember. . . .

Ythrae Daughter of Kosimarra Daughter of Shannivar stood watching with the other young women. Her gaze, clear as the sky after a storm, went to her father, Ishtotuch-chieftain, where he sat gray-faced and sweating in his chair of tooled camel-leather. From time to time, he stroked his left arm from shoulder to wrist as if to ease

271

a secret pain, a pain that came from no wound any man could see.

For the last cycle of the moon, the *enaree* had dosed the chieftain with foxflower and illbane; had painted dotted circles of protection in indigo paste around his eyes and navel; had forbidden him k'th and buttered tea; had in turns purged and fasted him. Now it was clear that ordinary measures had failed. Only the swearing of a false oath in the presence of a chieftain could resist natural healing. And only the *enaree* could divine the truth.

The wealth of a clan is not in its camels or armed might, the old poet had said, so many years ago his name was lost, *but in the vision of its* enaree. Yet behind their backs, people spoke of the "women's sickness" and called the *enarees* half-men.

Two young strong warriors, one of them Ythrae's childhood friend, Tenoshinakh, lowered themselves to the ground on either side of the chieftain and began drumming, not the passionate heartbeat of the dance, but slow, like the growl of a hunting cloud-leopard.

The flap to the *enaree's* tent lifted and the seer emerged. His hair was thin and unbound, his face bare as a woman's, the body beneath the ceremonial robes flat and spare.

He carried a bundle of salis branches and rolls of cured linden bark. As he circled the fire, he cast a handful of powdery stuff into the flame, causing it to flare and spark.

Ythrae knew the uses of the linden bark, for the enaree had used it to divine the cause of her baby brother's milk-fever.

The *enaree* halted before Ythrae. Her nostrils caught the odor of burnt orienna. She steeled herself to answer his piercing gaze. His eyes, bright under pale brows so shaggy the hairs curled and twined with his eyelashes, were a strange pellucid gray.

The *enaree* examined each member of their encampment. Some flushed coppery-red and a few hung their heads. *So guilt reveals itself for anyone with eyes to see,* she thought. *Where was the magic in that?*

The second time, the *enaree* carried two salis wands in each hand, waving them as he went. After a few moments, Ythrae caught the pattern, the way the freshly-stripped wood gathered energy and then smoothed it out.

The *enaree* walked the circle for a third time, shaking a fist-sized round box of fire-hardened leather from a camel's hump. From the rattling sounds within, Ythrae guessed it held Tabilit's Sacred Bones. She'd never seen them, only heard the same stories as everyone else, how the goddess in her compassion had cut off her own hand that the knucklebones, polished and preserved through the ages, might guide men to truth.

When the seer finished the third circuit, he withdrew to his tent, presumably to study the bones. The tribesmen let out their collective breath, for such a test might daunt the most stalwart warrior and there was no loss of pride in that. A few talked in low nervous voices, but no one ventured a joke.

Moments oozed by with infuriating slowness. The scent of orienna faded, a camel snored in the distance, a mother sat down to nurse her restive baby. At the picket lines, a pony squealed and made an abortive kick at its neighbor.

Ishtotuch looked paler and sicker on his chair. He slumped, then drew himself upright.

The *enaree* came back out of his tent. Ythrae expected him to make a solemn proclamation, point out the false-oath, or something equally dramatic. Instead, the seer approached her father the chief and whispered in his ear.

Ishtotuch pulled himself erect in his chair, though he could not entirely control the quaver in his voice. "There is no more to be done." He gestured to Tenoshinakh at his right side. "I will rest now."

Everyone sighed with relief, everyone but Ythrae. Natural healing, herbs and poultices, wards against evil, and therapeutic smoke; all of these could be understood and performed by most people, although they had special potency when an enaree did them. But to see falseness in a man's heart, to hear the music of the stars, to bridge the spiritual and material worlds—if that were not the special gift of the enarees, then all of their learning and sacrifice of their manhood was for nothing. This she could not believe, not when the stars called to her in her own dreams.

She started toward her father, but her path was blocked by people exchanging back-thumping hugs, others heading back to their own family groups. A camp dog got tangled in someone's feet and there was a good deal of squealing and shouting. By the time she'd pushed through, the *enaree* had disappeared and her father was halfway to his own tent, leaning heavily on Tenoshinakh.

"What happened?" she asked her father. "What did he say?"

With a stern expression, Tenoshinakh gestured at her that this was not the time to pester her father with questions.

"Don't you—" She bit off her words.

"No more concoctions!" Ishtotuch groaned. "All I need is rest."

Her father's words made sense. He looked exhausted as he sagged in Tenoshinakh's arms.

She would have to ask the *enaree* himself.

"Wait!" Tenoshinakh called after her. "Where are you going, you fool?"

His words drifted behind her, unanswered.

The *enaree's* tent was much like any other, tanned camel hide fitted over a frame of supple green salis wood. Others might be painted with the clan totem, the black-winged hawk; or pictographs of brave deeds in battle; or sometimes ornamented with trophies taken from the Geloni, who marched their armies and onager-drawn war carts across the steppes whenever they forgot what had always happened when they did. But this tent was dyed with blood-saffron in symbols that made Ythrae

feel both excited and restless. The door flap was tied
down.

She sat down where anyone who wanted to come in
or out would trip over her and composed herself to wait.

High sweet music, sweeter still than the tones of the
reed pipes, swept across the night sky. She reached up
and out to the stars, spreading herself across the heavens
as if her body were no more than whisper, a mist. . . .

Ythrae jerked awake. She was still sitting guard, her
hands already reaching for the bow and arrow case that
were not there, not outside the seer's tent. The *enaree*
stood over her. He stepped back, lifted the tent flap, and
invited her to enter with a minute tilting of his head.

Soft carpets, layers of them, covered the packed-dirt
floor and cushions lay piled for comfort. Though the
night was not cold, a brazier carved with the Meklavaran
Tree of Life gave off a curl of myrrh-thick smoke.

Ythrae followed the seer's invitation to sit on the
cushions, thinking that for all its privations, the life of
an *enaree* was not without pleasures.

The *enaree* lowered himself slowly, as if his joints hurt.
Ythrae's mother, Kosimarra, had told stories of him,
things which happened when she was a child, and still
older stories told by her own mother, Shannivar.

After greeting the *enaree* respectfully, Ythrae
broached the question of what had happened at the divi-
nation. Was there no false-oath in the gathering? Anyone could see that the ordinary signs of a guilty mind
had failed to reveal him? She had felt the magic gathered by the salis wands and she knew that orienna
smoke numbed the senses but sharpened the inner vision. And Tabilit's Sacred Bones—how could any mortal
man escape such power?

Or was her father's sickness simply a thing, like death,
that could not be cured?

"Your father will live or die as Tabilit wills." The
enaree's eyes turned opaque, like riverstone. "You see
much, Daughter of Kosimarra. You ask even more."

How it happened, she could not tell, but Ythrae found herself talking about the singing of the stars, the things she felt in salis wands and linden bark.

"If you were a boy—but you are not. I cannot give you this thing you ask."

Her father, Ishtotuch-chieftain, had made clear his desire for her to prove herself in a battle, marry, and raise lots of grandchildren. These were good things, proper things. Things she should want. Most of the time, and especially when she galloped her pony through the tall plainsgrass with Tenoshinakh at her side, she did want them.

Most of the time. But sometimes, when the stars sang their wordless songs, she wanted more. She had even thought of pleading with the *enaree* to teach her, or spying on him if he trained anyone else. But now, with the confusion of the night fresh in her mind, she was not sure the way of linden bark and orienna smoke, of reading the guilt of men and the entrails of animals, was what she wanted after all.

Gathering what was left of her dignity, Ythrae turned her back with deliberate rudeness and left the tent.

The next morning, Ythrae startled awake, momentarily confused. One of her nephews, her older sister's child, tugged at her sleeve and whispered.

"What?" she said with some gentleness, for she genuinely liked the boy. He was barely six, and the light which shone in his black eyes always had the power to soften her.

"Gran'da wants you. Mum says he's *pish*-ted."

Mum would probably have a word or two about that expression.

Ythrae slept in shirt and riding breeches, although she permitted herself a pallet on the carpeted floor of her mother's tent. She pulled on her boots and her long sleeveless vest, made of camelhair felt and embroidered with a stylized black-winged hawk.

The door flap to her father's tent was drawn half open,

not exactly an invitation. Within his tent, attended by his young men warriors, he lay in his low sling-frame bed, the wood black with age, its angles softened with furs. He saw her and struggled to rise, coughing. Tenoshinakh glared at her and bent over Ishtotuch, murmuring calming words.

There was only one reason Ishtotuch would summon her at this hour, in this manner.

That sexless, faithless *enaree!* He'd gone running to her father with a tale of how his only daughter wanted to become a eunuch!

Ythrae closed her eyes and prayed to Tabilit, to the father-god, to the spirits of the Geloni and the demons of Meklavar, to any celestial power that would listen. "I want grandchildren." Ishtotuch's words were hoarse with effort.

You already have them. You don't need them from me.
"Yes, Father-chief."

"It is time—you proved yourself in battle—so that you can marry."

"Yes, Father-chief."

"Tenoshinakh—go with her. The clan of the Wild Boar—two tens of years ago—raided our herds—"

"I know the story, Father!" *You have been waiting to use it as an excuse for another raid ever since I was born!*

"Hush, all will be well," Tenoshinakh murmured. "We will fight side by side, your warrior-daughter and I. Together we will drink the blood of the enemy at our wedding feast."

Ythrae opened her mouth, but no words came. Tenoshinakh took her arm and guided her out of the tent, respectfully facing the chief.

The camp already bustled with the morning's activity—heating water for barley porridge, milking the she-camels, making the day's fresh cheese, covering the pits of night-soil and digging new ones for today. A pack of puppies and barebottomed toddlers raced shrieking through the camp.

Tenoshinakh said, "We'll go together, just as we always said we would."

Ythrae, Tenoshinakh and three of their companions, young hotheads seized by glory-lust, headed toward to the country of the Boar clan. Gazelle bounded before them, and once they glimpsed a herd of snowbeasts moving ponderously across the rolling hills, their horns catching the sunlight. Dry winds brought the mixed aromas of late-blooming curlgrass, starflower, and shy convivial. Ahead, a stand of water-loving salis marked a spring. The ponies mouthed their bits, scenting water.

At the edge of the grove, prickles ran along Ythrae's scalp. She hauled on the reins to draw the pony to a walk, searching with her eyes and ears. Tenoshinakh glanced at her, puzzled, and motioned the others to halt.

They approached the spring, a circle of sparkling water. The scent, sweet and moist, swept through Ythrae. A breeze gusted and she caught another odor, acrid.

"What is it?" Tenoshinakh asked her.

"Can you smell it?" she said, frowning. "Something . . . bad."

He shrugged, and she saw that he could not sense as she did. All he knew was what his eyes and ears, his hunt-lore told him.

"Look!" One of the others pointed.

In the dappled shadows of the salis lay the half-mummified remains of two dogs and a pony.

Ythrae slipped from her pony's back and handed the reins to Tenoshinakh. One of the men muttered a protection against evil and another glanced at Ythrae with wide eyes.

No bones appeared to be broken. The ligaments had shortened as they dried, distorting the position of the bodies. Someone had removed the pony's gear, all except a noose of faded starflowers.

Someone else had died here, although he had been taken away, leaving no visible trace.

A child . . . a little boy . . .

In the darkness of her mind, Ythrae heard the wails of his parents and the bustle and clatter as they fled the grove.

It could so easily have been more dead, without the dog's warning.

On impulse, she put one hand on the dog's whitened pelvis. Tenoshinakh reached out to stop her, but too late. The moment she touched the bone with its scraps of leather-dry muscle, awareness jolted through her as blinding hard if she'd been struck by summer lightning.

"Poison?" Tenoshinakh asked. "Is the water poisoned?"

The acrid smell that was not a smell ran all through the spring. The body of the pony reeked with it. She'd heard of springs in the high alkali desert going bad and of streams fouled by disease, but this was neither.

With senses newly open, she heard the salis branches creaking a dirge. She went to the spring and squatted at the edge of the water, hesitating to touch it. A small bird fluttered close, its wings sending ripples across the surface. One tiny foot dipped into the water before she shooed it off. The bird settled on a nearby salis branch, scolding her. She watched, breath half-held, long enough to decide that contact with the water was safe.

She shoved one sleeve of her loose shirt above her elbow and plunged her hand into the water. It felt like ordinary water, cool and fresh.

She closed her eyes, fingertips still trailing in the water. Yes, there was a wrongness, a twisting. The substance remained the same, only the spirit had changed. Like a quivering in the marrow of her bones, she felt the water crying out to be itself again.

Not poison, but magic . . .

The acrid smell, she realized, was the arcane residue of burnt orienna. Someone—some human—had done this. She felt no trace of personality, only of festering anger.

Come to me! Sing to me! she prayed to the bright

unseen stars, to the goddess Tabilit. *Show me what to do!* The mournful song of the water ran all through her now, blending with the silent voices of the trees, the grasses, the birds overhead, the still bodies, the sorrow of the people who had owned them, the sharp grief of the parents of the child who had died, the restive thirst of the ponies.

As she closed her eyes, she felt herself drawn down into the spring, into something buoyant and misty. Her body swelled, her legs became a single powerful tail. Along her sides, gills sparkled like those of a magical fish. She opened her mouth and kept opening it, wide and wider. And as the mist-water flowed through her body, she felt its song shift, sadness bursting into joy. She had the strange sensation that she did nothing, that it was something beyond her, the stars or Tabilit or something beyond even them, working through her, gently guiding the water back into its true nature.

Guiding her to her true nature as well.

Something sang within her, a counterpart to the blended voices around her. She floated on the sound until it faded. Only then did she open her eyes.

She'd taken her hand from the water. She cupped a mouthful and sipped it. The water tasted delicious. She looked up, noted the men's horrified expressions, and smiled. "It's fine. The evil spell is no more."

"You purified the water? But only an *enaree* can do that!"

"Ythrae," said Tenoshinakh, fixing her with his level gaze, "is no ordinary woman."

Not anymore. Perhaps never again.

All the last few days, they found traces of recent human activity, the passage of a hunt, a trail of threaded pony tracks, a grove of false-carob stripped of its fruit. They made camp and broke out the last of their *k'th*.

Ythrae stretched out on her blanket. This far from home, she kept her bow and arrow case close to hand.

Her pony, still saddled, grazed on a long tether, rhythmi-
cally tearing up grass.

The stars still sang, but they no longer clawed at her
heart. *K'th*, as much as she had drunk this night, brought
mixed blessings. She didn't know what she would do
tomorrow night, when it was gone. If they fought hard
enough tomorrow, she'd be too tired to care.

She made a sign against an evil omen, calling on Tabilit, goddess of fire and hearth, but also protector of new
warriors. Tenoshinakh must have felt her stir, for he
reached out and touched her hair. Her body relaxed and
she drifted.

Not drifted, but walked. Not walked but floated, as if
the ground had gone misty. Her own body seemed to
be made of the same gauzy stuff, except for the amber-
gold jewel pulsing in her chest. She could almost see
through herself.

Ythrae found herself walking through a canyon,
although she could make out the contours of other hills
and other clefts. Gradually, she became aware that she
was not the only one on this path. Behind her—no, in
front of her—

She squinted, her shadow-eyes watering shadow-tears.
The image steadied, not a nightmarish scorpion shape
out of tales of Qr, but low and long, undulating with
power, its coat faintly mottled.

A cloud-leopard.

It gave no outward sign, but she sensed its awareness
of her. She walked behind it as naturally as if it had
been a black-winged hawk, her own clan totem.

On and on, the cloud-leopard strode at the same even
pace. On and on, she followed. The misty landscape rip-
pled past, one range of hills giving way to another until
she lost all sense of time or distance.

Ythrae's foot caught on an unexpectedly solid ripple
of cloud-stuff. Her feet dragged, gone suddenly heavy.
She cried out as she fell to her hands and knees. Sensation, like the chill of a summer's night, shocked through
her. The cloud-leopard hesitated, one paw raised in

midstride. Before she could scramble to her feet, the
beast disappeared in the fading hills.

Ythrae herself crouched on solid earth, gritty and
studded with rocks. Dark winds swirled around her and
her body quivered as if newly struck. Moon-sickness, the
old women called it, to wander from camp in her sleep.
The dream beast must have had a purpose in leading
her so far and alone.

Relieved that at least she'd had the sense to keep her
bow and arrow case with her, she straightened up and
oriented herself.

"Yi-yi-yi!" came a triumphant, ululating cry.

A pony neighed wildly. Battle-shouts echoed from the
direction of the camp. Ythrae recognized Tenoshinakh's
voice, hoarse with sleep. Pausing only long enough to
string her bow and notch an arrow, she sprinted
toward them.

Loose dirt scattered beneath Ythrae's boots. Air
whipped her braided hair. Fire seared her lungs. She
skidded into the darkened camp. Her eyes watered from
the smoke of suddenly doused embers. She searched for
a target, an enemy.

Nothing.

Shadowy forms moved too quickly for her to make
out, the rump of the last departing pony. Hoofbeats
faded in the distance. A groan came from the camp. She
knelt, found the man by moonlight. He was one of hers.
Her fingertips came away sticky.

"Caught—in our own trap," he whispered.

"How badly are you hurt?" She fumbled for her pack
of supplies, then realized it was still strapped to her pony
and her pony gone with the others.

"They left . . . us . . . for dead. All but . . . Teno . . ."

"Tenoshinakh! What have they done to him?"

"Taken." Death rattled in his throat.

Ythrae realized she could do nothing more for him.
She rocked back on her heels.

Taken could mean only one thing. She must act
quickly.

*   *   *

Tracking the Boar clan's raiding party was easy enough, even by moonlight. They rode brazenly, confident that they had left no one alive at their backs. The trampled tracks led Ythrae to a stream, its near bank churned with mud. She drank, whispering her thanks to the stars. They hung above her in their slow whirling dance, singing secrets she could not quite understand.

The sentries around the Boar encampment were few and distracted, their attention focused on the ritual clearly about to unfold. From the center of the camp came voices, slurred with drink, and the mingled smells of camel meat and k'th. To Ythrae, creeping from one hiding place to the next, the scene bore an uncanny resemblance to the enaree's judgment not so very long ago. As she watched, she realized that the young man now preparing for his initiation must be the son of the chief and that the man whose blood he intended to drink was Tenoshinakh.

Tenoshinakh sagged in his bonds, spread-eagled on a frame of green-cut salis. He lifted his head. Firelight glinted off his eyes. He snarled something, Ythrae could not catch what.

She lifted her eyes to the sky. It must be close now to the time when dawn and dusk lay equally far. Stars burned even more brightly now that the moon had set, swirling in their eternal dance.

Swirling . . .

A familiar, inarticulate longing rose within her, like a flame, like thirst. But she was no longer an untried child, dreaming of things she had no names for. Purifying the spring had changed her, left her more than what she was and less than what she must become. She had touched the spirit of the waters, she had heard the bones lament, she had cried out to the very stars . . . and they had answered her.

O bright stars, sing to me now!

Swirling . . .

Ythrae blinked in surprise. Her heart stuttered as first

one and then another star left their places. Downward
they streaked. Their beauty, like the dancing of rain-
bows, like the drumbeat of mountains, drew her. She
wanted to fling her arms wide, to let their music pierce
her to the core.

"Look!" came from the encampment. "The stars are
weeping!"

"An omen!"

Men scrambled to their feet to point upward and exclaim. The chieftain's son drew a long curved knife and
poised it at the base of Tenoshinakh's throat.

Acting on bold instinct, Ythrae jumped into the circle
of firelight. Men cried out in surprise; a few, including
some women, stumbled as they reached for their weapons. A dog yelped as someone tripped backward over
it. The chieftain shouted for the sentries.

Tabilit's Holy Thumbs! What had she gotten herself
into now? Ythrae touched her bow in its case slung over
her back, then realized she had not time to draw it.
Maybe a diversion . . .

Improvising wildly, praying that the Boar warriors
were too drunk and too confused to realize she was but
a single woman, Ythrae cavorted around the firepit.

" 'Ware!" she called in her deepest, most growly
voice. " 'Ware the anger of the stars!"

Screams of terror answered her. Only the enaree
moved to block her path. He lifted his staff, hung with
the skulls of snakes and rodents, with cloud-leopard
fangs and other jangling things.

So the eunuch thought to exorcise her, as if she were
a bad dream or a swarm of locusts? For an instant, her
eyes met his, glassy with *k'th* and orienna smoke, re-
flecting red.

" 'Ware! 'Ware!" Brazenly, she arched her back to
accentuate the contours of her breasts. "Or this will happen to you!"

The *enaree* fell to the ground, his arms and legs jerk-
ing as if pulled in a dozen directions at once. She
plucked his staff from his twitching fingers and swung it

over her head like the long pikestaff called *inata*, which
the Geloni used.

"Tabilit's Demon Daughter! Aieee, she's come to
seize us all!" a man screamed and rushed from the camp.

Not even the chief's son stood for more than a heartbeat. They bolted—some for their tents, others into the
night. Ponies squealed and hoofbeats disappeared into
the darkness.

"Cowards!" Tenoshinakh's voice sounded weedy and
hoarse. She rushed in, sliced through the strips of camel
hide binding him.

"Escape now, talk later!" She caught him as he staggered against her. "Pray they've left us a pony or two."

Two docile-looking beasts stood, tethers hanging loose
from their rope halters, lipping the last of the sheaf of
wild plains barley. By some miracle, Ythrae was able to
half-drag, half-hoist Tenoshinakh on to the unsaddled
back of the shorter beast. The second pony lifted its
head with a grunt of resignation when she vaulted on
board. Pulling on the lead line of Tenoshinakh's pony,
she booted hers into a rolling lope.

Beyond the circle of the encampment, the night took
on a strange, iridescent brilliance. She saw every stone,
every clump of curlgrass and starflowers. Every beating
heart, of hare or lizard or far-off sleeping hawk. Every
spring, bubbling over with delight. Behind her, scattered
men fought their way through drunken confusion.

At her side, Tenoshinakh sat easily on his pony, a
good man, an ordinary man.

Nothing lay between them but days of easy travel,
living on what she could shoot, basking in the summer's
warmth. She thought of Tenoshinakh taking her into his
arms, imagined pledging themselves with body and whispered words.

Thought of the children that would come, the raids
and heroic deeds he would ride away to, thought of endless circles of seasons blending together into a blur of
babies, camel's milk, weaving, the songs of men.

She pulled her pony to a walk.

"What is it?" Tenoshinakh said.

In a few hours, it would be light enough for him to make his own way. She handed him the bow and arrow case.

"I can't take that! What are you doing?"

"You need it more than I do," she said, turning her pony's head north instead of southwest, toward their own clan.

"What—Ythrae! Where are you going?"

"Go home. Don't follow me. Tell my father it has nothing to do with him." Tell the enaree—what? That she would learn the songs of the stars without him? It wasn't worth the breath.

He went on without her, wise enough to know that he must leave her to her own journey. He truly believed, after the manner of men, that once this madness had passed, she would come back to him.

Within a few minutes, the sound of his pony's hooves died to stillness. A bat flew overhead, diving and swooping, a tiny mote of warmth. She wanted to laugh, to throw her arms wide to the wonder of the night.

The days ahead of her would shorten and plainsgrass turn first golden, then brown, then gray. The pony would grow hard and lean. Perhaps she would meet families whose clan-tokens she had never seen before and bargain with them for another bow and a winter jacket of thick soft camelhair felt. One of the bright-cheeked girls might sell her a polished amber chip of the kind called Tabilit's Golden Tears, and she'd wear it on a thong around her neck because it made her think of the way her own heart had pulsated with the honey-gold color after she purified the spring.

At night, she would lie out under these very stars. Sometimes she would listen to the noises of the earth, feel the slow rotation of the skies, the air shifting along with its heat, the movement of plants, the quick percussive deaths of mice. And sometimes the stars would sing to her their stories, so filled with beauty that her heart would ache, even as it did now.

It came to her as she rode through the luminous night that perhaps she was not becoming an enaree, but something entirely else. Something the wide world had never known before, a woman who sang with the stars.

THE DAY THEY RAN OUT OF PRINCESSES

by Gail Sosinsky Wickman

Gail Sosinsky Wickman has been a newspaper copyeditor, English teacher, corporate newsletter editor, doughnut seller, and polka band performer. She has a B.A. in Journalism and an M.A. in English Literature. She's currently a stay-at-home mom, which gives her hours and hours of free time to write—and she says that if anyone buys that, she'll have sold her second fantasy.

She has two children, Harrison and Molly, and lives with her husband, Randy, in Cadott, Wisconsin, where they are building a house in the woods.

Last October she won a local contest for a 200-word mystery story, but this is her first professional sale.

Darla dug methodically at the ground at the base of the great, iron Beast Stake. The chain that bound her to the ornate, ten-foot pole clanked and clattered, rubbing her left wrist, which was already bloody from her initial attempts to pull her hand free. That was the trouble with being a drudge, muscles where they weren't desirable on a woman. If she'd been born a skinny-handed princess, she's have easily pulled free of the manacle.

If she'd been born a skinny-handed princess, they never would have had to use chains.

This morning, the first time the royal escort had brought her up the mountain, she'd been bound to the stake with a silken cord. Perhaps bound was not the

288

proper word. The guards were forbidden to harm any royal person—even a newly made princess by decree—and so out of habit the cord had been tied loosely, so as not to impede her circulation. It had taken mere moments to free herself, and she had climbed the gate and run down the narrow road so fast that she had rounded a bend and run straight into the hands of the royal party that had escorted her.

When King Tirrod had seen Darla, he had looked more confused than angry. None of his daughters had ever left her post. Each had dutifully given the requisite scream as the beast approached, then loudly shouted the courageous last words she had composed during the previous ten to 18 years, words that were, of course, painstakingly recorded by the chronicler even as the beast consumed their author.

Except, of course, for the last few princesses, who had been, of necessity, too young to come up with anything memorable—or intelligible.

The second time the royal retinue dragged her up the mountain, her hands and feet had been tightly bound with ropes. Darla had been lucky that time. The beast had not come immediately, and she'd been able to cut the ropes on the leaves that decorated the Beast Stake. This time she tried to leave the road as soon as the terrain allowed, but the guards were watching for her. She wanted to scream at herself for wasting her first escape.

She was not likely to be so lucky this third time. Darla pushed up the soiled silk of her sleeve. The cloth unnerved her. It slipped and wound itself around her like a spiderweb around a fly, yet she felt naked. She yearned for the weight of her homespun, but she'd been made a princess, so silk it was. King Tirrod was probably afraid homespun would give the beast indigestion.

Darla grasped the Beast Stake, avoiding the sharp ornamental edges, and strained to shift its position, pushing, pulling, twisting. Perhaps there was a sharp point on

the end that she could use as a weapon. She'd aim for
the eyes.

The dirt. That would be a weapon against eyes, too,
but when she'd scraped together all she'd dug up, the
pathetic pile barely contained two or three handfuls.

She choked back a sob and lifted her face to the cool
afternoon breeze, willing her eyes free of tears. Nothing
in life had prepared her for this. Until yesterday she'd
been a serving drudge in the women's quarters, a busy
place until these past few months. She'd scrubbed and
laundered and fetched for the queens and princesses,
and if it was annoying to have to jump every time a
princess said, "Eeww! Potgirl, take this and empty it!"
at least food had been plentiful, and her bed had been
warm and her own.

And her bed her own. Darla thumped an angry fist
against her thigh. If she'd known the trouble virginity
could cause, she'd have had done with it. There were a
dozen at least who would have been eager to help, and
two or three of them young or good-looking.

Darla wiped the dirt from her hands and stood. She
kicked at the ground with her heel, but all she did was
hurt her foot. She pulled and pushed the stake again, to
no avail. She strained to the edge of her tether and
touched the high cliff wall to her west. The sun-warmed
granite was white with small flecks that glinted in the
light. The castle below was made of the same stone, and
people called it the Diamond Keep because of its beauty
and flash.

To the north, the royal road slanted downward, locked
by a heavy iron gate, climbable, as she'd already learned,
but if she tried with the beast behind her, it would pick
her off like a grape off a vine. Two small steps to the
east of the stake lay the sheer drop to the castle below.
She peered over the edge at the crenelated walls, sharply
pointed towers, and thatched roofs of the outbuildings,
the fresh repairs standing out golden against the aged
straw. Here and there, close to a building, she could see
the forms of the other peasants, too frightened to come

into the open when the beast was expected, yet more frightened that one of their own was to be sacrificed.

Closed in on three sides, Darla forced herself to face the fourth—the path to the beast's lair. Some called the beast a dragon, but Darla doubted that was what it was. Knights slew dragons as a rite of passage; none worth his sword was without a box full of scales and teeth. If it were a dragon, some fledgling with spurs would have taken it as a trophy long ago.

The old men in the castle's stable spoke of giant, purplish feathers that occasionally fell after the beast had eaten a princess. The old herb woman, who had come from across the mountains as a maiden, told of fleeing a great beast that made a rattling, sucking sound like a child with a cold in its nose.

Darla began to shake in rage and terror. She could see the king, flanked by the prince and the chronicler, watching out the window of the tallest tower, and she shouted, "Couldn't you have sired more daughters?"

Through the chill air, the chronicler's voice rose. "You're supposed to scream first."

Darla stomped her foot in frustration and began digging at the ground again with her broken, bleeding nails.

Her complaint really hadn't been fair. The beast had been appearing for hundreds of years, but when it made its first appearance during King Tirrod's reign, his knights had been busy fighting against a lowland neighbor and were unavailable to chase the monster back to its lair as had been done for generations. He'd bought time with a princess sacrifice, a matter the First Lady still held against him, but it did give the king the Grand Idea. Usually, when the creature made its appearance every ten to twenty years, the ruling king would lose as many as half a dozen good knights fighting it off. Why should he waste his expensively trained men on beast battles when appeasement was so easy?

The Queen, now the First Lady, resisted the plan. She had neither the desire to produce princesses simply to lose them, nor the willingness to share the women's

quarters with other queens, even if they were subordi-
nate to her and even if their sole purpose was to provide
the necessary volume of princesses. She agreed finally
after much solicitous attention by the king and an iron-
clad law that only princes born of her blood could inherit
the throne.

The king had reacted to her agreement with enthusiasm, so much so that at one point Tirrod's accountant
had balked at paying the support of so many princesses,
to say nothing of the nobles' tax complaints. When the
beast showed up after eleven years, many of the lords
pointed out that one princess had been quite sufficient.
The grousing continued until the monster returned—a
mere three years later. Then a year later. Then every
few months. The last princess, a toddler who had had
the charming habit of latching on to Darla's skirt as she
swept, had been gone no more than a week when the
beast's demanding roar could be heard in the early
evenings.

Tirrod was desperate. He didn't even have a princess
in the making—at least none any queen would admit
to—with which to tempt the beast. He had been dis-
cussing possible solutions with the First Lady when
Darla had walked into the chamber with a freshly
cleaned pot and found herself summarily ennobled.

Enprincessed? Darla sat back on her heels and wiped
her running nose with the back of her hand. It didn't
matter what it was called. She knew what had been done
to her.

She sat beside the Beast Stake and shivered. The
shade crept beyond her perch, out across the valley
below as the sun sank slowly behind the mountain, mut-
ing the gold of the fields. If the beast didn't show up
soon, she'd never see what killed her. An irrational fear
rose in her, an anger at being killed by an unknown. She
felt as helpless as the smith, William Caird, who had
fallen to the red line sickness after a small cut on his
finger had swollen his hand hard as the stone beneath
her.

It had been years since he'd died, but she still mourned his loss. Others missed him too, though for his work. He'd had no child and had but one apprentice, Cedric, who had great strength but none of Master Caird's feel for metal nor skill with horses. Tirrod had sent word with every traveler who came to the Diamond Keep, but travelers were few, and free smiths valued enough where they were that none were willing to take the long journey around the mountain as the traders did, nor the dangerous shortcut through the beast's territory. Finally, Tirrod had pressed Ann Caird, the master's widow, to try shoeing the horses and making those pieces that required more skill than strength. She had often helped William and did the work well enough, but she had no enthusiasm, for the women gossiped meanly within her hearing, and the men spoke to her only of business, and in that tried to cheat her.

Darla felt guilty, now that she, too, had been cast out. She had spoken no word of friendship to Ann since she began her work, despite the fact that Darla saw her whenever one of the queens or princesses required the repair of a belt buckle or brooch.

In truth, Darla spent as little time as possible with Mistress Caird in order to lessen her own pain, for she missed the woman's husband terribly. Although an excellent weapons maker, he had a talent for making jewelry from precious metals, much to the delight of the queens. Darla had frequently run back and forth picking up new pieces or dropping off broken pieces for repair. In her life surrounded by women, he was like a strange and wonderful beast, like the giant brown bear from the herb woman's homeland.

When she was very little, he would set her on a stool close enough to the fire to be thoroughly warmed, yet far enough away that no spark hit her. If it were near midday and Mistress Caird brought his lunch, he would break his loaf and give her part to eat while she watched him work.

His muscled fingers shaped the soft metals with grace

and confidence, forming lilies, violets or tendrils of ivy.
If she'd been told to hurry, he'd lift her from the stool
as soon as he'd finished and pat her cheek with his
warm, hard hand.

"Hold it fast, Darla," he'd say. "You've strong
hands, too."

Sometimes, on quiet days, she would stay and watch
him work the weapons and tools. The smoke, the sparks,
the flare of flames and groan of the bellows could have
been plucked whole from a priest's sermon of hell, but
Darla had never known a truer heaven. Even on the
cold rock, tied by iron to iron, she could see William
Caird, the sweat dripping from his matted brow, glisten-
ing on his muscled arm. She could see him swinging the
great hammer, striking iron, swinging again to the top
of his arc—

Darla's eyes snapped open in the encroaching dusk.
Master Caird had found power at the top of his swing;
perhaps she would find power at the top of the Beast
Stake.

She began to climb, grasping leaves and flowers as
finely rendered as any Caird had ever made. She could
feel her flesh tear as she stepped on the iron thorns, but
this was one more chance, one more hope. At the top
was an enormous rose, multipetaled and exceedingly
beautiful. Caird would have loved to have seen it, for
though the queens frequently requested roses on jewelry,
he'd always said he hadn't mastered that shape.

Darla anchored herself to the rose one-handed, her
chain being too short for two, and began to sway her body
back and forth. Tears of frustration coursed her face by
the time she heard the first, blessed groan of metal. A
desperate laugh broke through her lips as she flung herself back and forth, scrambling for purchase when her
blood-slicked feet slipped from the thorns. Bit by bit,
the metal began to twist. It wouldn't be long before the
iron broke.

Her struggles were so intense that she never heard the
beast's approach.

Darla screamed as she looked up into a great toothless mouth, gaping to pluck her from the Beast Stake like meat from a skewer.

She jumped.

The ornamental iron tore her skin and silk alike as the monster's maw closed on the sharp iron rose. It screamed—a rattle of sucked mucus—and its three eyes waved at the ends of two-foot stalks.

Struggling to catch her breath, Darla looked up at an enormous winged slug. Its pale gray flesh sparkled with slime that glistened silver in the light of the rising moon. One immense purplish-black wing stretched half as wide as the king's audience chamber, while the other beat against the white loch wall. A darker slime dripped from the beast's injured mouth, and it backed off, complaining in its snot-rattle growl.

Darla rose, keeping the stake between herself and the beast. She knew now why there'd been no trophy hunters. No lady would let any lord, however dear, hang such fetid wings in the hall—and what else was there to display? Its head was simply a tapering point, the three eyes dancing like afterthoughts. Its body was that of a bloated slug, its skin stretched taut as an over-filled grain sack.

Darla jerked once on her chain. The stake had been so close to breaking. Perhaps, given the monster's confusion, she'd have time to climb the gate.

The iron held.

The beast slid toward her, around the pole. Darla backed away, circling twice before she realized she was simply shortening her chain. There was nowhere to go, no weapon to pierce the mass of flesh. Even the handfuls of dirt were out of reach. If the beast had a true head, she might be able to strangle it with the chain, but she could see no proper target save the eyes, and destroying those would not save her. The creature knew where dinner was.

She was going to die. The only question was how.

Darla stood with the sheer drop to her back, a cold

smile on her face. If she couldn't save her life, she could hand the king's problem right back to him. She stepped off.

She screamed as the iron manacle ripped her left wrist, and reflexively her right hand grabbed the chain. To her amazement, the iron held.

The beast rattled and roared above her, dripping spittle and gore, which turned the chain links as slippery as refrozen ice. She could feel the monster push at the chain, but it had no limbs with which to pull her back up.

Eventually, it backed off, and her wild pendulum swinging began to slow. Her arms ached, and her fingers were numb. Blood flowed freely down her left arm. She could imagine the beast's confusion. What princess had ever fought before? She looked down at the lighted tower, where the king, his son and the chronicler stood in silhouette. What would Tirrod do if she survived the encounter? Would he make her face the monster again? Would he simply leave her hanging here?

The quiet of the beast fell about Darla like the breath of a sick person. Pain shot through her shoulders, and she thanked God she carried no more weight than she did, even as she begged for a miracle to deliver her.

With a great roar, the beast was suddenly above her, the tuberous body launching over her head, the massive wings cupping the air. Darla screamed as its tail hit her, knocking loose her right hand's hold.

Screams echoed from the castle below. The wind from the beating wings gagged Darla with the stench of swamp gas and rotted fish. She caught the chain again and fought to pull herself up over the lip of the cliff as the beast circled over the castle and flew toward her, its drooping tail knocking slates from the queens' tower.

As she rolled herself onto the granite ledge, she saw the beast's flight falter, the wings beating faster and faster with shorter and shorter strokes. The pulpy body, fattened on its abundance of princesses, writhed in a desperate attempt to creep on air. With a gurgling roar, the monster fell, impaling itself on the king's high tower.

The beast's death convulsions snapped the stone, and Darla could hear the screams of Tirrod and the others as they fell to the courtyard below.

Darla woke desperately fighting against silk wrapped around her body. The movement reignited the pain that sleep had banked. She groaned, but the sound came out thin and wavery through lips stuck to her teeth.

"Hush, hush, Your Majesty," said a woman's soft voice, and a cool wet rag delicately touched Darla's lips. She cracked open her gummed eyes.

"Mistress Caird," she whispered, letting her eyes fall closed again.

"Shh, Your Majesty," the woman said, brushing Darla's hair from swollen lips and eyes. "I'm that, and here to care for you until you're well enough to choose those you want about you. If you would, the herb woman left a drink to ease the swelling and the pain. Will you swallow?"

Darla slowly nodded once, and felt a strong arm lift her and a cup touch her lips. Peppermint—not enough to mask the bitterness of some other herb, but refreshing to her slimy mouth.

Slime.

Darla shivered.

"There, there, Your Majesty." Darla heard the cup set down and felt the softness of the pillows beneath her. A waft of cool air brushed her as the silken covers were lifted and straightened.

"Oh," Darla said, opening her eyes and lifting her hand toward the woman. "I must go outside."

Comprehension crossed the other's face.

"Don't be foolish, Your Majesty," she said. "Let me help."

As Mistress Caird helped her to the chamber pot, lights reeled before Darla's eyes. She closed them, only to bring into focus the tympanic thumping in her skull. She reached for her head and would have fallen if Mistress Caird hadn't caught her.

"There, there, Your Majesty," she said, patting Darla's head.

"What did you call me?"

"Your Majesty." Darla could hear the smug satisfaction in the woman's voice.

Darla looked up at her through a curtain of waltzing lights.

"I don't understand."

The older woman's warm chuckle filled the room. "The king and the prince were killed by the beast." She chucked Darla lightly under the chin. "Long live the queen."

"This castle is full of queens."

"All by marriage."

"But what of their sons?"

"Which of the thirty-seven would you choose? The two eldest were born a day apart, the elder to the third wife, the younger to the second. Who has the better claim? You are the only legal heir. Princess by decree."

A shiver raced along Darla's spine as she considered this new monster.

"I've no talent for ruling."

"Not yet, perhaps, but you know how to watch and think. I saw you sitting with my William." Her face softened in remembrance.

Darla started to shake her head and winced. "The council will never accept me."

"The council will because the people have. Lass, you killed the beast! Chained and abandoned, with naught but your native wit!"

"And that's why you would serve me?"

Darla watched as a look of remembered pain settled on the other woman.

"Nay," she said quietly. "I serve you for the service you did my William. He said the forging of the Beast Stake was the greatest evil he ever committed. He wept every time a princess was taken to it and turned his head in shame from every rose he saw. You broke that evil. He must rest easier, think you not?"

"Aye, he must," Darla said, surprised she had not recognized the work for his. She felt warmed by this first show of fealty and laid her hand upon the other woman's arm.

"But, Your Majesty, I'd best see you rest." She helped Darla arrange her night dress and walked her to the bed. "Sleep now if you can, Your Majesty. There's a delegation of merchants to see you tomorrow. That pass hasn't been safe for five hundred years, and they're all eager to cut their travel time in half."

The words washed over Darla without meaning, and her worries slipped from her mind as lightly as the covers were slipped over her shoulder.

"Mistress Caird," Darla said as she drifted toward sleep. "As queen, I can make any law I want, right?"

"I'd imagine so, Your Majesty," the woman said from the chamber door.

"Then I decree that from now on, all queens must empty their own pots."

"That's a generous law, Your Majesty," the smiling woman said, closing the door with her free hand.

TAKING FLIGHT
by Susan Wolven

Susan says that she considers herself lucky because she actually makes her living as a writer. She's right, she is lucky; very few of us can make a living writing. She started as a secretary in the Marketing Department at the Twentieth Century Fox Film Corporation in New York ten years ago, and is now in Los Angeles overseeing copy development for Fox's domestic home video and interactive game releases.

She says, however, that it's a real thrill to see her own story in print, as opposed to writing copy for video sleeves, ads and brochures which focuses on someone else's story. Yes, I'd say that makes quite a difference.

She wishes to dedicate this story to her friend and neighbor, Deborah Wheeler, who always believed in her ability as a writer—even when she herself began to doubt.

It's funny the way things work out; I published Deborah's first story in *Sword and Sorceress I*. If Deborah is my literary daughter, does that make Susan my literary granddaughter?

S aria had been dead for a week when her missing 'tsunee flew into the village, a message tied to its leg. The hawk cried out once as it circled overhead.

:Home:

Feeding her pigeons, Lei had to grasp the coop for support, overcome with the dizzying sensation her sister had flown back from the dead.

:Grayhawk!:

:Lei! PainLonelyAfraid:

Although Lei had linked with Grayhawk once before,

she cringed under the onslaught of feelings now pushing against her mind. She quickly severed the link, gasping as the pressure in her head subsided.

Grayhawk spiraled downward as pigeons rose like a locust cloud and flew for the nearest trees. The hawk landed awkwardly in the now empty coop, huddling in silent exhaustion, one wing slightly askew. Lei saw its small heart beating, saw where an arrow had pierced clear through its wing.

With trembling fingers, she untied Saria's message. *So now I will know what was more important than being with me on my name day. What need took you down the southern road only to fall to a bandit's arrow through your heart.* But Lei's initial anger had long faded and her vision blurred as she read the familiar scrawl.

CROSDEN'S CROSSING. SOLSTICE SUNRISE. WONDERS!

The cooing of the birds faded as Lei stared at the paper clutched between her fingers. She could almost sense her sister's excitement in the hurried scrawl, smell the cinnamon tea Saria always kept in the pouch with her paper.

"Did they watch you write this, my sister, then shoot you and Grayhawk as you parted ways?" Lei whispered.

"What does it say?"

Lei spun around with a small cry.

Nathon, the village healer, stood directly behind her, his eyes fixed upon the scrap of paper in Lei's hand. "Well?" he repeated, leaning heavily upon his walking stick.

"She wanted me to meet her at Crosden's Crossing at sunrise . . . on my name day." Lei straightened her shoulder as a small group began to gather. She held up the message so everyone could see. "She did not forget."

"Tradition says she comes to you," Nathon said softly.

Lei's eyes widened. "The winter sickness left her twice as many patients. Her route had more than doubled."

"Yes, but she knew you feared leaving this village.

Why ask you to meet her someplace so far away?" Nathon shrugged. "Her actions have left you with nothing."

Lei blinked in surprise. "I have Grayhawk."

"Pah!" Nathon pulled himself up as tall as his crippled back allowed. "A clever bird that gathers herbs!"

And guides lost and frightened souls to their place in the spirit world. But Lei said nothing.

"Since Saria was the last of your family, the elders will give you your true name and you shall be apprenticed to me." Nathon smiled as the crowd murmured approval. "Now go home and rest, young woman."

Lei felt panic stir deep in her stomach as Nathon moved away, drawing the crowd behind him. She glanced down at Saria's message, the ink now blurred with the sweat from her hand. But one word stood out clearly.

Wonders!

Carefully, Lei tucked Saria's final message into the small pouch hanging around her neck, a gift from Saria's last trip home. She brought the pouch up to her nose, inhaling deeply, letting its spicy smell overwhelm her: a smell that spoke of exotic marketplaces full of strange and wonderful teas, medicines, and magics that could cure anyone of anything.

I could straighten Nathon's back. But she knew better than to reveal that Saria had taught her such magic.

Our secret.

Lei looked into the pigeon coop. "We know their fear blinds them, don't we, friend."

Grayhawk stared back unflinchingly as Lei suddenly gasped and fell to her knees. *As my own fear binds me here!*

Lei looked around the never-changing village square with its small wood-and-mud-baked homes and cluttered marketplace. So familiar. So safe.

"Saria," Lei whispered again as realization shook her. "What other wonders were you going to share with me?"

The wind soughing through the trees whispered the

question back as the sky turned from deepest indigo to black, and the first star appeared low on the horizon over the southern road.

Saria! As Lei stared at the glittering star, she took a deep breath and slowly lowered her defenses. An instant later she felt another heart beat slow and sure in her breast, felt a gentle awareness slip into her mind.

:LeiCome: Grayhawk struggled to her feet as Lei put on Saria's leather gauntlet and held out her arm.

:You are right, brave one. Come:

It did not take Lei long to pack her few belongings. And as others gathered around their fires for the evening meal, Lei slipped through the shadows with a small pack on her back, Saria's medicine pouch over her shoulder and a 'tsunee warm inside her cloak. As she reached Nathon's hut, she circled it once, casting a small, healing spell—a slight tingle Nathon would remember when he awoke the next morning, his back a little stronger.

Lei smiled. *Perhaps he will speak of it when I return.*

She crept on, reaching the edge of the village unchallenged. The road to Crosden's Crossing shone bright in the moonlight, the dark forest on either side seeming to guard the way so that Lei could take no wrong turn. She took one hesitant step as Nathon's voice came back to her. *She gave you nothing?*

"No," Lei whispered back. "She gave me knowledge."

:KnowledgePowerFreedom:

:Yes, Grayhawk! She gave me freedom:

Lei laughed as the warm night air blew back her hair, astonished she had ever feared the night or the road leading out of her village.

THE VISION THAT APPEARED

by Katherine L. Rogers

Katherine Rogers is thirty-four years old and has a Master's degree in Archaeology from Boston University. She worked on prehistoric and historic sites in the U.S. and once did a survey in Greece, but she is not currently pursuing a career in archaeology. Instead she pursues her two daughters—ages 19 months and 3-and-1/2 years—all the time. That's enough pursuing for anybody—or for several bodies. And if I say any more now, the introduction will be longer than the story.

The last faint sounds of music and laughter faded as Claudia carefully shut the door to the library. Missing the music and dancing of a Midsummer's Eve party was a painful decision, but she had a chance to work magic tonight. This might be the only occasion to try the spell she had found in the chest in the library. By the date on the parchment she knew it was old, but the writing was still clear. "A Spell to See" it was called. Claudia was thrilled to discover that the spell was designed to be used by someone without special training.

Claudia's branch of the family had no wizards. There were the old stories of course, about how Claudia's Great-Great-Great-Great-Grandmother, Lady Margaret Reed, had been courted by a famous wizard and then rejected him. He had later married Margaret's younger sister.

Claudia knew the story was true; she had a distant cousin at the Wizard's College. If Lady Margaret had been anything like Claudia's grandmother, it was a wonder a wizard had even bothered with her. (Grandmother called magic a "frivolous pursuit.") Still, the note at the top of the page said it was a gift to Lady Margaret Reed from "The Wizard Egbert, the Magnificent." The spell was to be performed on Midsummer's Eve by "a young unmarried woman" and could only be used once by any person. It would reveal "A Wonderful Vision" to the caster.

Claudia's anticipation mounted. She felt so daring sneaking off to cast a spell. "Certainly Mother never tried anything like this," Claudia scoffed. Her mother was unsympathetic to Claudia's protests over the unfairness of having a cousin at the Wizard's College while she had to stay home and learn "Domestic Engineering." "Magic is overrated," her mother always insisted. Claudia would not believe it. Magic was grand, magic was important. "A Wonderful Vision." What would be revealed?

Claudia retrieved the parchment from the closet. She reviewed the spell, took a deep breath, and chanted the words that would be her one taste of magic. What marvels she was going to see! A shiver ran through her body as she completed the spell. She lifted her hand and pointed at the octagonal window in the North wall. It shimmered and wavered. Still clutching the parchment, Claudia moved closer and held her breath as the glass cleared. At first she saw only her own reflection peering back expectantly. Then it changed. As she looked, the reflection became that of another young woman—her mother! Then Aunt Hildegarde, her grandmother, another young lady, and another, each holding the parchment. The images changed like the riffling of pages in a book finally stopping with an image of Lady Margaret herself.

Lady Margaret, too, held the parchment, and gazed in shock and dismay at the "wonderful vision" of a hundred pink parrots rising into the night sky to spell out the words "Marry Me, Egbert."

Incredulous, Claudia shook her head. Mother was right, magic was overrated.

MARION ZIMMER BRADLEY

THE DARKOVER NOVELS

☐ DARKOVER LANDFALL	UE2234—$3.99
☐ HAWKMISTRESS!	UE2239—$4.99
☐ STORMQUEEN!	UE2310—$5.99
☐ TWO TO CONQUER	UE2174—$4.99
☐ THE HEIRS OF HAMMERFELL	UE2451—$4.99
☐ THE SHATTERED CHAIN	UE2308—$5.99
☐ THENDARA HOUSE	UE2240—$5.99
☐ CITY OF SORCERY	UE2332—$5.99
☐ REDISCOVERY*	UE2529—$4.99
☐ THE SPELL SWORD	UE2237—$3.99
☐ THE FORBIDDEN TOWER	UE2373—$4.99
☐ STAR OF DANGER	UE2607—$4.99
☐ THE WINDS OF DARKOVER & THE PLANET SAVERS	UE2630—$4.99
☐ THE BLOODY SUN	UE2603—$4.99
☐ THE HERITAGE OF HASTUR	UE2413—$4.99
☐ SHARRA'S EXILE	UE2309—$5.99
☐ EXILE'S SONG	UE2705—$6.99
☐ THE SHADOW MATRIX (hardcover)	UE2743—$21.95
☐ THE WORLD WRECKERS	UE2629—$4.99

*with Mercedes Lackey

Don't Miss These Exciting DAW Anthologies

THEY'RE COMING TO GET YOU. . . .
ANTHOLOGIES FOR NERVOUS TIMES

☐ **FIRST CONTACT** UE2757—$5.99
   Martin H. Greenberg and Larry Segriff, editors

In the tradition of the hit television show "The X-Files" comes a fascinating collection of original stories by some of the premier writers of the genre, such as Jody Lynn Nye, Kristine Kathryn Rusch, and Jack Haldeman.

☐ **THE UFO FILES** UE2772—$5.99
   Martin H. Greenberg, editor

Explore close encounters of a thrilling kind in these stories by Gregory Benford, Ed Gorman, Peter Crowther, Alan Dean Foster, and Kristine Kathryn Rusch.

☐ **THE CONSPIRACY FILES** UE2797—$5.99
   Martin H. Greenberg and Scott Urban, editors

We all know that we never hear the whole truth behind the headlines—let Douglas Clegg, Tom Monteleone, Ed Gorman, Norman Partridge and Yvonne Navarro unmask the conspirators and their plots—if the government lets them. . . .

☐ **BLACK CATS AND BROKEN MIRRORS** UE2788—$5.99
   Martin H. Greenberg and John Helfers, editors

From the consequences of dark felines crossing your path to the results of carelssly smashed mirrors, authors such as Jane Yolen, Michelle West, Charles de Lint, Nancy Springer and Esther Friesner dare to answer the question, "What happens if some of those long-treasured superstitions are actually true?"

Prices slightly higher in Canada. **DAW 215X**

Mercedes Lackey

The Novels of Valdemar